# Mr. PANtS

*Ahhhhhhh!*

VUUMBA

ZOOM!

# SLACKS, CAMERA, ACTION!

**WORDS BY**
## SCOTT MCCORMICK

**PICTURES BY**
## R. H. LAZZELL

PUFFIN BOOKS
An Imprint of Penguin Group (USA)

FOR MY MOM, WHO WAS EVEN MORE EXCITED
ABOUT THIS THAN I WAS.
". . . THE . . ."                                    —S.M.


FOR MY FAMILY, FRIENDS, AND CHOCOLATE CHIP
COOKIES EVERYWHERE.                    —R.H.L.

PUFFIN BOOKS
Published by the Penguin Group
Penguin Group (USA) LLC
375 Hudson Street
New York, New York 10014

USA * Canada * UK * Ireland * Australia * New Zealand * India * South Africa * China

penguin.com
A Penguin Random House Company

First published in the United States of America by Dial Books for Young Readers,
an imprint of Penguin Young Readers Group, 2015
Published by Puffin Books, an imprint of Penguin Young Readers Group, 2015

Text copyright © 2015 by Scott McCormick
Pictures copyright © 2015 by R. H. Lazzell

THE LIBRARY OF CONGRESS HAS CATALOGED THE DIAL BOOKS EDITION AS FOLLOWS:
McCormick, Scott, date.
Mr. Pants : slacks, camera, action! / words by Scott McCormick ; pictures by R. H. Lazzell.
pages cm
Summary: Mr. Pants is determined to win a film contest, but his sisters and their friends are not eager to participate.
ISBN 978-0-8037-4009-9 (hardcover)
[1. Brothers and sisters—Fiction. 2. Cats—Fiction. 3. Video recordings—Production and direction—Fiction.
4. Behavior—Fiction.]
I. Lazzell, R. H., illustrator. II. Title. III. Title: Slacks, camera, action!
PZ7.M47841437Mr 2015   [E]—dc23   2013038372

Puffin Books ISBN 978-0-14-751711-1

Manufactured in China

1  3  5  7  9  10  8  6  4  2

# CONTENTS

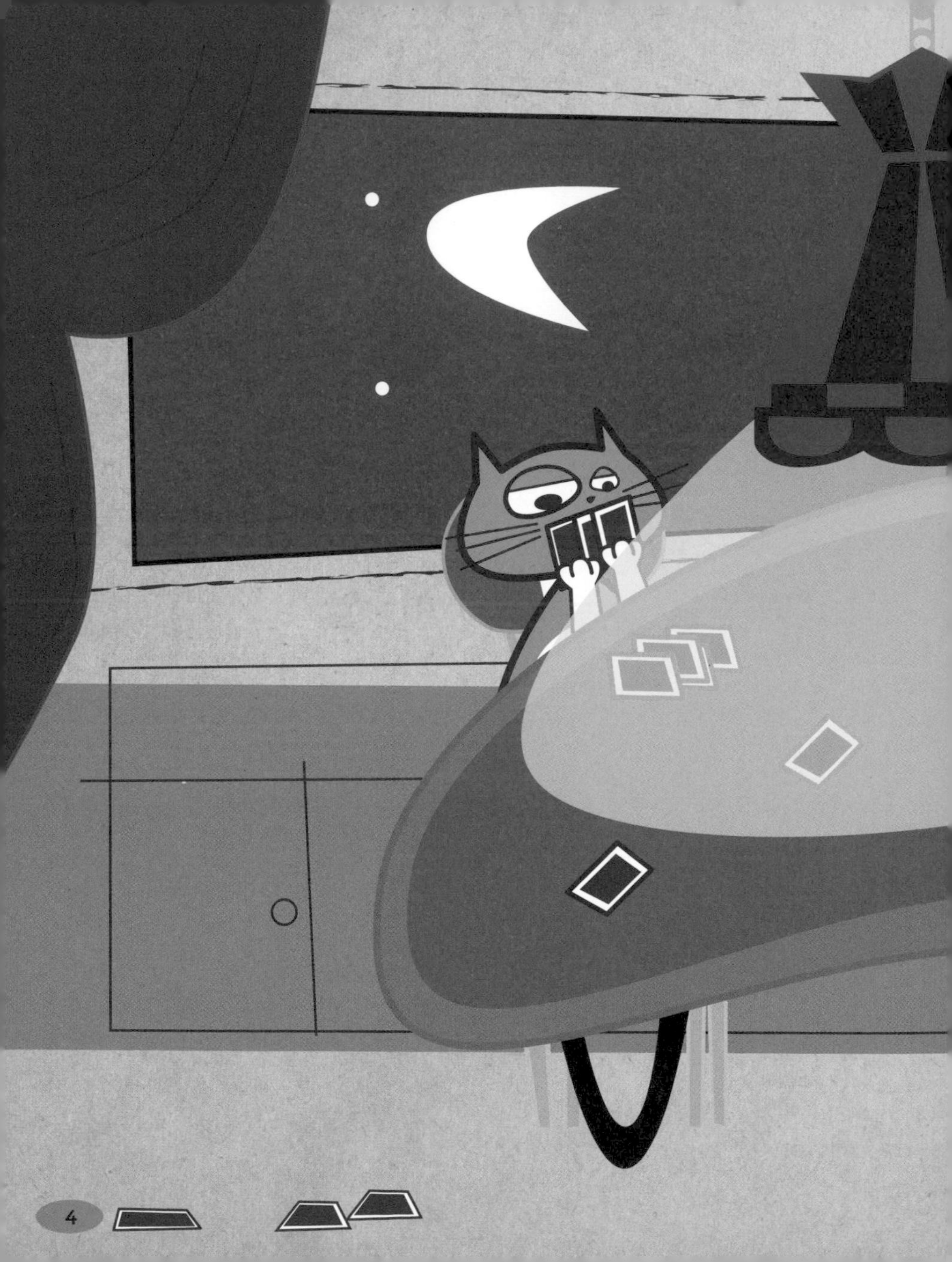

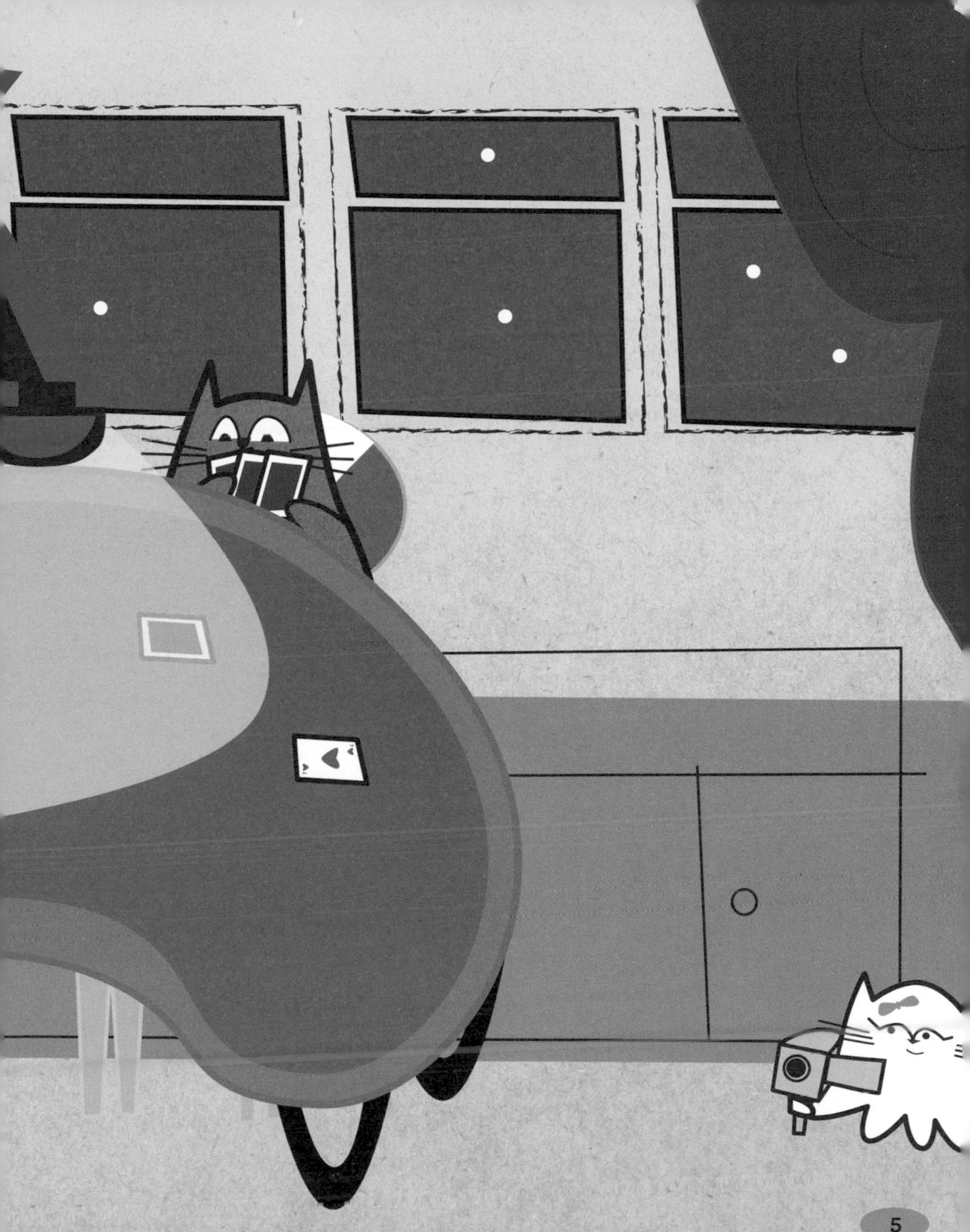

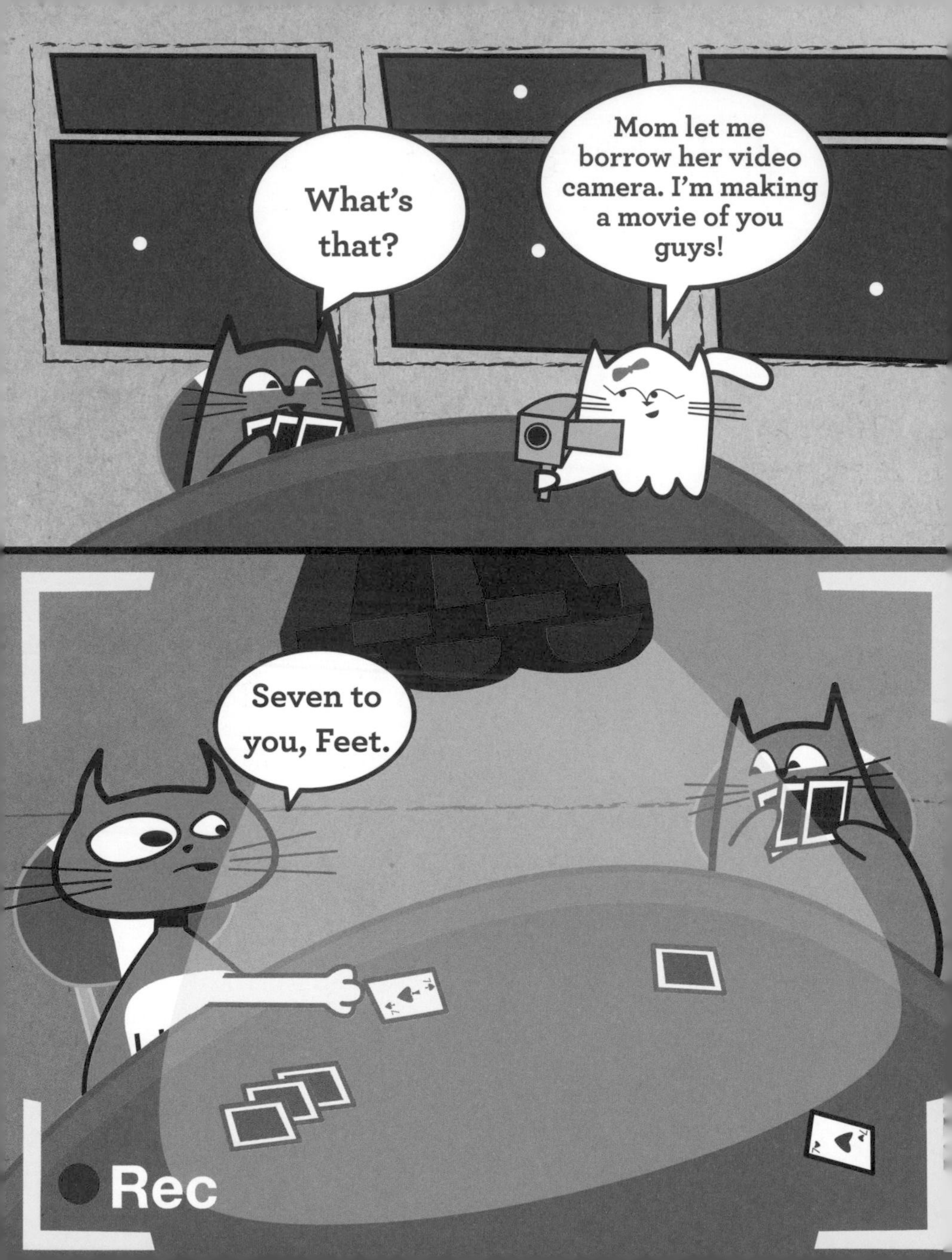
What's that?
Mom let me borrow her video camera. I'm making a movie of you guys!
Seven to you, Feet.
Rec

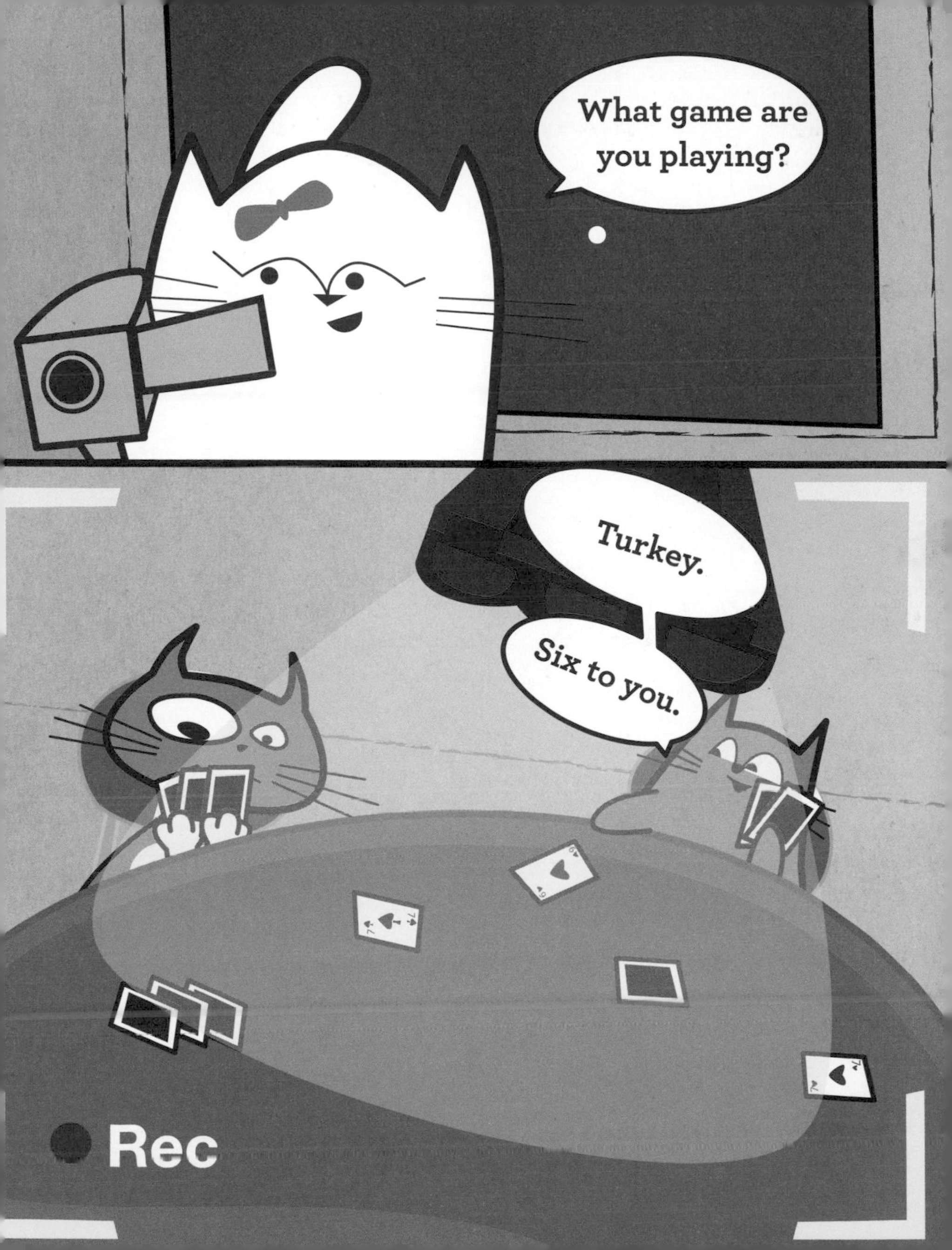
What game are you playing?
Turkey.
Six to you.
Rec

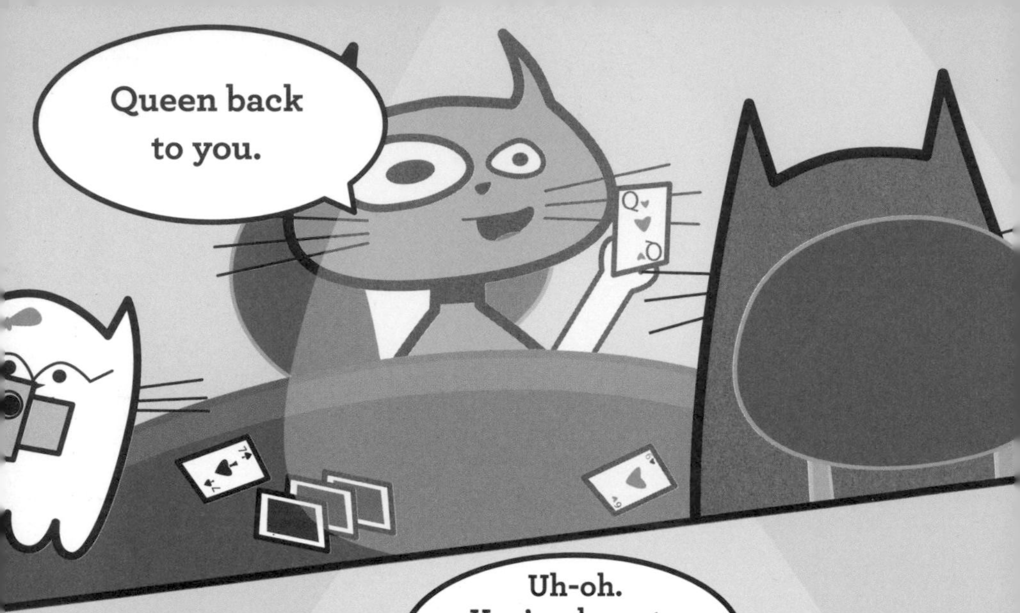
Queen back
to you.

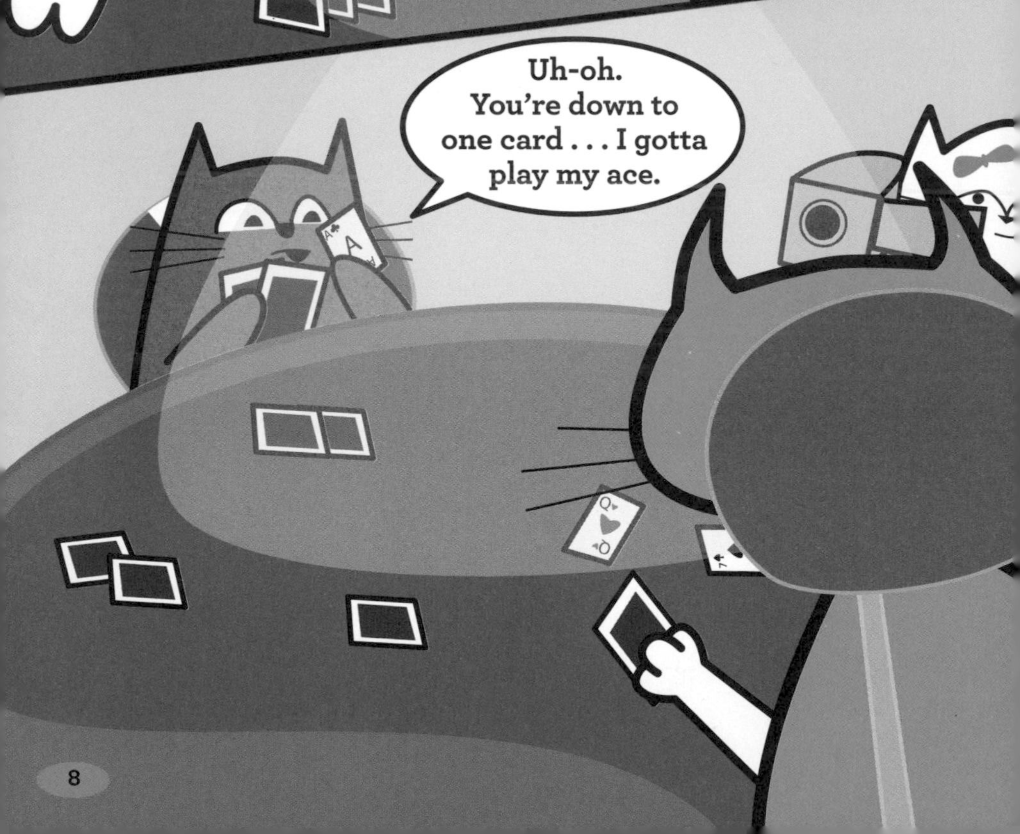
Uh-oh.
You're down to
one card . . . I gotta
play my ace.

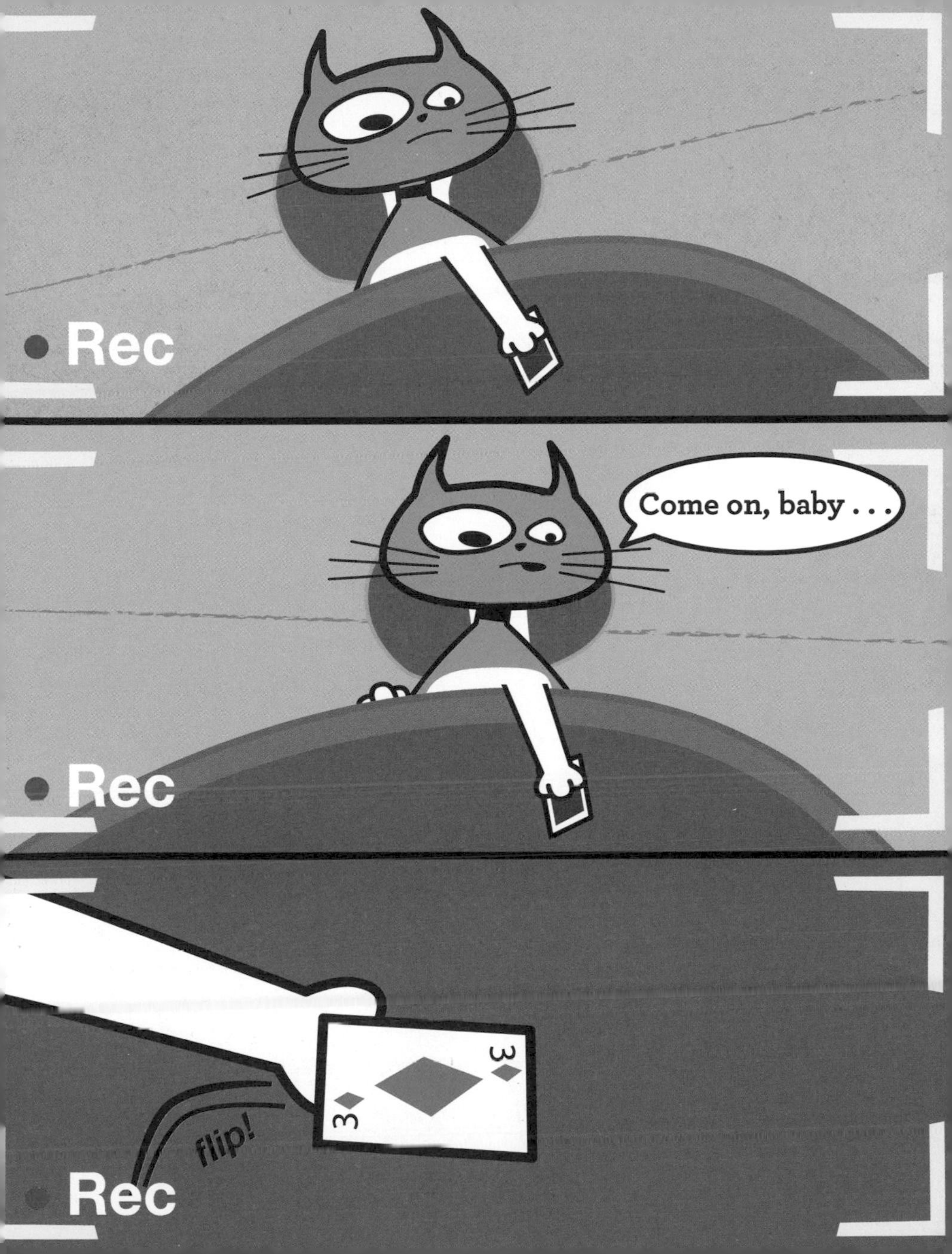
Rec
Come on, baby . . .
Rec
3
3
flip!
Rec

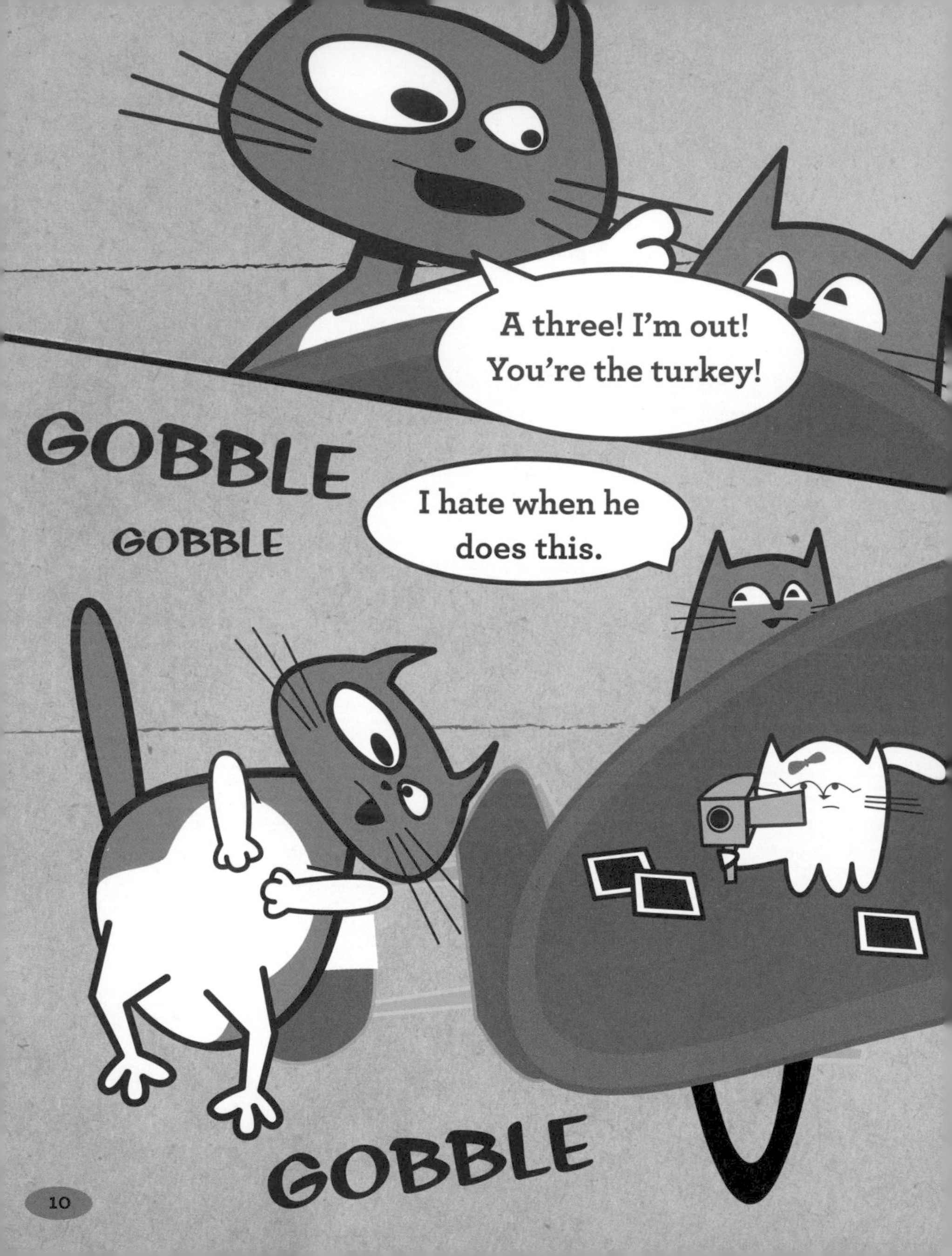
A three! I'm out!
You're the turkey!
GOBBLE
GOBBLE
I hate when he
does this.
GOBBLE

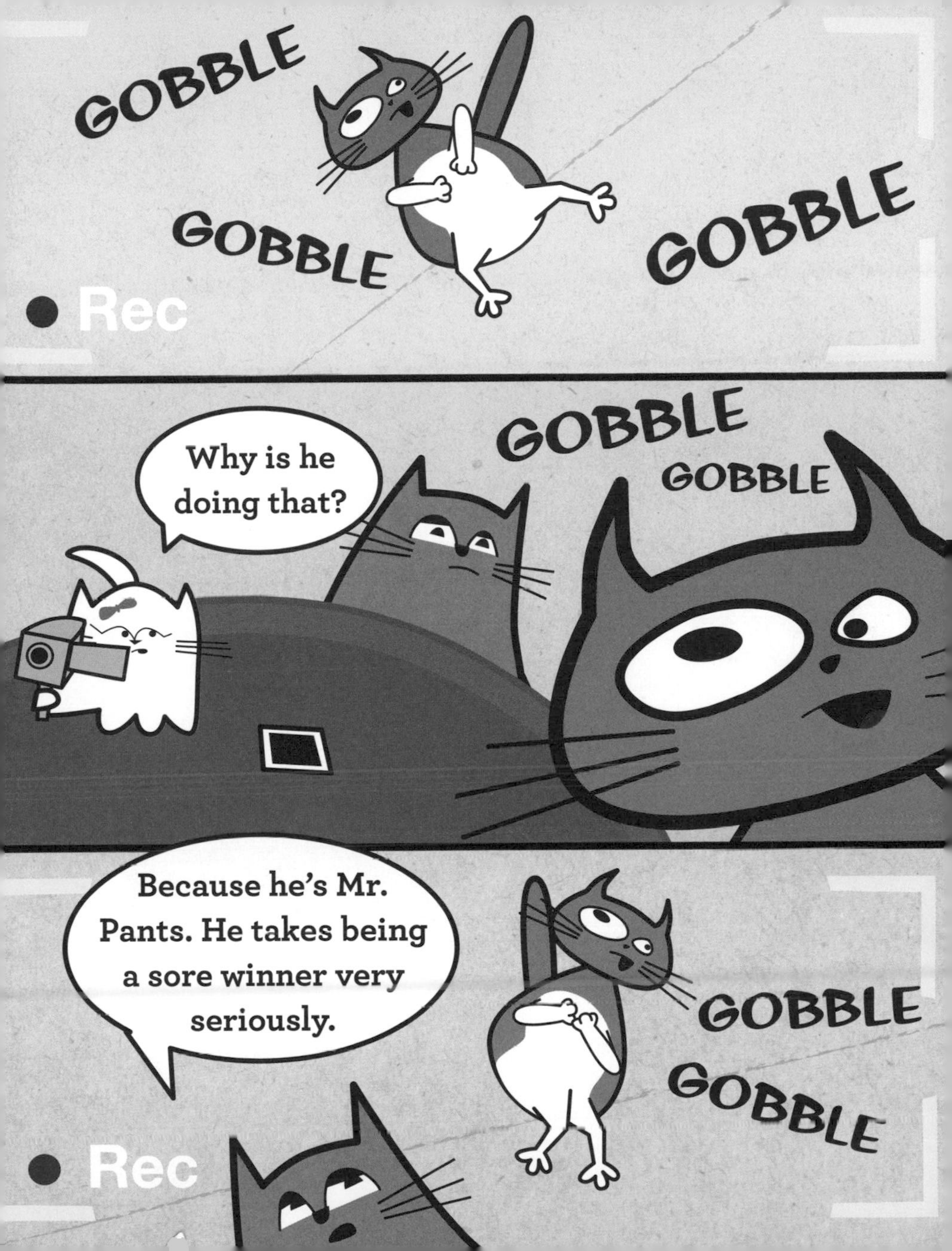
GOBBLE
GOBBLE
GOBBLE
Rec
Why is he doing that?
GOBBLE
GOBBLE
Because he's Mr. Pants. He takes being a sore winner very seriously.
GOBBLE
GOBBLE
Rec

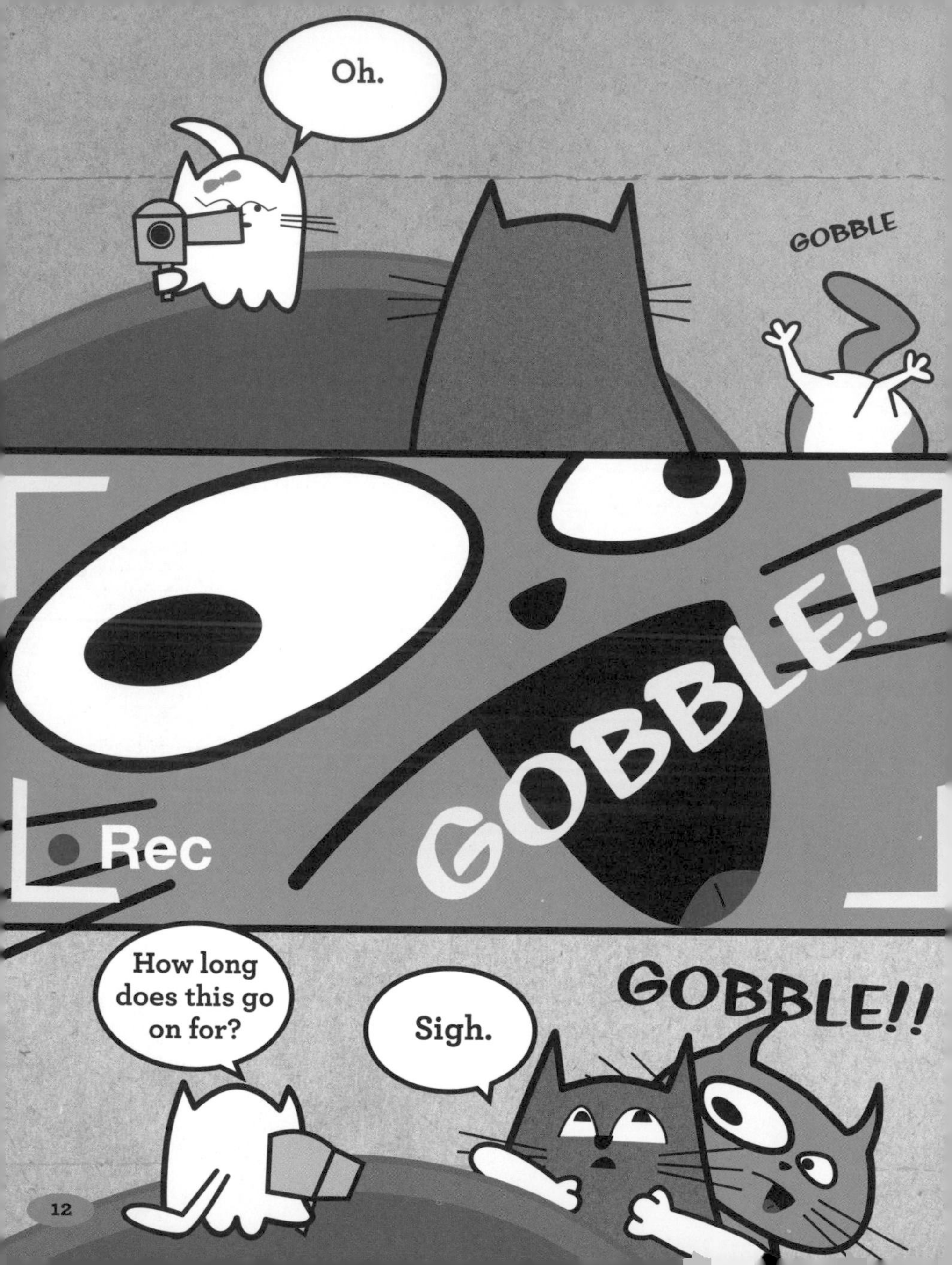

Oh.
GOBBLE
Rec
GOBBLE!
How long does this go on for?
Sigh.
GOBBLE!!

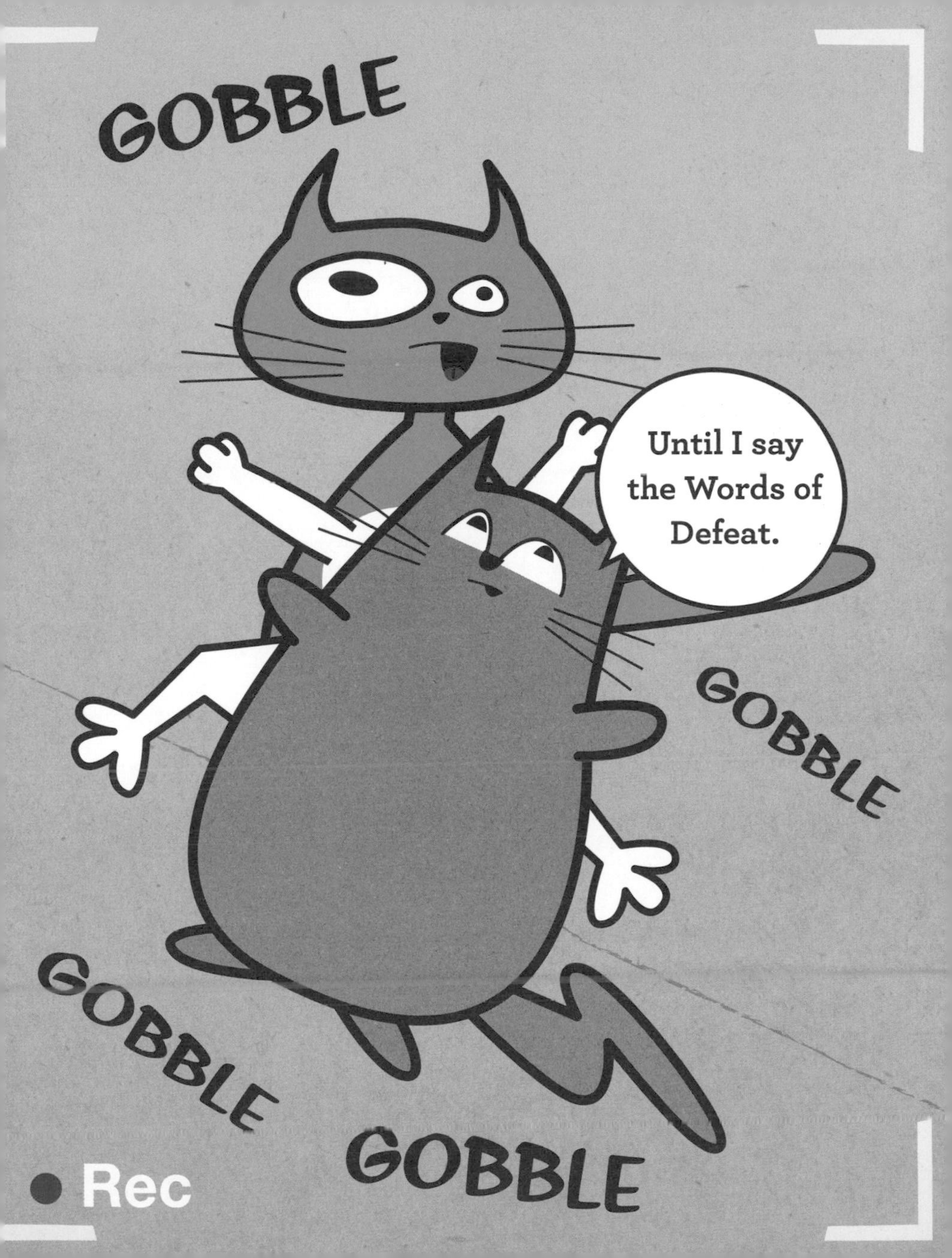
GOBBLE
Until I say the Words of Defeat.
GOBBLE
GOBBLE
GOBBLE
• Rec

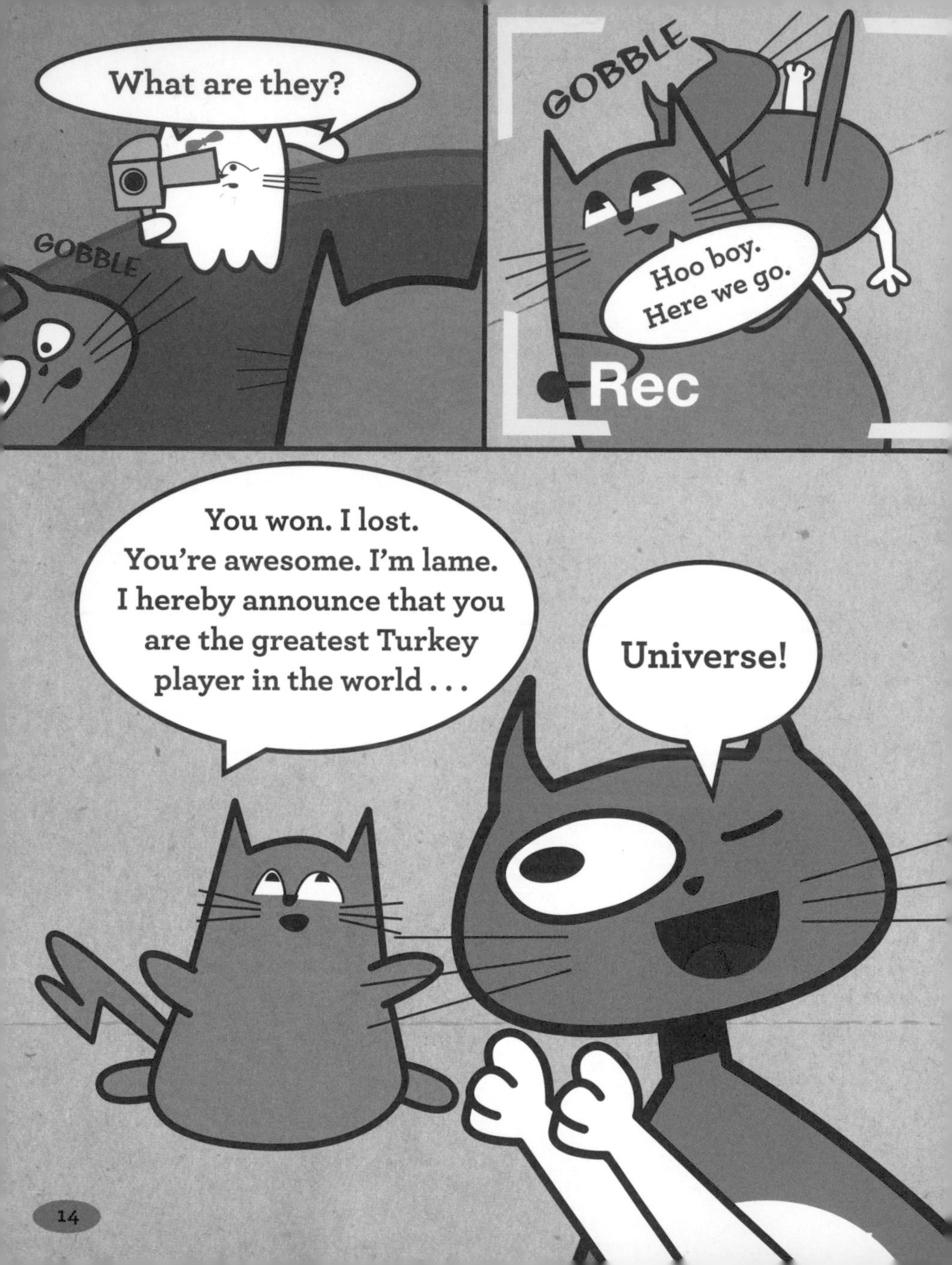
What are they?
GOBBLE
GOBBLE
Hoo boy. Here we go.
Rec
You won. I lost. You're awesome. I'm lame. I hereby announce that you are the greatest Turkey player in the world . . .
Universe!

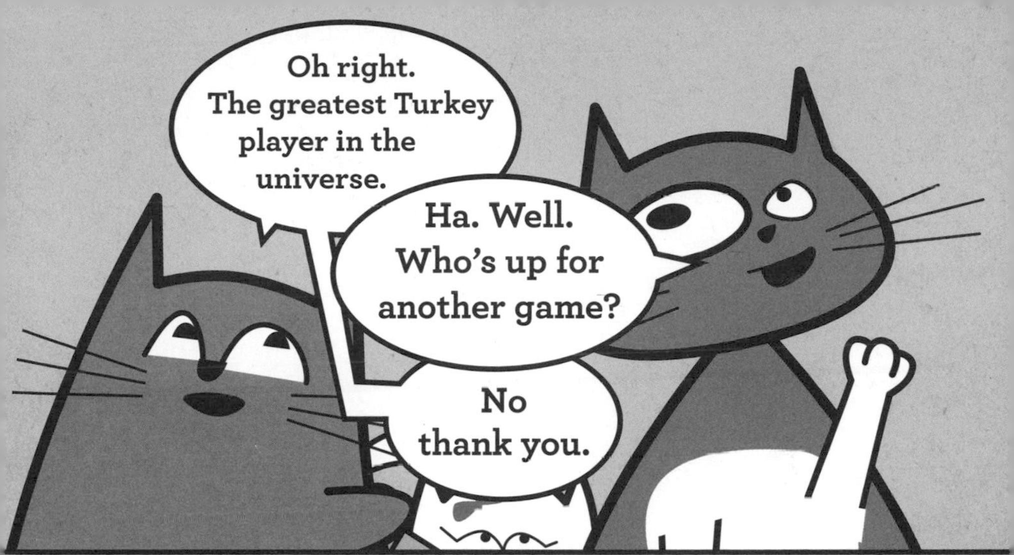
Oh right.
The greatest Turkey
player in the
universe.
Ha. Well.
Who's up for
another game?
No
thank you.

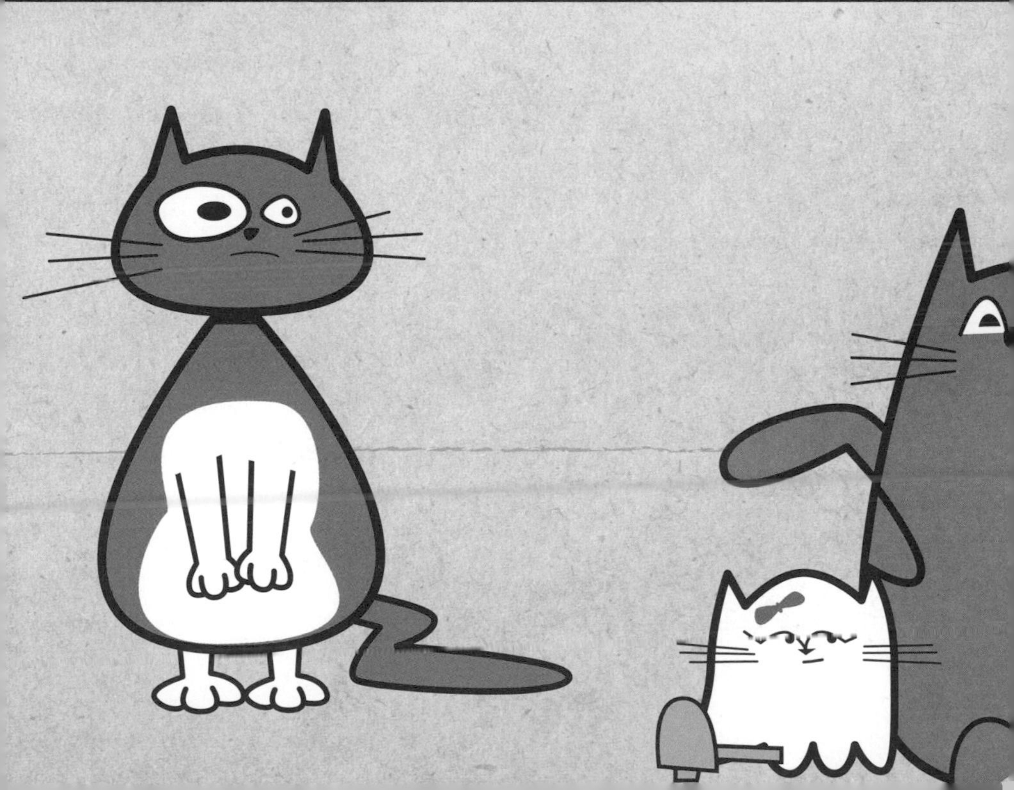

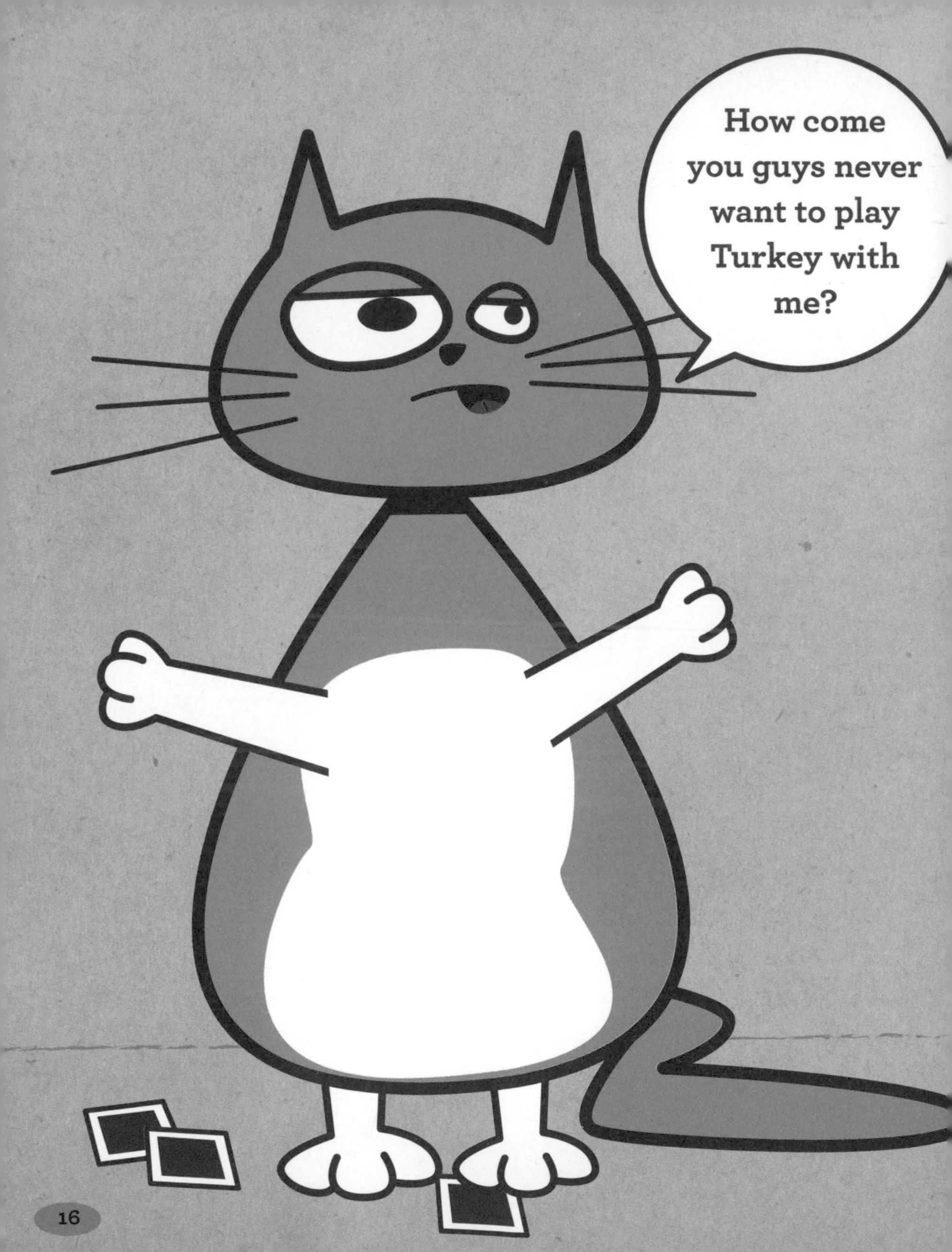
How come you guys never want to play Turkey with me?

# Chapter One:
# THE CONTEST

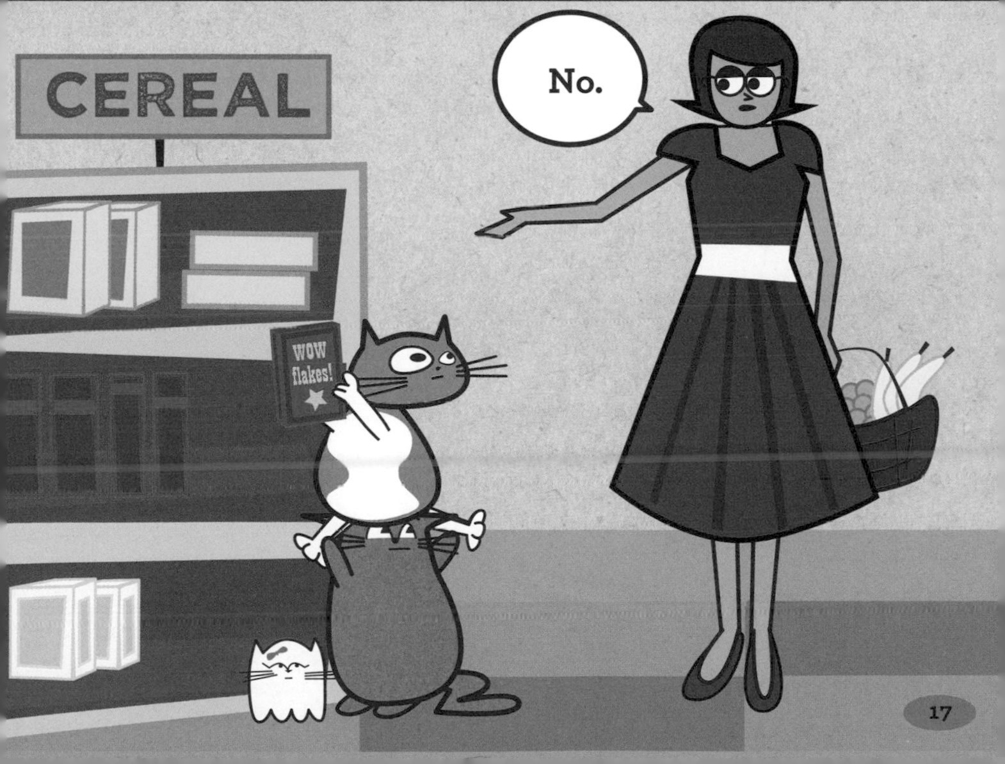
CEREAL
No.
WOW
flakes!

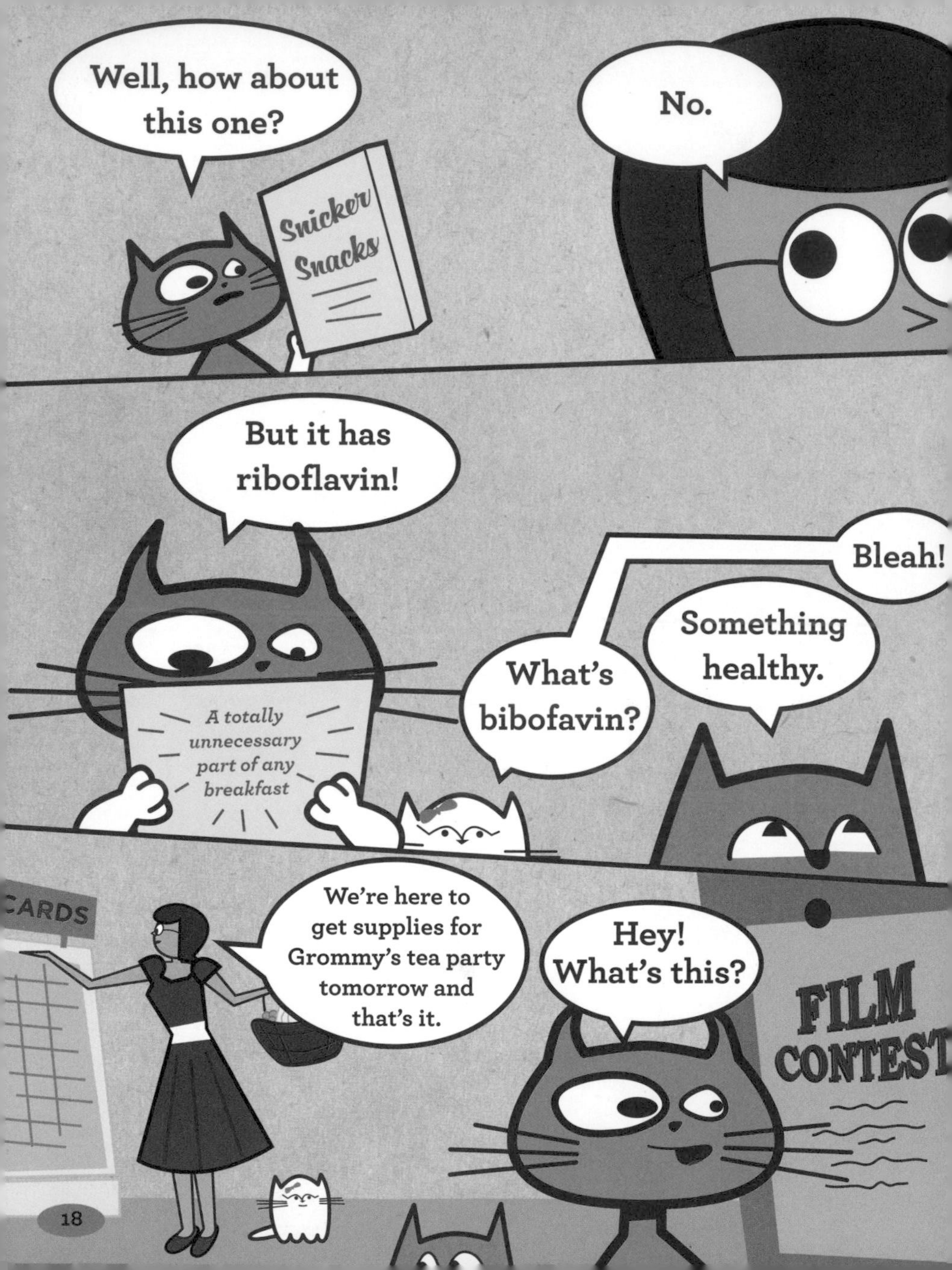

Well, how about this one?
Snicker Snacks
No.
But it has riboflavin!
A totally unnecessary part of any breakfast
What's bibofavin?
Bleah!
Something healthy.
CARDS
We're here to get supplies for Grommy's tea party tomorrow and that's it.
Hey! What's this?
FILM CONTEST

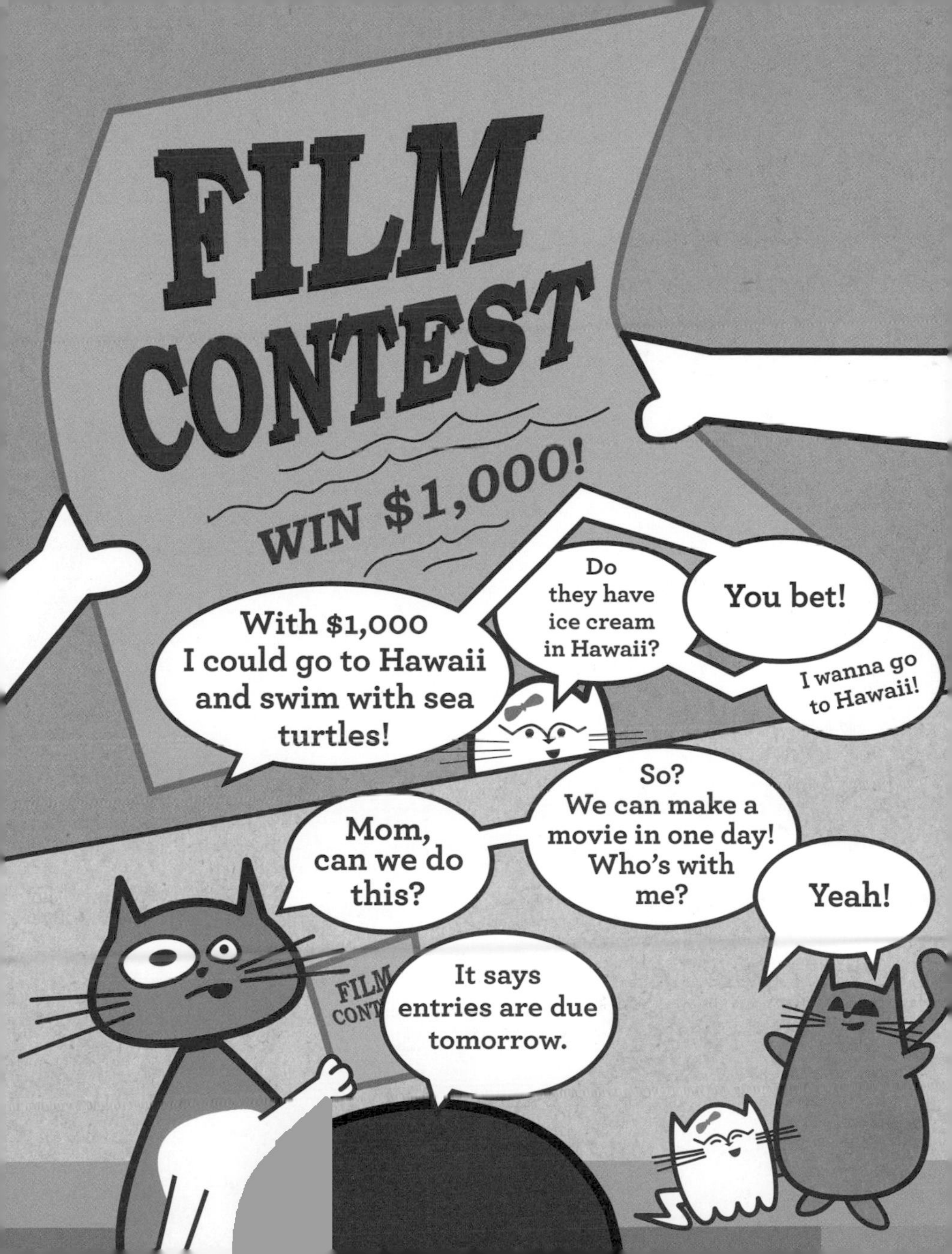
FILM CONTEST
WIN $1,000!
With $1,000 I could go to Hawaii and swim with sea turtles!
Do they have ice cream in Hawaii?
You bet!
I wanna go to Hawaii!
Mom, can we do this?
So? We can make a movie in one day! Who's with me?
Yeah!
It says entries are due tomorrow.

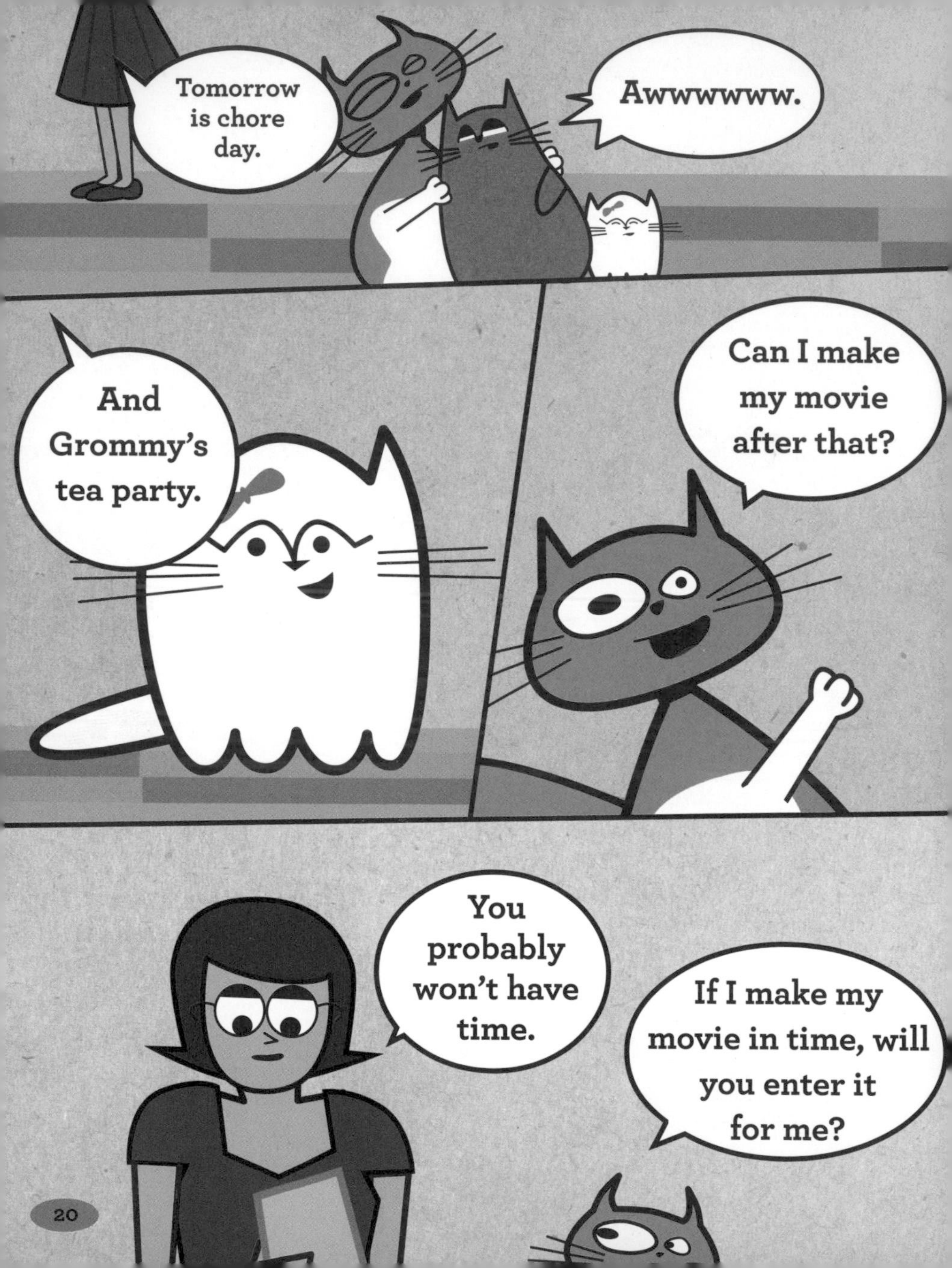
Tomorrow is chore day.
Awwwwww.
And Grommy's tea party.
Can I make my movie after that?
You probably won't have time.
If I make my movie in time, will you enter it for me?

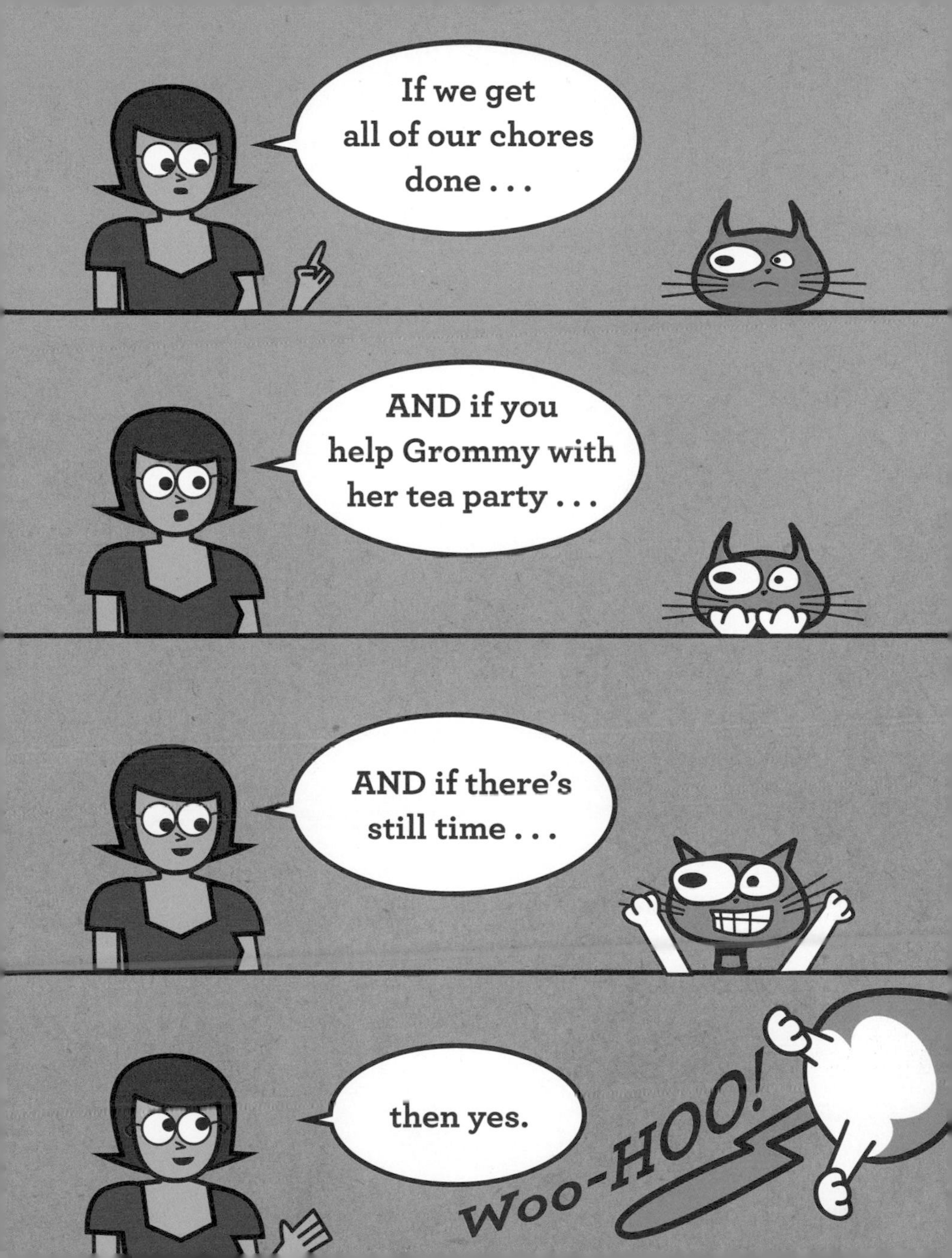
If we get all of our chores done . . .
AND if you help Grommy with her tea party . . .
AND if there's still time . . .
then yes.
Woo-HOO!

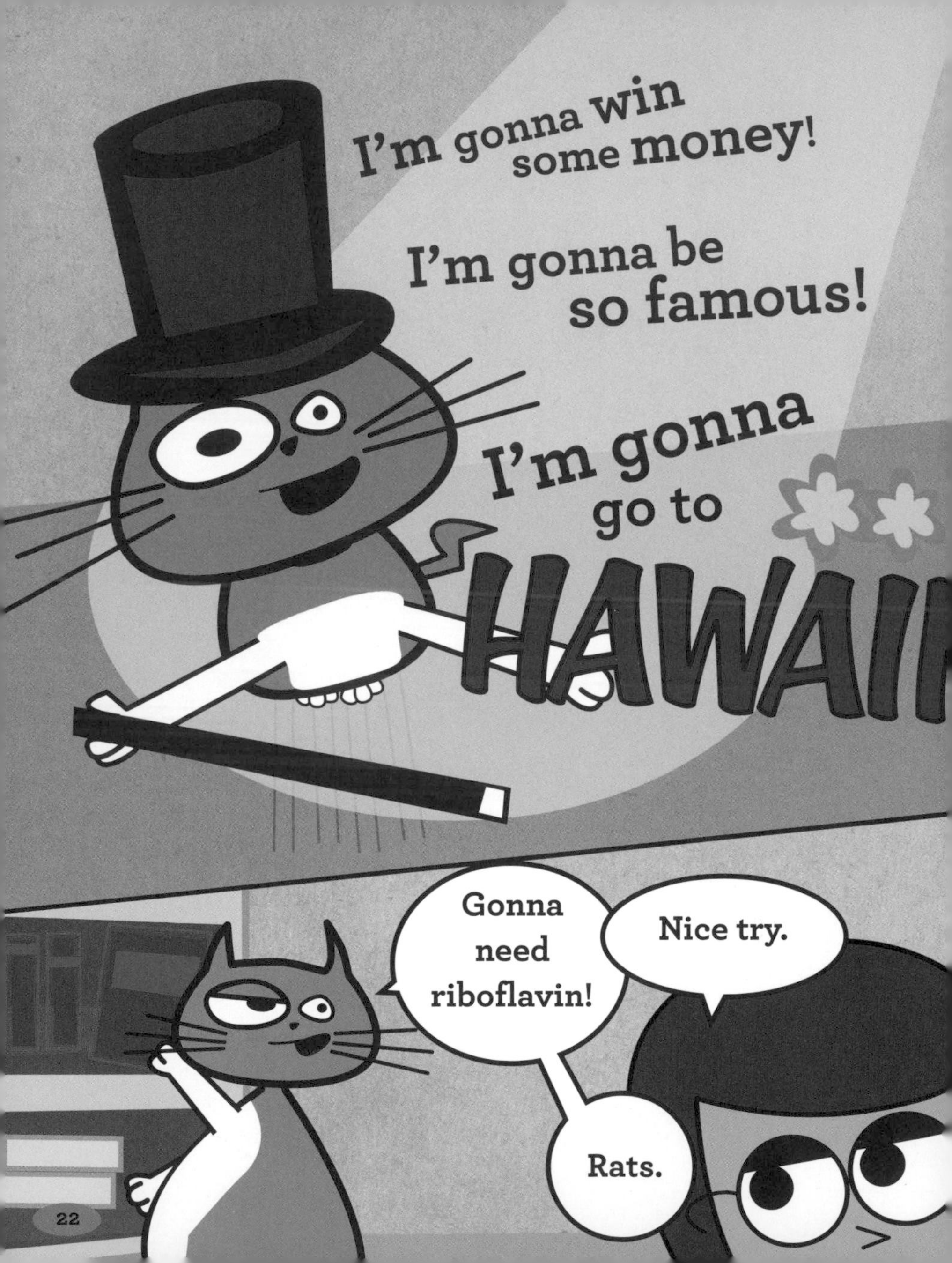
I'm gonna win some money!
I'm gonna be so famous!
I'm gonna go to
HAWAII
Gonna need riboflavin!
Nice try.
Rats.

# Chapter Two:
# THE HONESTLY BOMB

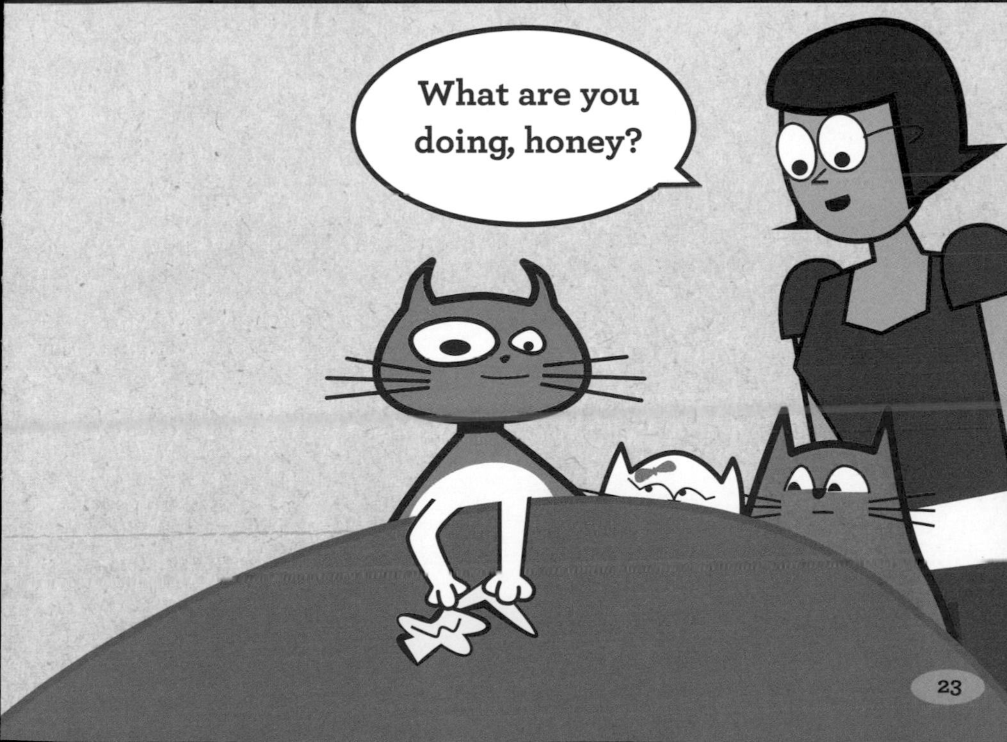
What are you doing, honey?

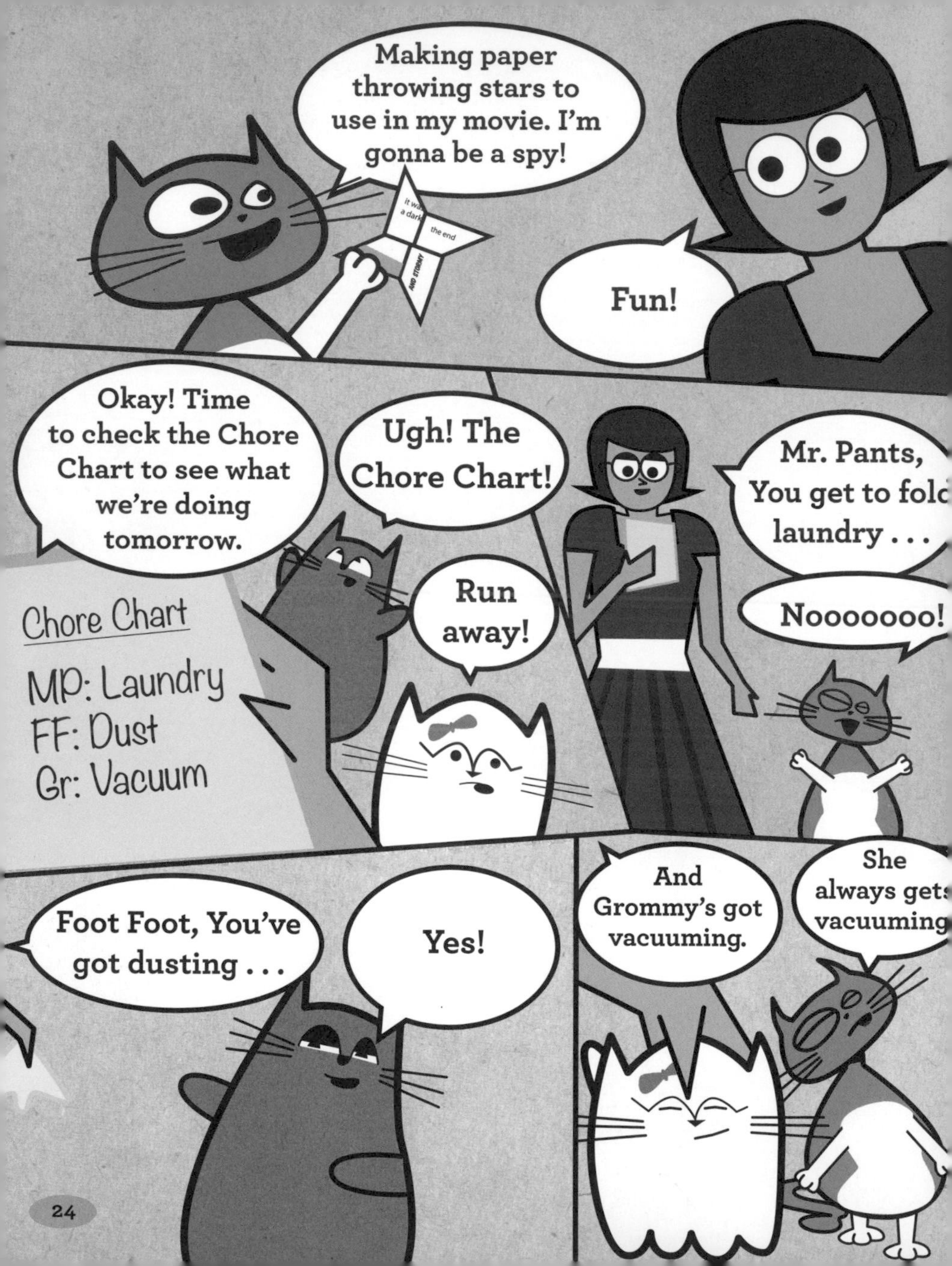

Making paper throwing stars to use in my movie. I'm gonna be a spy!
it wa a dark
the end
AND STORMY
Fun!
Okay! Time to check the Chore Chart to see what we're doing tomorrow.
Ugh! The Chore Chart!
Chore Chart
MP: Laundry
FF: Dust
Gr: Vacuum
Run away!
Mr. Pants, You get to fold laundry . . .
Noooooo!
Foot Foot, You've got dusting . . .
Yes!
And Grommy's got vacuuming.
She always gets vacuuming

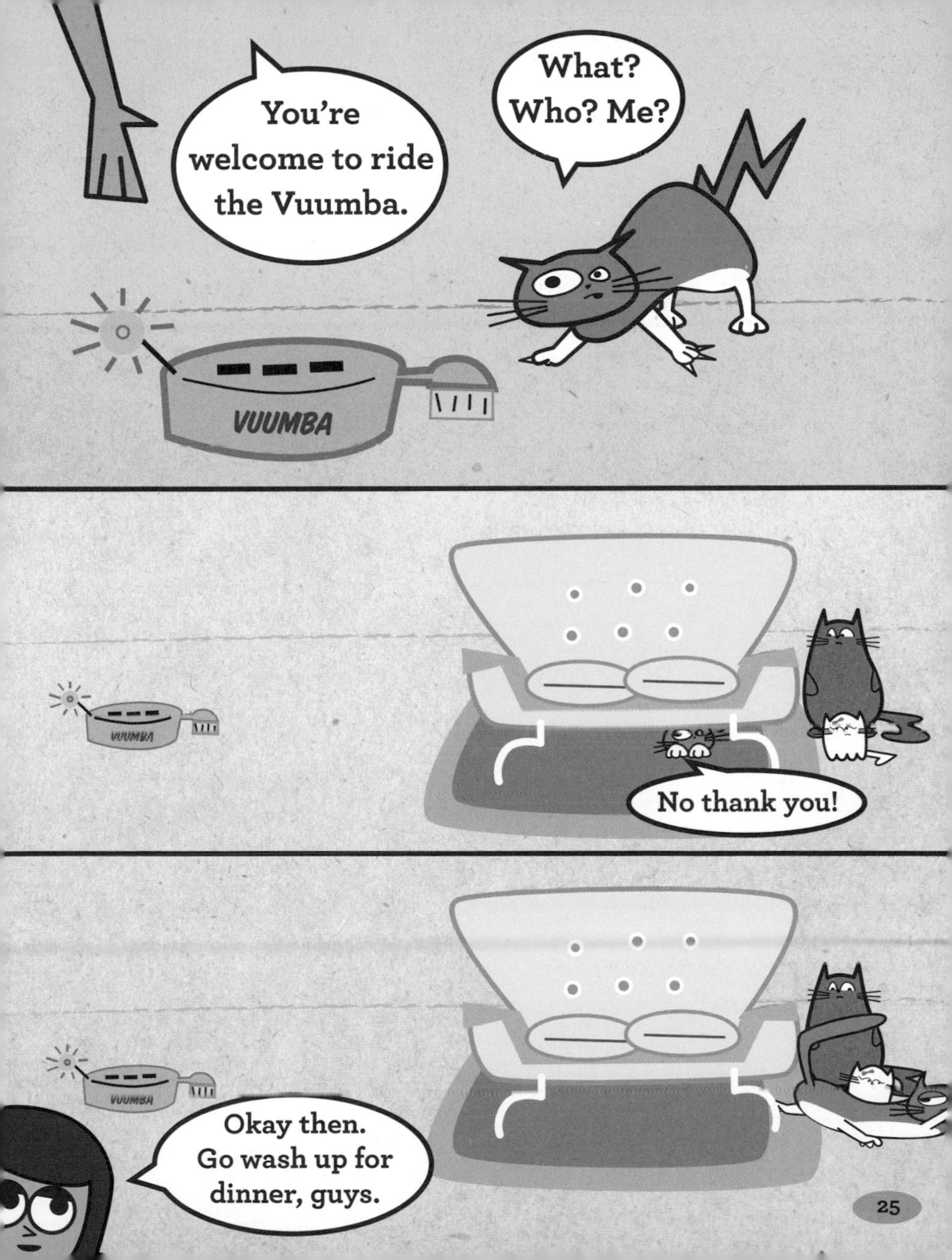

You're welcome to ride the Vuumba.
What? Who? Me?
VUUMBA
VUUMBA
No thank you!
VUUMBA
Okay then. Go wash up for dinner, guys.

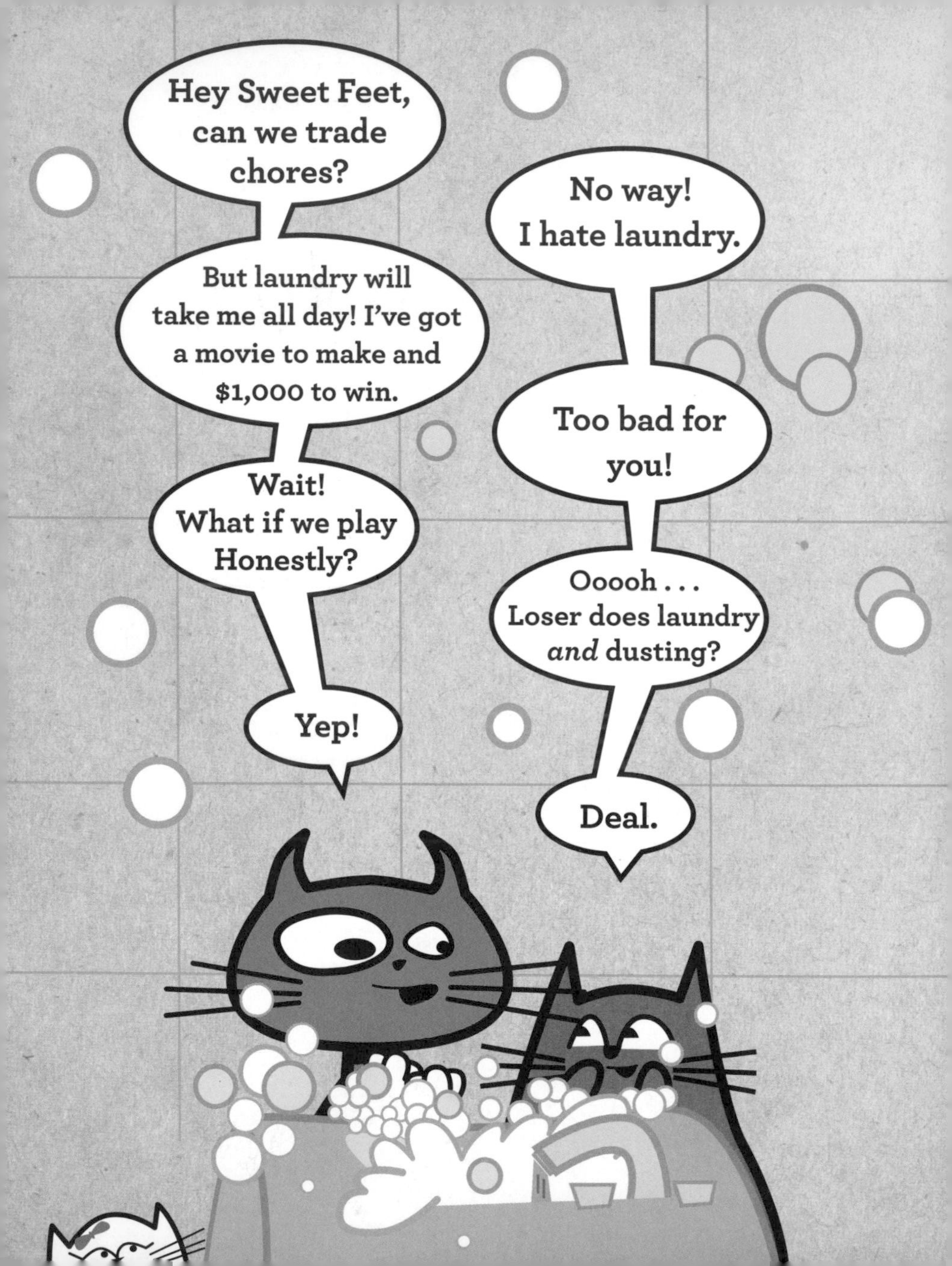
Hey Sweet Feet, can we trade chores?
No way! I hate laundry.
But laundry will take me all day! I've got a movie to make and $1,000 to win.
Too bad for you!
Wait! What if we play Honestly?
Ooooh . . . Loser does laundry *and* dusting?
Yep!
Deal.

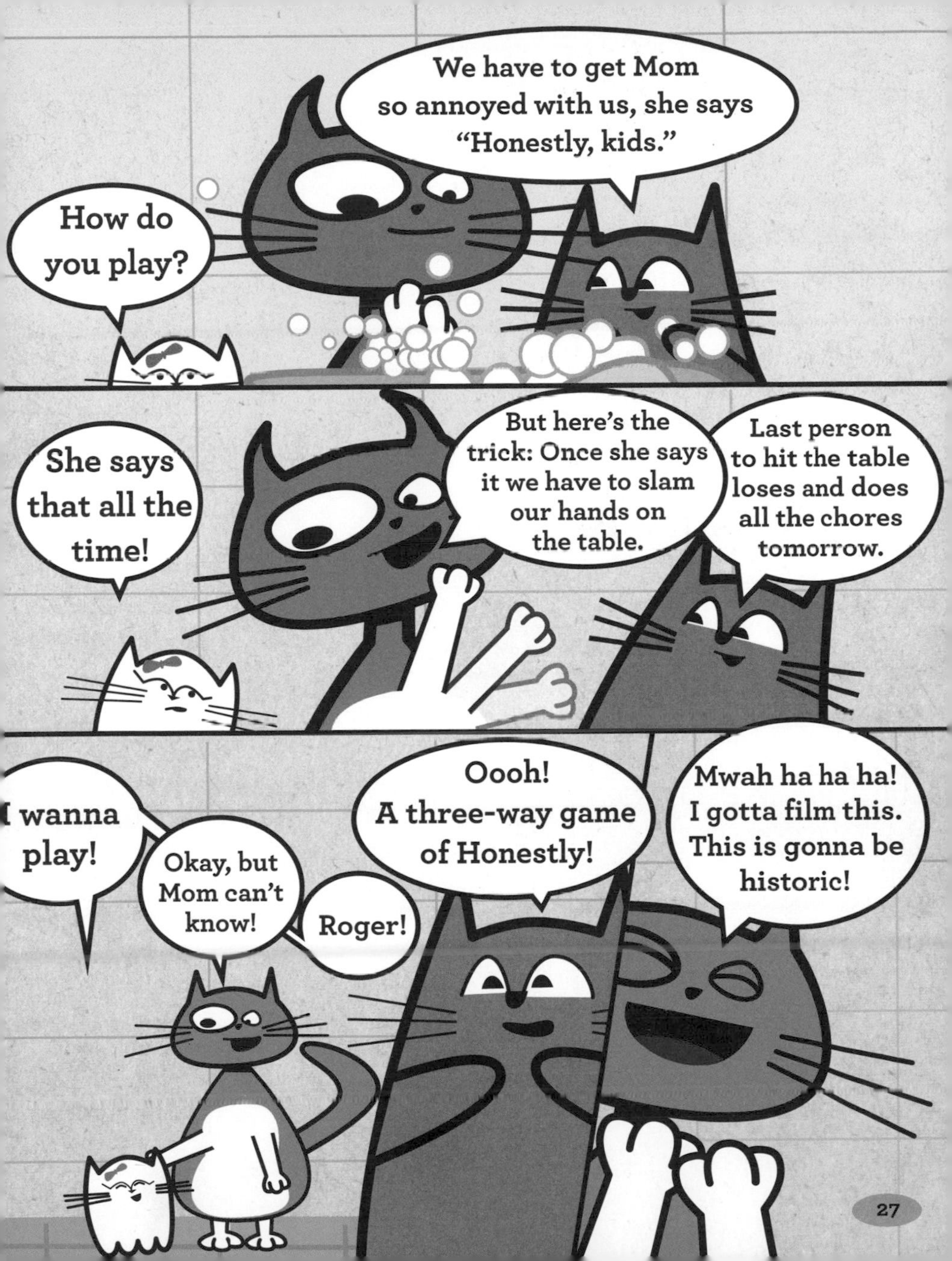
We have to get Mom so annoyed with us, she says "Honestly, kids."
How do you play?
She says that all the time!
But here's the trick: Once she says it we have to slam our hands on the table.
Last person to hit the table loses and does all the chores tomorrow.
I wanna play!
Okay, but Mom can't know!
Roger!
Oooh! A three-way game of Honestly!
Mwah ha ha ha! I gotta film this. This is gonna be historic!

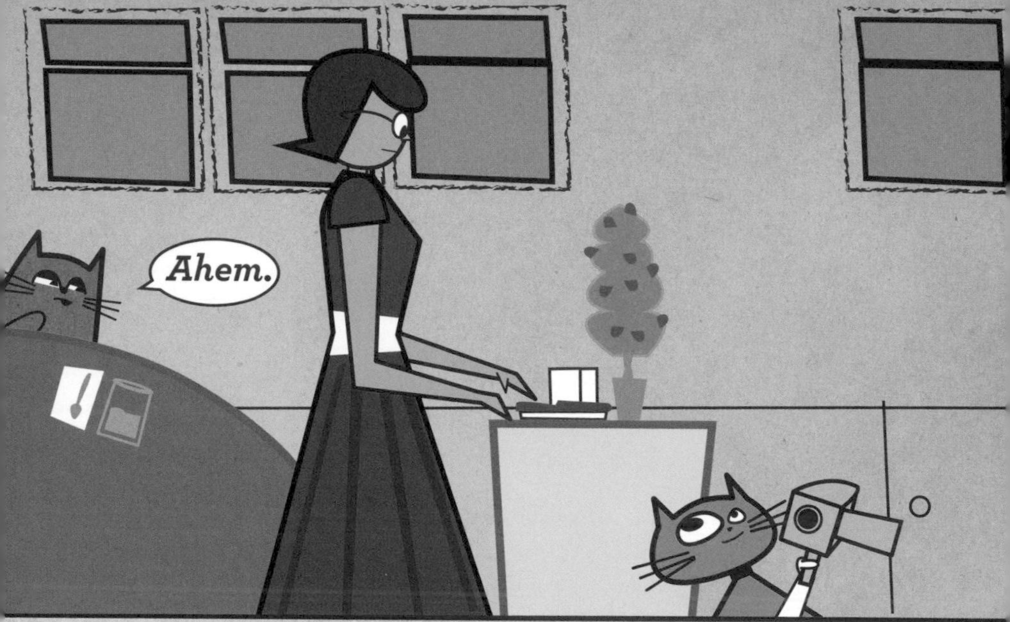
Ahem.

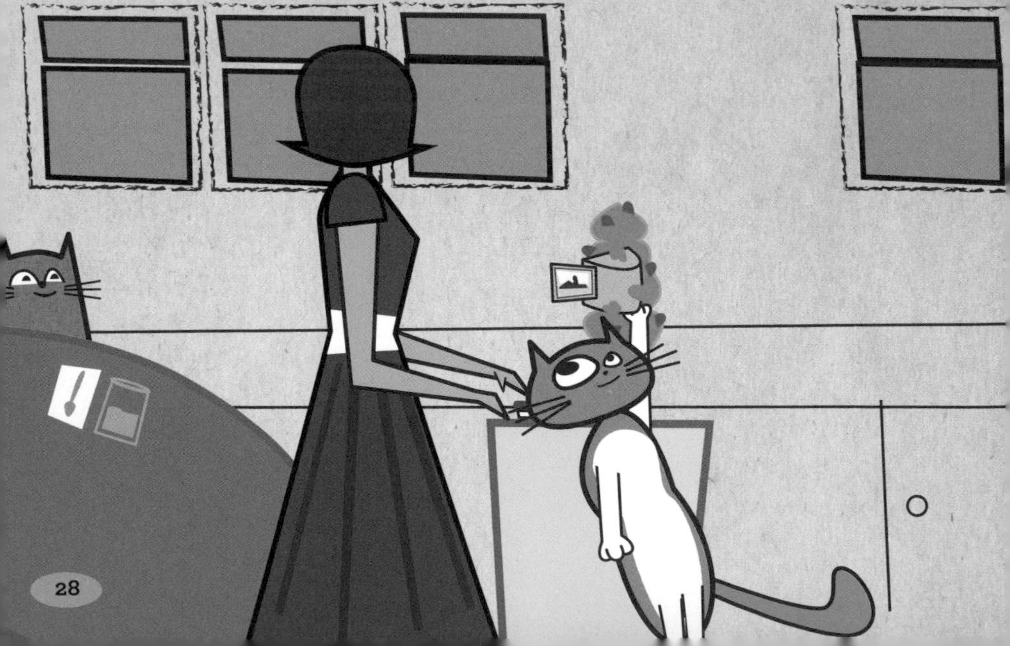

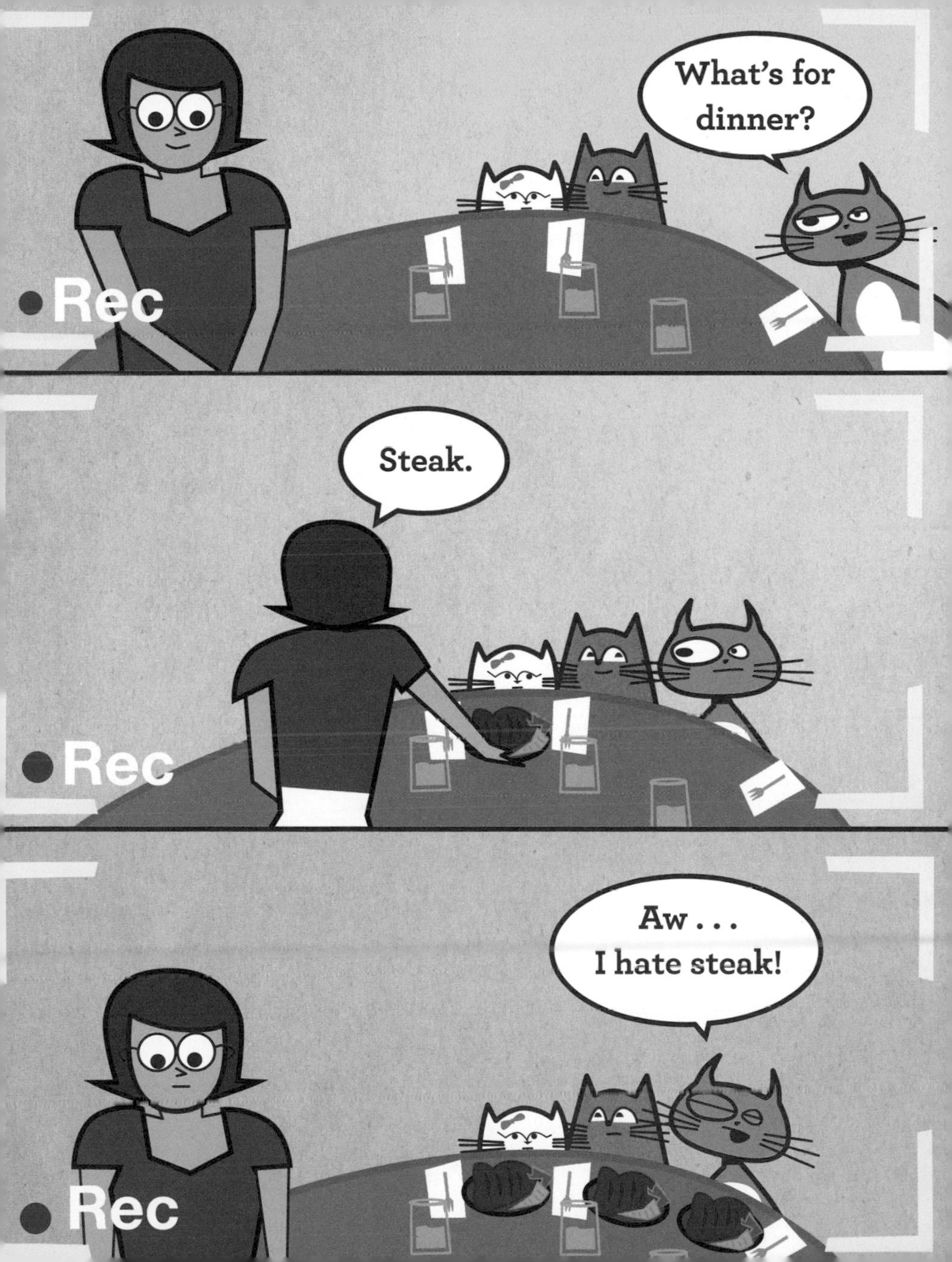
Rec
What's for dinner?
Rec
Steak.
Rec
Aw . . .
I hate steak!

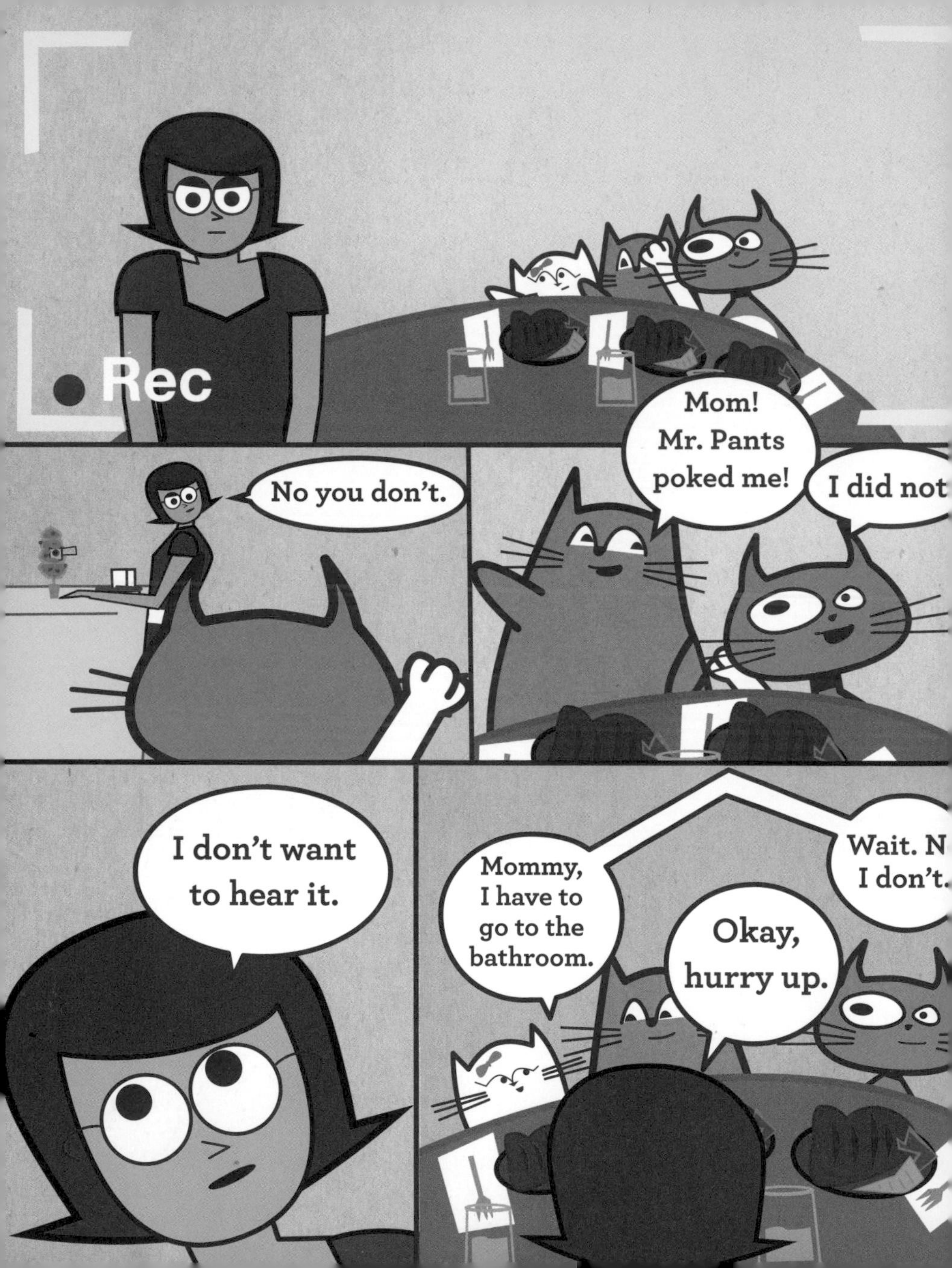
Rec
No you don't.
Mom! Mr. Pants poked me!
I did not
I don't want to hear it.
Mommy, I have to go to the bathroom.
Wait. N I don't.
Okay, hurry up.

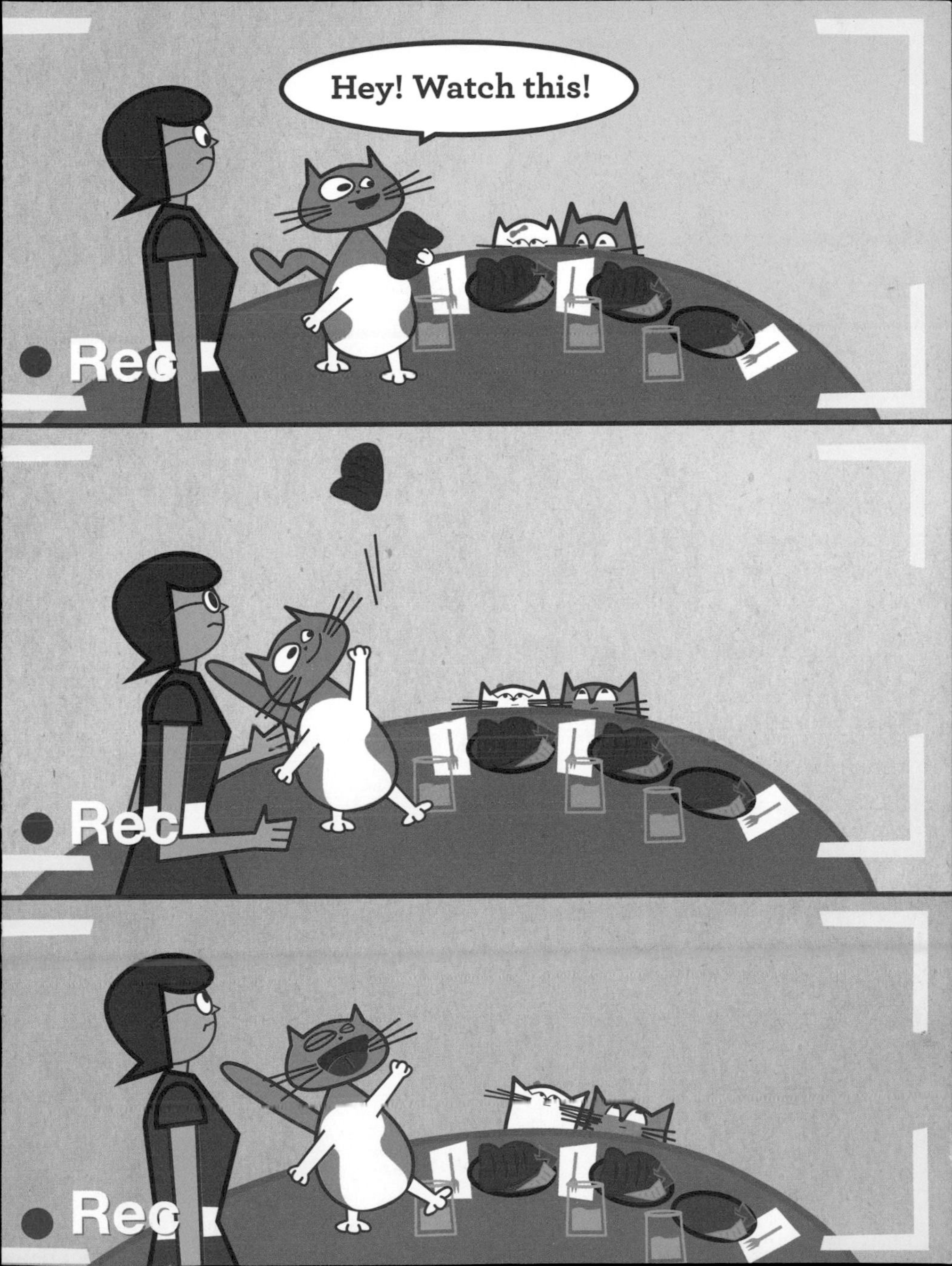
Hey! Watch this!
Rec
Rec
Rec

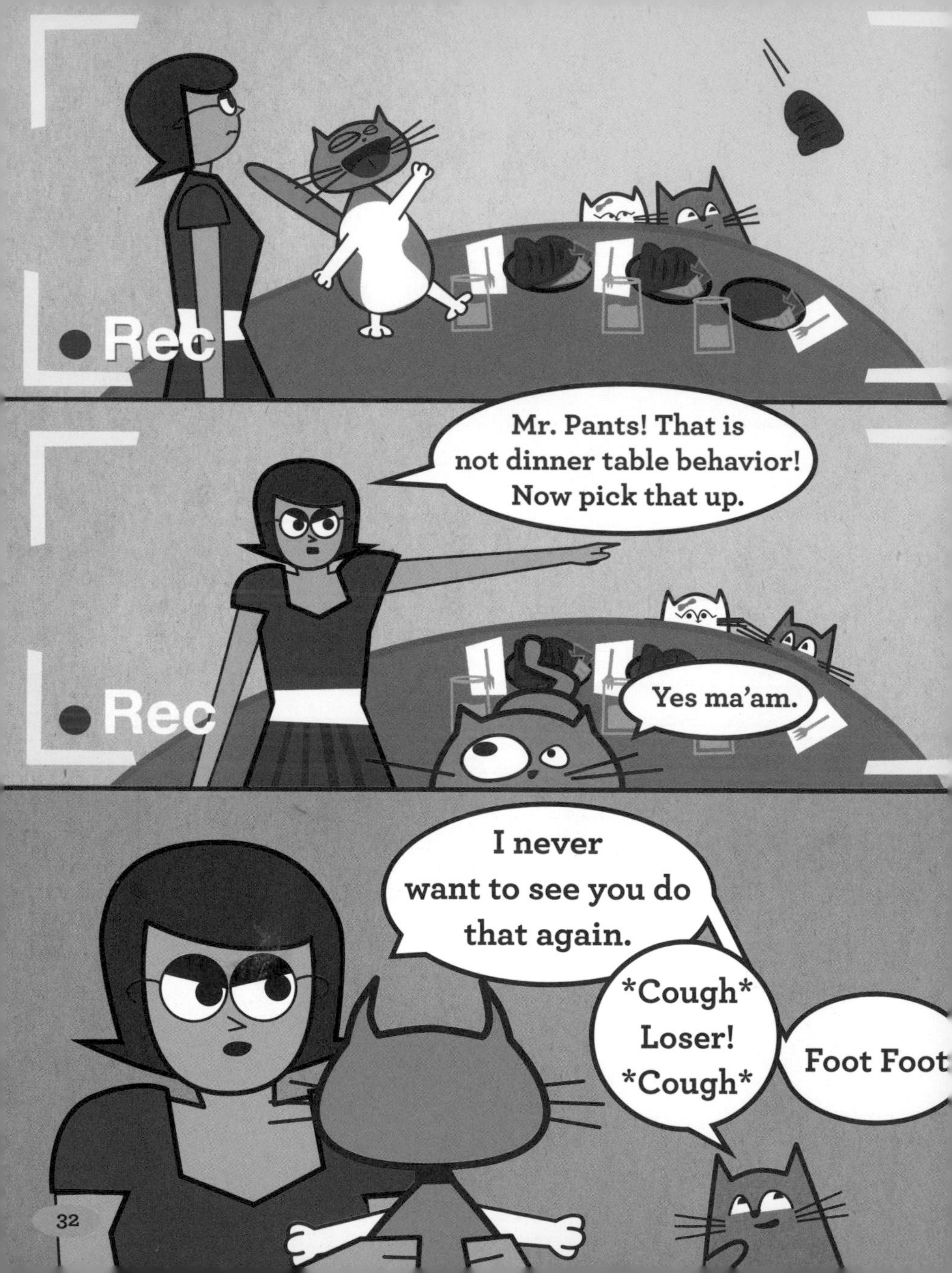
●Rec
Mr. Pants! That is not dinner table behavior! Now pick that up.
Yes ma'am.
●Rec
I never want to see you do that again.
*Cough* Loser! *Cough*
Foot Foot

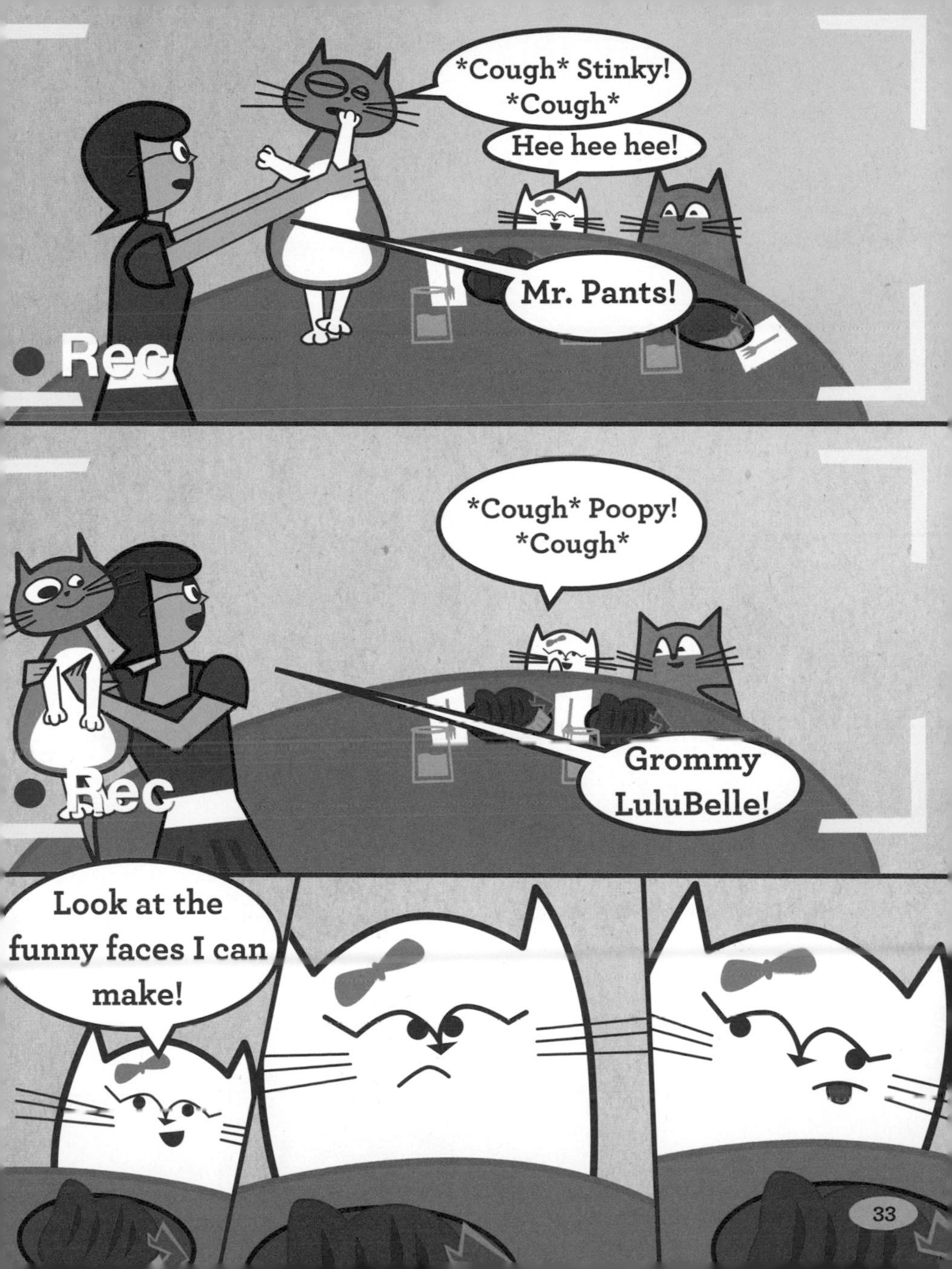

*Cough* Stinky! *Cough*
Hee hee hee!
Mr. Pants!
Rec
*Cough* Poopy! *Cough*
Grommy LuluBelle!
Rec
Look at the funny faces I can make!

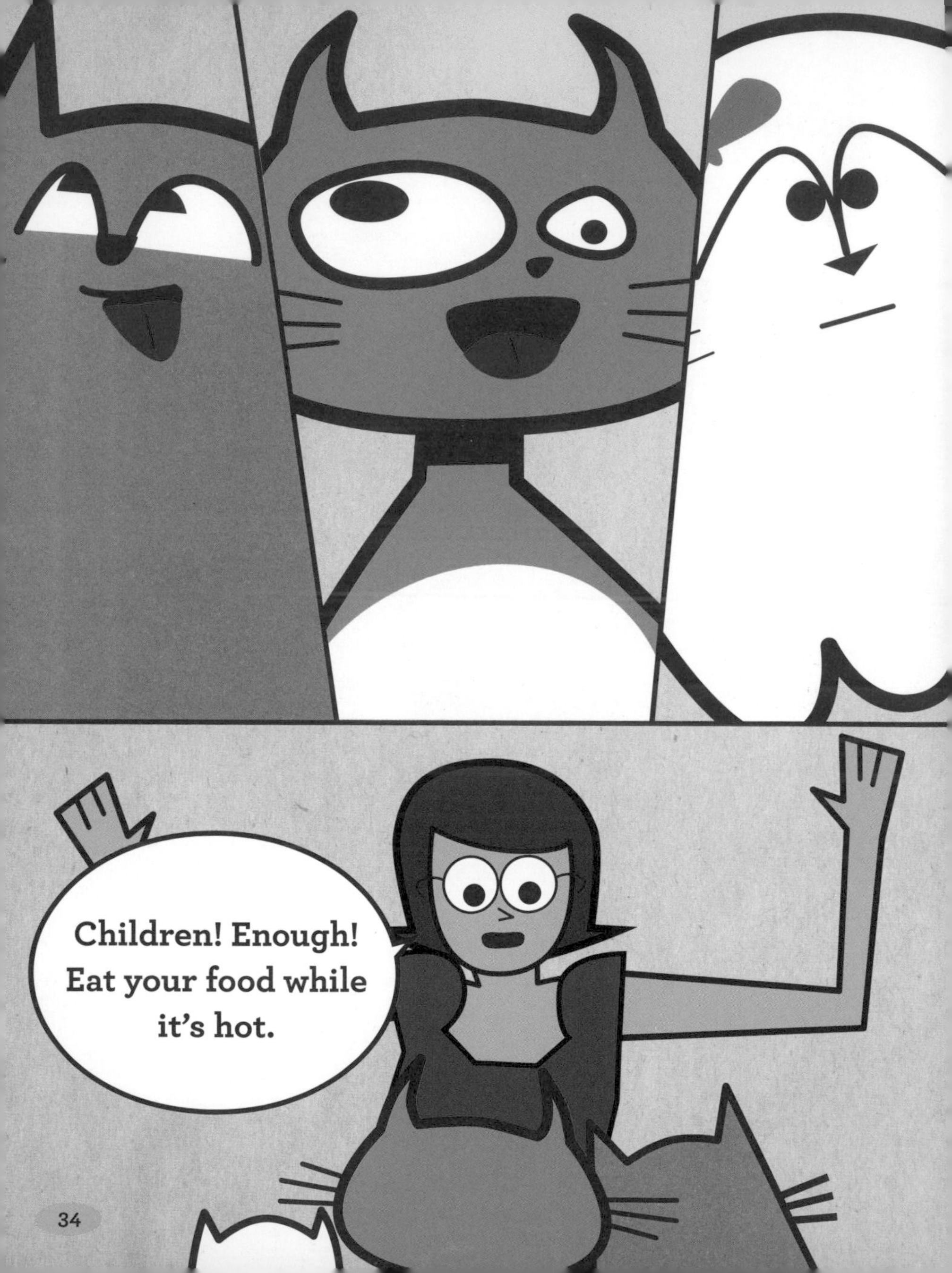
Children! Enough! Eat your food while it's hot.

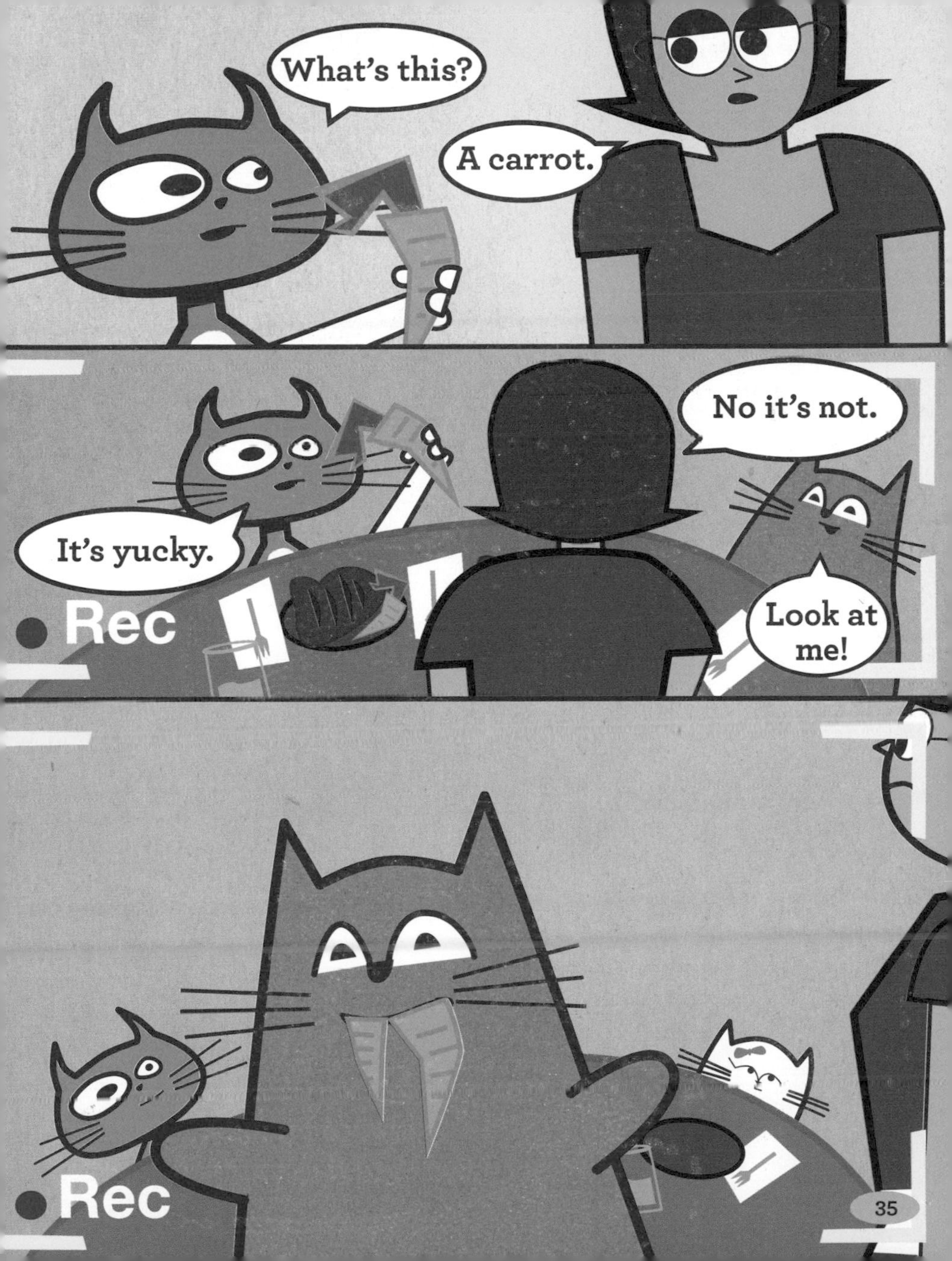
What's this?
A carrot.
No it's not.
It's yucky.
Look at me!
Rec
Rec

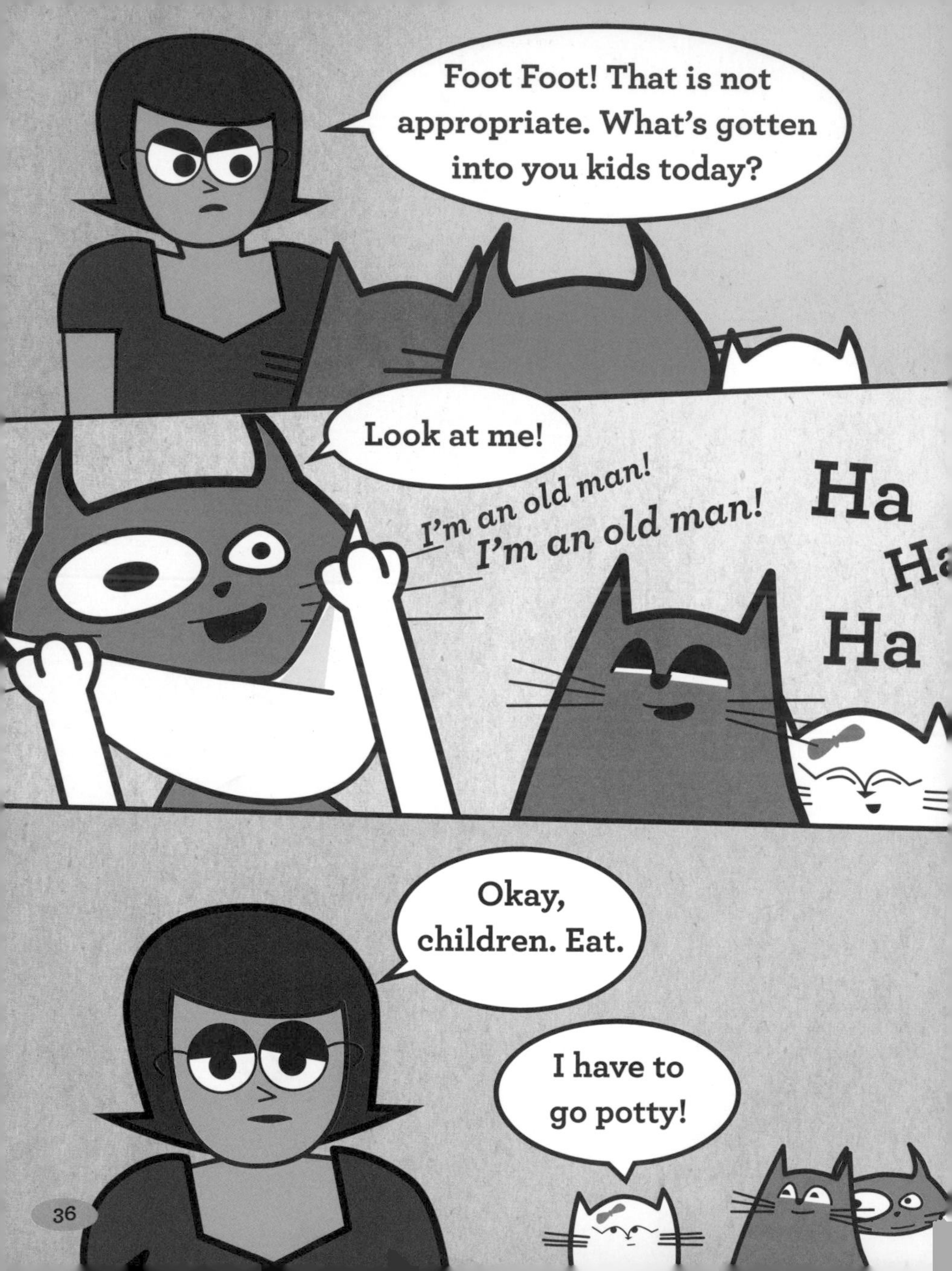

Foot Foot! That is not appropriate. What's gotten into you kids today?
Look at me!
I'm an old man!
I'm an old man!
Ha
Ha
Ha
Okay, children. Eat.
I have to go potty!

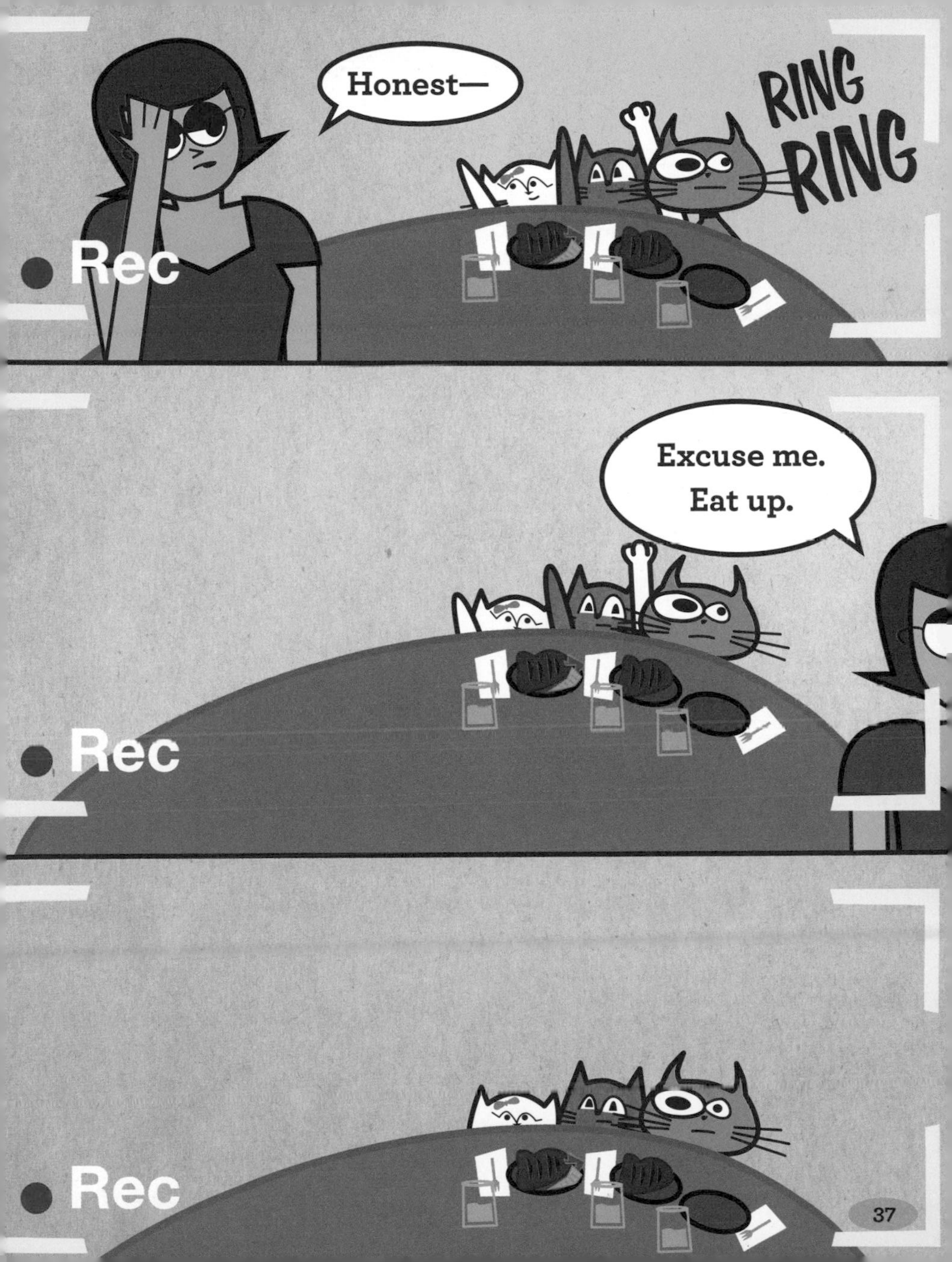
Honest—
RING
RING
Rec
Excuse me.
Eat up.
Rec
Rec

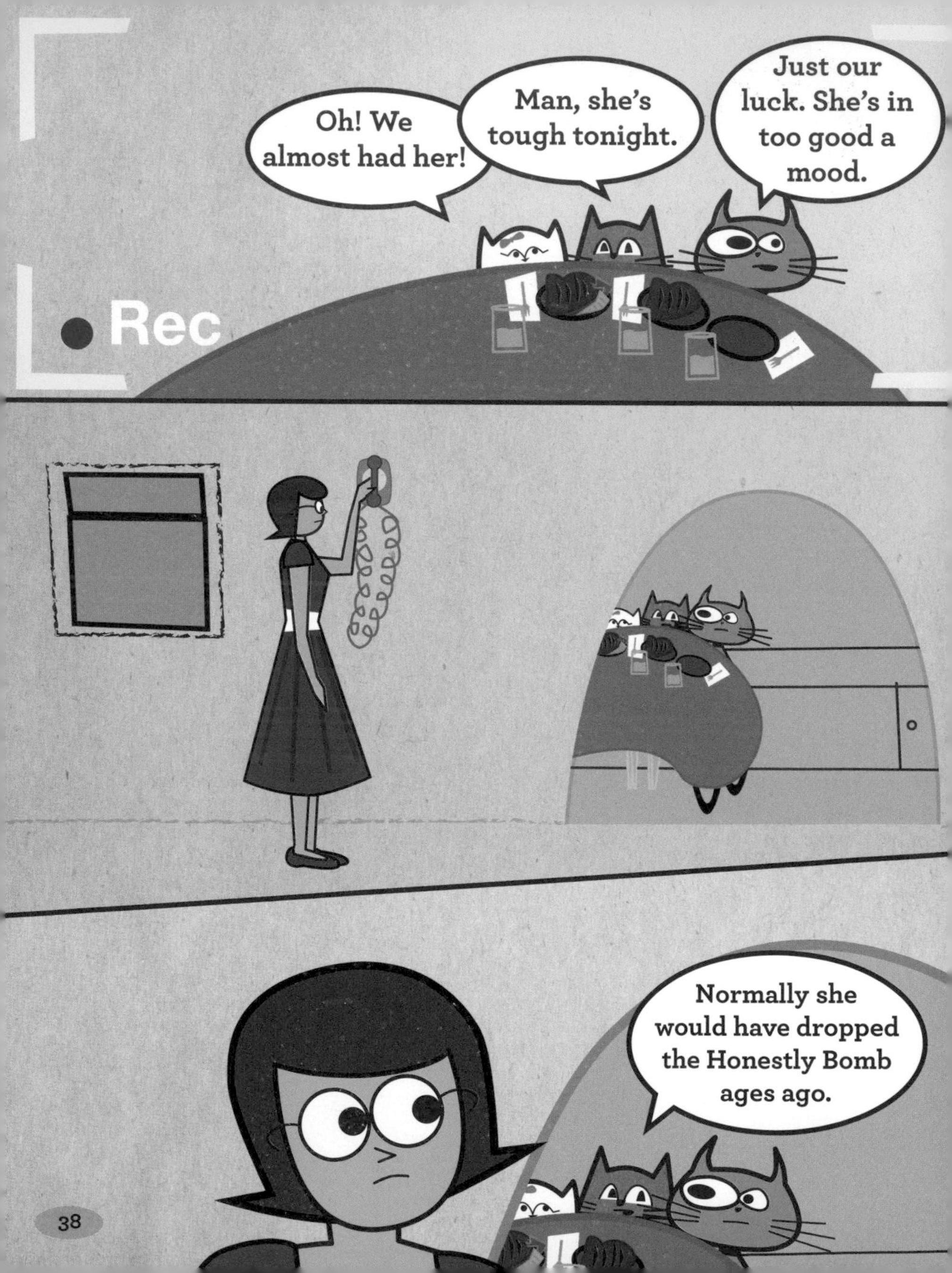
Oh! We almost had her!
Man, she's tough tonight.
Just our luck. She's in too good a mood.
Rec
Normally she would have dropped the Honestly Bomb ages ago.

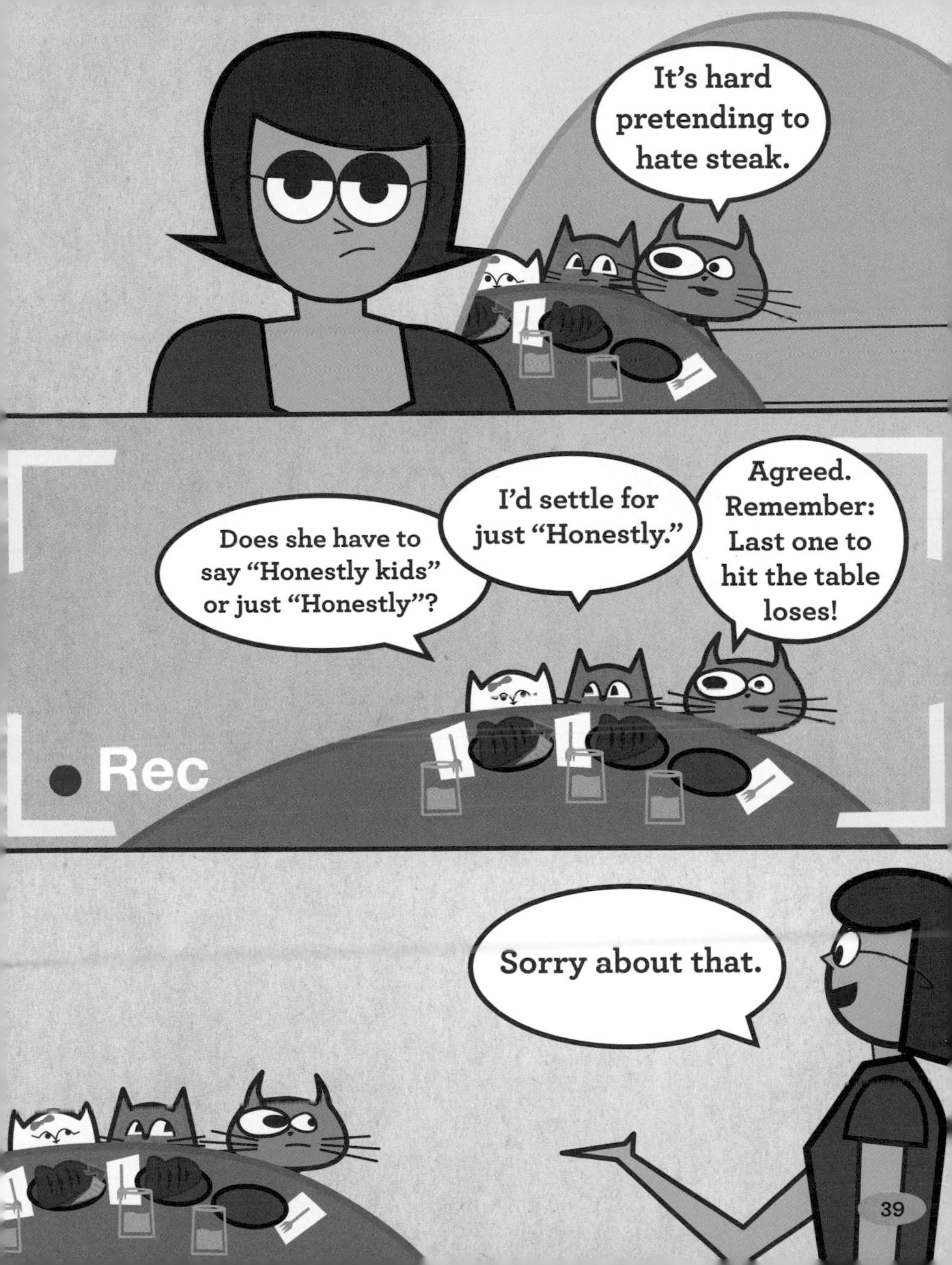
It's hard pretending to hate steak.
Does she have to say "Honestly kids" or just "Honestly"?
I'd settle for just "Honestly."
Agreed. Remember: Last one to hit the table loses!
Rec
Sorry about that.

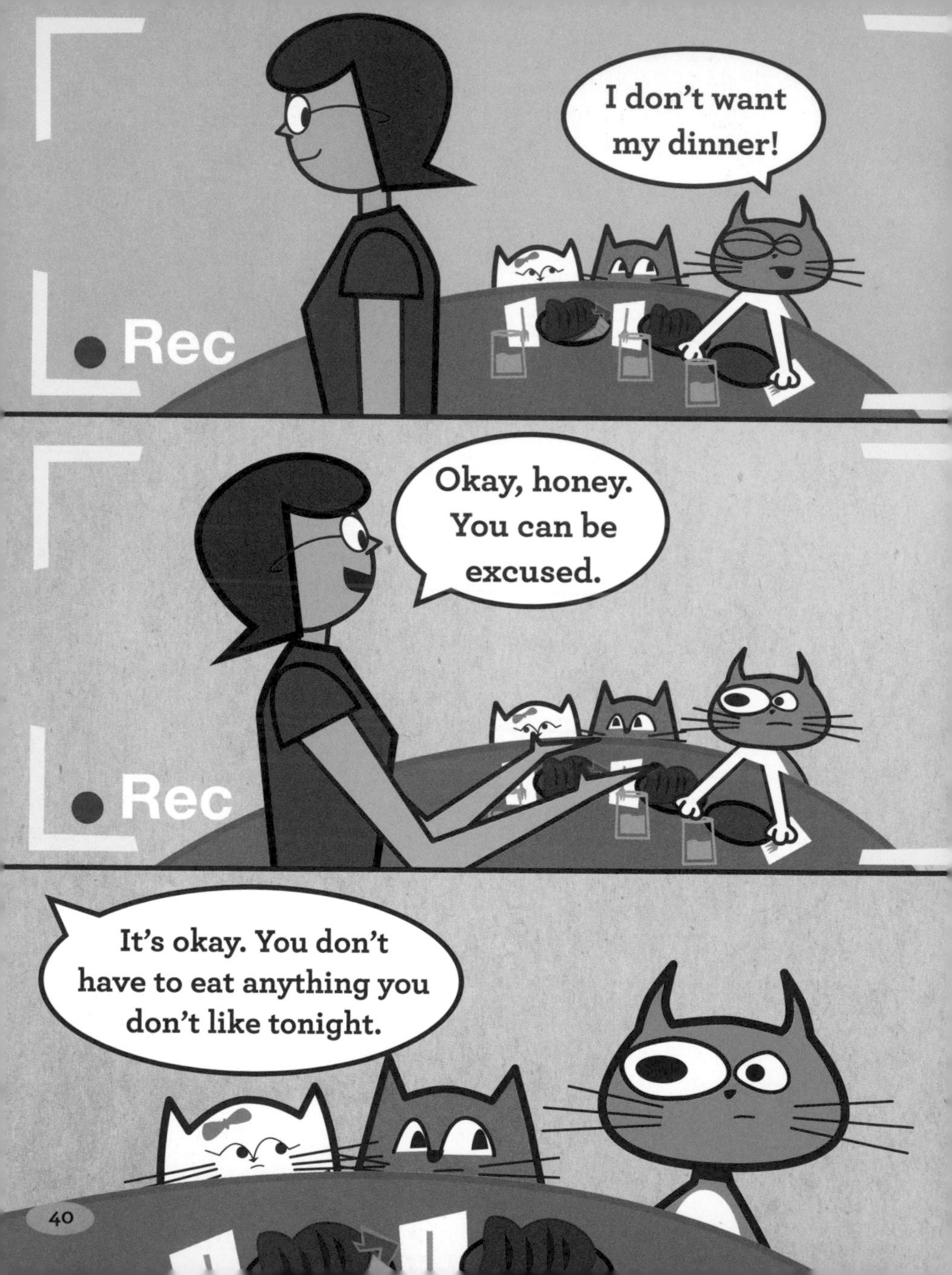
I don't want my dinner!
Rec
Okay, honey. You can be excused.
Rec
It's okay. You don't have to eat anything you don't like tonight.

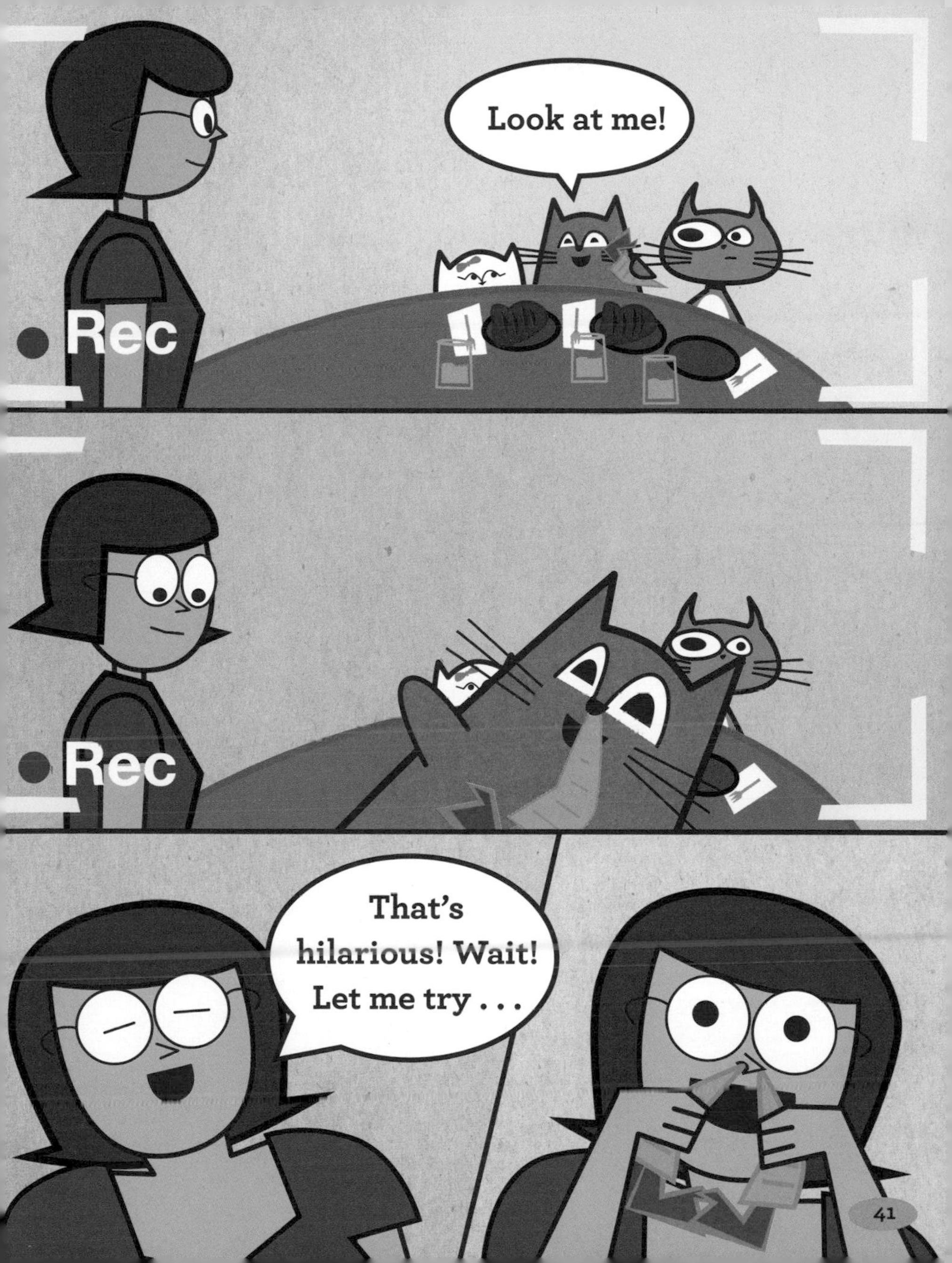
Look at me!
Rec
Rec
That's hilarious! Wait! Let me try . . .

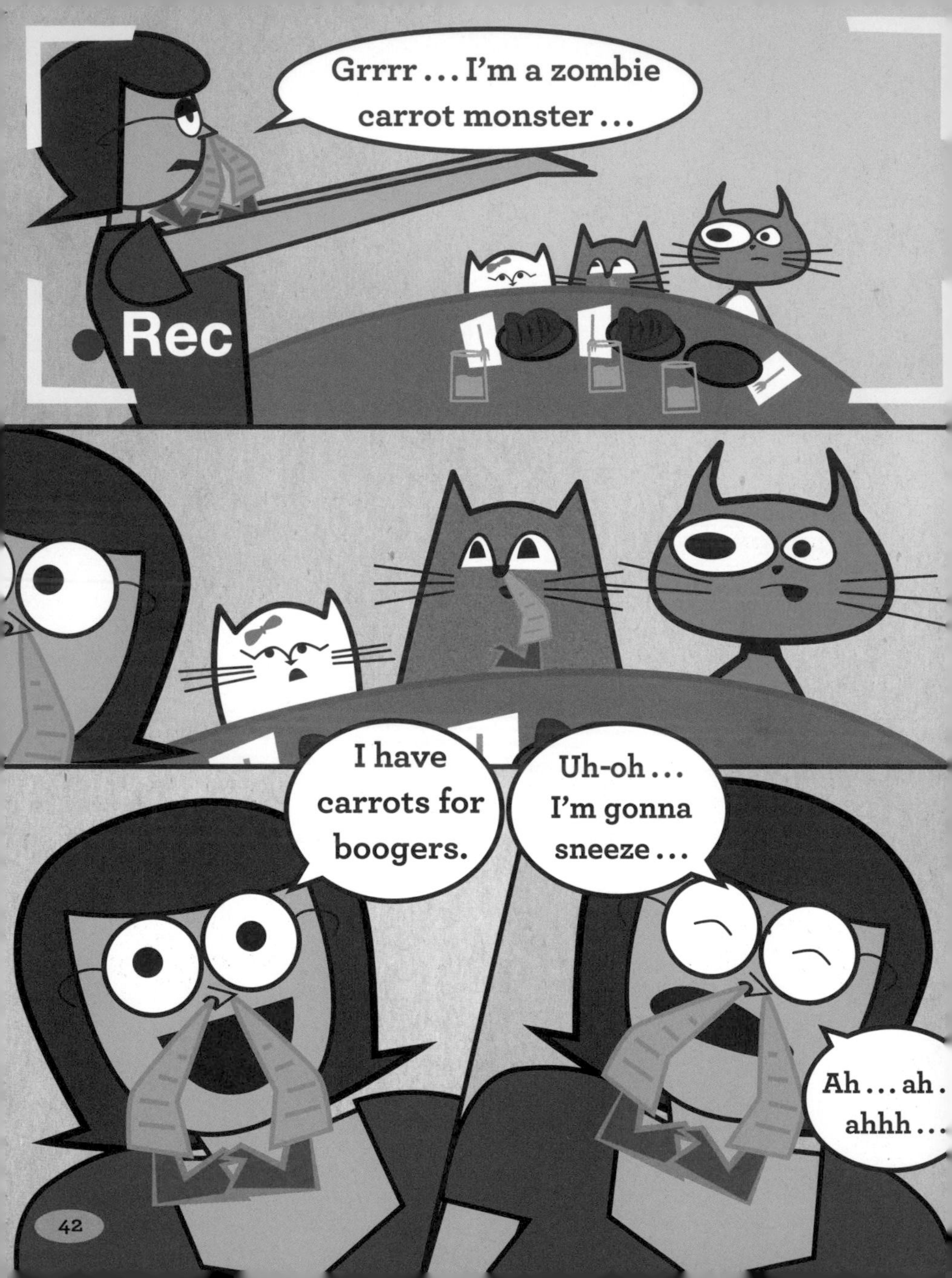
Grrrr . . . I'm a zombie carrot monster . . .
Rec
I have carrots for boogers.
Uh-oh . . . I'm gonna sneeze . . .
Ah . . . ah . . . ahhh . . .

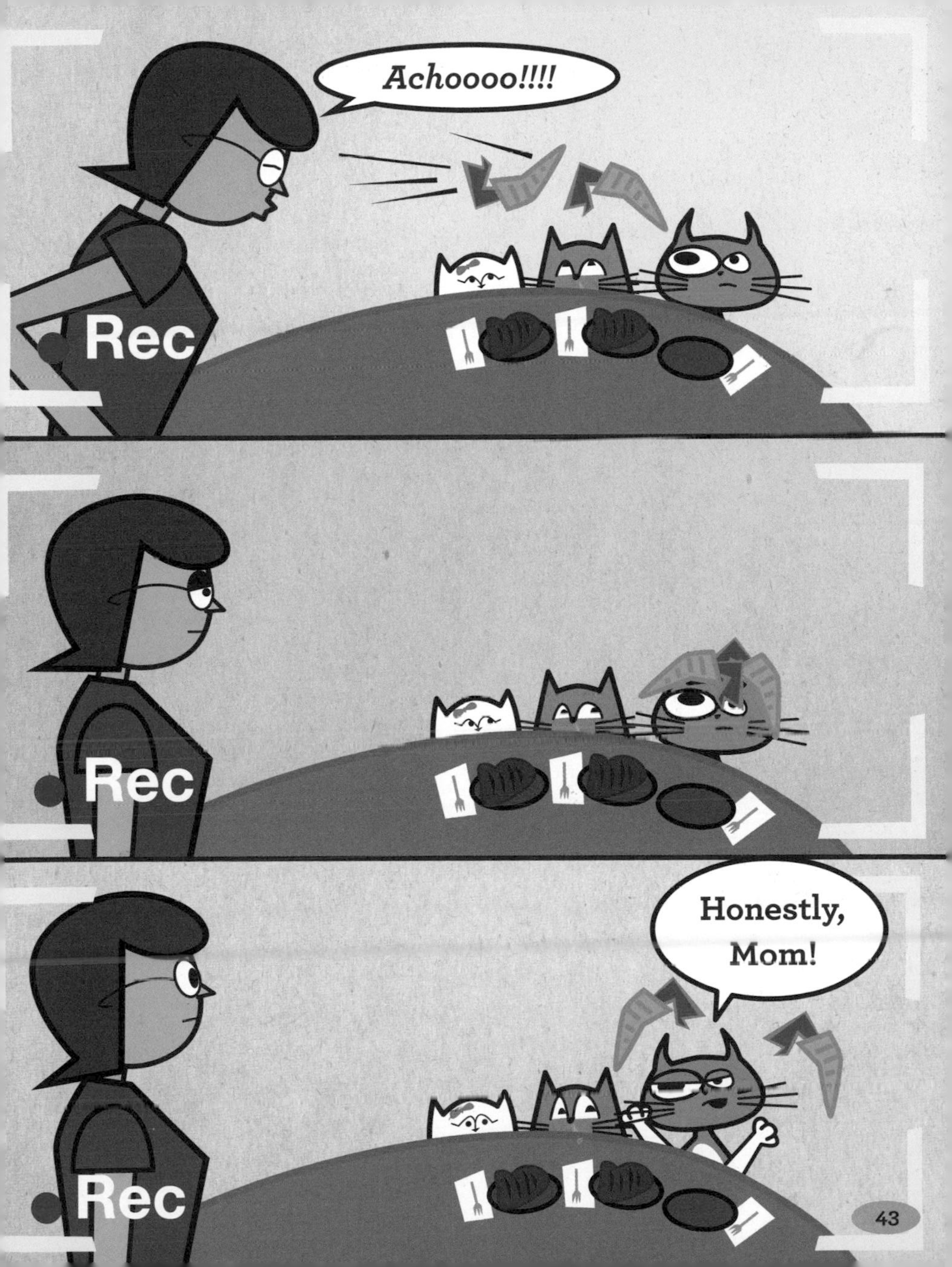
Achoooo!!!!
Rec
Rec
Honestly, Mom!
Rec

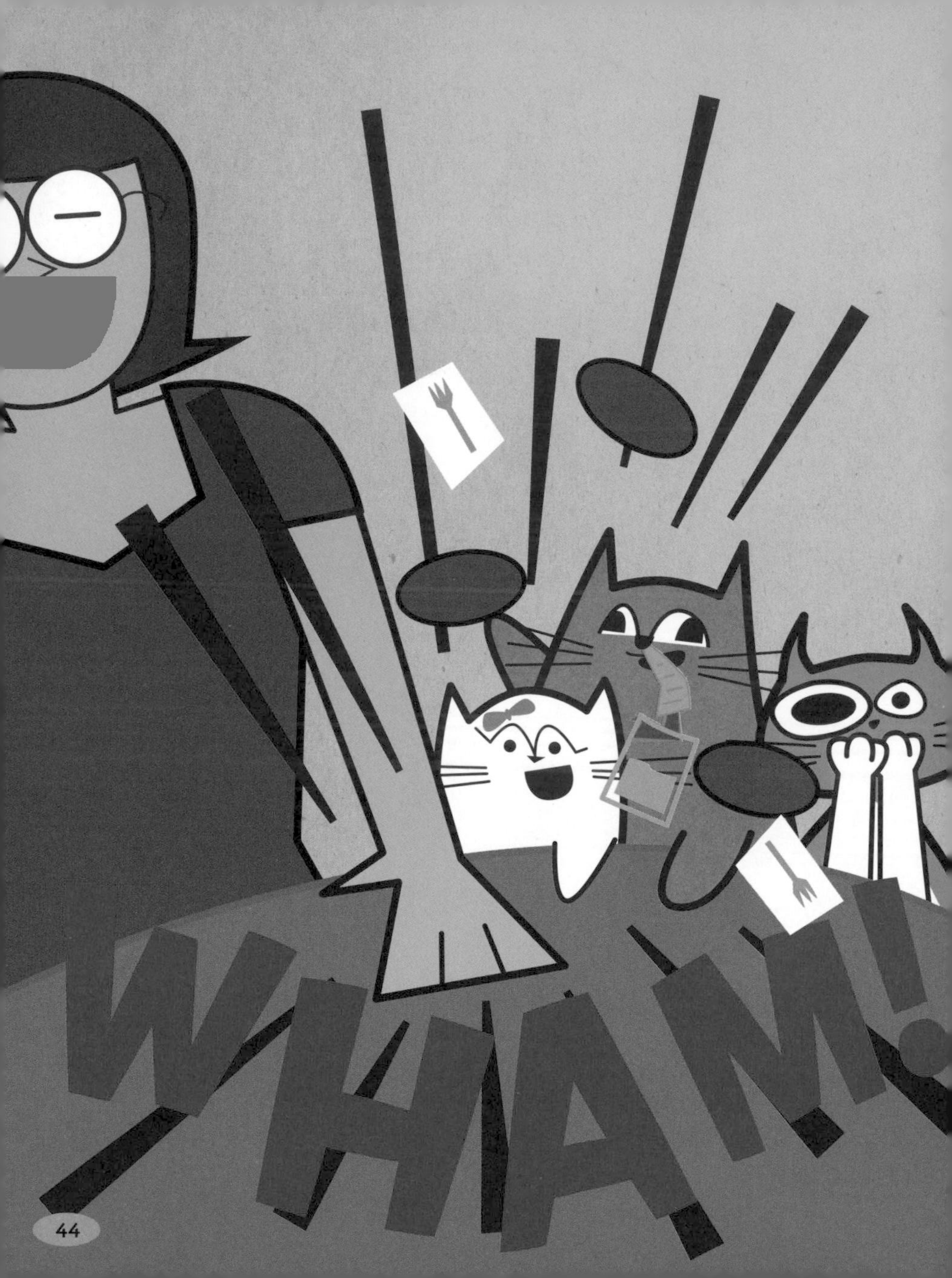
WHAM!

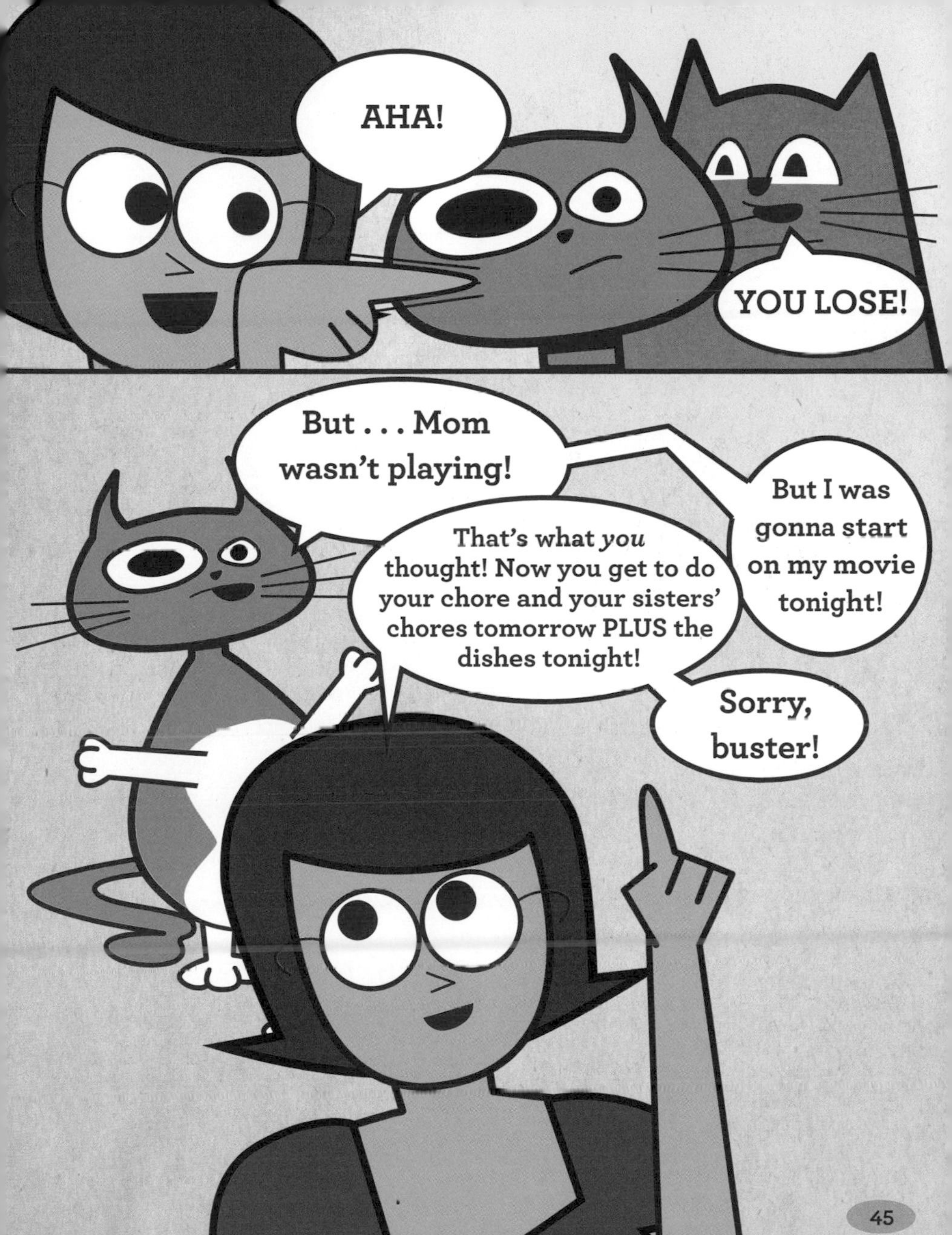
AHA!
YOU LOSE!
But . . . Mom wasn't playing!
But I was gonna start on my movie tonight!
That's what *you* thought! Now you get to do your chore and your sisters' chores tomorrow PLUS the dishes tonight!
Sorry, buster!

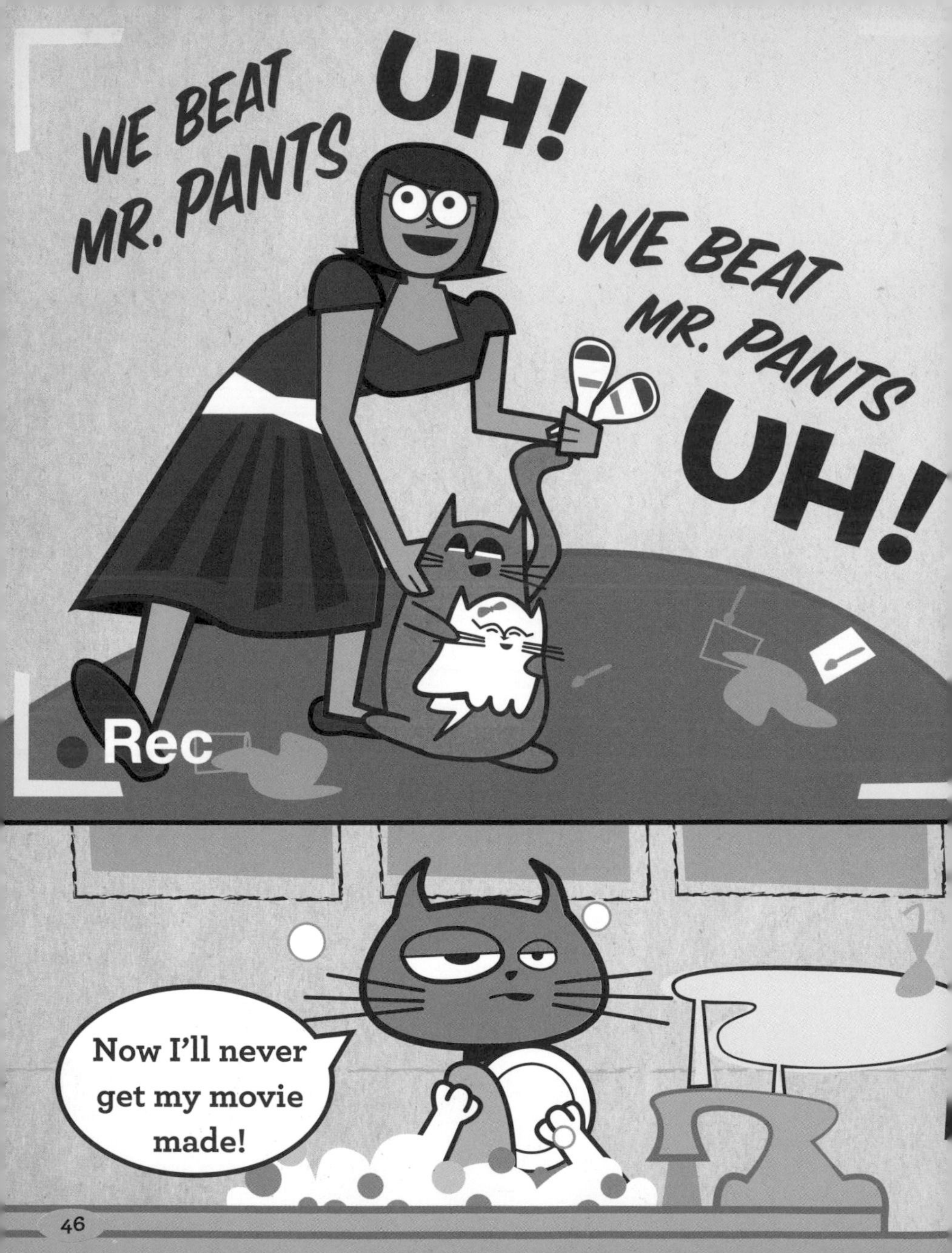
WE BEAT MR. PANTS UH!
WE BEAT MR. PANTS UH!
Rec
Now I'll never get my movie made!

# Chapter Three:
# BUM-BUM'S VUUMBA BOOM

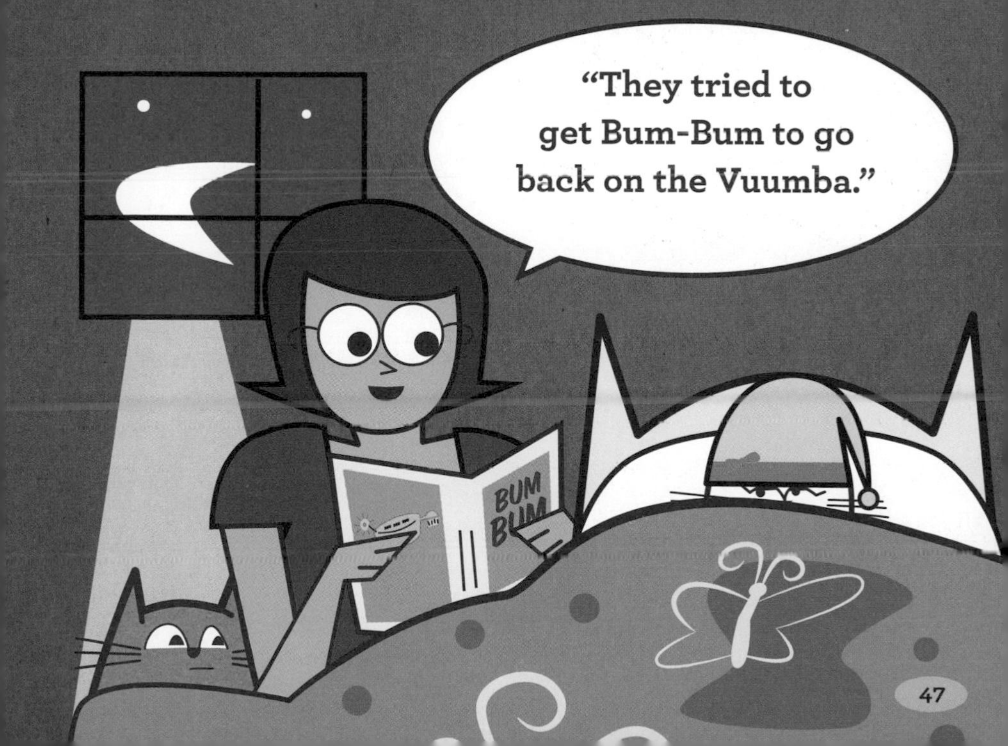
"They tried to get Bum-Bum to go back on the Vuumba."
BUM

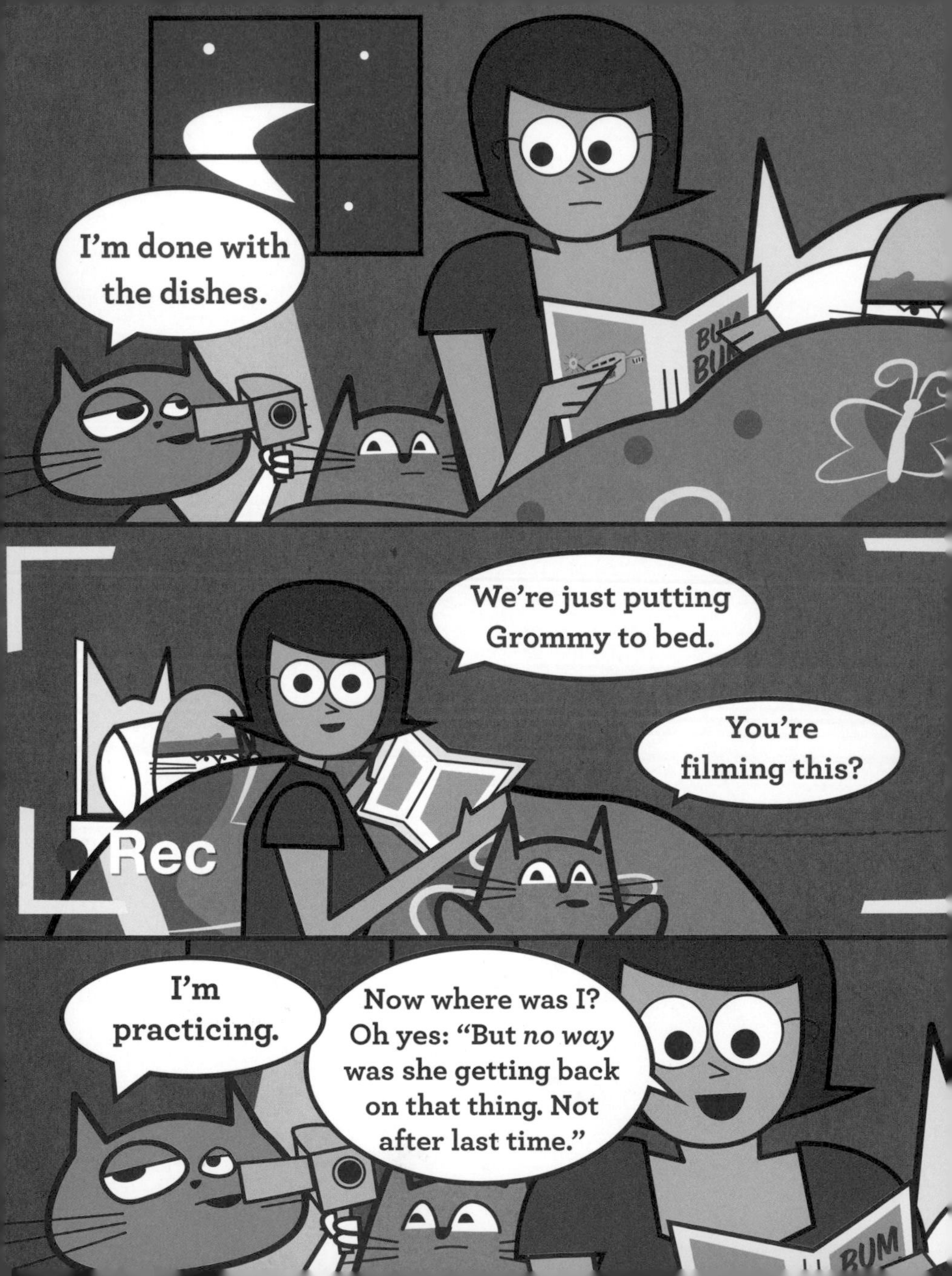
I'm done with the dishes.
BUM BUM
We're just putting Grommy to bed.
You're filming this?
Rec
I'm practicing.
Now where was I? Oh yes: "But *no way* was she getting back on that thing. Not after last time."
BUM

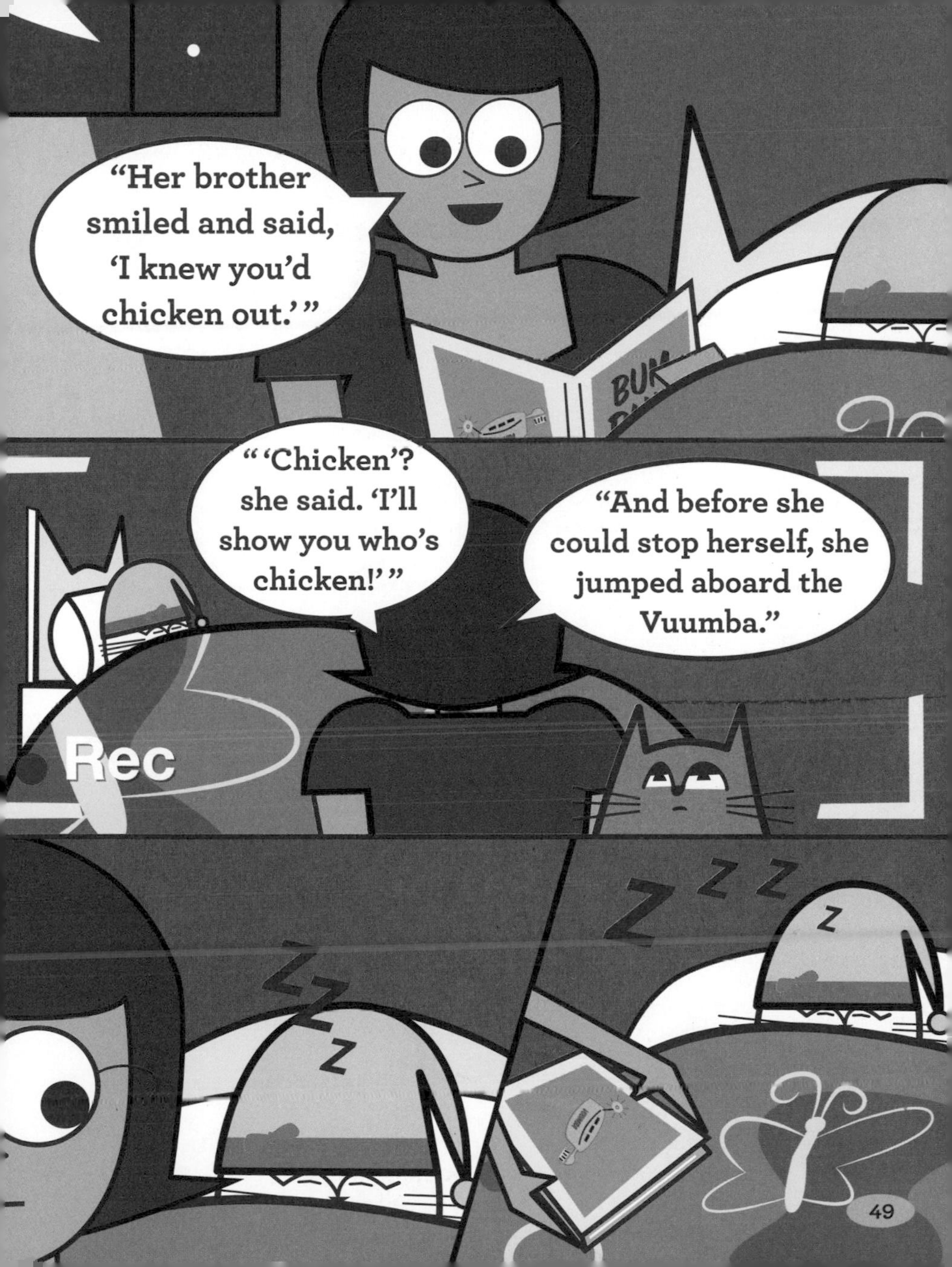
"Her brother smiled and said, 'I knew you'd chicken out.' "
BUM
" 'Chicken'? she said. 'I'll show you who's chicken!' "
"And before she could stop herself, she jumped aboard the Vuumba."
Rec
Z Z Z
Z
Z
Z
Z

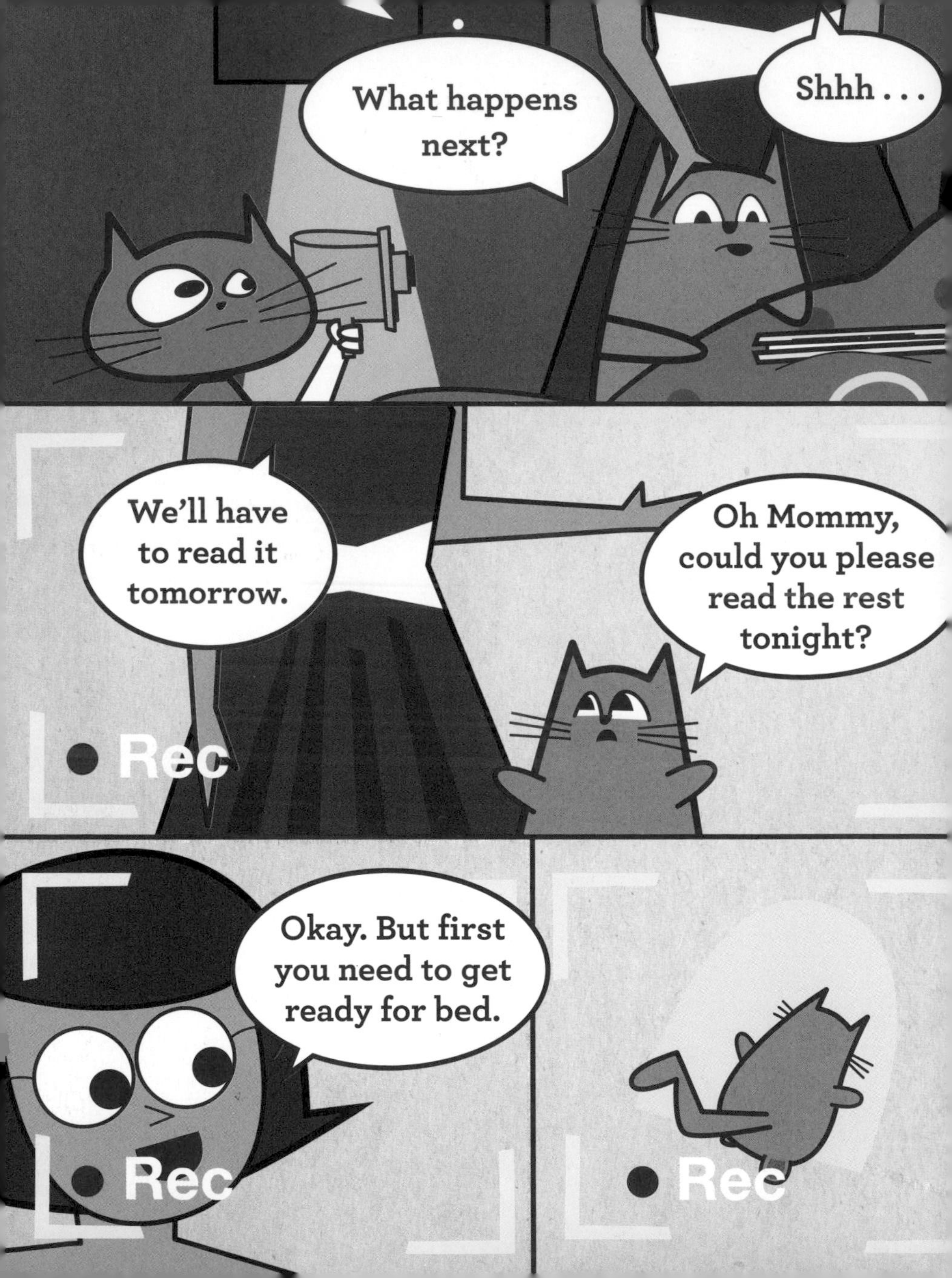
What happens next?
Shhh . . .
We'll have to read it tomorrow.
Oh Mommy, could you please read the rest tonight?
Rec
Okay. But first you need to get ready for bed.
Rec
Rec

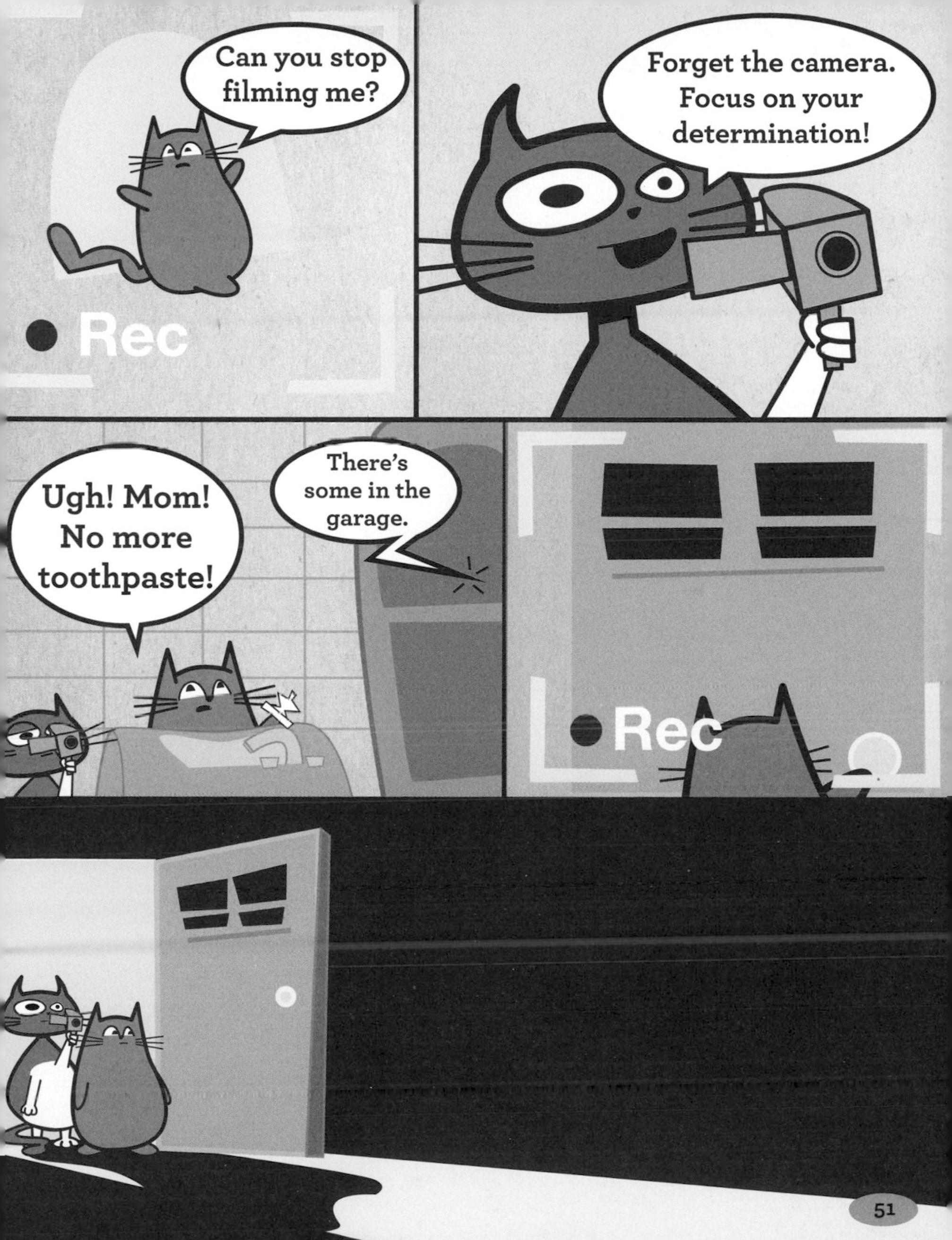
Can you stop filming me?
Rec
Forget the camera. Focus on your determination!
Ugh! Mom! No more toothpaste!
There's some in the garage.
Rec

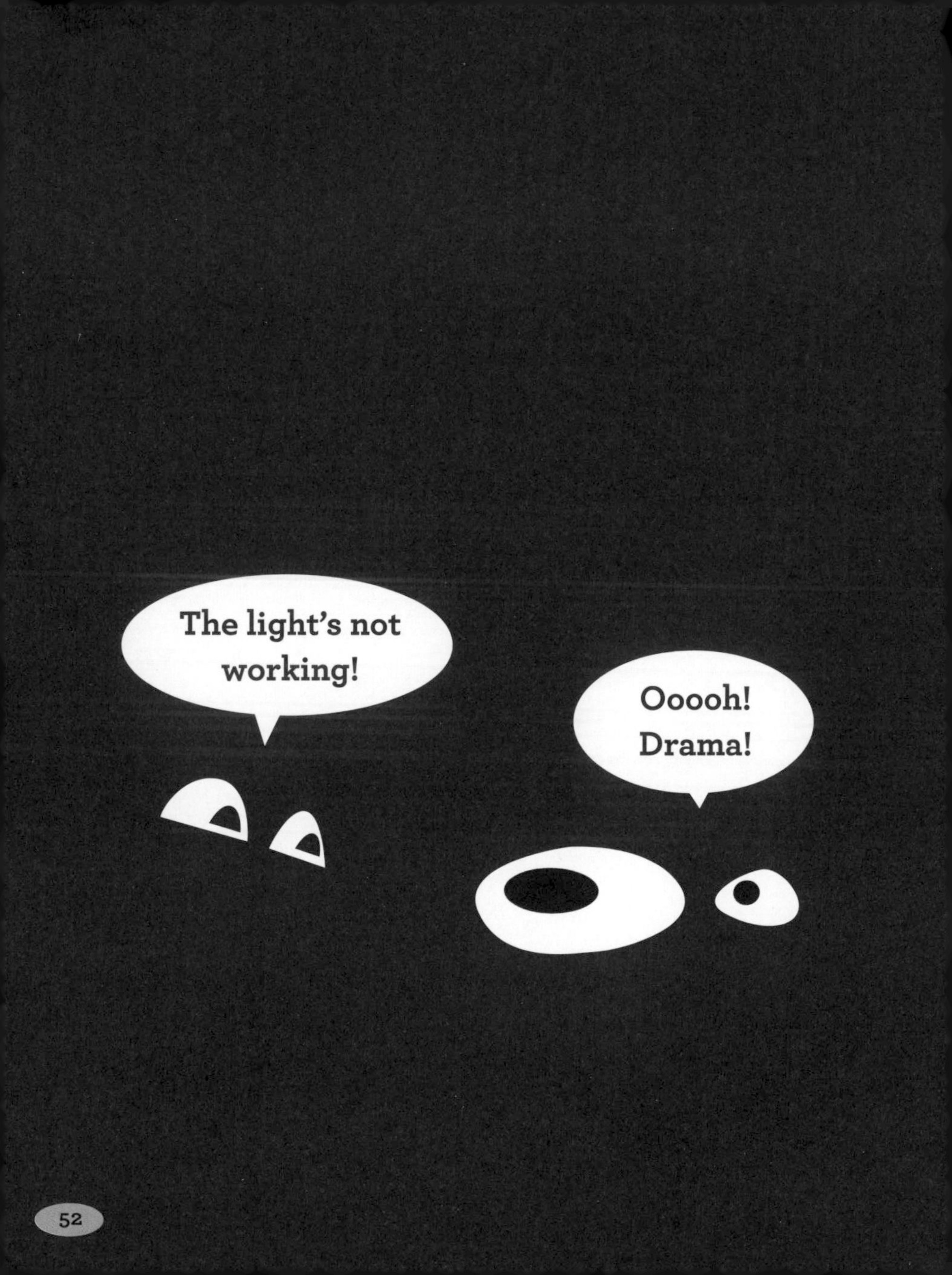
The light's not working!
Ooooh! Drama!

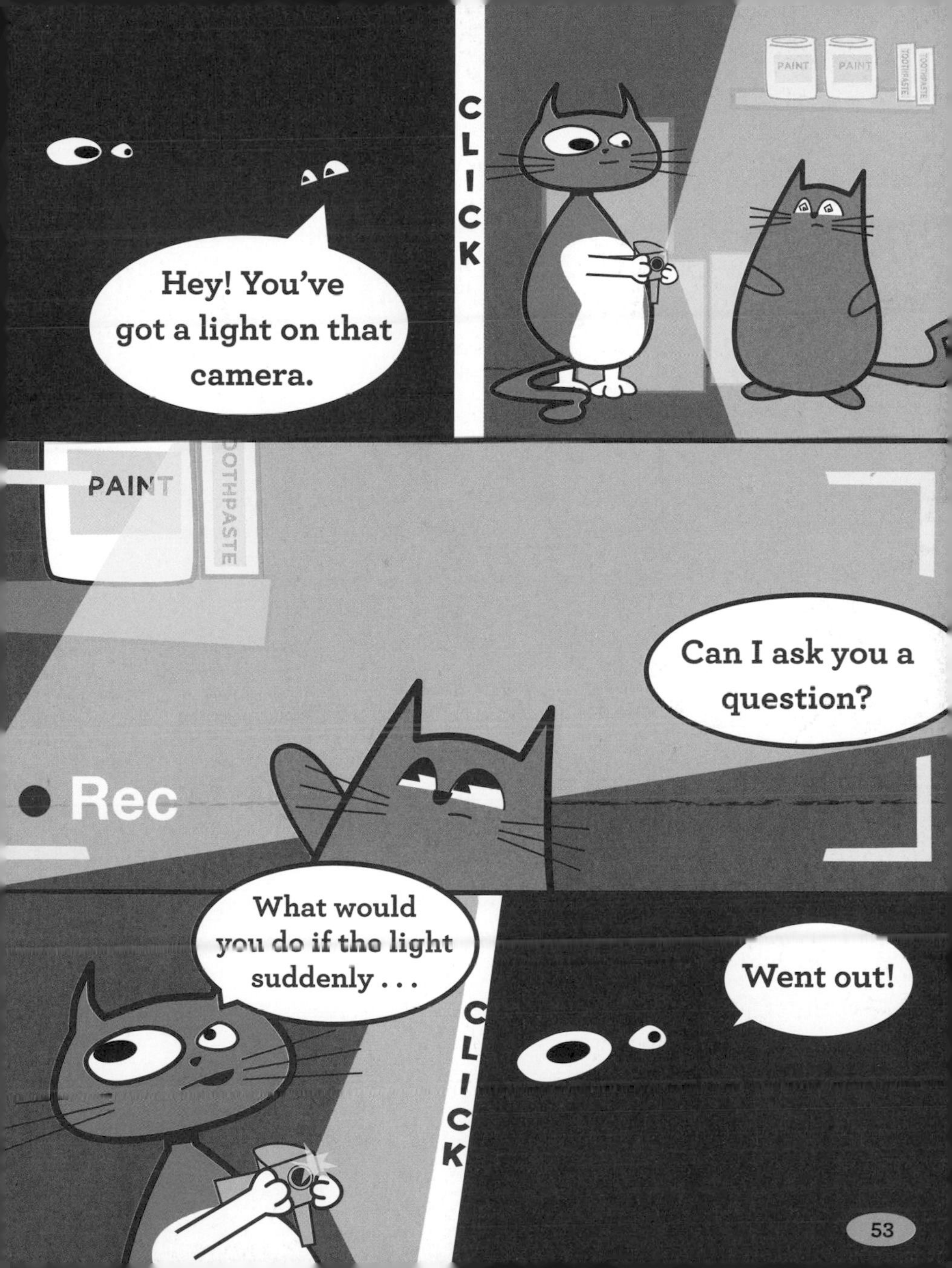
Hey! You've got a light on that camera.
CLICK
PAINT
PAINT
TOOTHPASTE
TOOTHPASTE
PAINT
TOOTHPASTE
Can I ask you a question?
Rec
What would you do if the light suddenly . . .
CLICK
Went out!

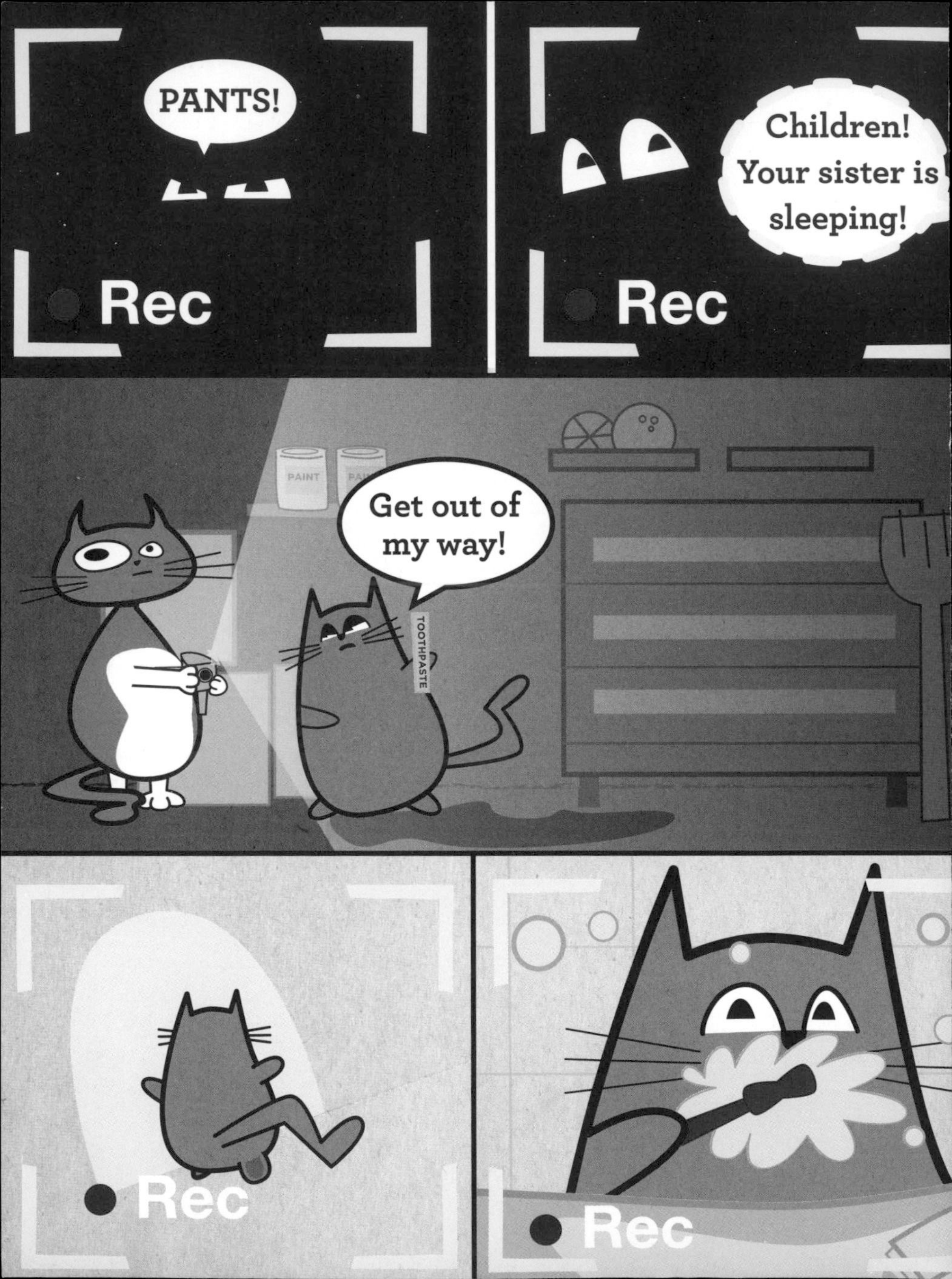
PANTS!
Rec
Children! Your sister is sleeping!
Rec
PAINT
Get out of my way!
TOOTHPASTE
Rec
Rec

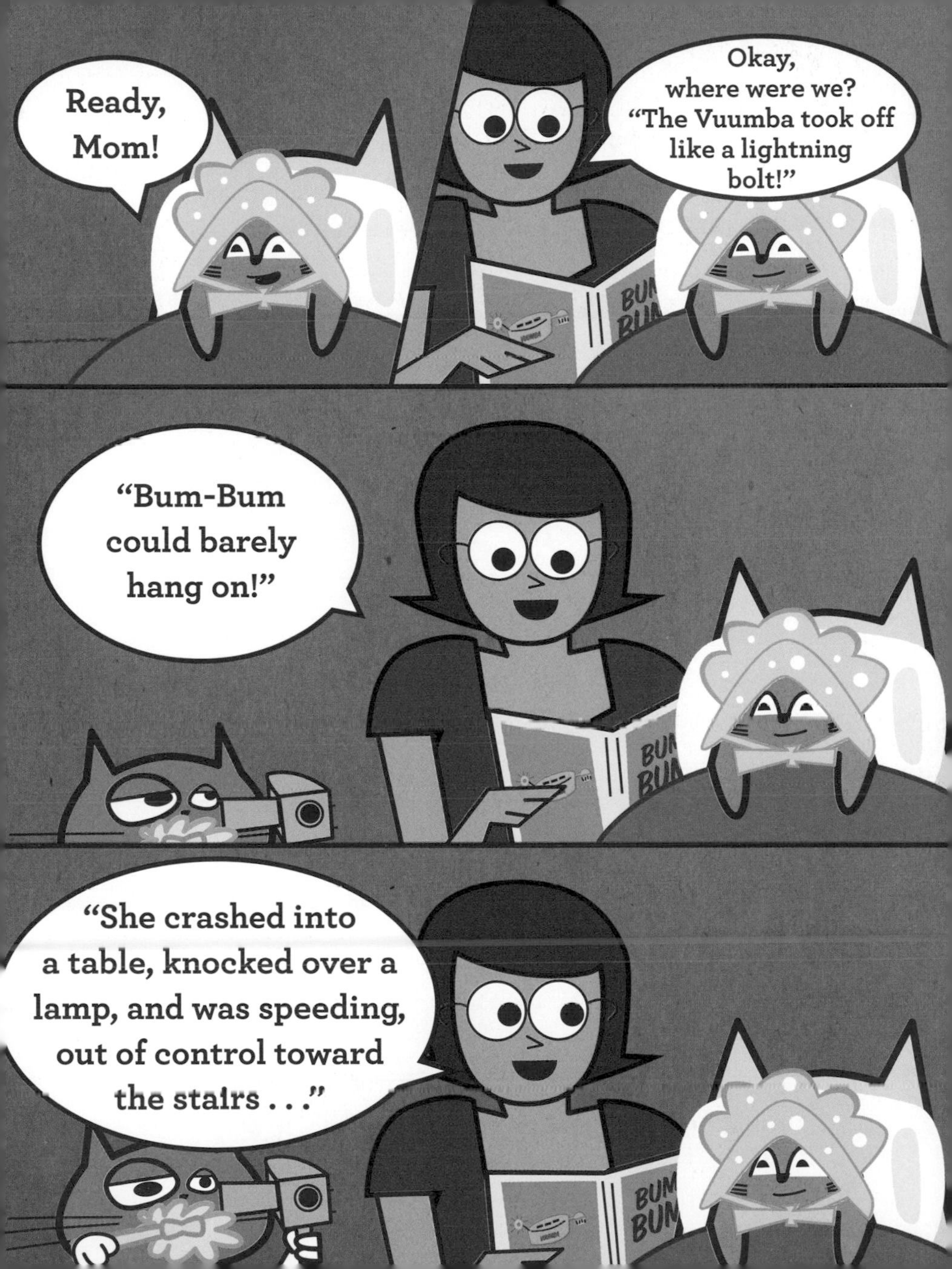
Ready, Mom!
Okay, where were we? "The Vuumba took off like a lightning bolt!"
BUM BUM
"Bum-Bum could barely hang on!"
BUM BUM
"She crashed into a table, knocked over a lamp, and was speeding, out of control toward the stairs . . ."
BUM BUM

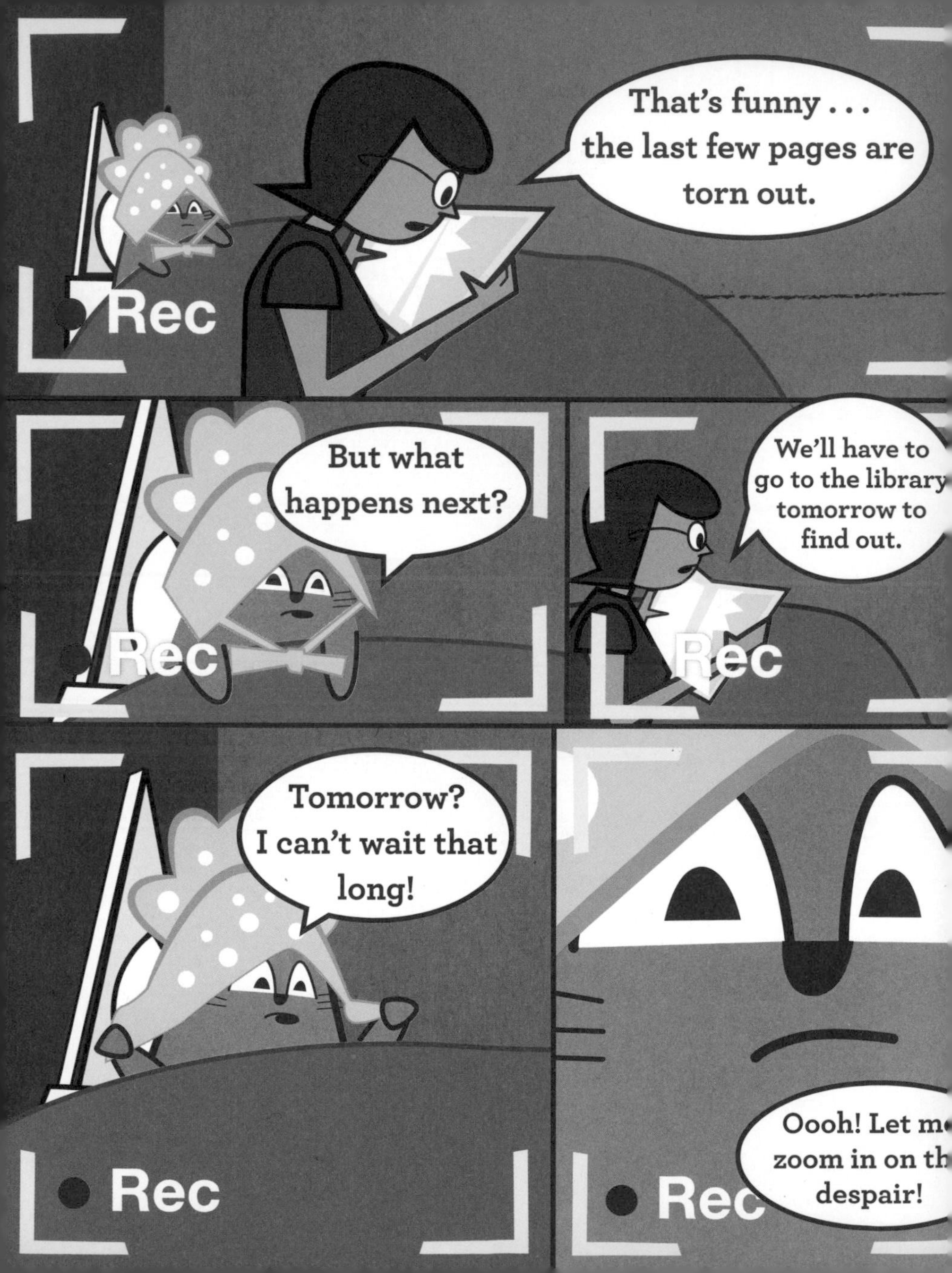

That's funny . . . the last few pages are torn out.
Rec
But what happens next?
Rec
We'll have to go to the library tomorrow to find out.
Rec
Tomorrow? I can't wait that long!
Rec
Rec

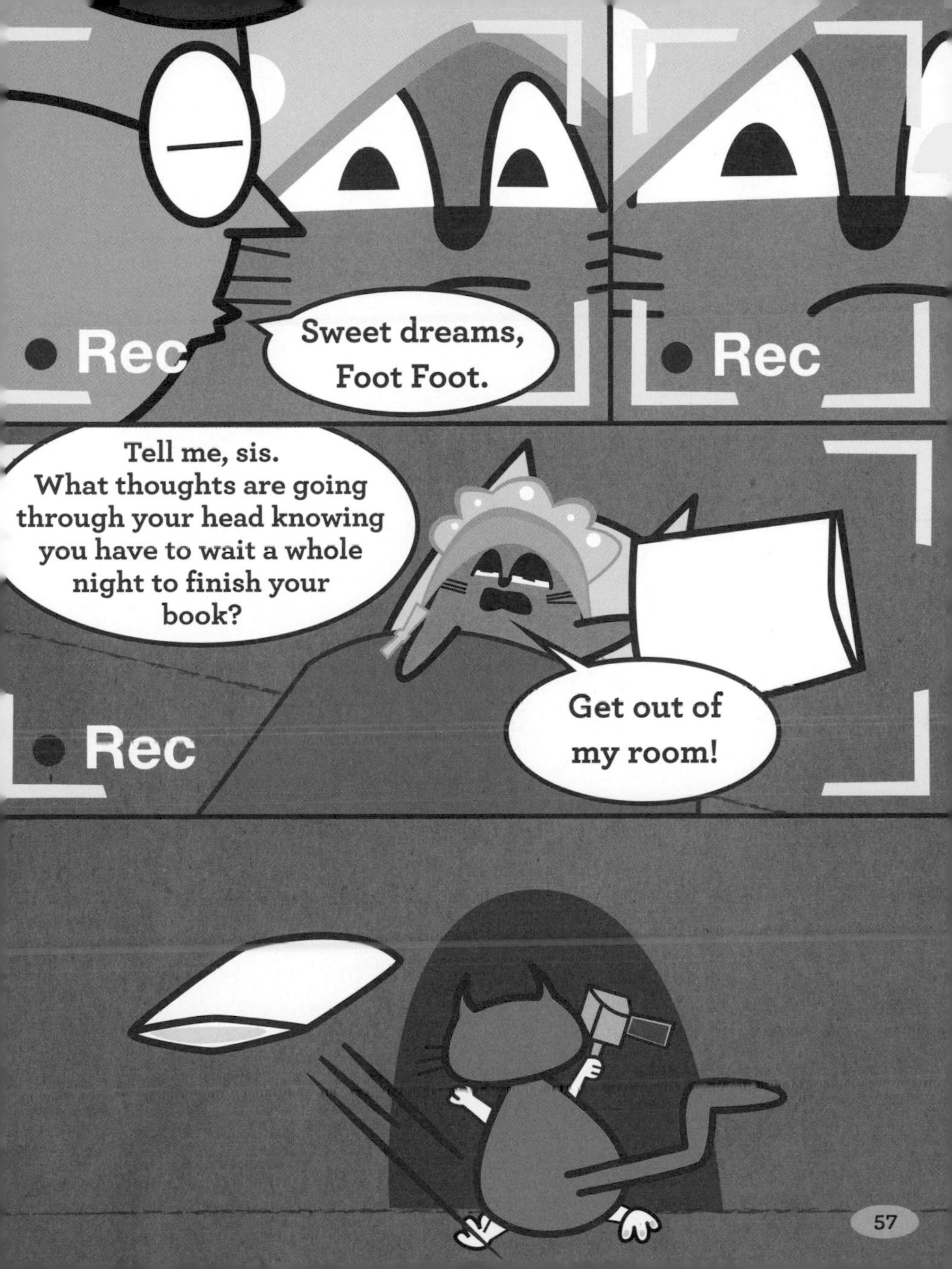
Rec
Sweet dreams, Foot Foot.
Rec
Tell me, sis. What thoughts are going through your head knowing you have to wait a whole night to finish your book?
Get out of my room!
Rec

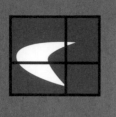
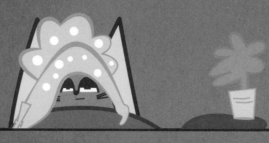

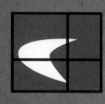

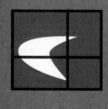

Pants!

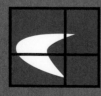

WHOOSH

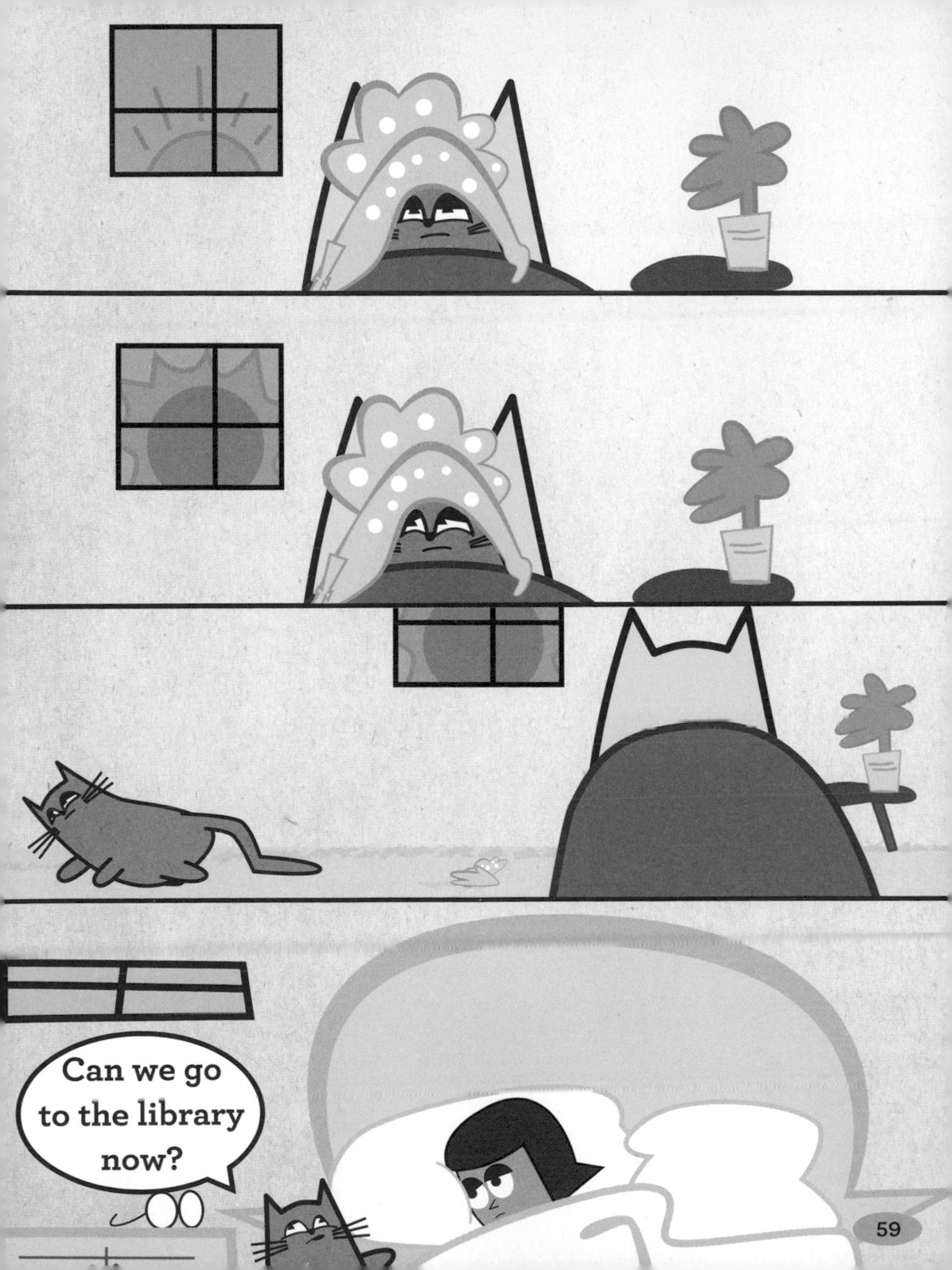
Can we go to the library now?

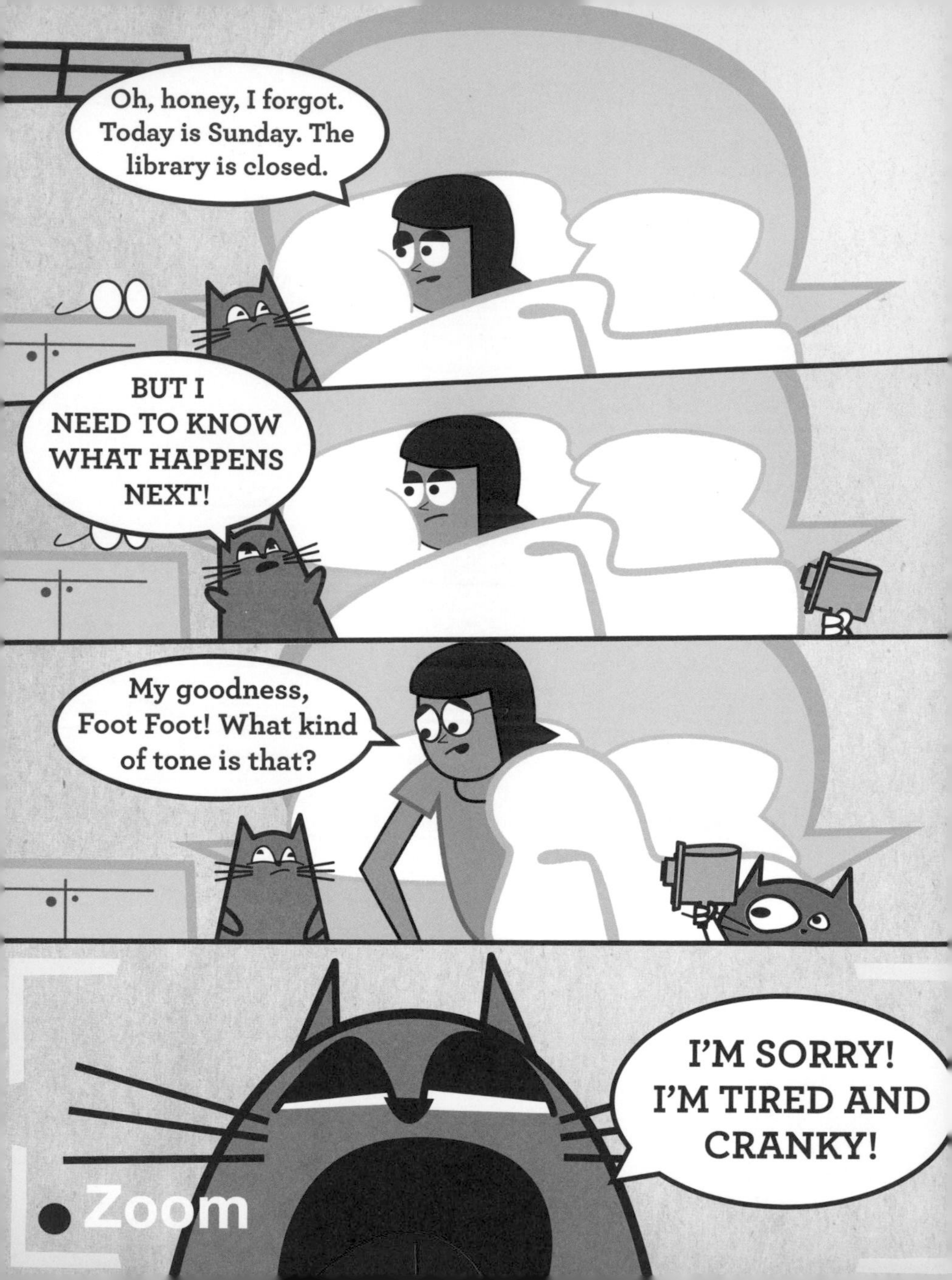

Oh, honey, I forgot. Today is Sunday. The library is closed.
BUT I NEED TO KNOW WHAT HAPPENS NEXT!
My goodness, Foot Foot! What kind of tone is that?
I'M SORRY! I'M TIRED AND CRANKY!
Zoom

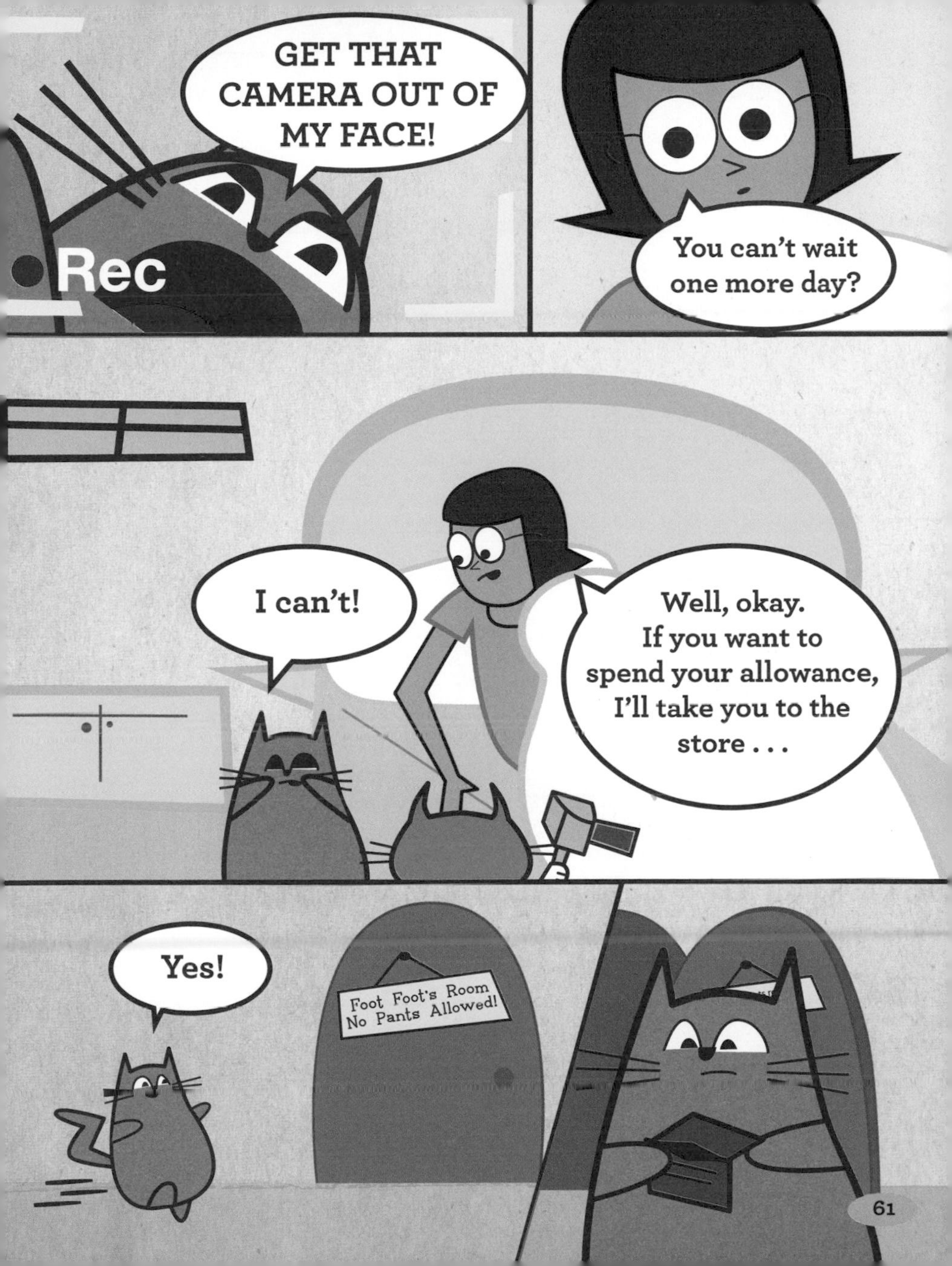
GET THAT CAMERA OUT OF MY FACE!
Rec
You can't wait one more day?
I can't!
Well, okay. If you want to spend your allowance, I'll take you to the store . . .
Yes!
Foot Foot's Room
No Pants Allowed!

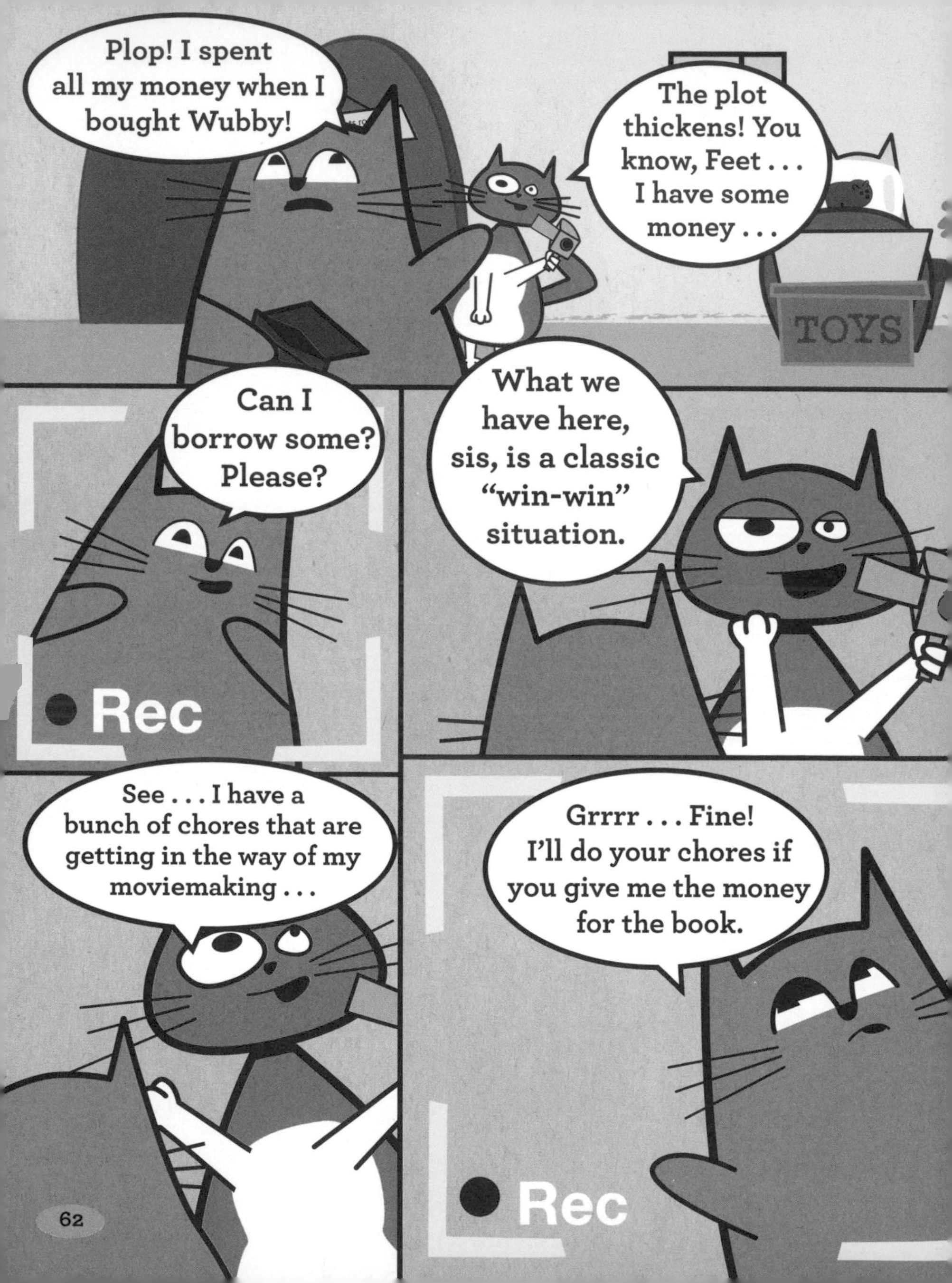

Plop! I spent all my money when I bought Wubby!
The plot thickens! You know, Feet . . . I have some money . . .
TOYS
Can I borrow some? Please?
Rec
What we have here, sis, is a classic "win-win" situation.
See . . . I have a bunch of chores that are getting in the way of my moviemaking . . .
Grrrr . . . Fine! I'll do your chores if you give me the money for the book.
Rec

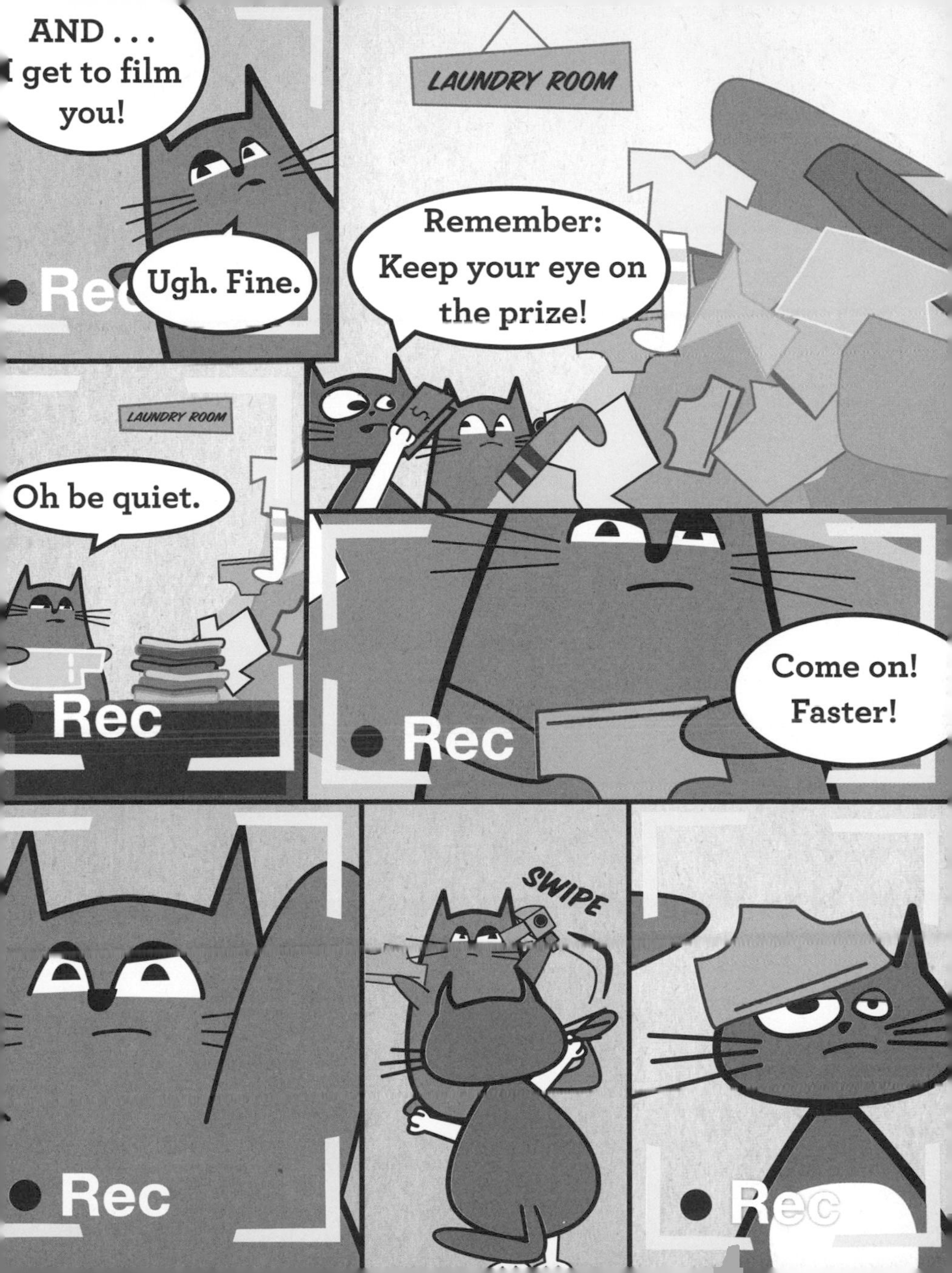
AND . . . I get to film you!
Rec
Ugh. Fine.
LAUNDRY ROOM
Remember: Keep your eye on the prize!
LAUNDRY ROOM
Oh be quiet.
Rec
Rec
Come on! Faster!
Rec
SWIPE
Rec

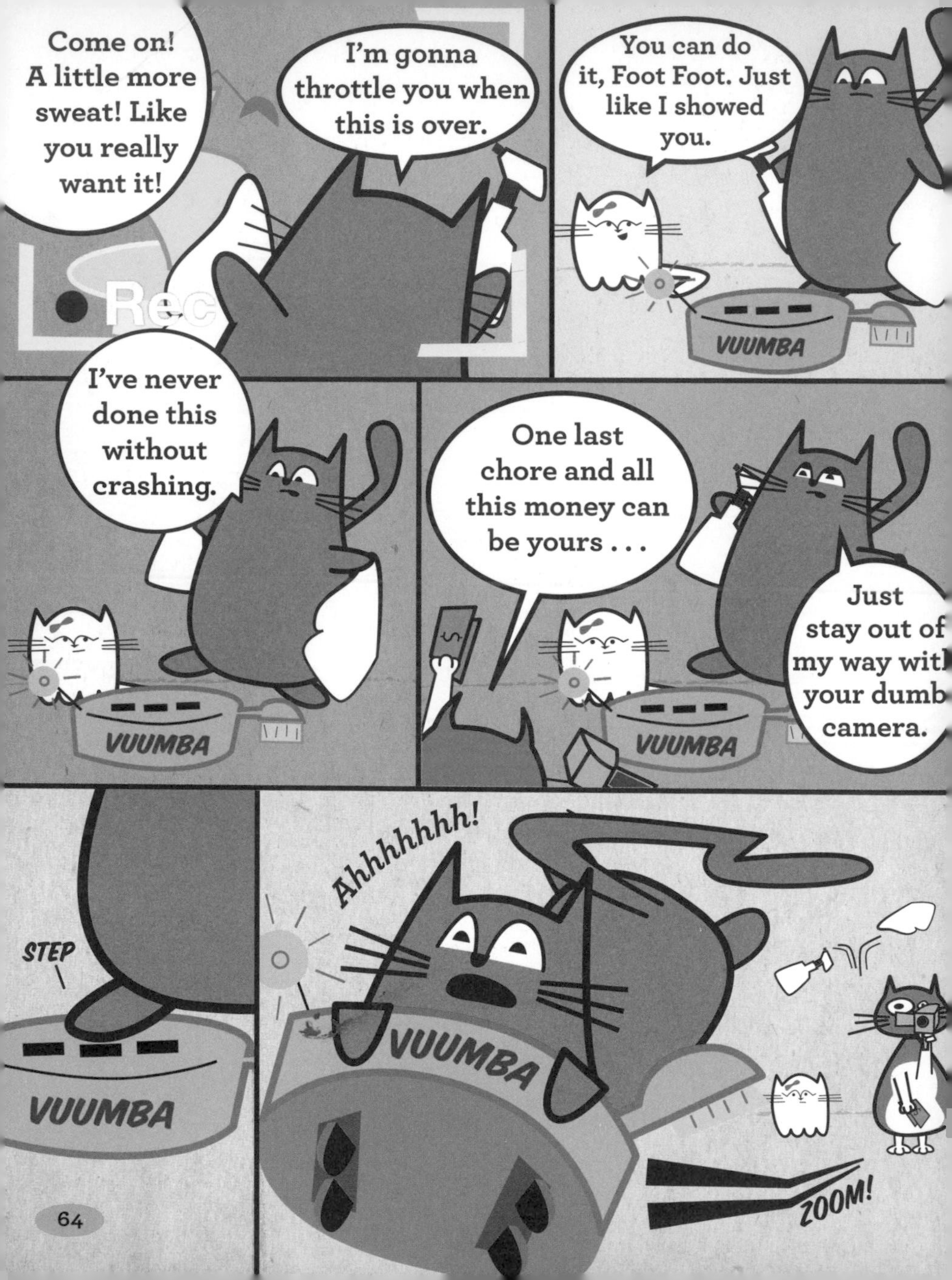

Come on! A little more sweat! Like you really want it!
Rec
I'm gonna throttle you when this is over.
You can do it, Foot Foot. Just like I showed you.
VUUMBA
I've never done this without crashing.
VUUMBA
One last chore and all this money can be yours . . .
Just stay out of my way with your dumb camera.
VUUMBA
STEP
VUUMBA
Ahhhhhhh!
VUUMBA
ZOOM!

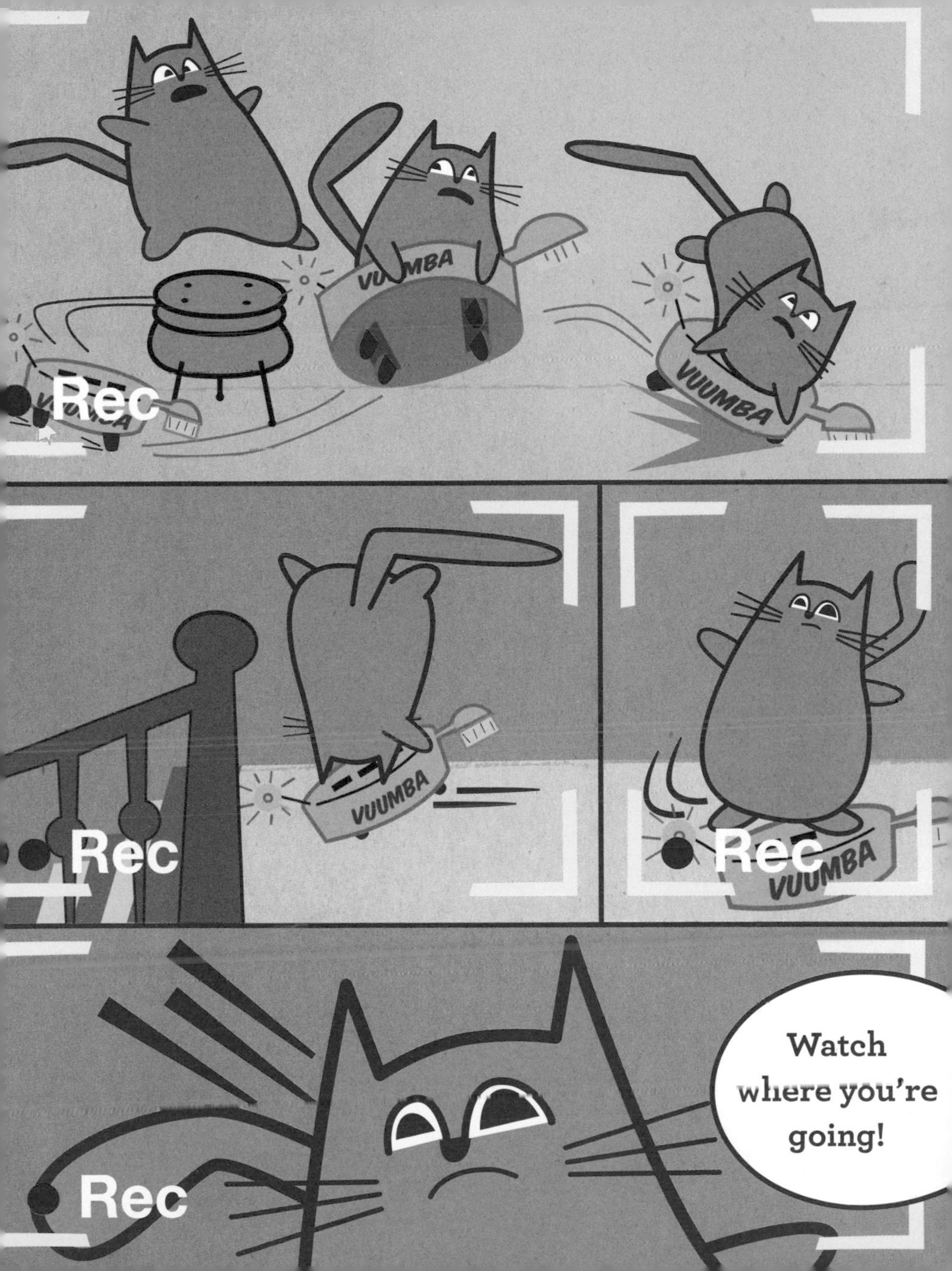
VUUMBA
Rec
VUUMBA
VUUMBA
Rec
VUUMBA
Rec
VUUMBA
Rec
Watch where you're going!

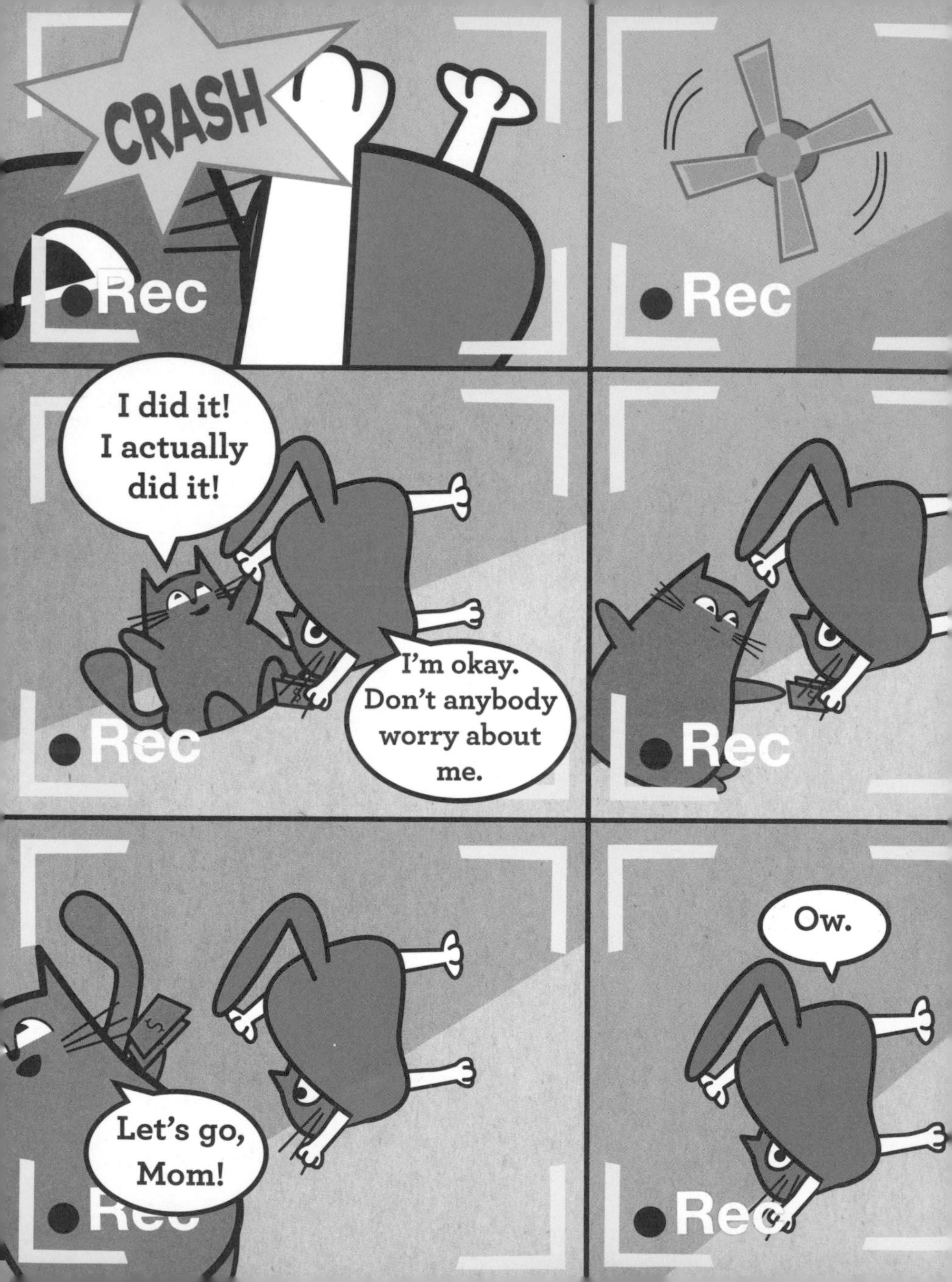
CRASH
Rec
Rec
I did it! I actually did it!
I'm okay. Don't anybody worry about me.
Rec
Rec
Let's go, Mom!
Ow.
Rec

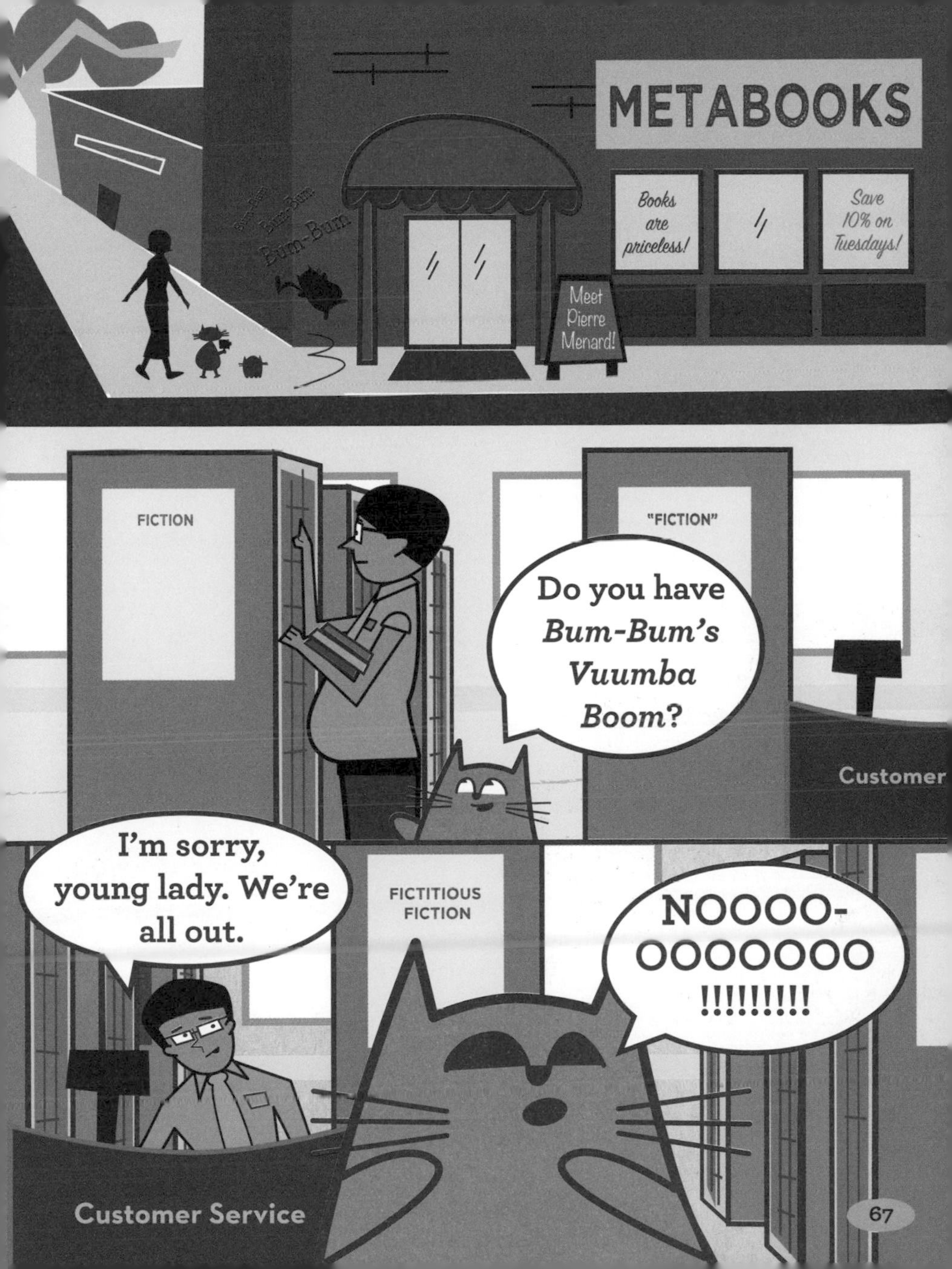
METABOOKS
Books are priceless!
Save 10% on Tuesdays!
Meet Pierre Menard!
Bum-Bum
FICTION
"FICTION"
Do you have *Bum-Bum's Vuumba Boom*?
Customer
I'm sorry, young lady. We're all out.
FICTITIOUS FICTION
NOOOO-OOOOOOO!!!!!!!!!
Customer Service

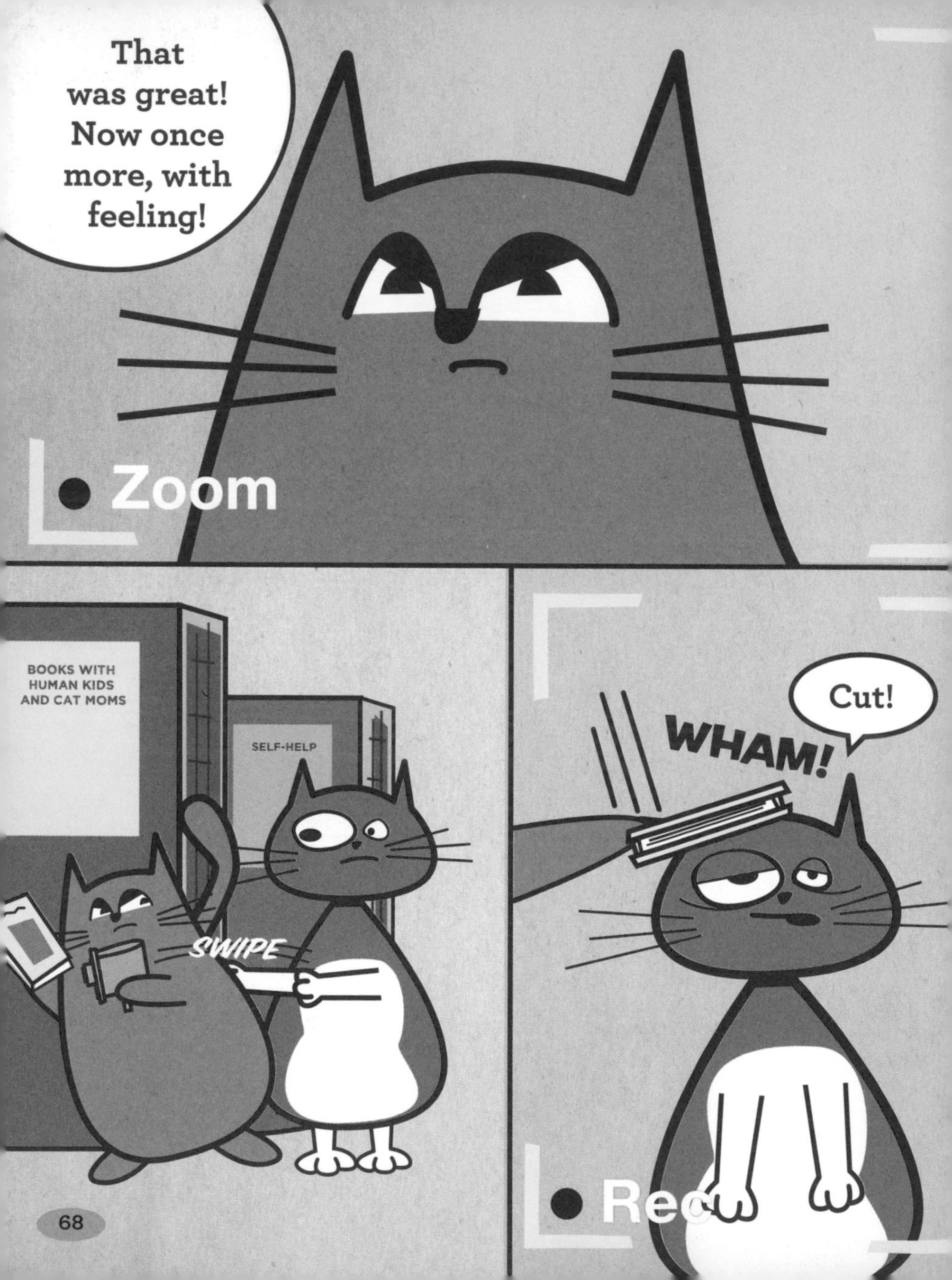
That was great! Now once more, with feeling!
Zoom
BOOKS WITH HUMAN KIDS AND CAT MOMS
SELF-HELP
SWIPE
Cut!
WHAM!
Rec

# Chapter Four: TEA TIME TROUBLES

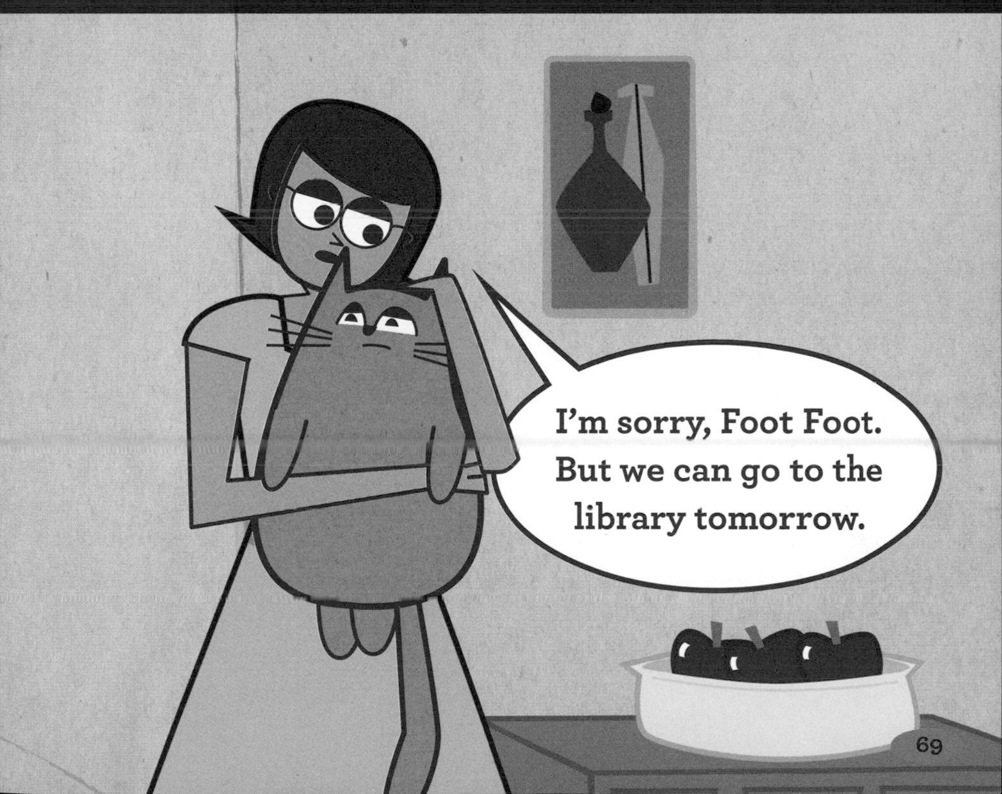
I'm sorry, Foot Foot. But we can go to the library tomorrow.

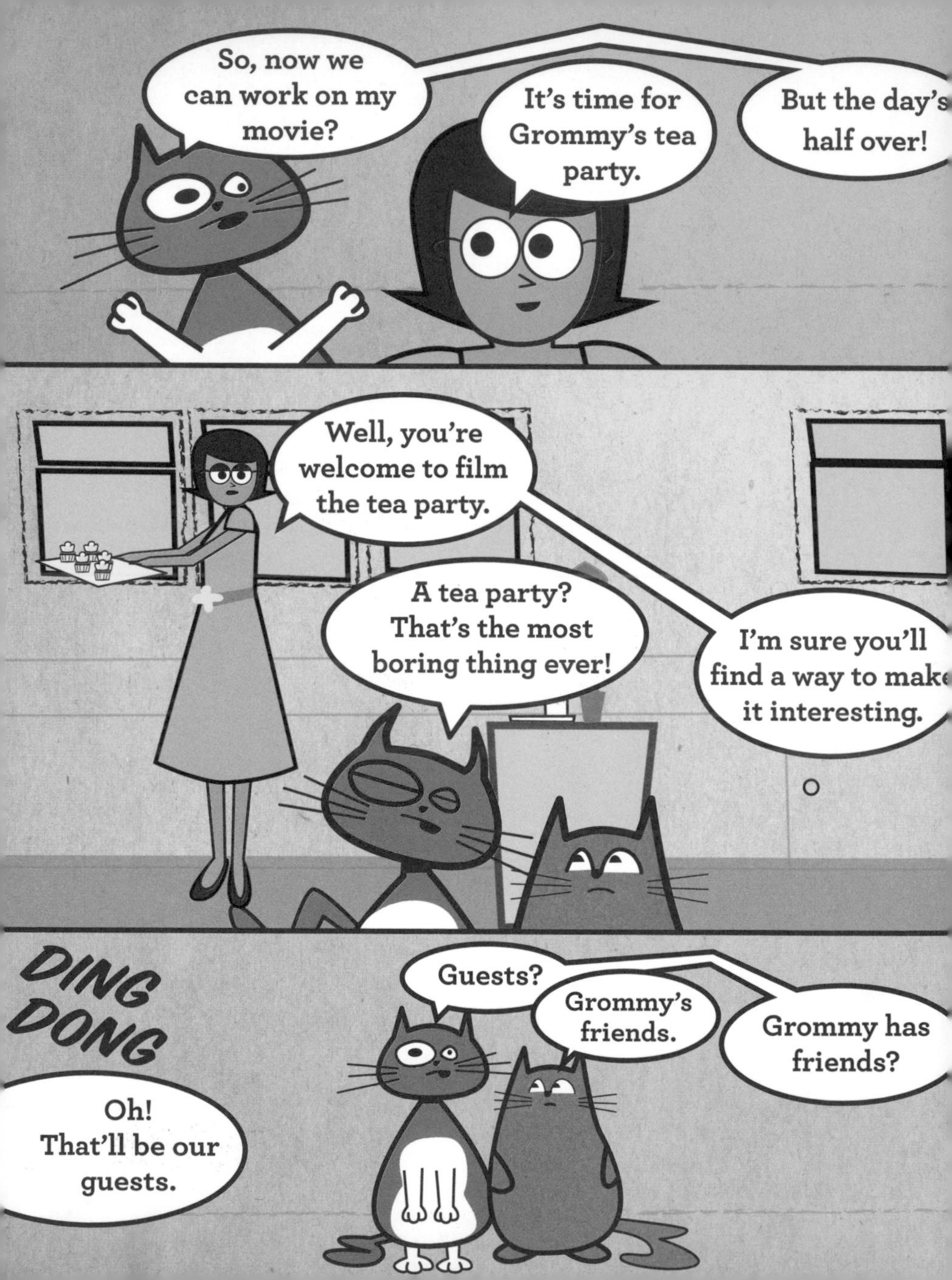
So, now we can work on my movie?
It's time for Grommy's tea party.
But the day's half over!
Well, you're welcome to film the tea party.
A tea party? That's the most boring thing ever!
I'm sure you'll find a way to make it interesting.
DING DONG
Oh! That'll be our guests.
Guests?
Grommy's friends.
Grommy has friends?

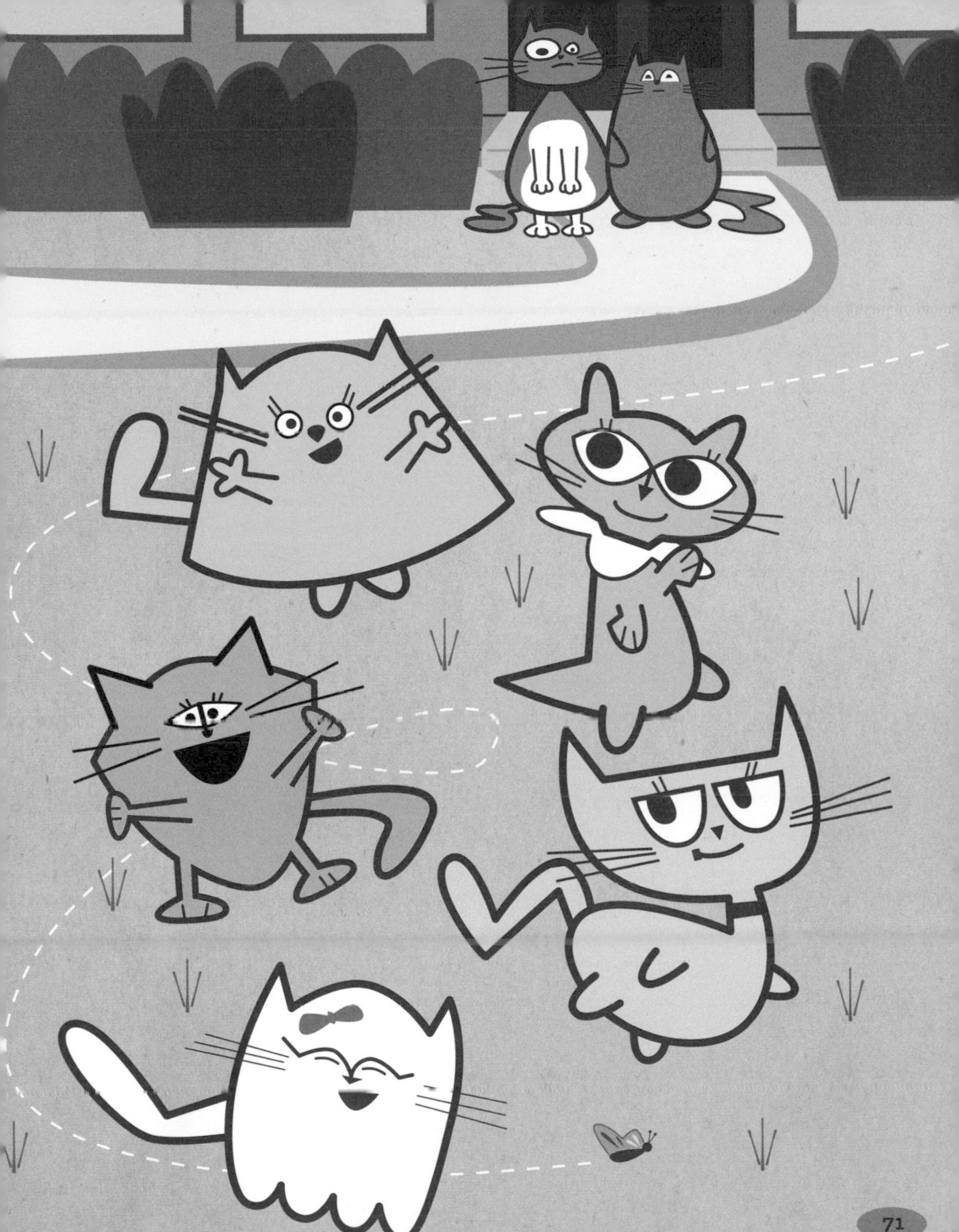

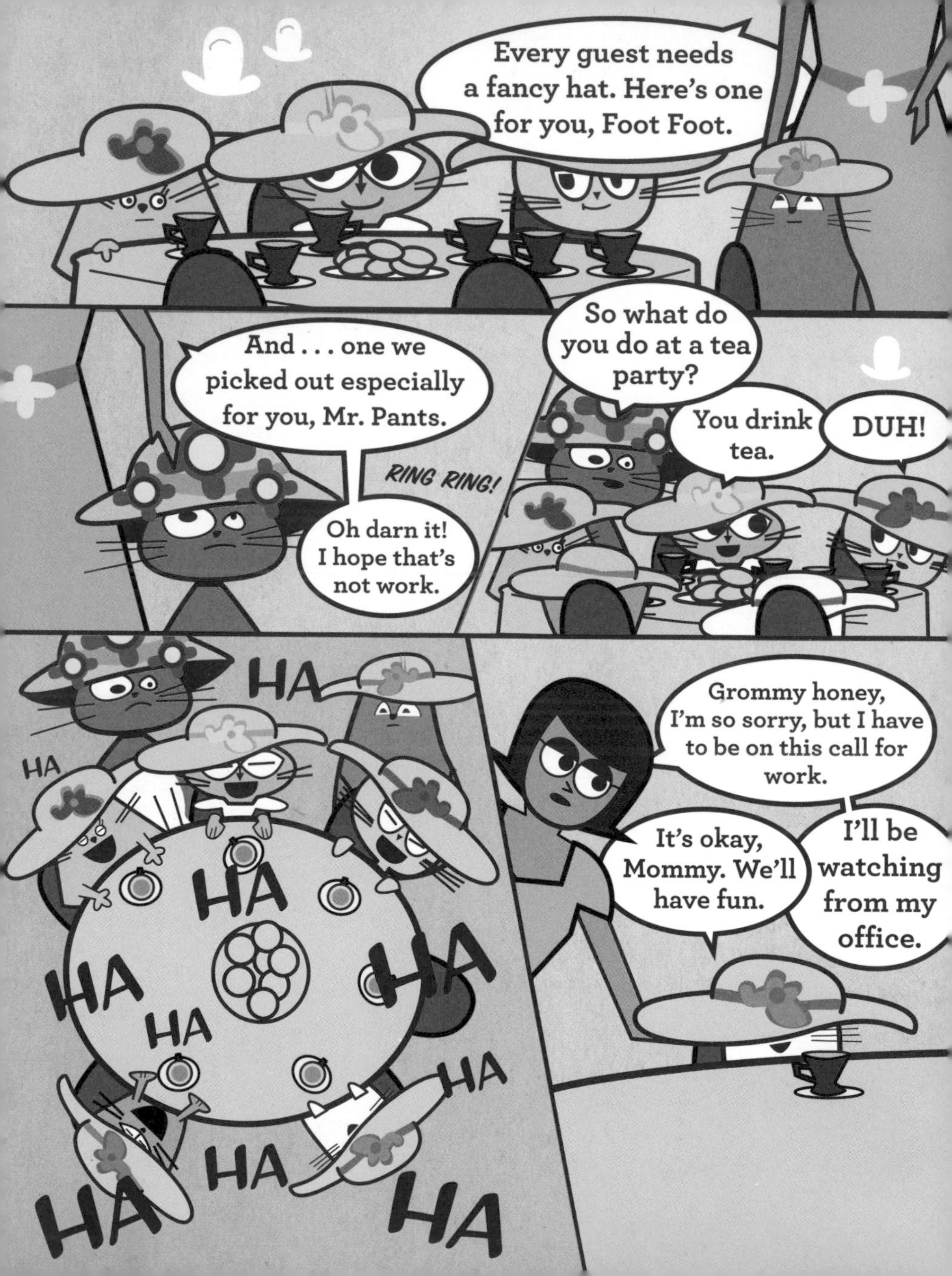

Every guest needs a fancy hat. Here's one for you, Foot Foot.
And . . . one we picked out especially for you, Mr. Pants.
RING RING!
Oh darn it! I hope that's not work.
So what do you do at a tea party?
You drink tea.
DUH!
HA
HA
HA
HA
HA
HA
HA
HA
HA
HA
Grommy honey, I'm so sorry, but I have to be on this call for work.
It's okay, Mommy. We'll have fun.
I'll be watching from my office.

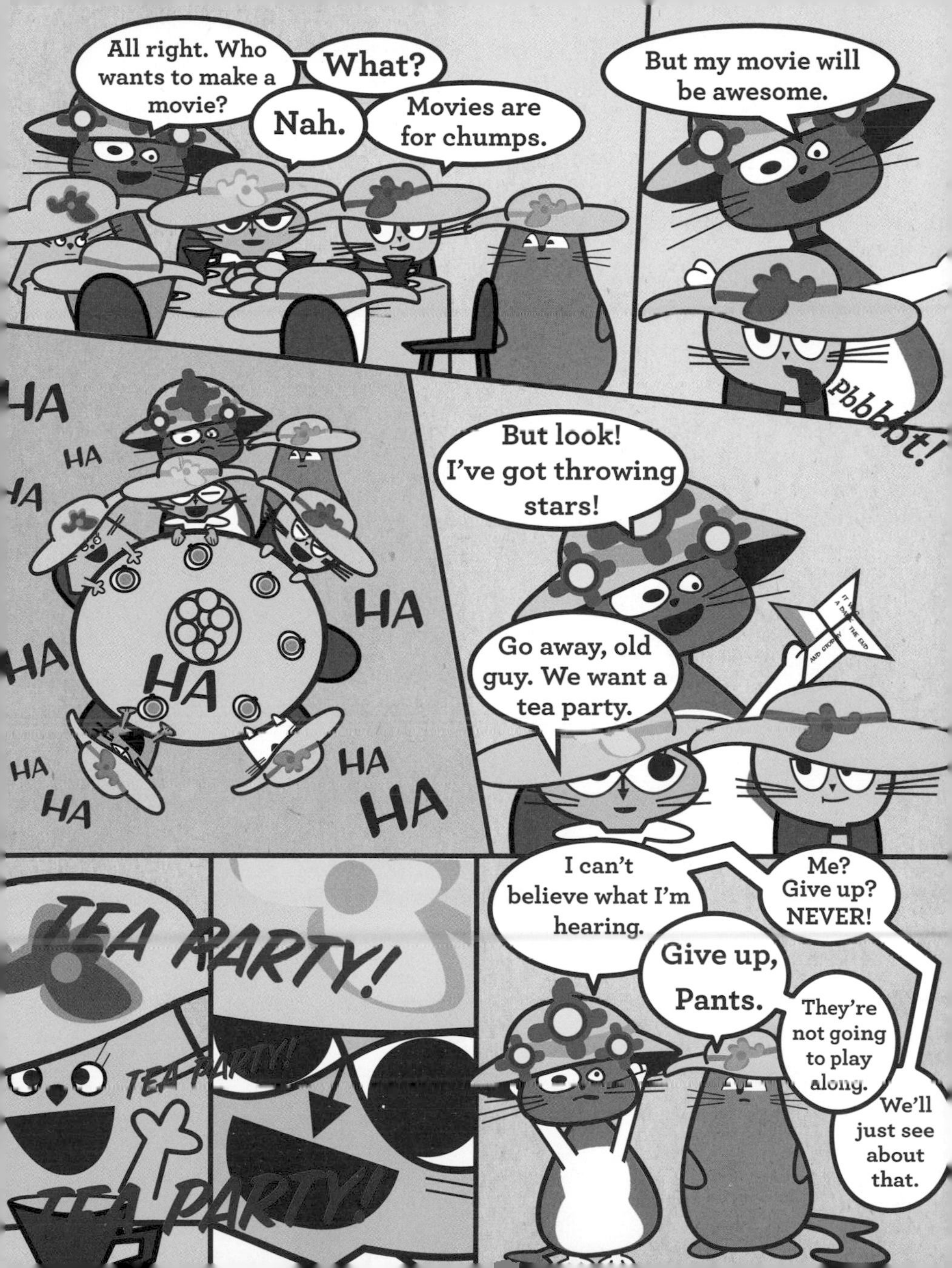
All right. Who wants to make a movie?
What?
Nah.
Movies are for chumps.
But my movie will be awesome.
Pbbbbt!
HA
HA
HA
HA
HA
HA
HA
HA
HA
HA
But look! I've got throwing stars!
Go away, old guy. We want a tea party.
TEA PARTY!
TEA PARTY!
TEA PARTY!
I can't believe what I'm hearing.
Give up, Pants.
Me? Give up? NEVER!
They're not going to play along.
We'll just see about that.

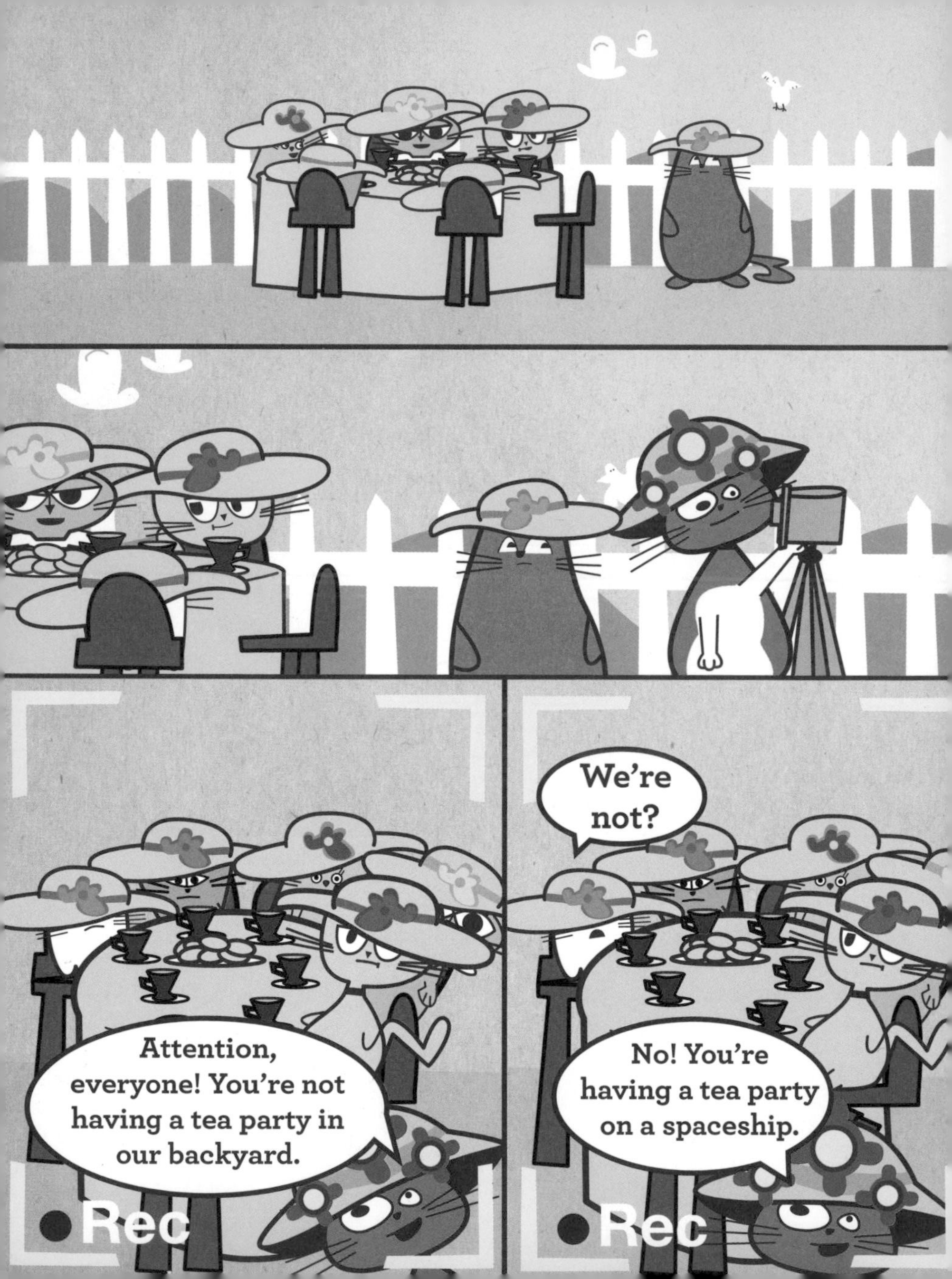
Attention, everyone! You're not having a tea party in our backyard.
We're not?
No! You're having a tea party on a spaceship.
Rec
Rec

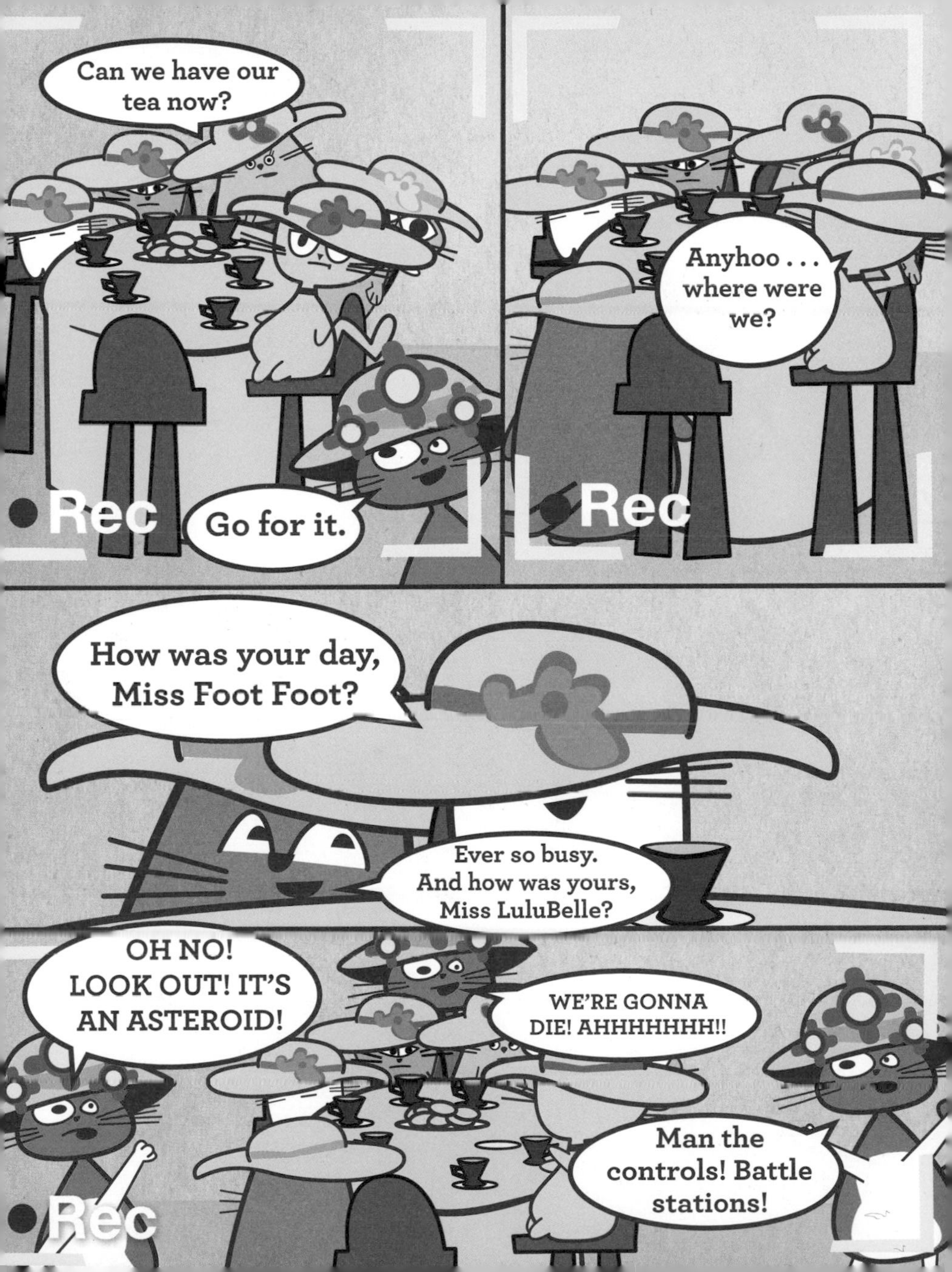
Can we have our tea now?
Rec
Go for it.
Anyhoo . . . where were we?
Rec
How was your day, Miss Foot Foot?
Ever so busy. And how was yours, Miss LuluBelle?
OH NO! LOOK OUT! IT'S AN ASTEROID!
WE'RE GONNA DIE! AHHHHHHH!!
Man the controls! Battle stations!
Rec

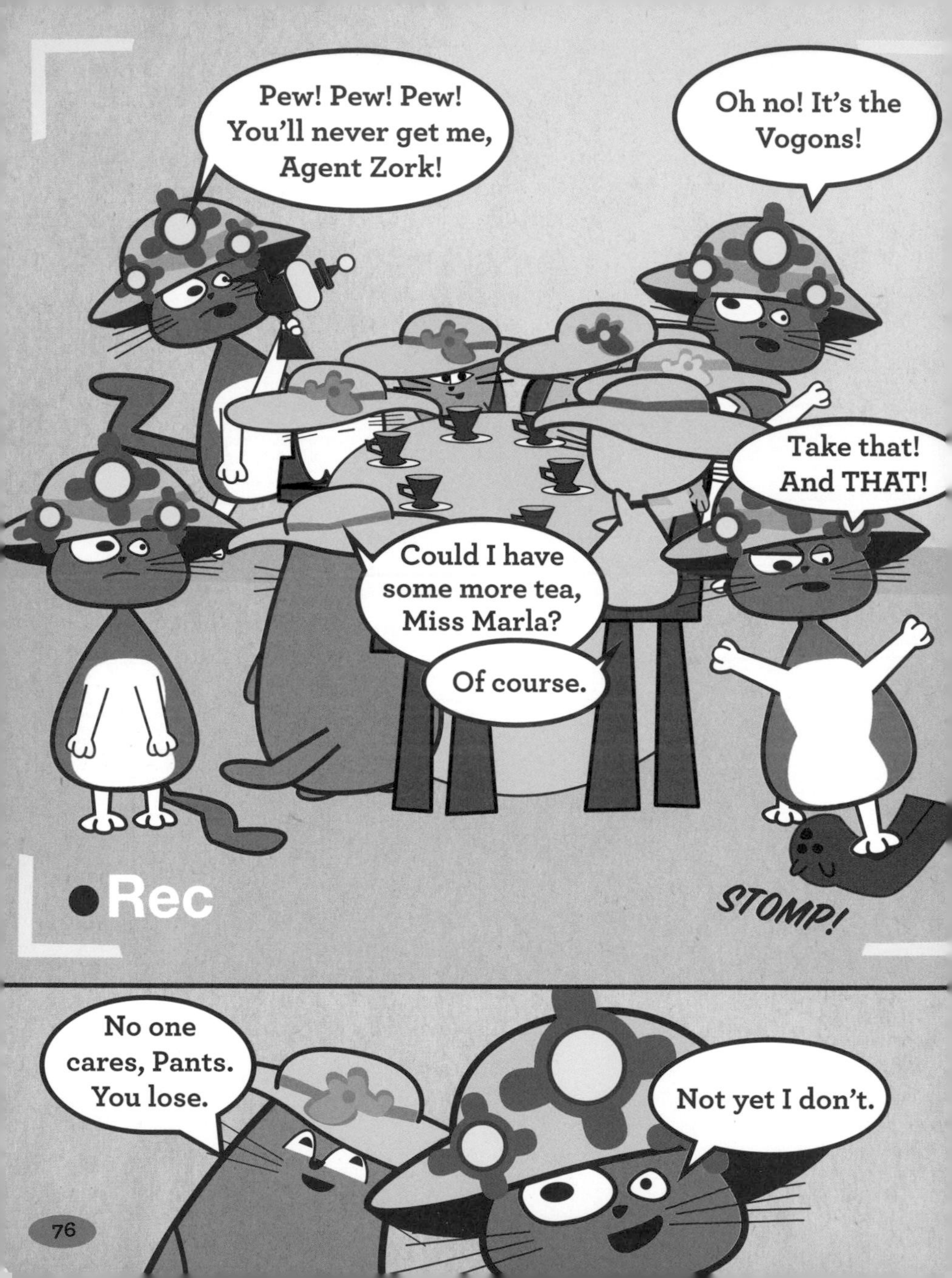
Pew! Pew! Pew! You'll never get me, Agent Zork!
Oh no! It's the Vogons!
Take that! And THAT!
Could I have some more tea, Miss Marla?
Of course.
Rec
STOMP!
No one cares, Pants. You lose.
Not yet I don't.

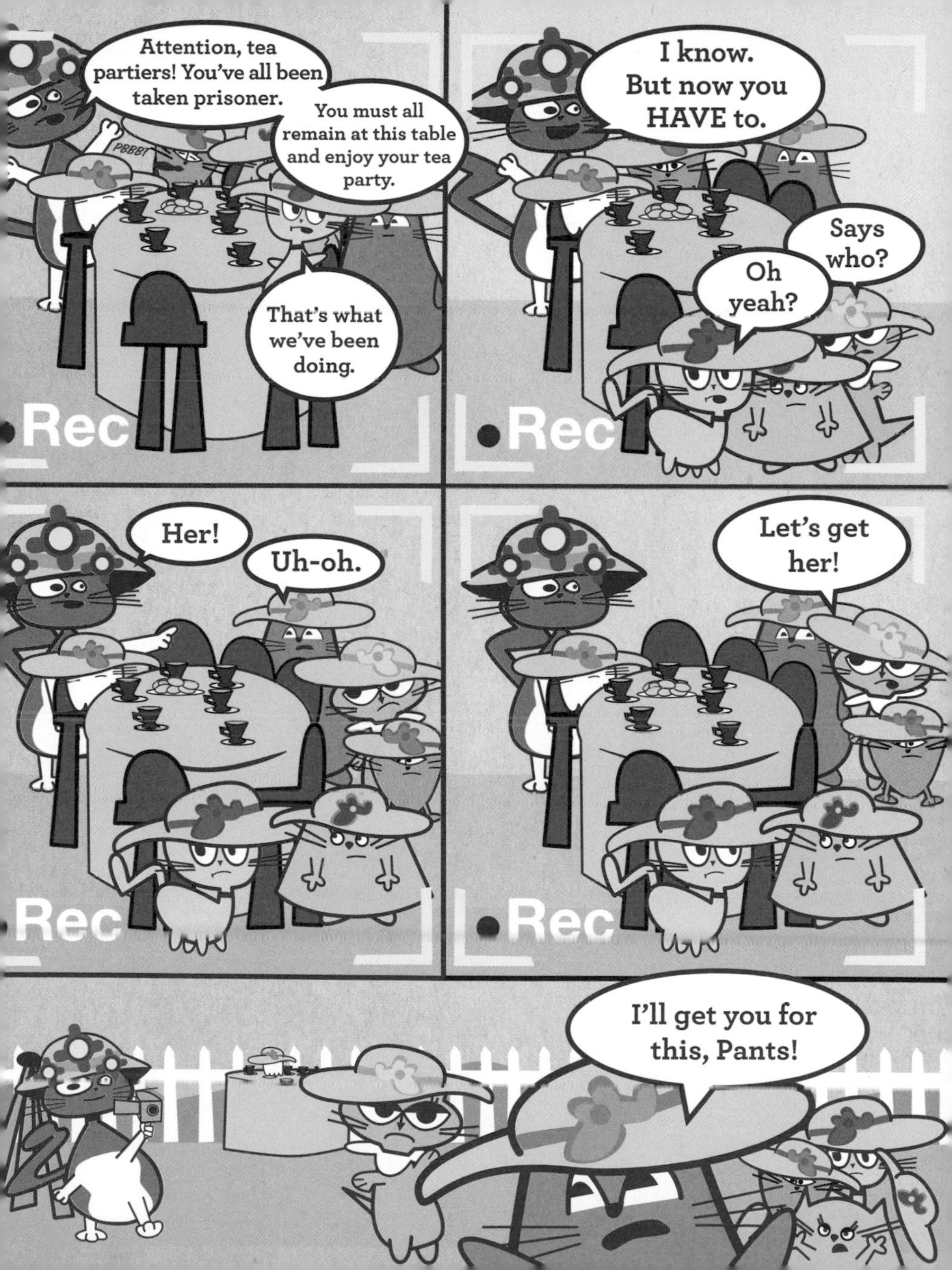
Attention, tea partiers! You've all been taken prisoner.
You must all remain at this table and enjoy your tea party.
PBBBT
That's what we've been doing.
Rec
I know. But now you HAVE to.
Says who?
Oh yeah?
Rec
Her!
Uh-oh.
Rec
Let's get her!
Rec
I'll get you for this, Pants!

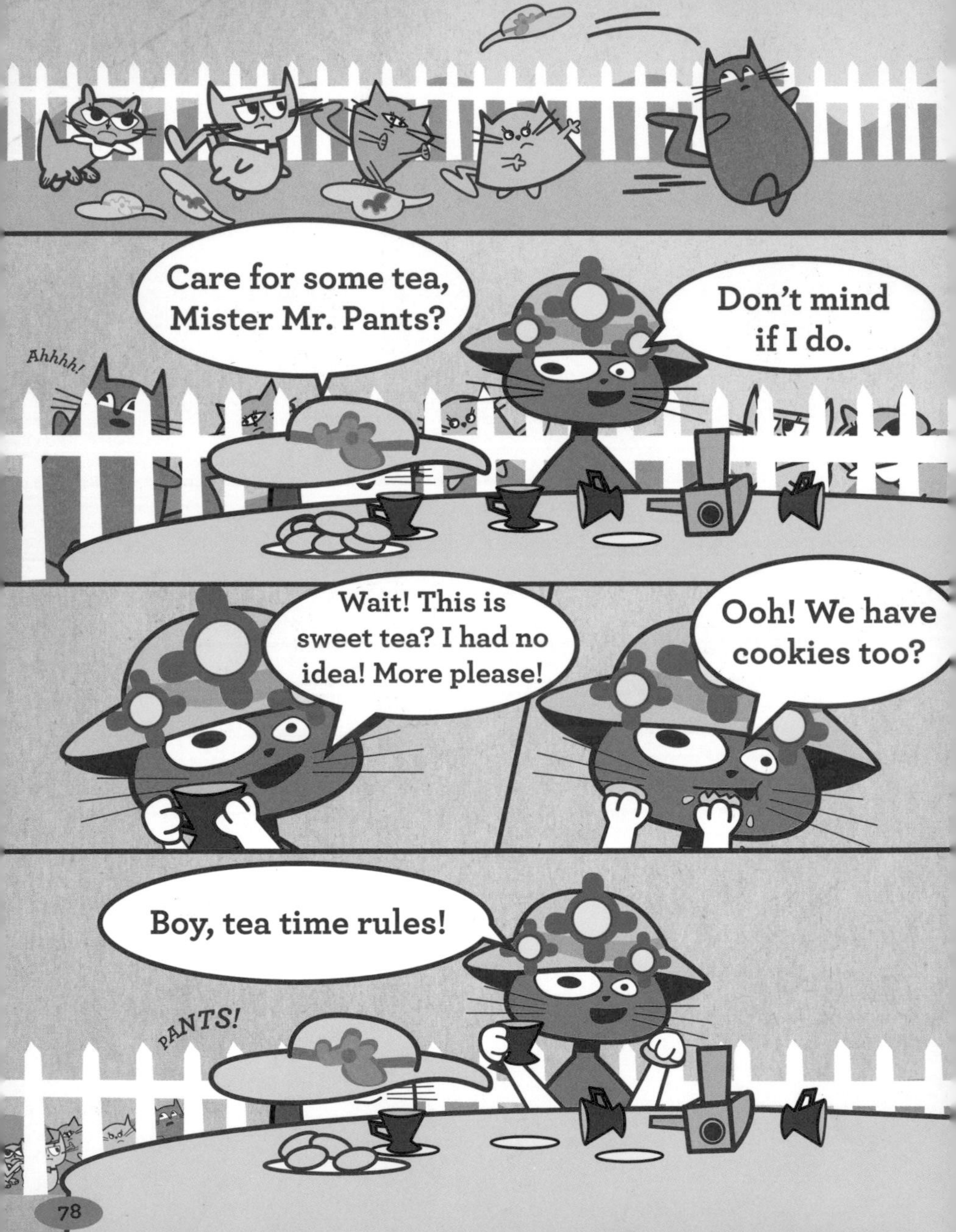
Care for some tea, Mister Mr. Pants?
Don't mind if I do.
Ahhhh!
Wait! This is sweet tea? I had no idea! More please!
Ooh! We have cookies too?
Boy, tea time rules!
PANTS!

# Chapter Five:
# THE SPY WHO PANTSED ME

That was the best tea party ever!

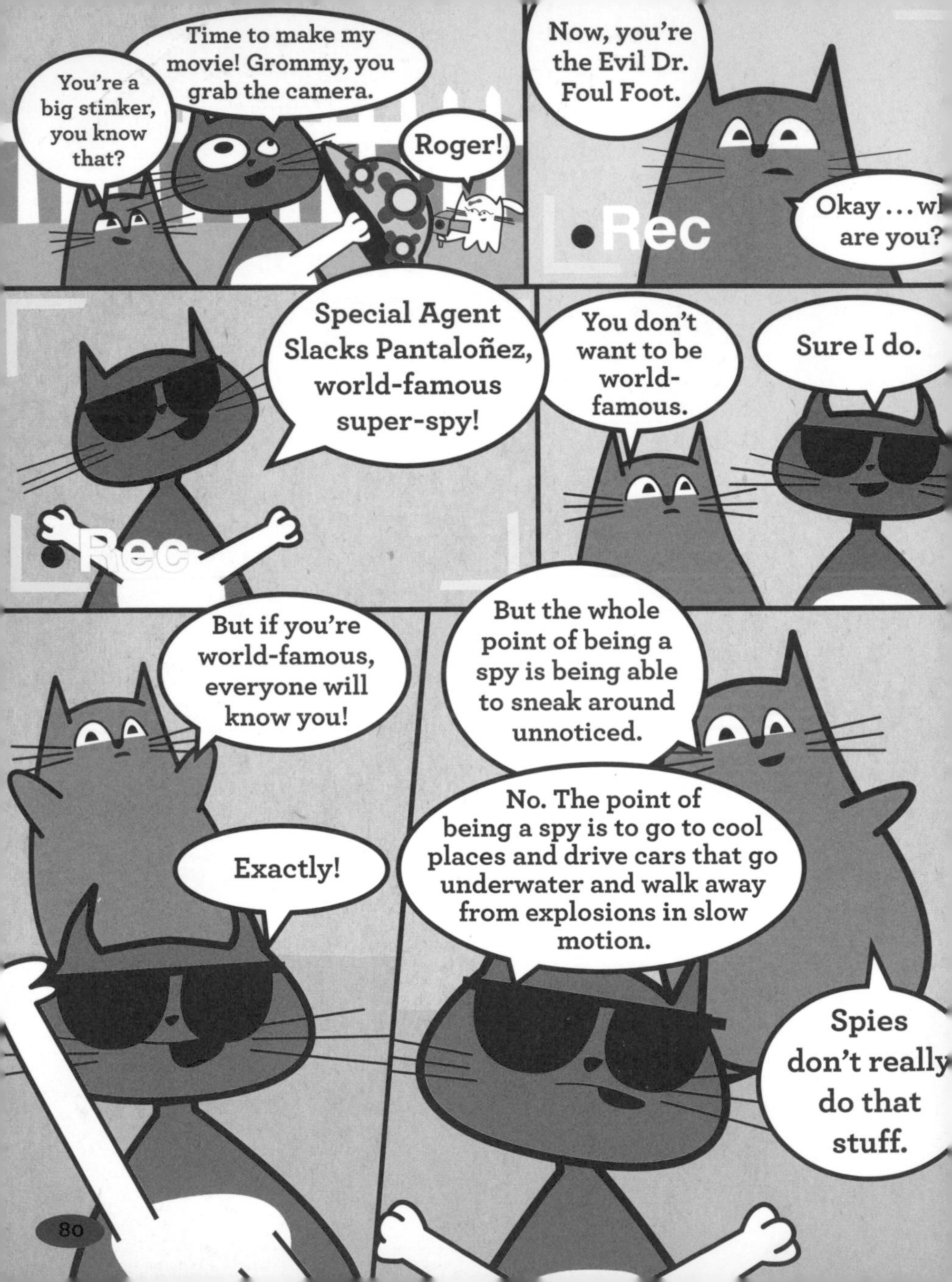

Time to make my movie! Grommy, you grab the camera.
You're a big stinker, you know that?
Roger!
Now, you're the Evil Dr. Foul Foot.
Rec
Okay . . . wh are you?
Special Agent Slacks Pantaloñez, world-famous super-spy!
Rec
You don't want to be world-famous.
Sure I do.
But if you're world-famous, everyone will know you!
Exactly!
But the whole point of being a spy is being able to sneak around unnoticed.
No. The point of being a spy is to go to cool places and drive cars that go underwater and walk away from explosions in slow motion.
Spies don't really do that stuff.

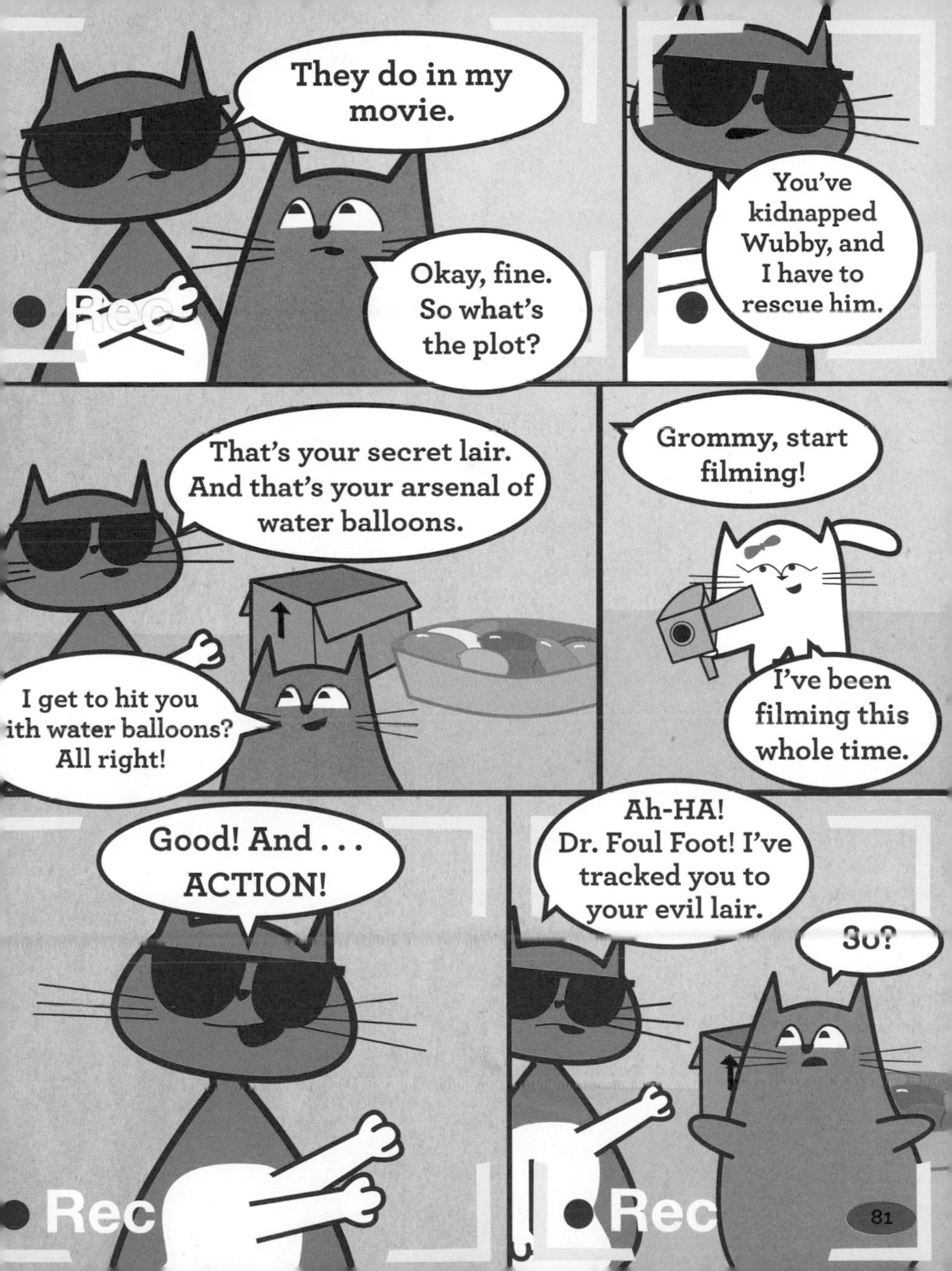
They do in my movie.
Okay, fine. So what's the plot?
Rec
You've kidnapped Wubby, and I have to rescue him.
That's your secret lair. And that's your arsenal of water balloons.
I get to hit you ith water balloons? All right!
Grommy, start filming!
I've been filming this whole time.
Good! And . . . ACTION!
Rec
Ah-HA! Dr. Foul Foot! I've tracked you to your evil lair.
So?
Rec

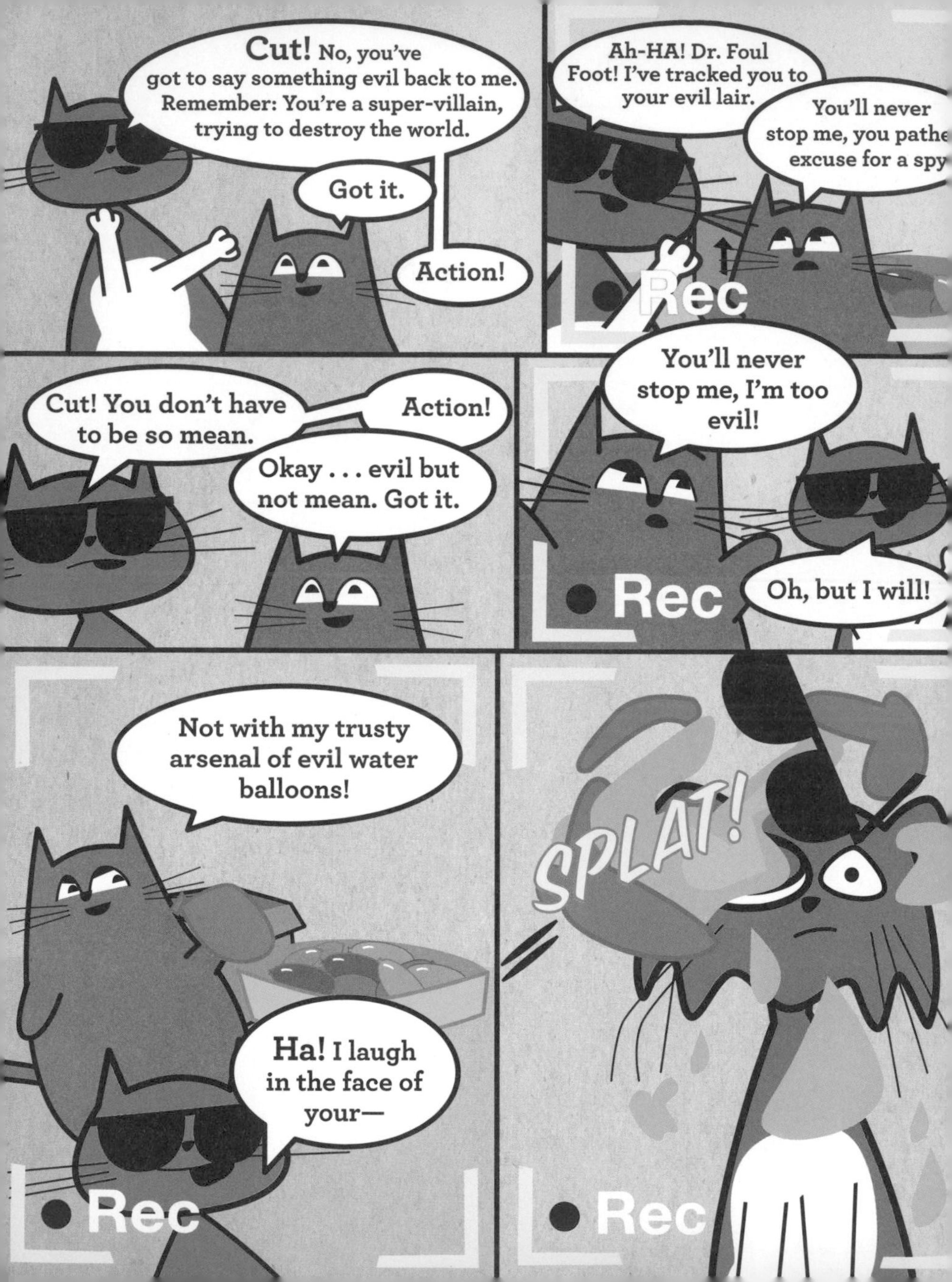
Cut! No, you've got to say something evil back to me. Remember: You're a super-villain, trying to destroy the world.
Got it.
Action!
Ah-HA! Dr. Foul Foot! I've tracked you to your evil lair.
You'll never stop me, you pathe excuse for a spy
Rec
Cut! You don't have to be so mean.
Action!
Okay . . . evil but not mean. Got it.
You'll never stop me, I'm too evil!
Oh, but I will!
Rec
Not with my trusty arsenal of evil water balloons!
Ha! I laugh in the face of your—
Rec
SPLAT!
Rec

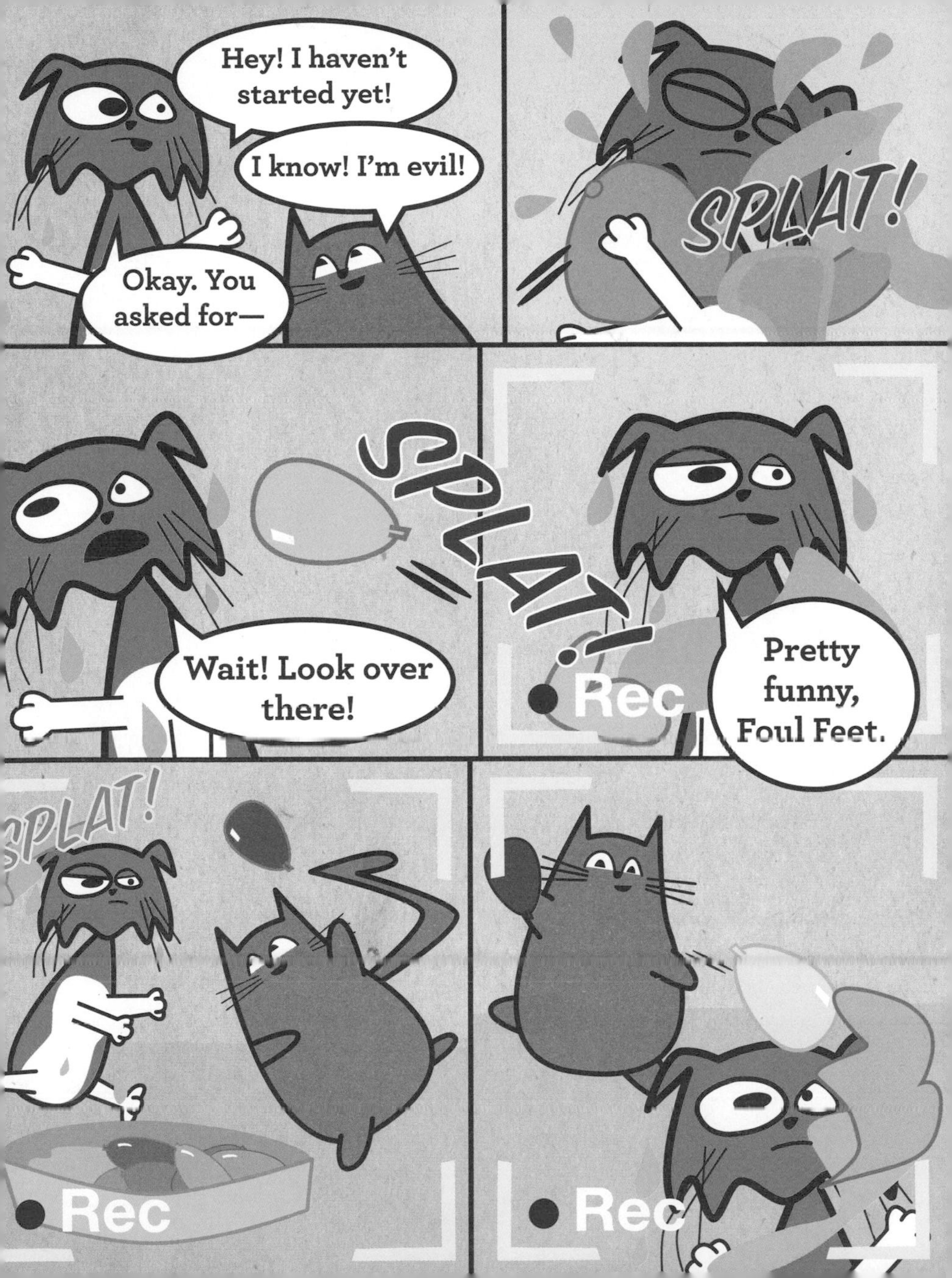

Hey! I haven't started yet!
I know! I'm evil!
Okay. You asked for—
SPLAT!
SPLAT!
Wait! Look over there!
Rec
Pretty funny, Foul Feet.
SPLAT!
Rec
Rec

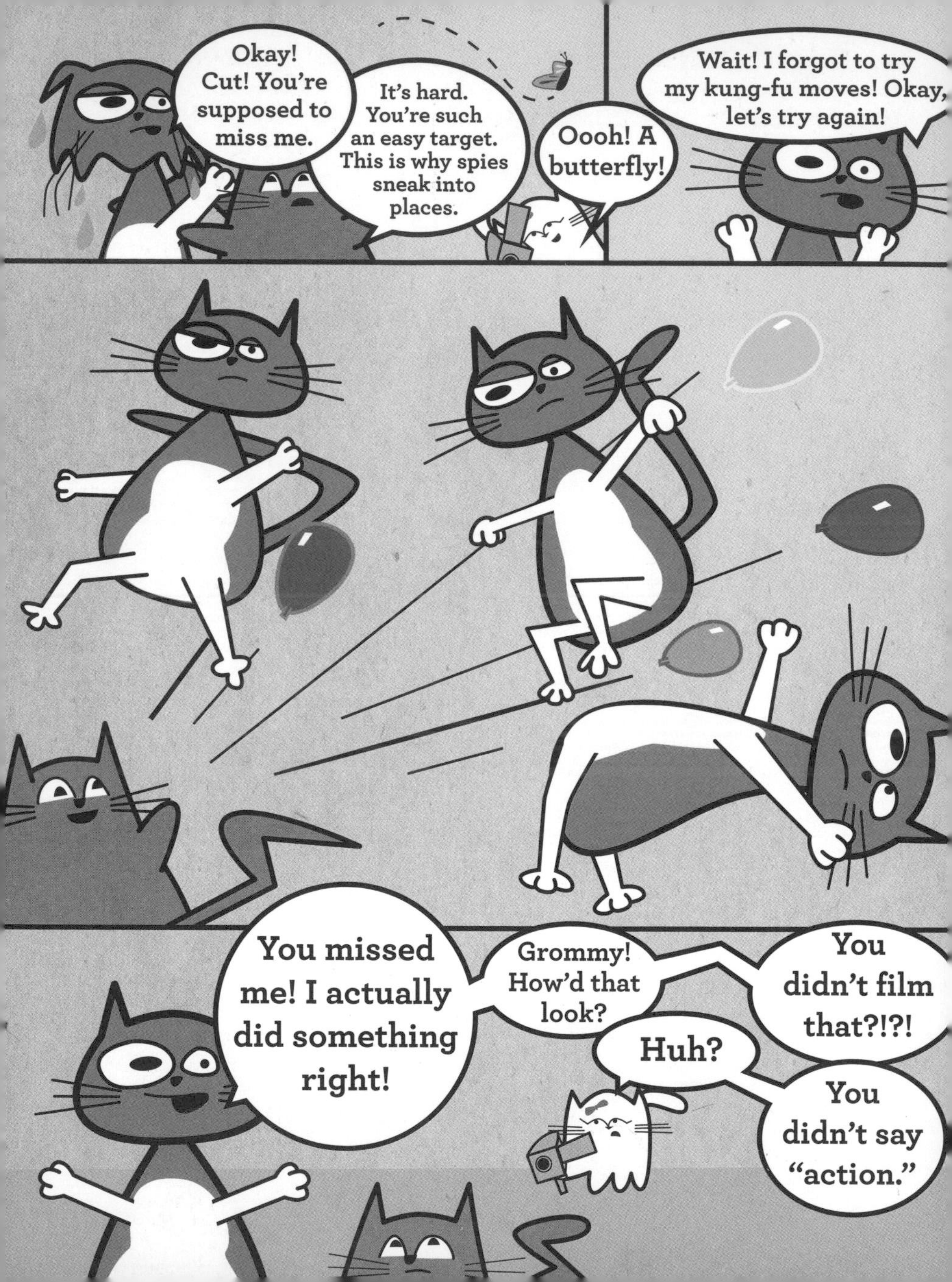
Okay! Cut! You're supposed to miss me.
It's hard. You're such an easy target. This is why spies sneak into places.
Oooh! A butterfly!
Wait! I forgot to try my kung-fu moves! Okay, let's try again!
You missed me! I actually did something right!
Grommy! How'd that look?
Huh?
You didn't film that?!?!
You didn't say "action."

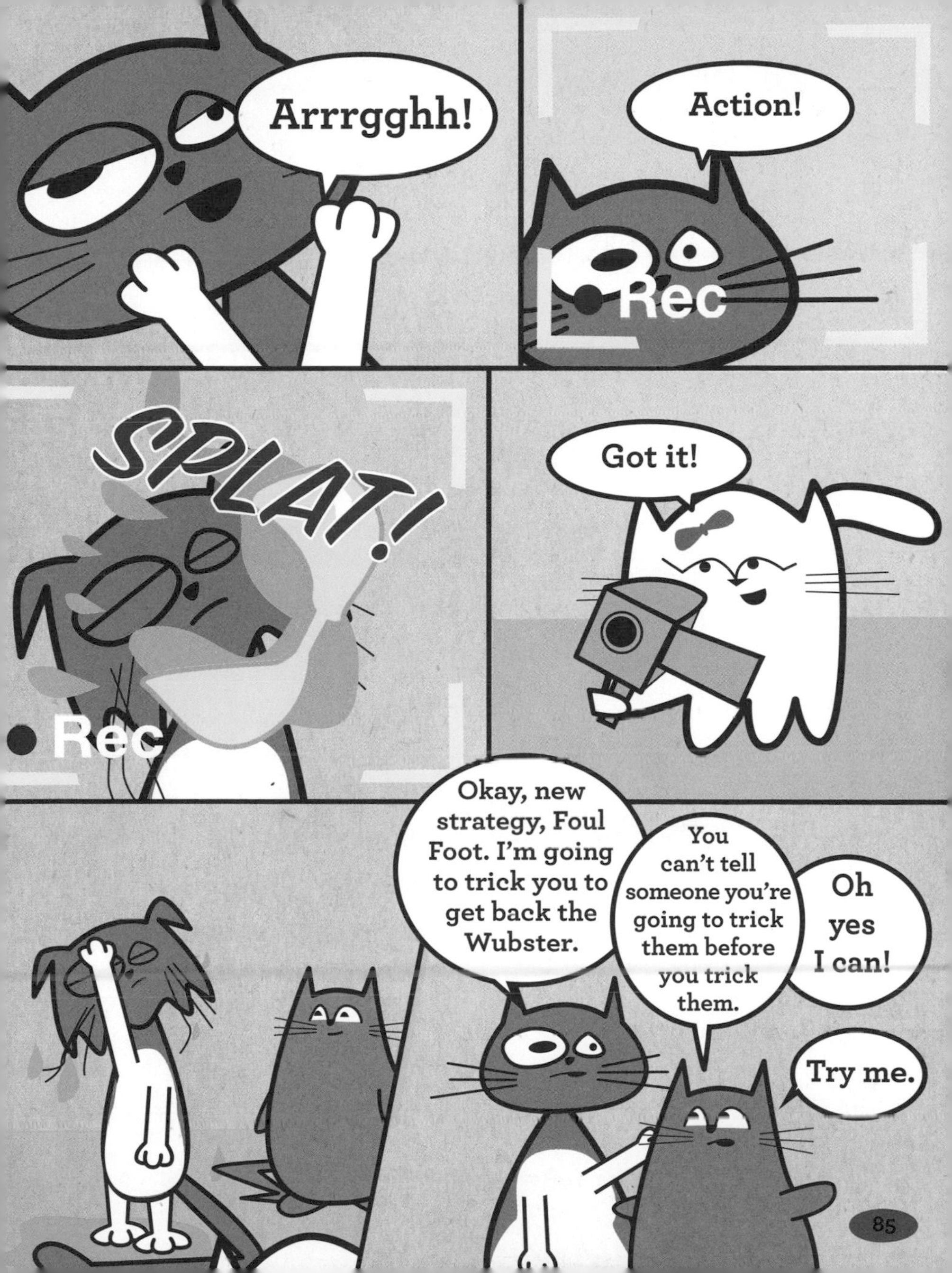

Arrrgghh!
Action!
Rec
SPLAT!
Rec
Got it!
Okay, new strategy, Foul Foot. I'm going to trick you to get back the Wubster.
You can't tell someone you're going to trick them before you trick them.
Oh yes I can!
Try me.

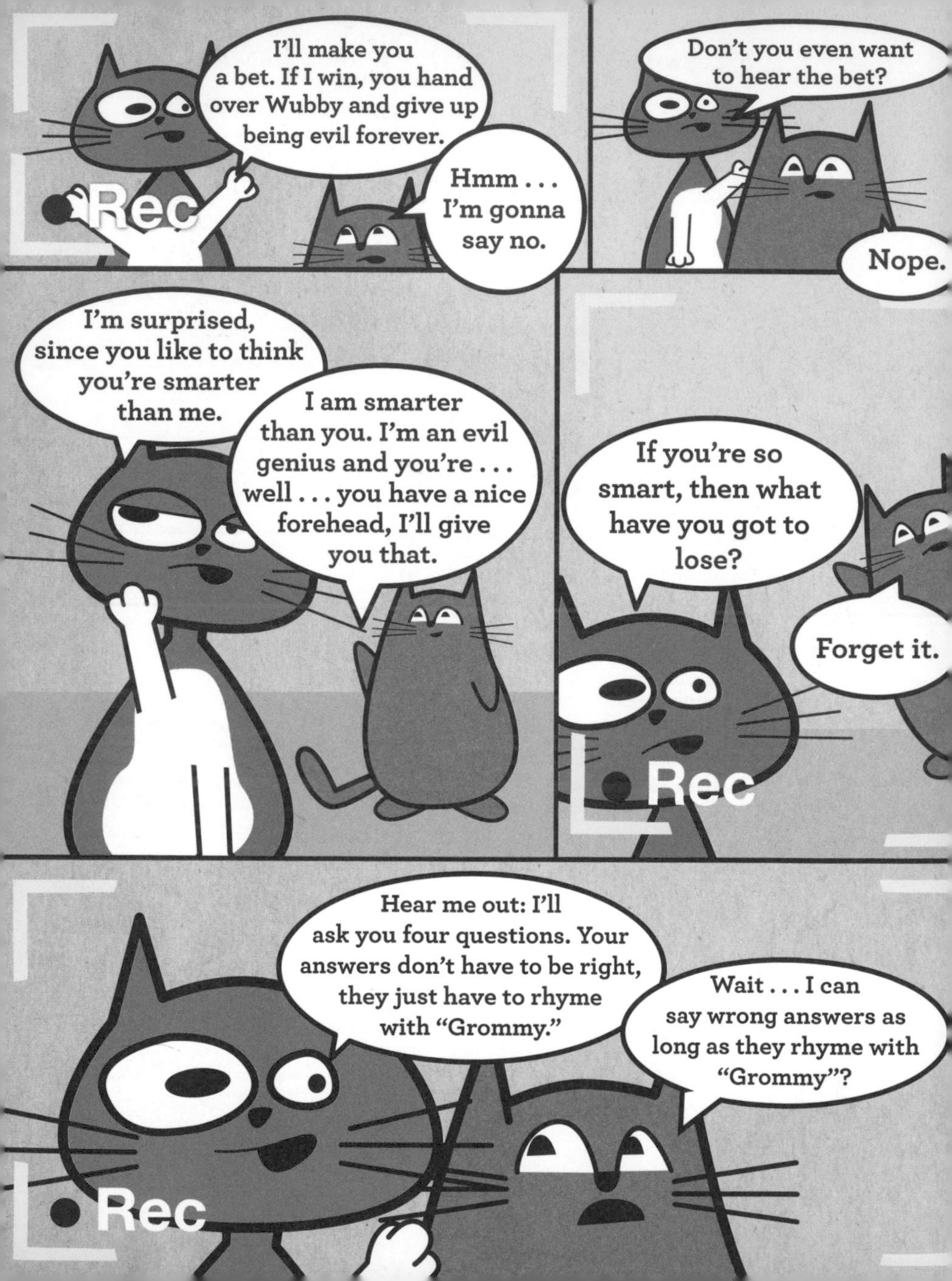
I'll make you a bet. If I win, you hand over Wubby and give up being evil forever.
Rec
Hmm . . . I'm gonna say no.
Don't you even want to hear the bet?
Nope.
I'm surprised, since you like to think you're smarter than me.
I am smarter than you. I'm an evil genius and you're . . . well . . . you have a nice forehead, I'll give you that.
If you're so smart, then what have you got to lose?
Forget it.
Rec
Hear me out: I'll ask you four questions. Your answers don't have to be right, they just have to rhyme with "Grommy."
Wait . . . I can say wrong answers as long as they rhyme with "Grommy"?
Rec

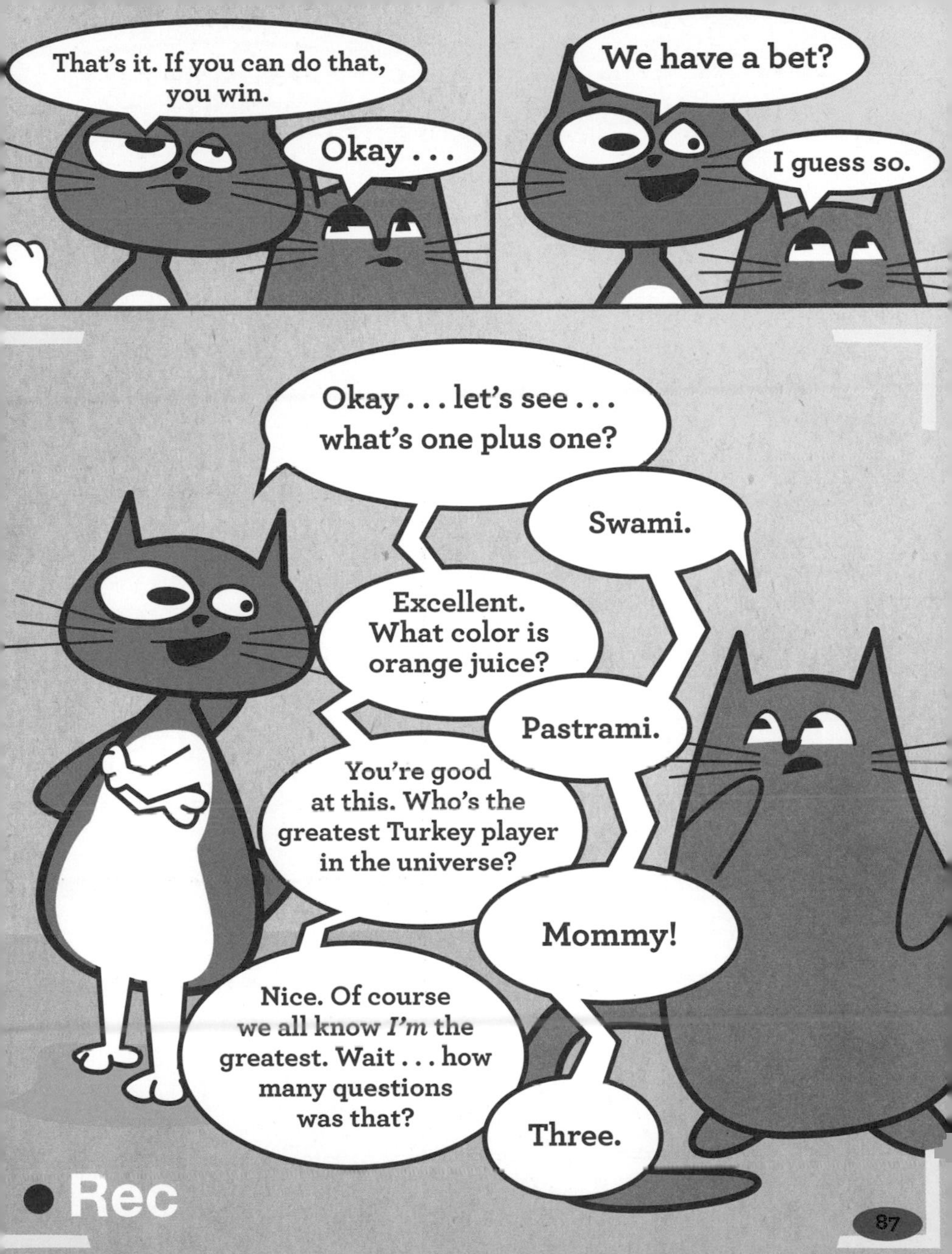
That's it. If you can do that, you win.
Okay . . .
We have a bet?
I guess so.
Okay . . . let's see . . . what's one plus one?
Swami.
Excellent. What color is orange juice?
Pastrami.
You're good at this. Who's the greatest Turkey player in the universe?
Mommy!
Nice. Of course we all know *I'm* the greatest. Wait . . . how many questions was that?
Three.
• Rec

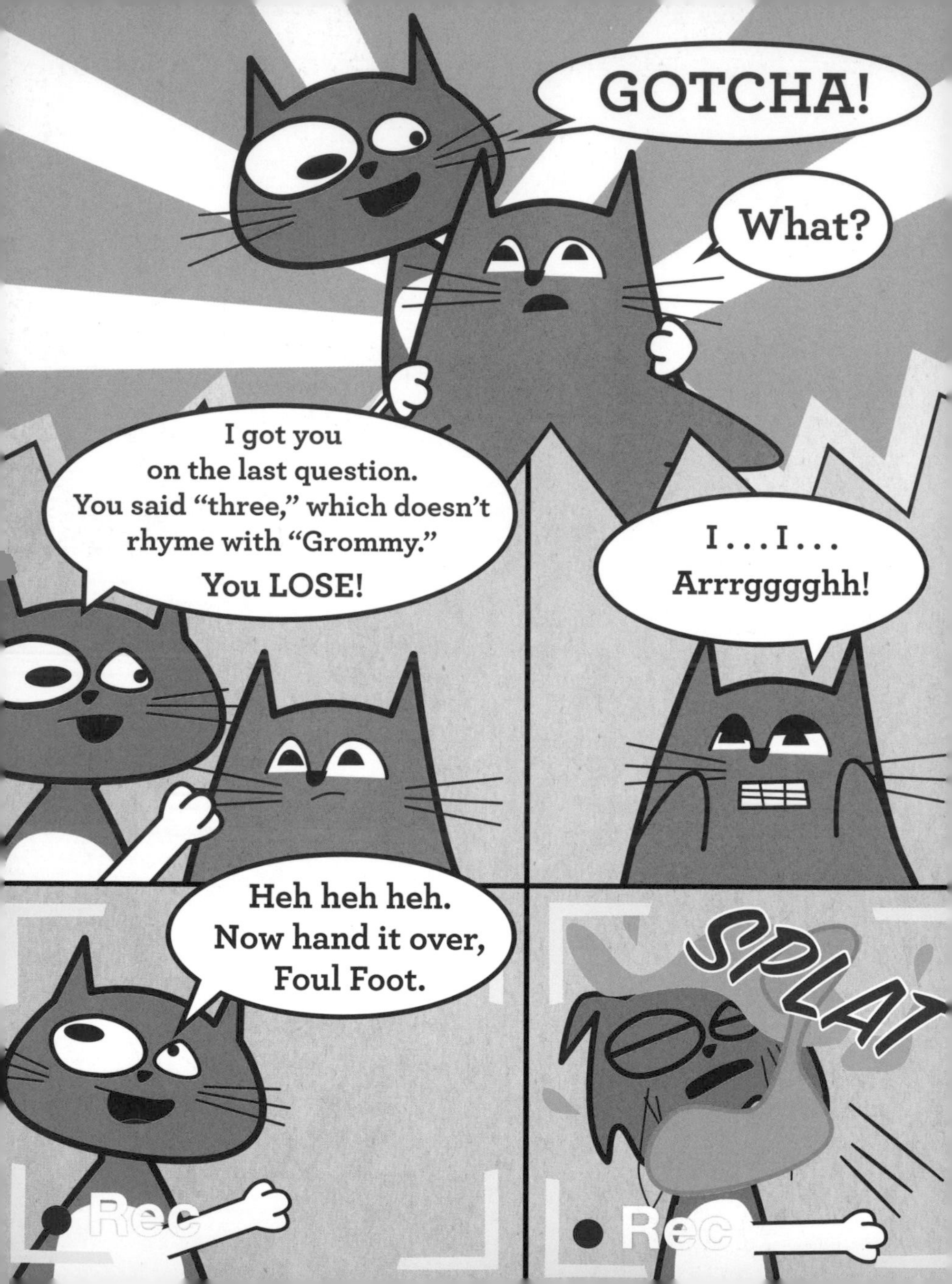
GOTCHA!
What?
I got you on the last question. You said "three," which doesn't rhyme with "Grommy." You LOSE!
I . . . I . . . Arrrggggghh!
Heh heh heh. Now hand it over, Foul Foot.
Rec
SPLAT
Rec

# Chapter Six:
# BUM-BUM OVERDUB

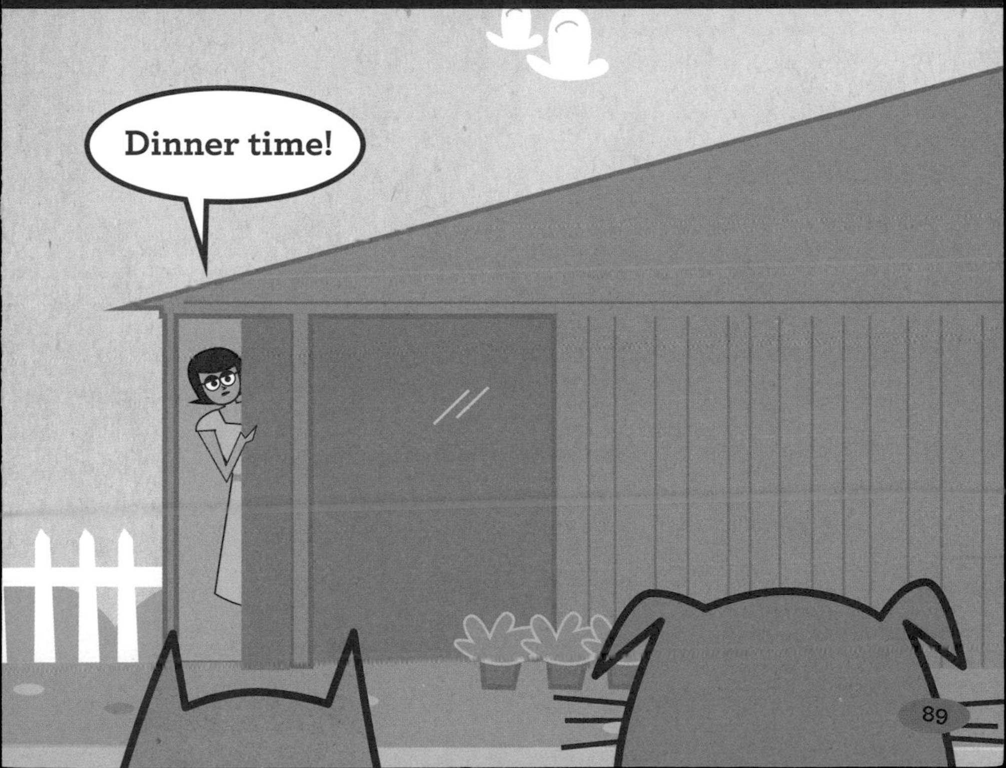
Dinner time!

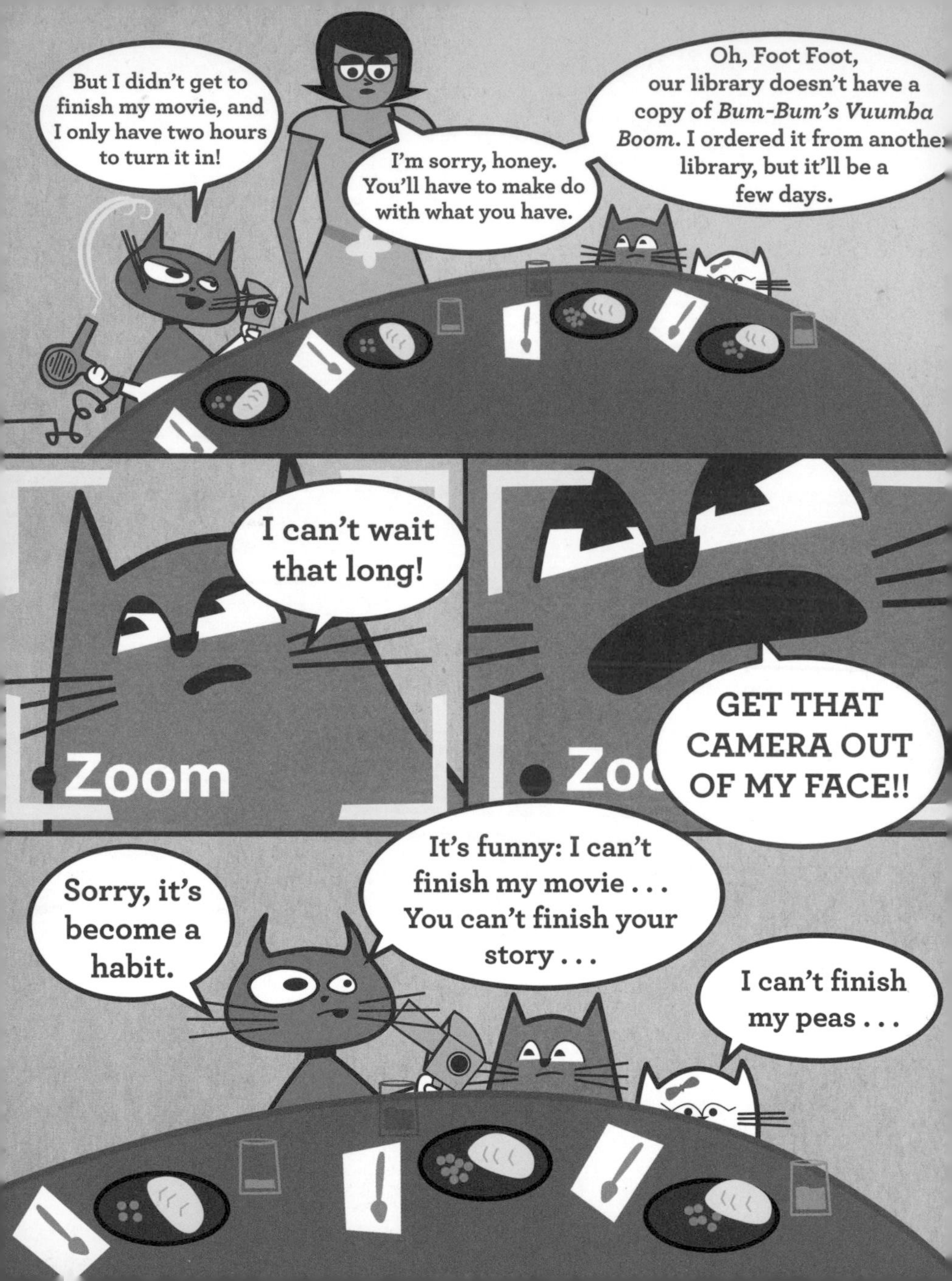
But I didn't get to finish my movie, and I only have two hours to turn it in!
I'm sorry, honey. You'll have to make do with what you have.
Oh, Foot Foot, our library doesn't have a copy of *Bum-Bum's Vuumba Boom*. I ordered it from another library, but it'll be a few days.
I can't wait that long!
Zoom
GET THAT CAMERA OUT OF MY FACE!!
Sorry, it's become a habit.
It's funny: I can't finish my movie . . . You can't finish your story . . .
I can't finish my peas . . .

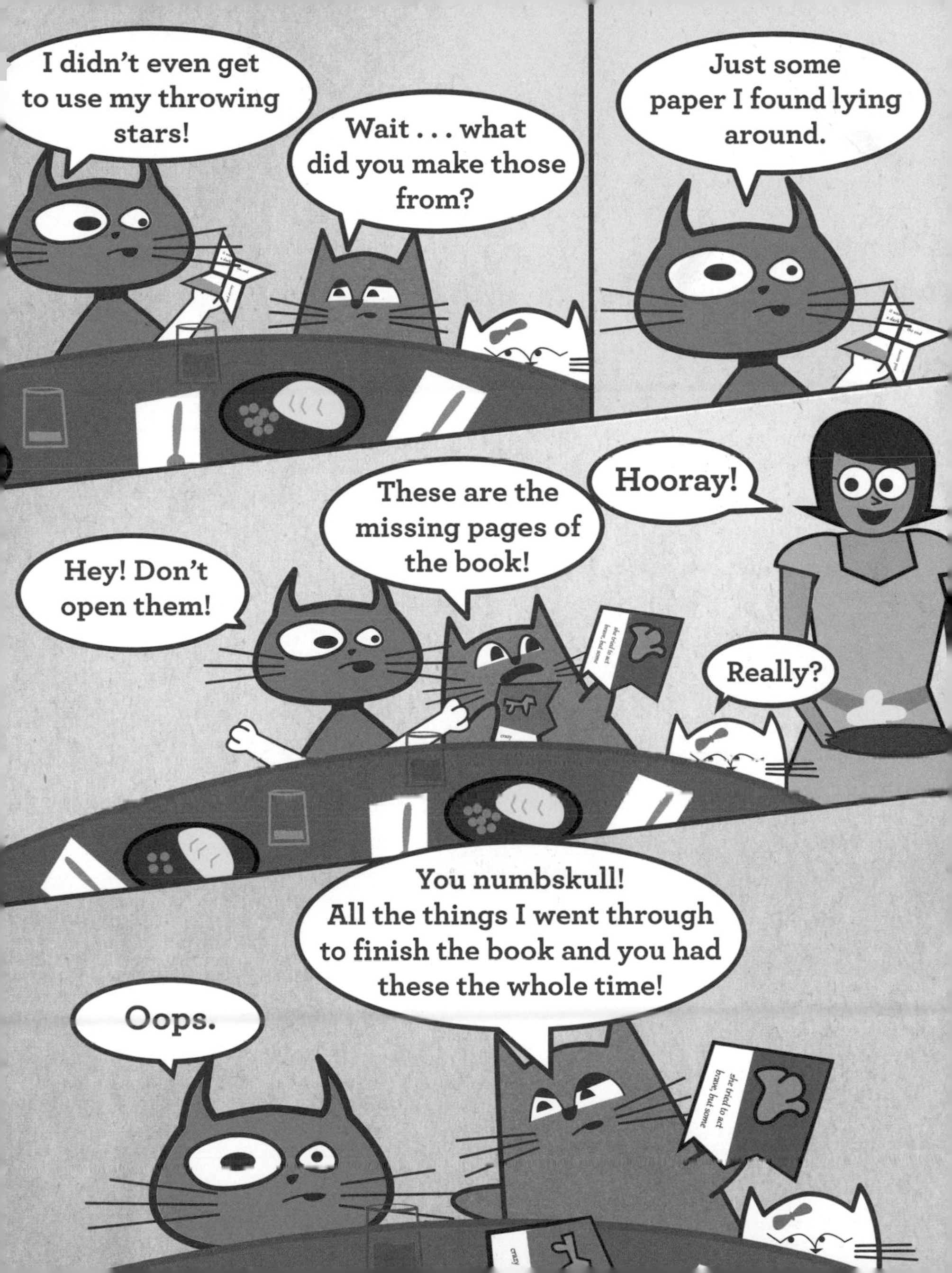

I didn't even get to use my throwing stars!
Wait . . . what did you make those from?
Just some paper I found lying around.
These are the missing pages of the book!
Hey! Don't open them!
Hooray!
Really?
You numbskull! All the things I went through to finish the book and you had these the whole time!
Oops.
she tried to act brave, but some
crazy

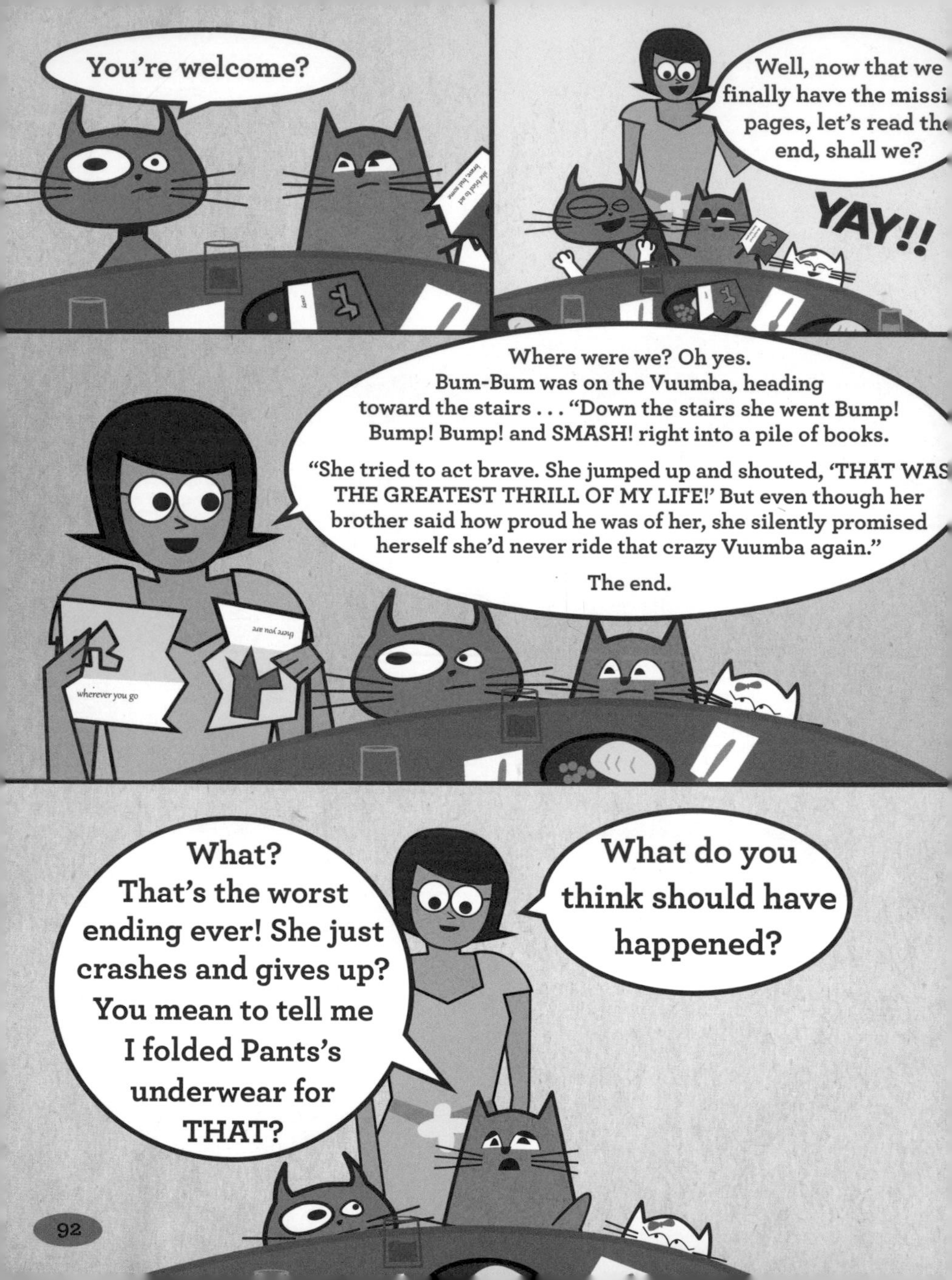
You're welcome?
Well, now that we finally have the missi pages, let's read th end, shall we?
YAY!!
Where were we? Oh yes. Bum-Bum was on the Vuumba, heading toward the stairs . . . "Down the stairs she went Bump! Bump! Bump! and SMASH! right into a pile of books.
"She tried to act brave. She jumped up and shouted, 'THAT WAS THE GREATEST THRILL OF MY LIFE!' But even though her brother said how proud he was of her, she silently promised herself she'd never ride that crazy Vuumba again."
The end.
wherever you go
What? That's the worst ending ever! She just crashes and gives up? You mean to tell me I folded Pants's underwear for THAT?
What do you think should have happened?

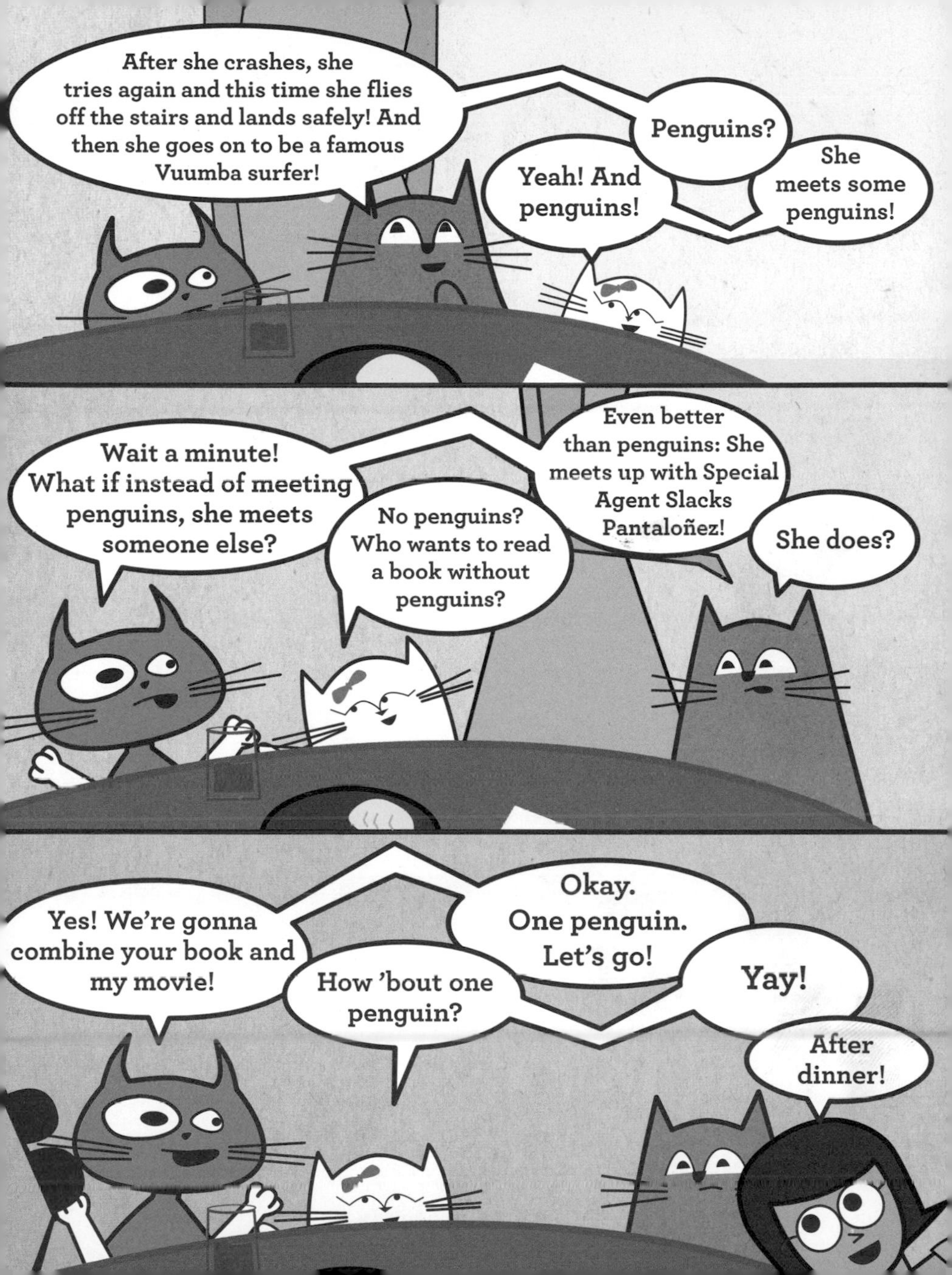
After she crashes, she tries again and this time she flies off the stairs and lands safely! And then she goes on to be a famous Vuumba surfer!
Penguins?
Yeah! And penguins!
She meets some penguins!
Wait a minute! What if instead of meeting penguins, she meets someone else?
No penguins? Who wants to read a book without penguins?
Even better than penguins: She meets up with Special Agent Slacks Pantaloñez!
She does?
Yes! We're gonna combine your book and my movie!
How 'bout one penguin?
Okay. One penguin. Let's go!
Yay!
After dinner!

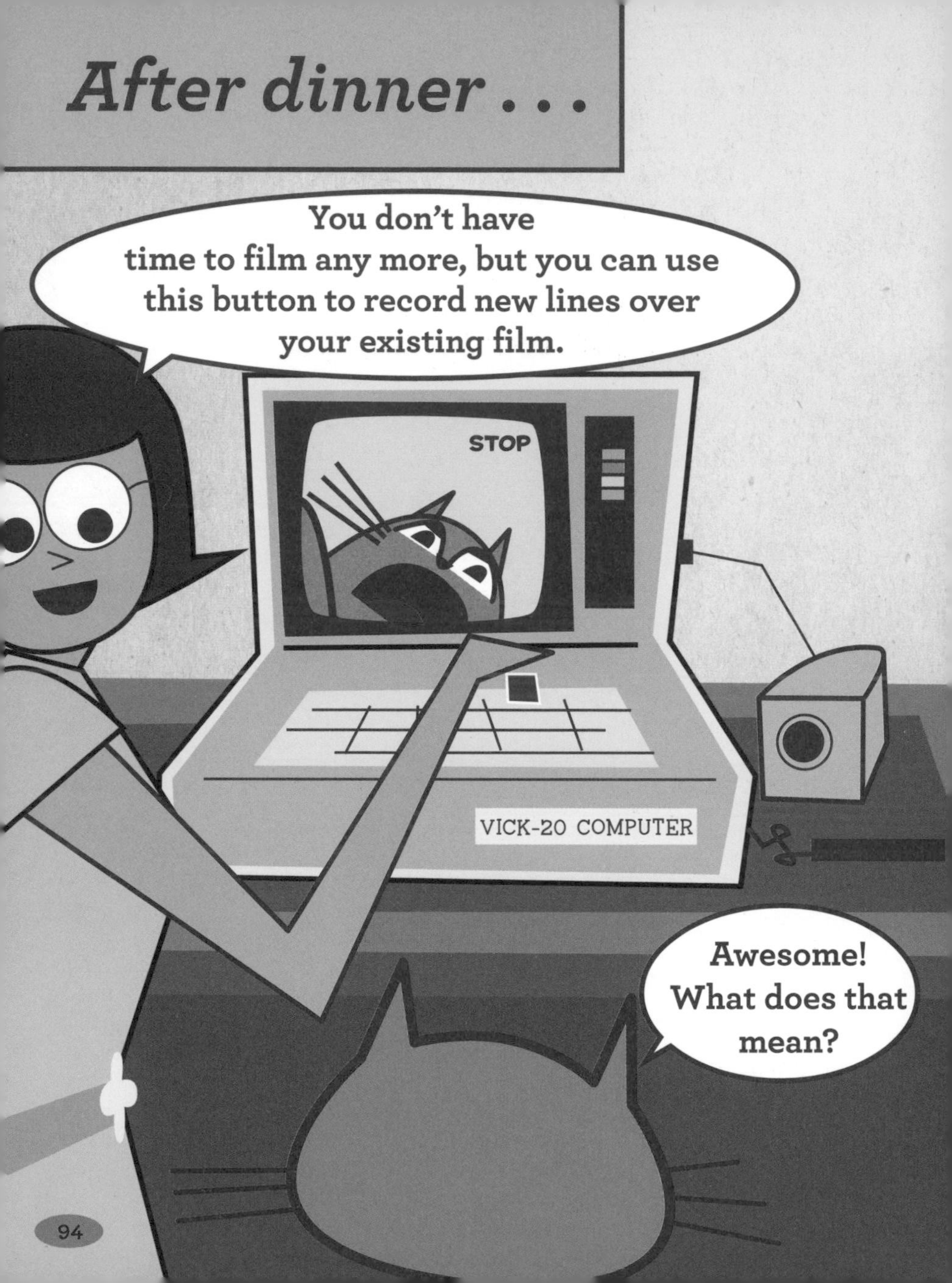
After dinner . . .
You don't have time to film any more, but you can use this button to record new lines over your existing film.
STOP
VICK-20 COMPUTER
Awesome! What does that mean?

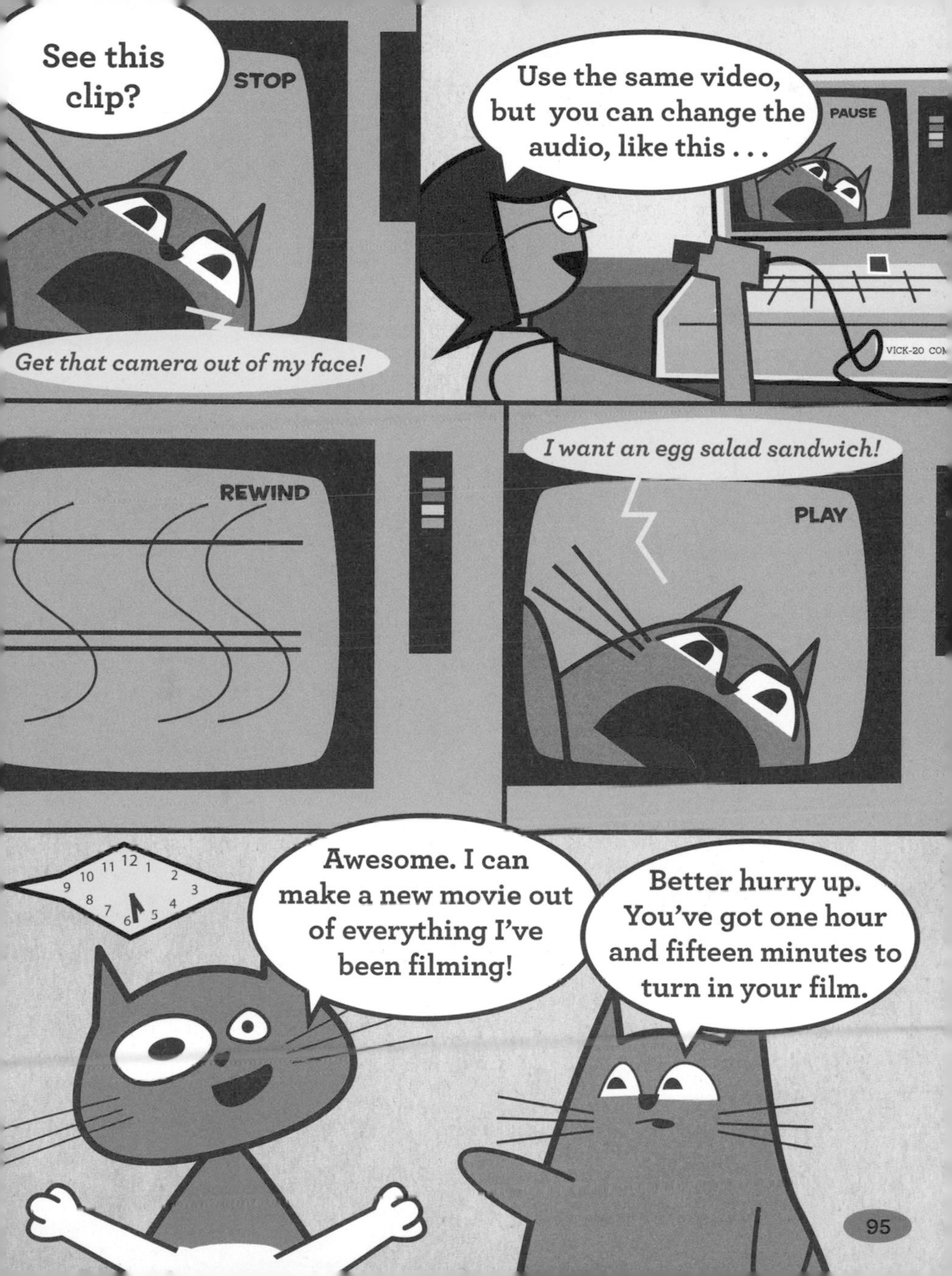
See this clip?
STOP
Get that camera out of my face!
Use the same video, but you can change the audio, like this . . .
PAUSE
VICK-20 CO
REWIND
I want an egg salad sandwich!
PLAY
Awesome. I can make a new movie out of everything I've been filming!
Better hurry up. You've got one hour and fifteen minutes to turn in your film.

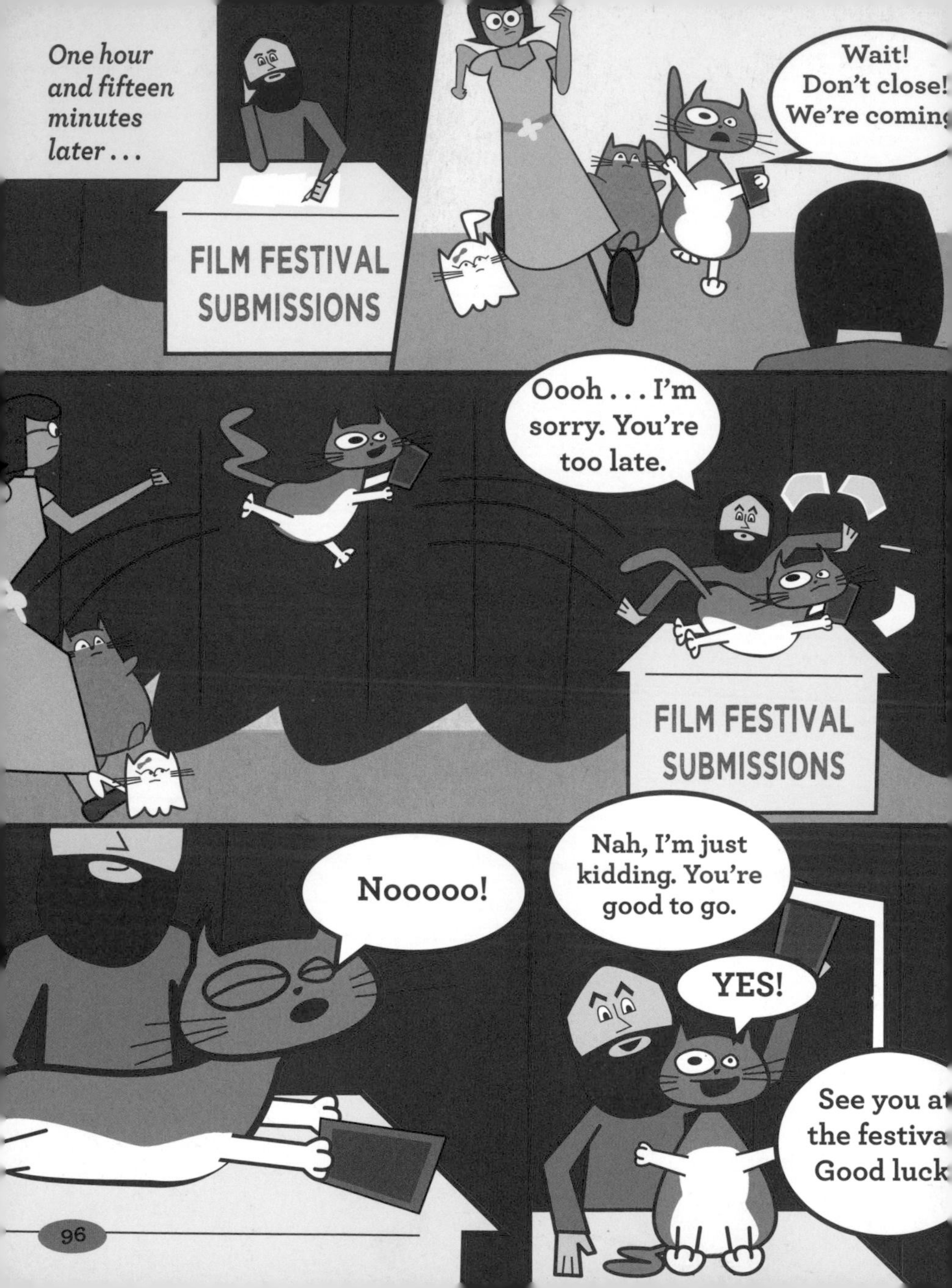
One hour and fifteen minutes later . . .
FILM FESTIVAL SUBMISSIONS
Wait! Don't close! We're coming
Oooh . . . I'm sorry. You're too late.
FILM FESTIVAL SUBMISSIONS
Nooooo!
Nah, I'm just kidding. You're good to go.
YES!
See you at the festiva Good luck

# Chapter Seven: DOUBLE-O-AWESOME

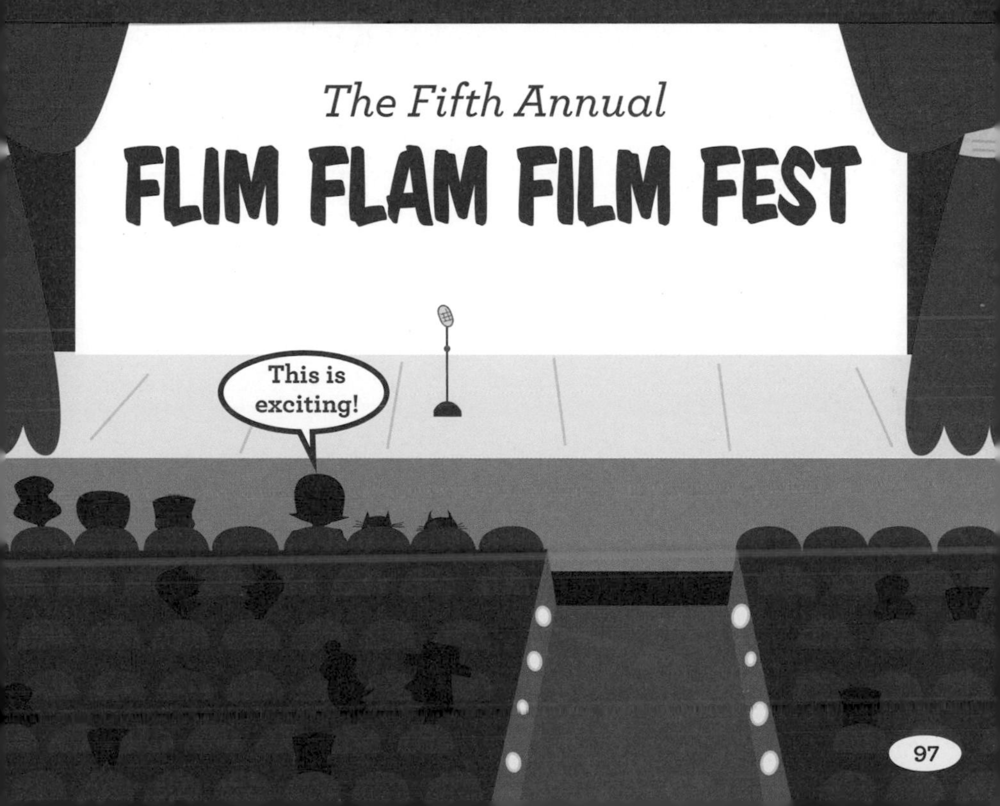
The Fifth Annual
FLIM FLAM FILM FEST
This is exciting!

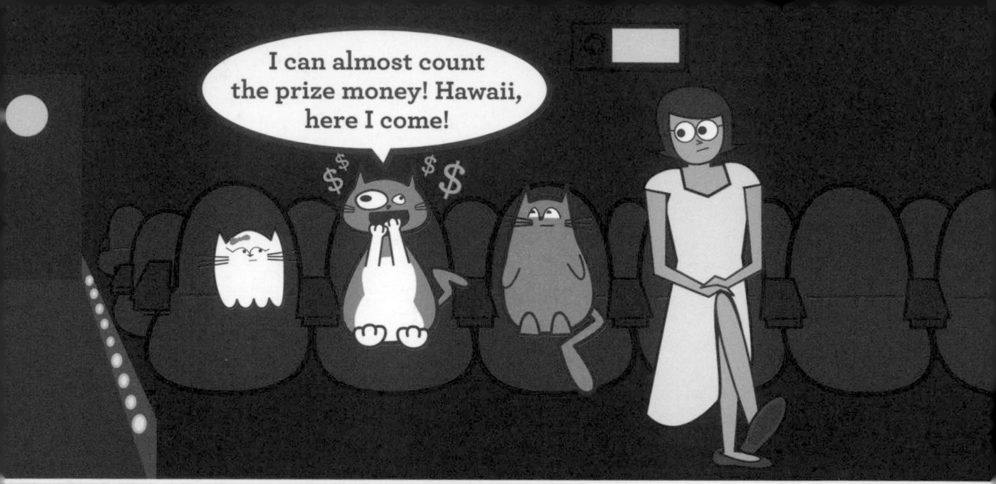
I can almost count the prize money! Hawaii, here I come!

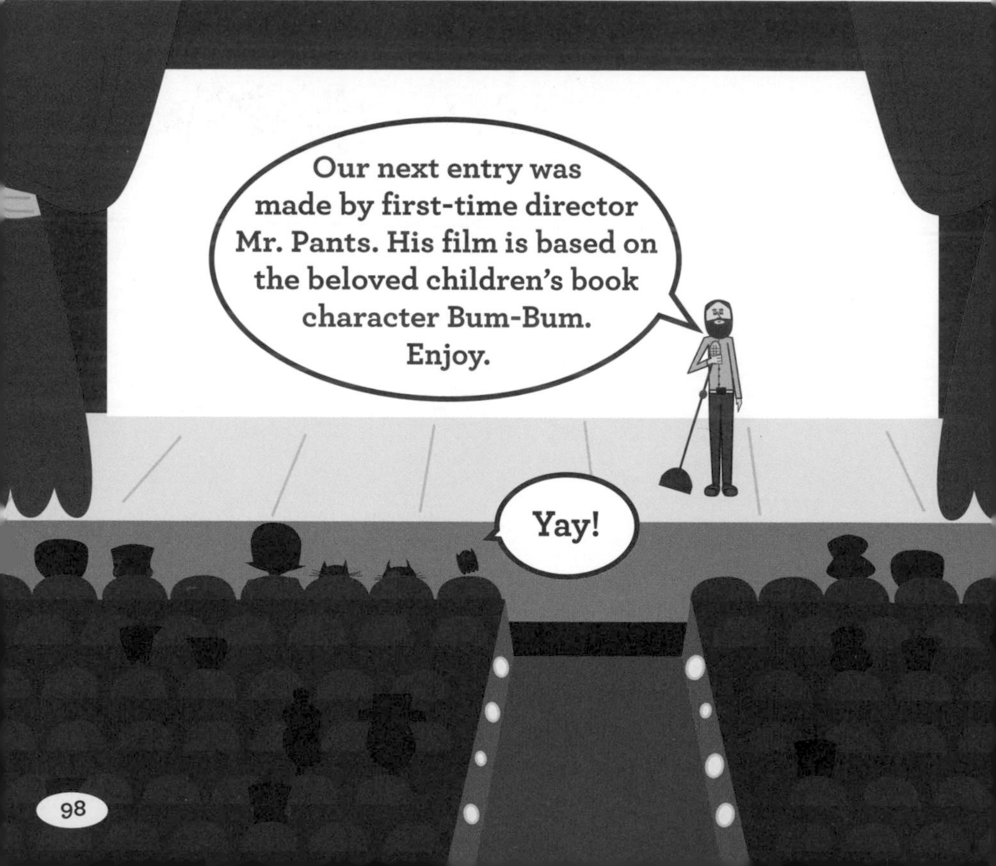
Our next entry was made by first-time director Mr. Pants. His film is based on the beloved children's book character Bum-Bum. Enjoy.
Yay!

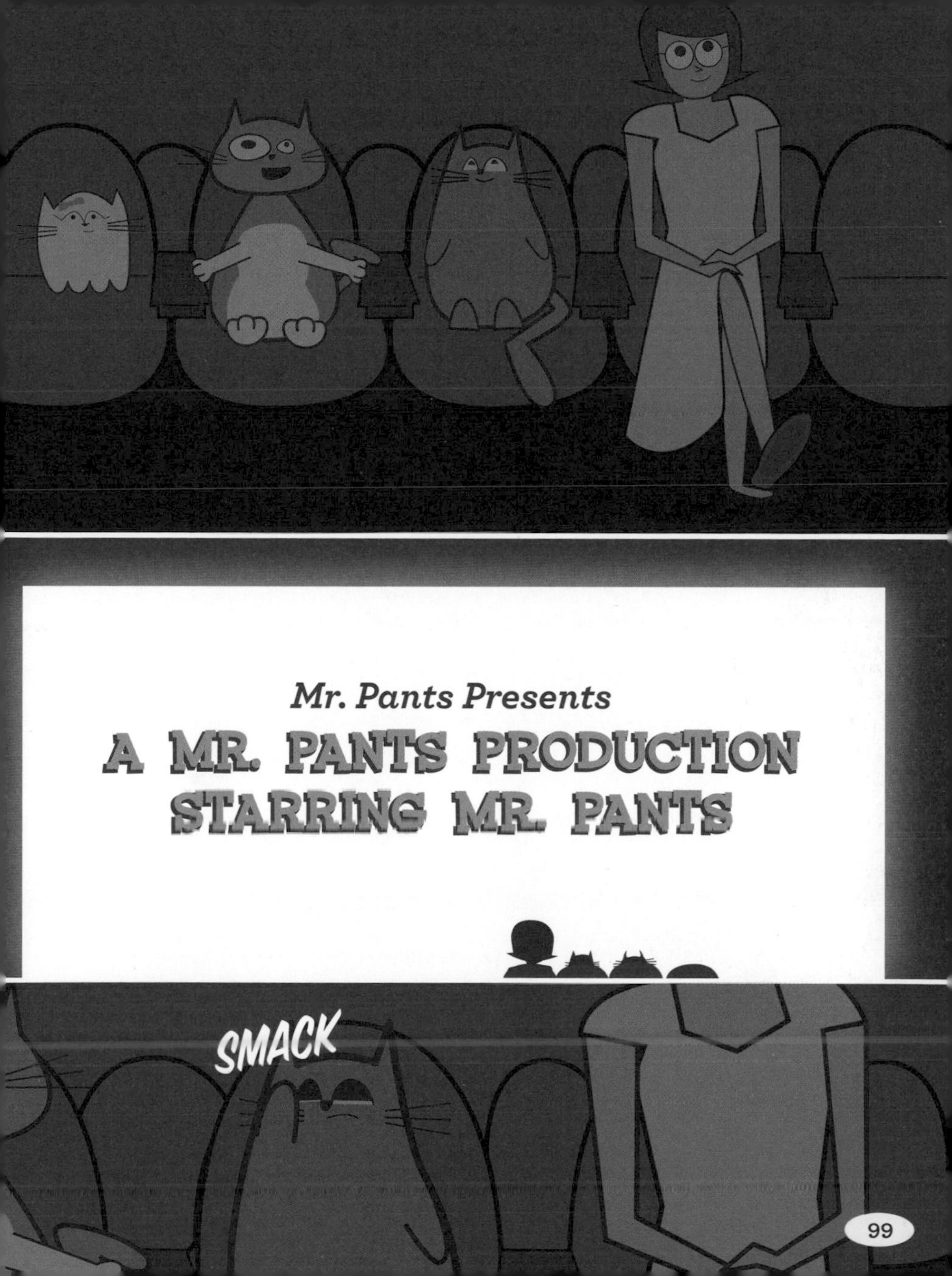

Mr. Pants Presents
A MR. PANTS PRODUCTION
STARRING MR. PANTS
SMACK

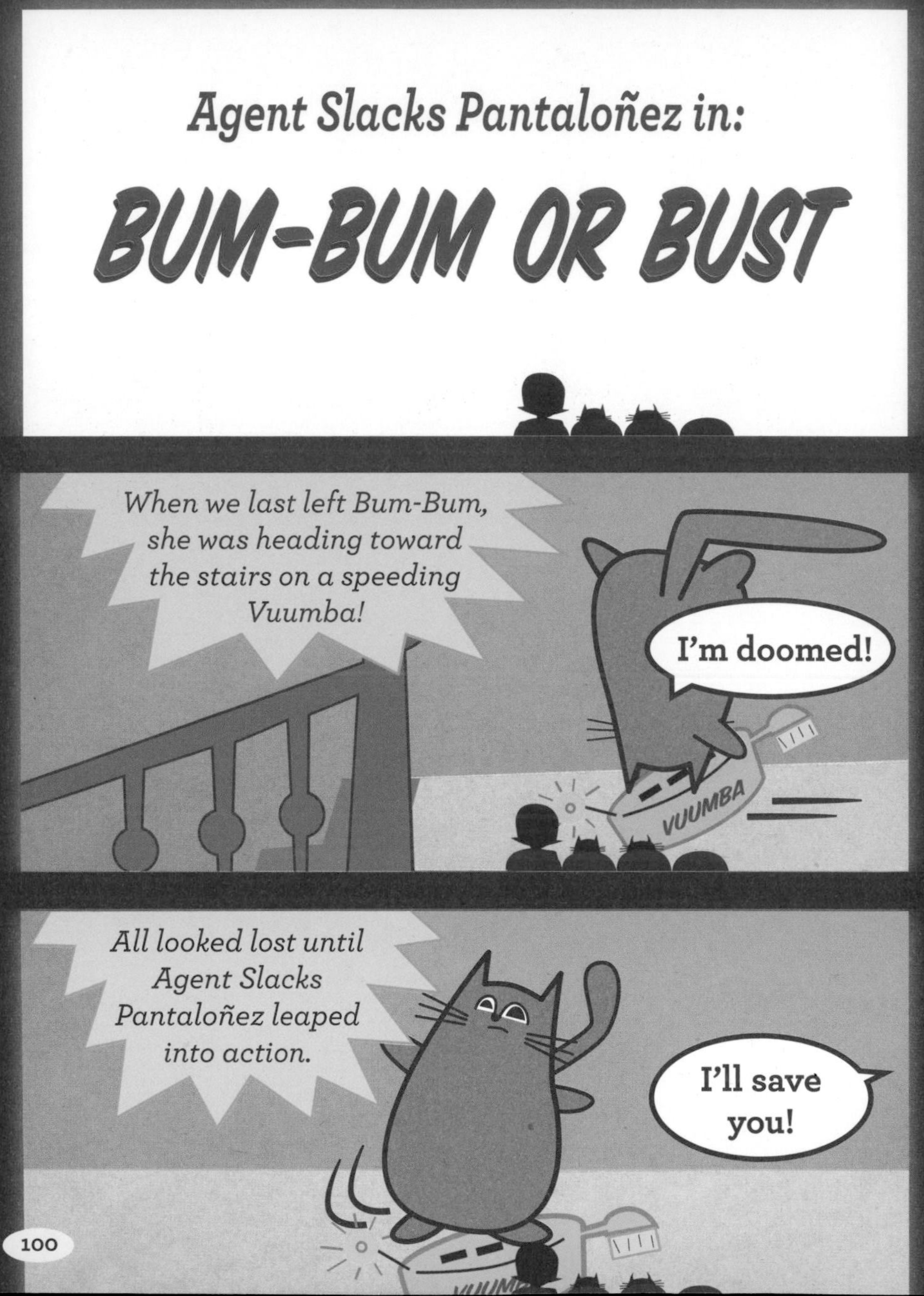
Agent Slacks Pantaloñez in:
BUM-BUM OR BUST
When we last left Bum-Bum, she was heading toward the stairs on a speeding Vuumba!
I'm doomed!
VUUMBA
All looked lost until Agent Slacks Pantaloñez leaped into action.
I'll save you!

Oh, my hero!

You're welcome!

BUT! Dazed from his crash, Slacks unwittingly revealed the secret missile launch codes.

I'll take these, thank YOU!

Hmmm . . . Why would Bum-Bum want the secret codes? Unless . . .

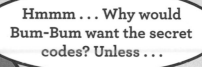

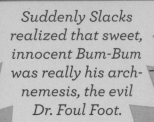

Suddenly Slacks realized that sweet, innocent Bum-Bum was really his arch-nemesis, the evil Dr. Foul Foot.

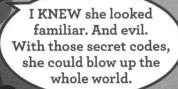

I KNEW she looked familiar. And evil. With those secret codes, she could blow up the whole world.

That would be bad!

Raise your hand if you want me to save the world.

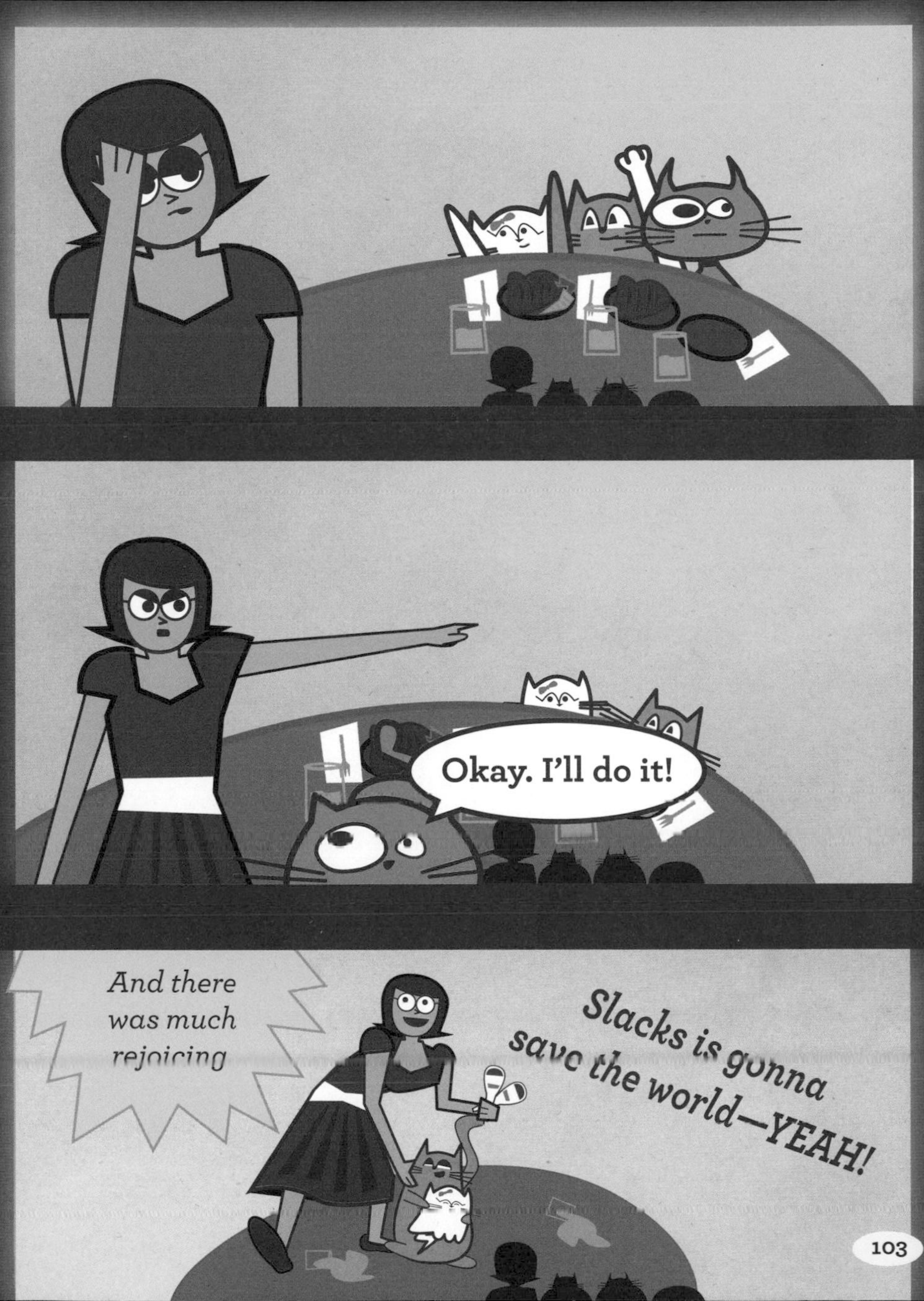
Okay. I'll do it!
And there was much rejoicing
Slacks is gonna save the world—YEAH!

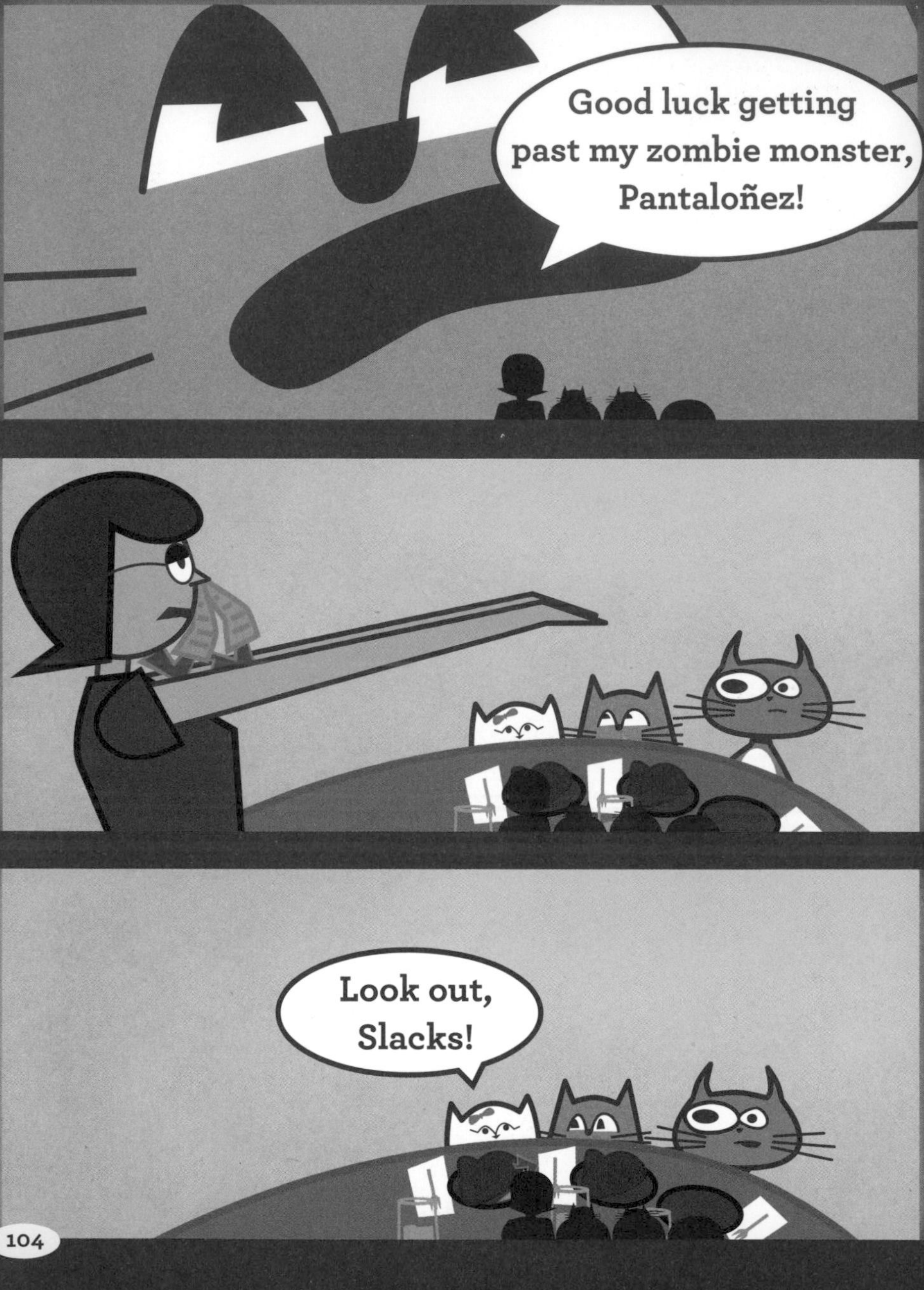
Good luck getting past my zombie monster, Pantaloñez!
Look out, Slacks!

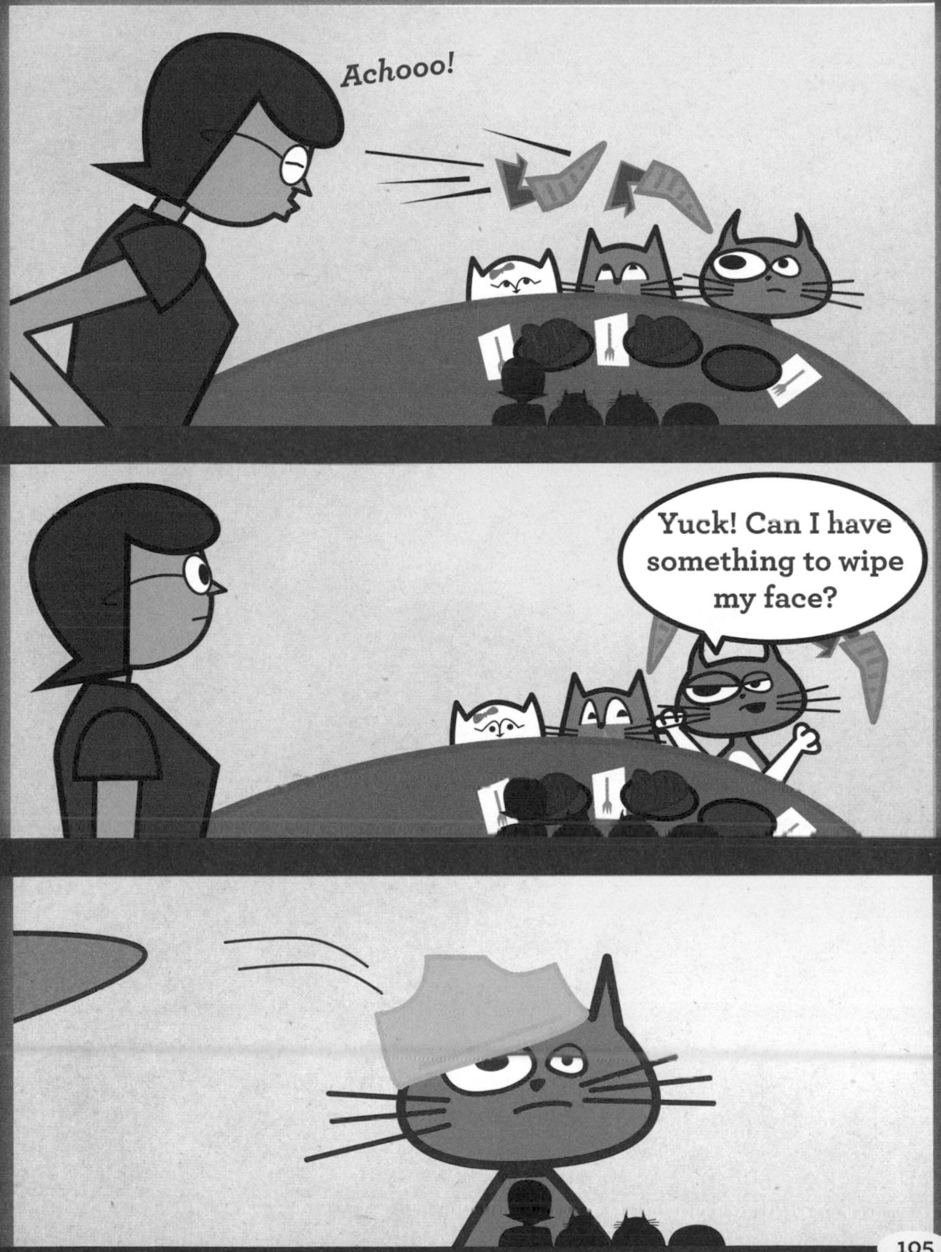
Achooo!
Yuck! Can I have something to wipe my face?

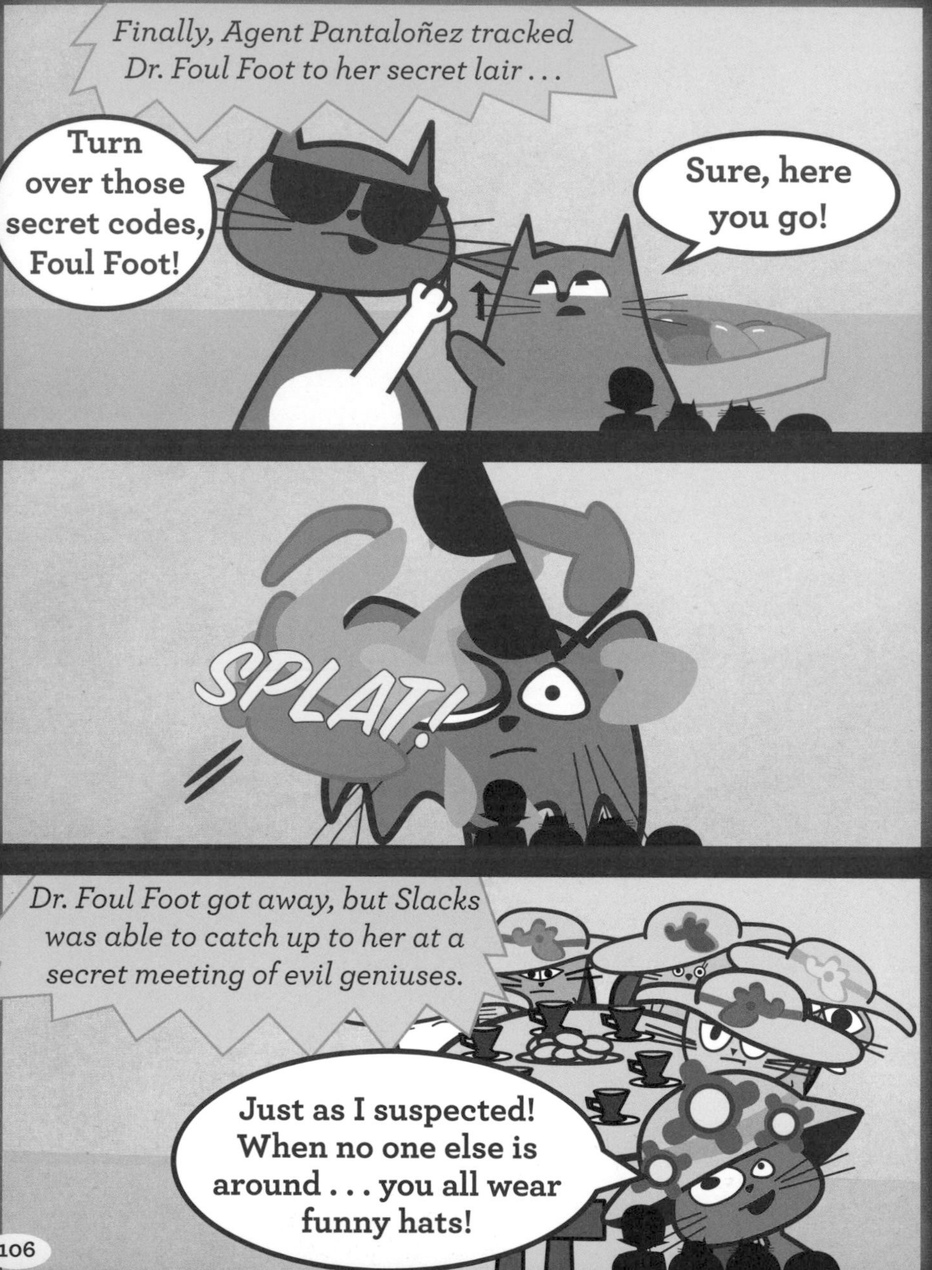
Finally, Agent Pantaloñez tracked Dr. Foul Foot to her secret lair . . .
Turn over those secret codes, Foul Foot!
Sure, here you go!
SPLAT!
Dr. Foul Foot got away, but Slacks was able to catch up to her at a secret meeting of evil geniuses.
Just as I suspected! When no one else is around . . . you all wear funny hats!

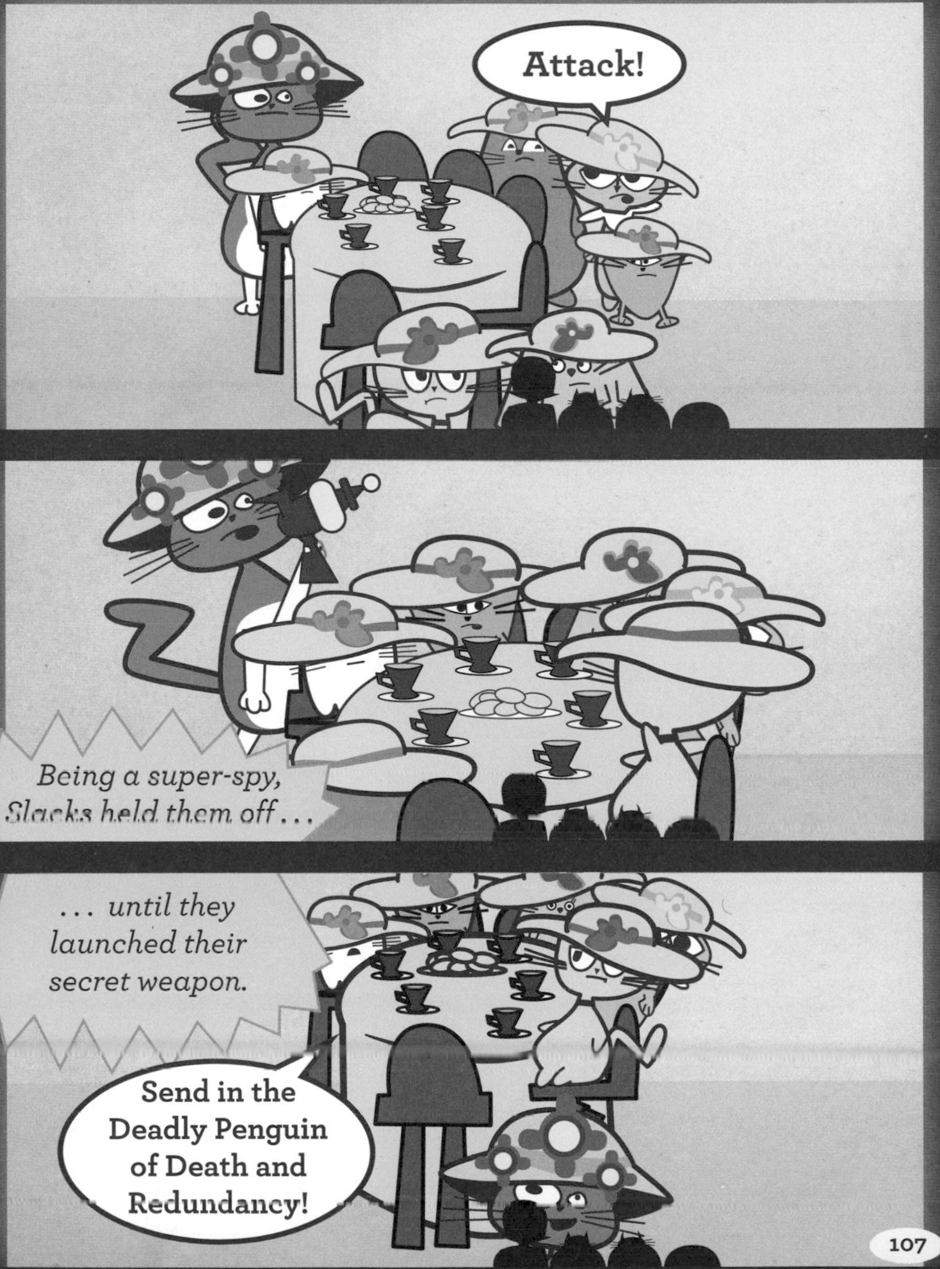
Attack!
Being a super-spy, Slacks held them off . . .
. . . until they launched their secret weapon.
Send in the Deadly Penguin of Death and Redundancy!

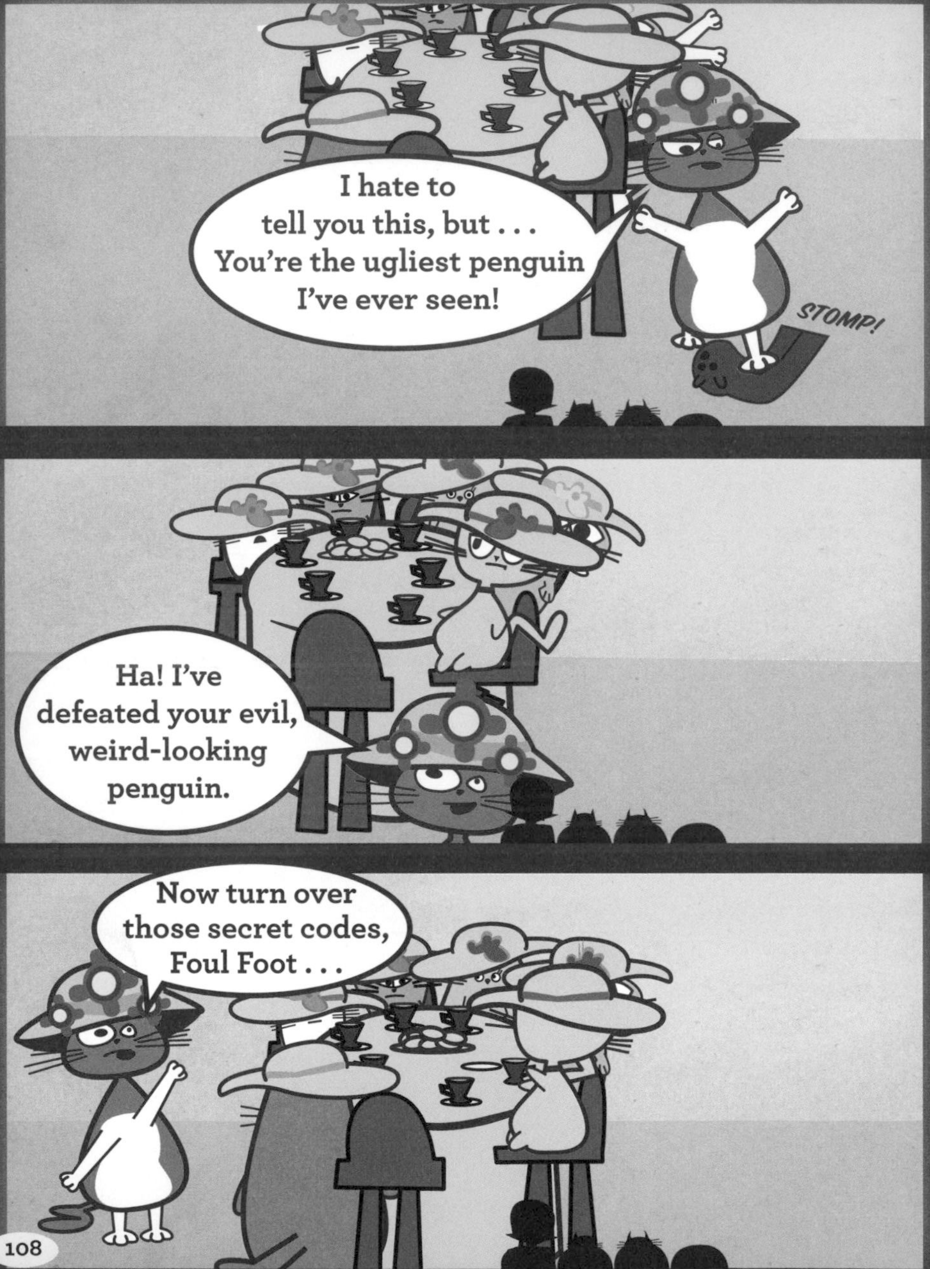
I hate to tell you this, but . . . You're the ugliest penguin I've ever seen!
STOMP!
Ha! I've defeated your evil, weird-looking penguin.
Now turn over those secret codes, Foul Foot . . .

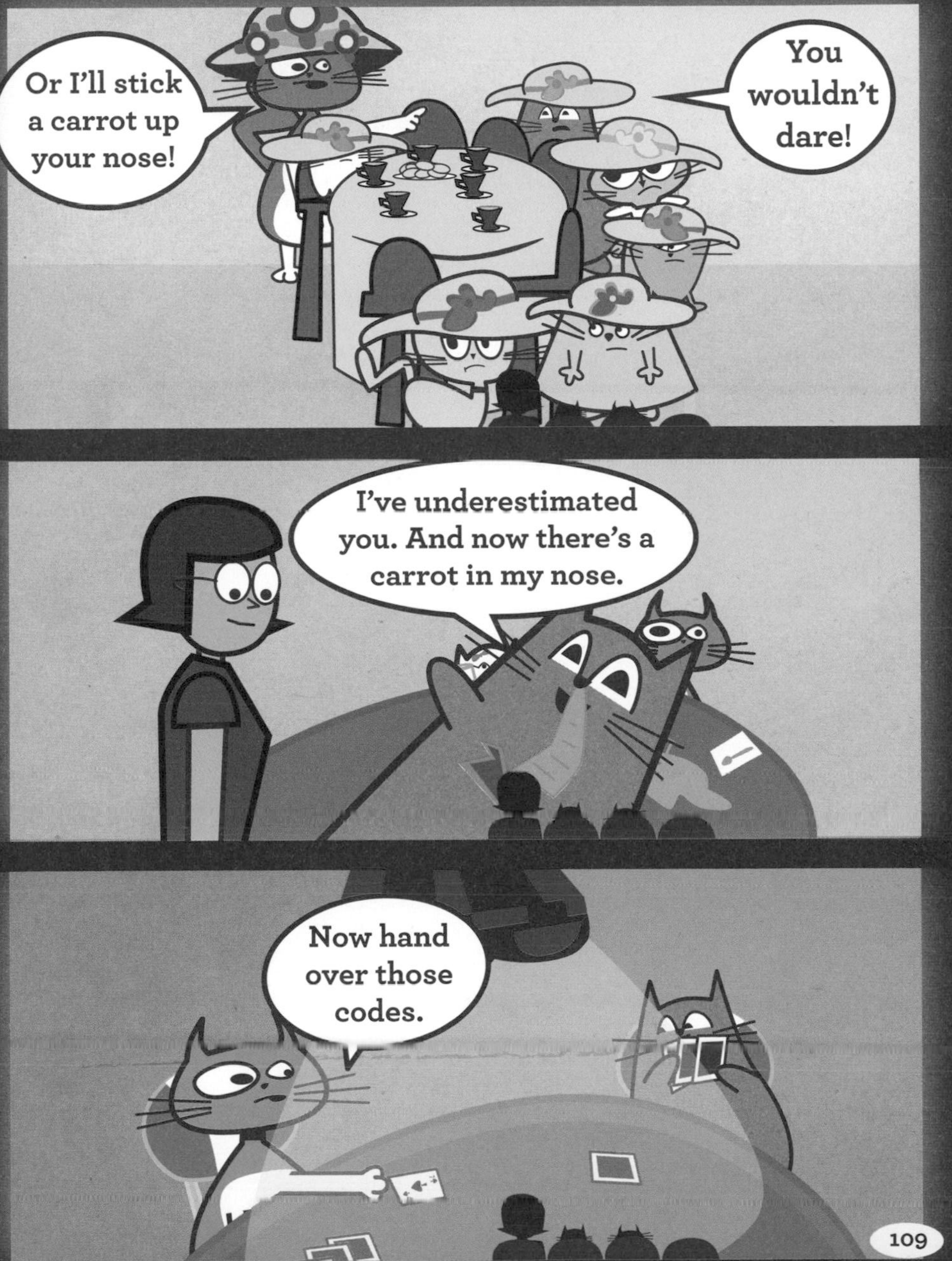
Or I'll stick a carrot up your nose!
You wouldn't dare!
I've underestimated you. And now there's a carrot in my nose.
Now hand over those codes.

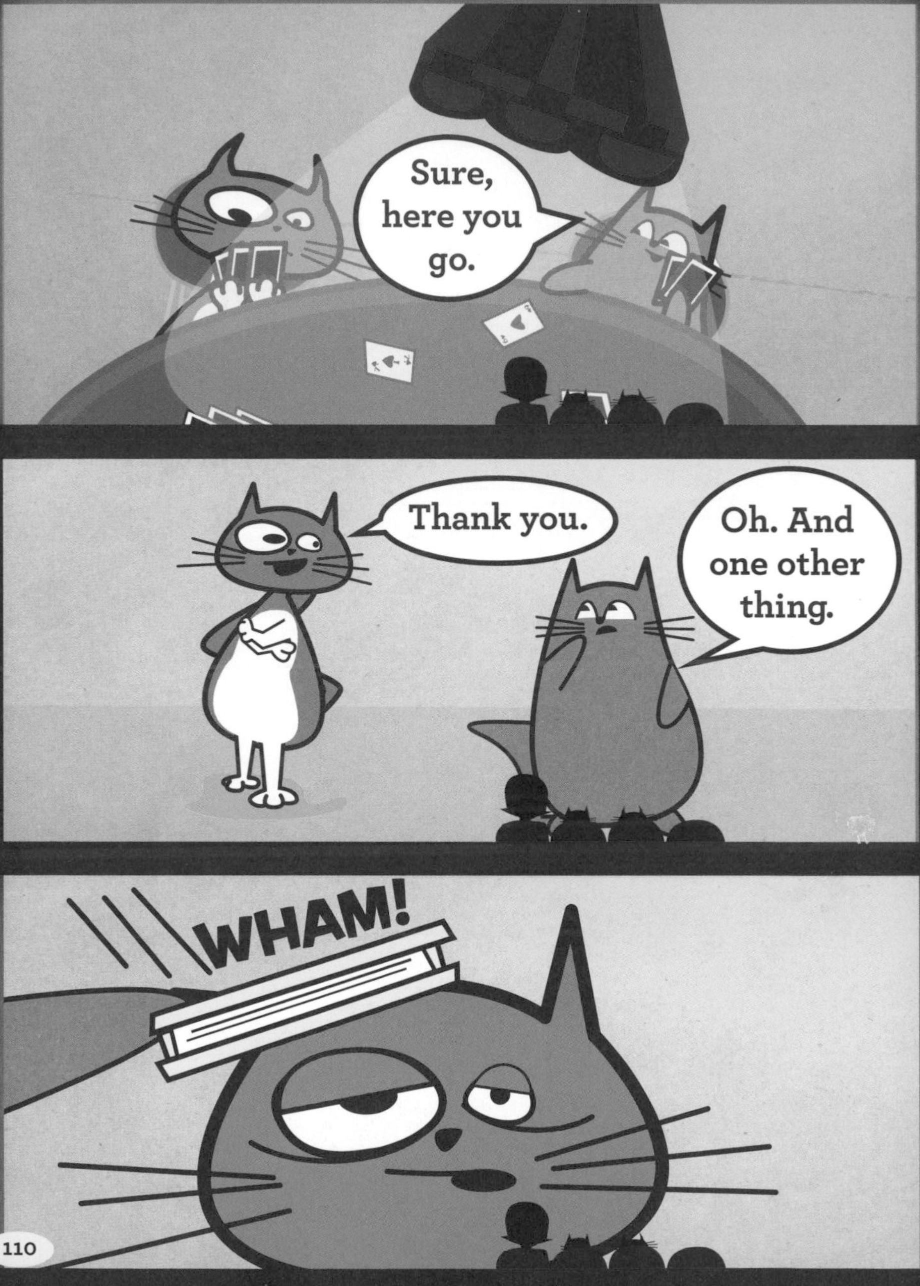
Sure, here you go.
Thank you.
Oh. And one other thing.
WHAM!

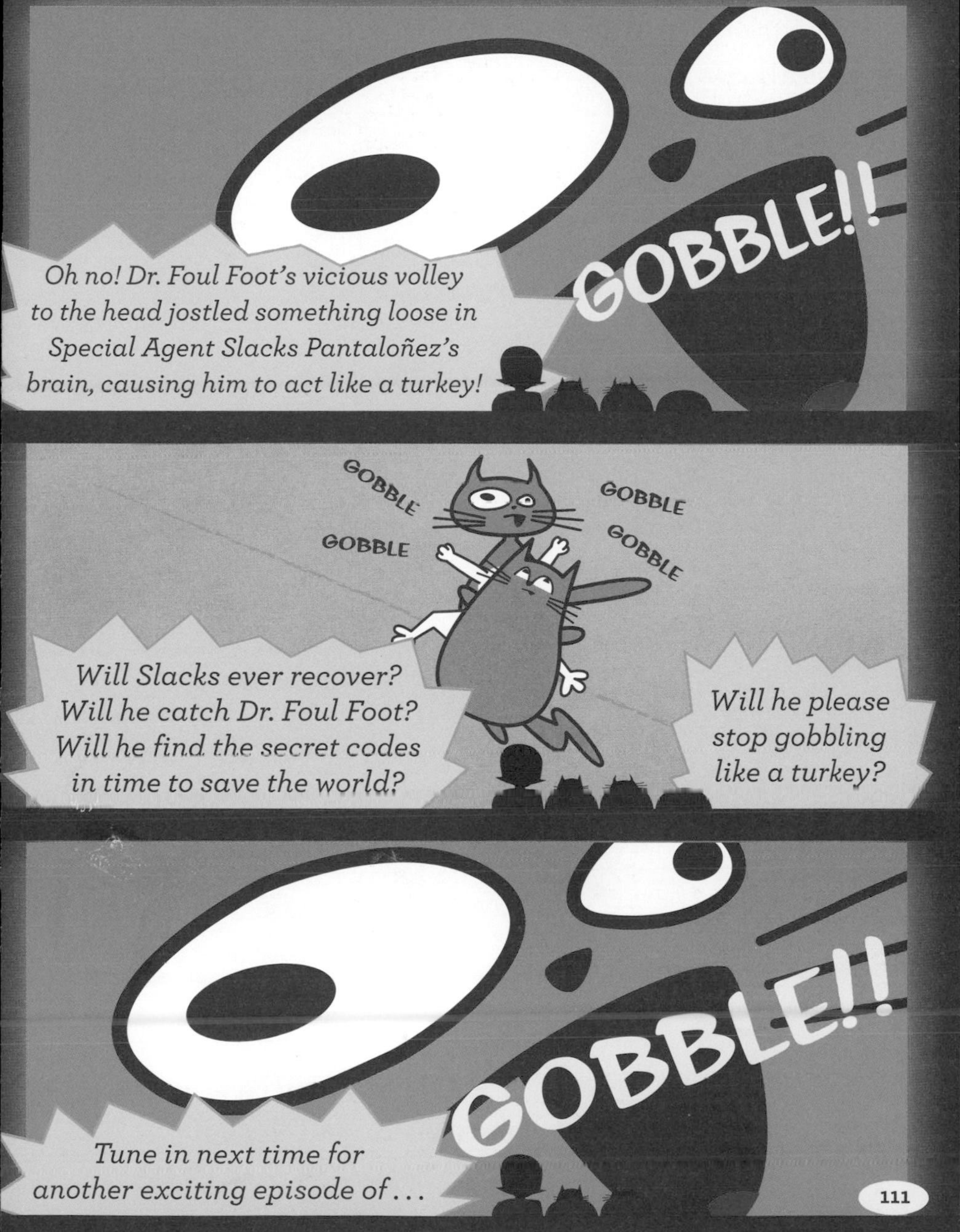
GOBBLE!!
Oh no! Dr. Foul Foot's vicious volley to the head jostled something loose in Special Agent Slacks Pantaloñez's brain, causing him to act like a turkey!
GOBBLE
GOBBLE
GOBBLE
GOBBLE
Will Slacks ever recover? Will he catch Dr. Foul Foot? Will he find the secret codes in time to save the world?
Will he please stop gobbling like a turkey?
GOBBLE!!
Tune in next time for another exciting episode of . . .

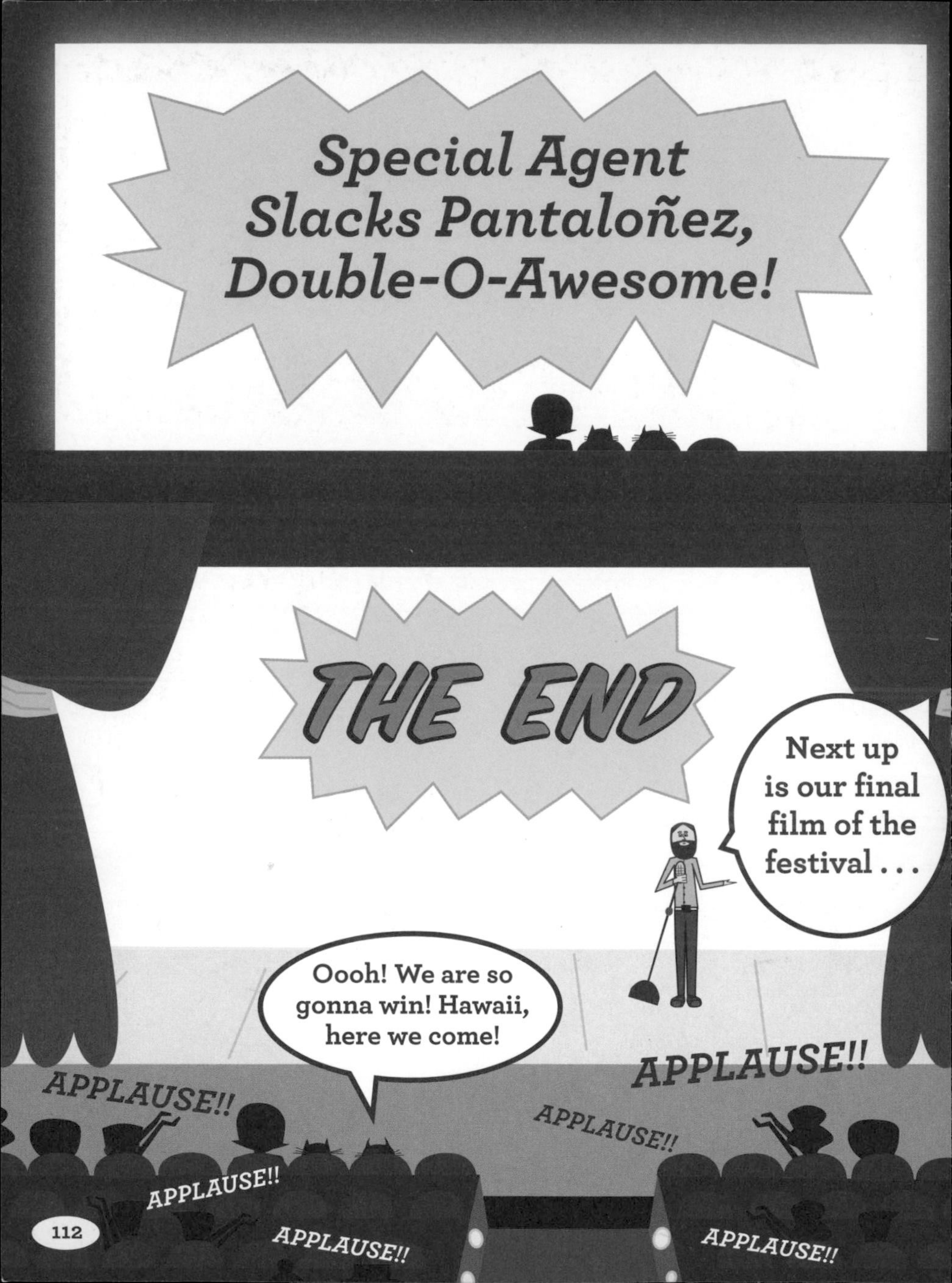
Special Agent Slacks Pantaloñez, Double-O-Awesome!
THE END
Next up is our final film of the festival . . .
Oooh! We are so gonna win! Hawaii, here we come!
APPLAUSE!!
APPLAUSE!!
APPLAUSE!!
APPLAUSE!!
APPLAUSE!!
APPLAUSE!!

# Chapter Eight:
# AND THE SORE WINNER IS...

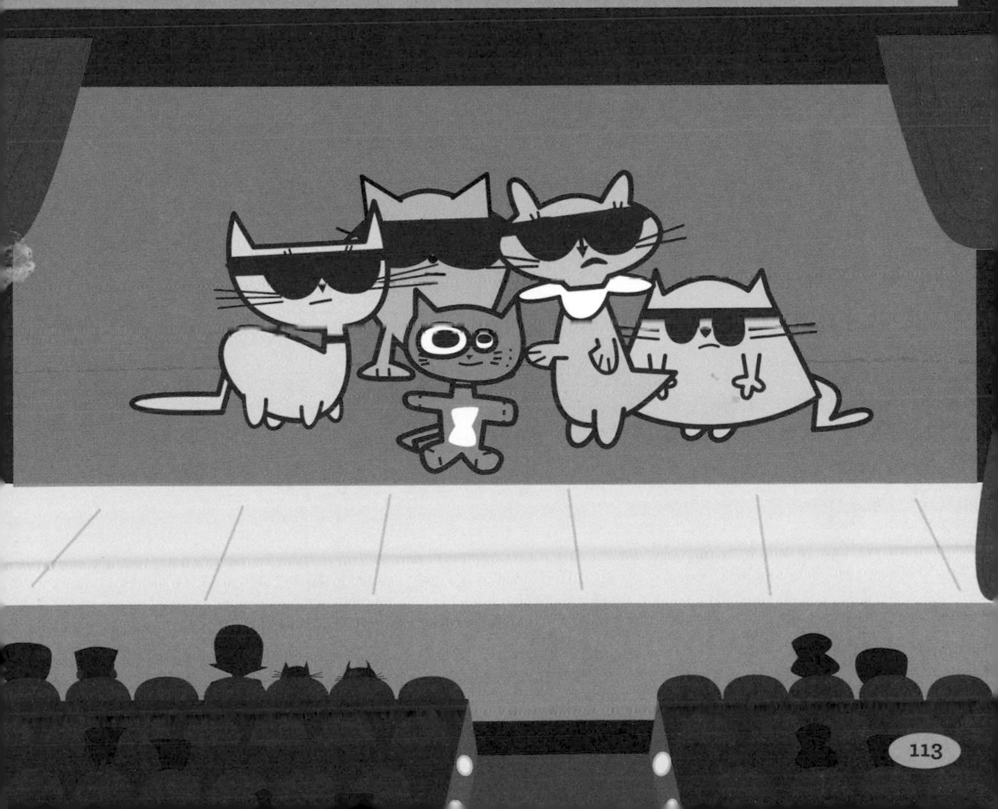

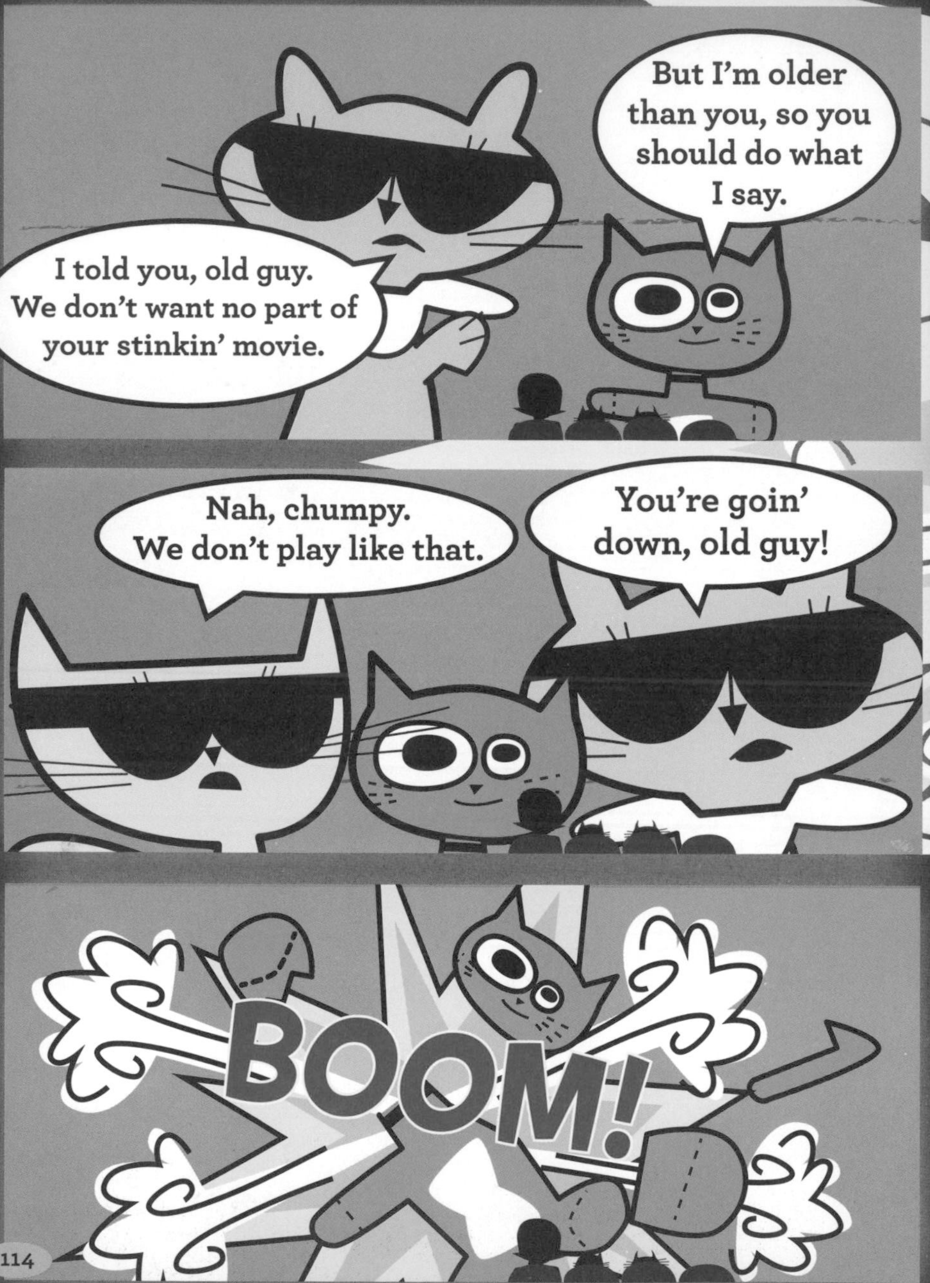
But I'm older than you, so you should do what I say.
I told you, old guy. We don't want no part of your stinkin' movie.
Nah, chumpy. We don't play like that.
You're goin' down, old guy!
BOOM!

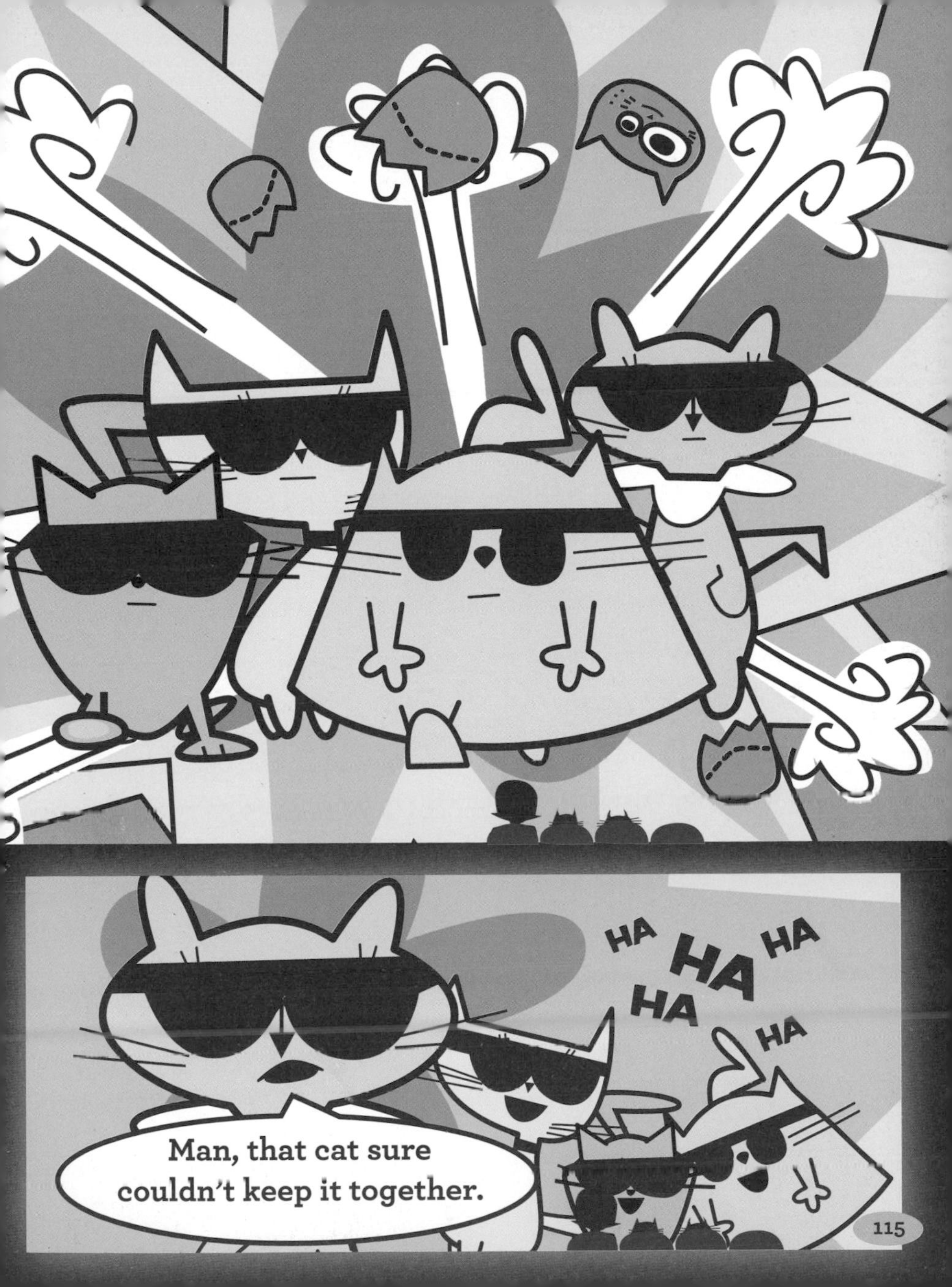
HA
HA
HA
HA
HA
Man, that cat sure couldn't keep it together.

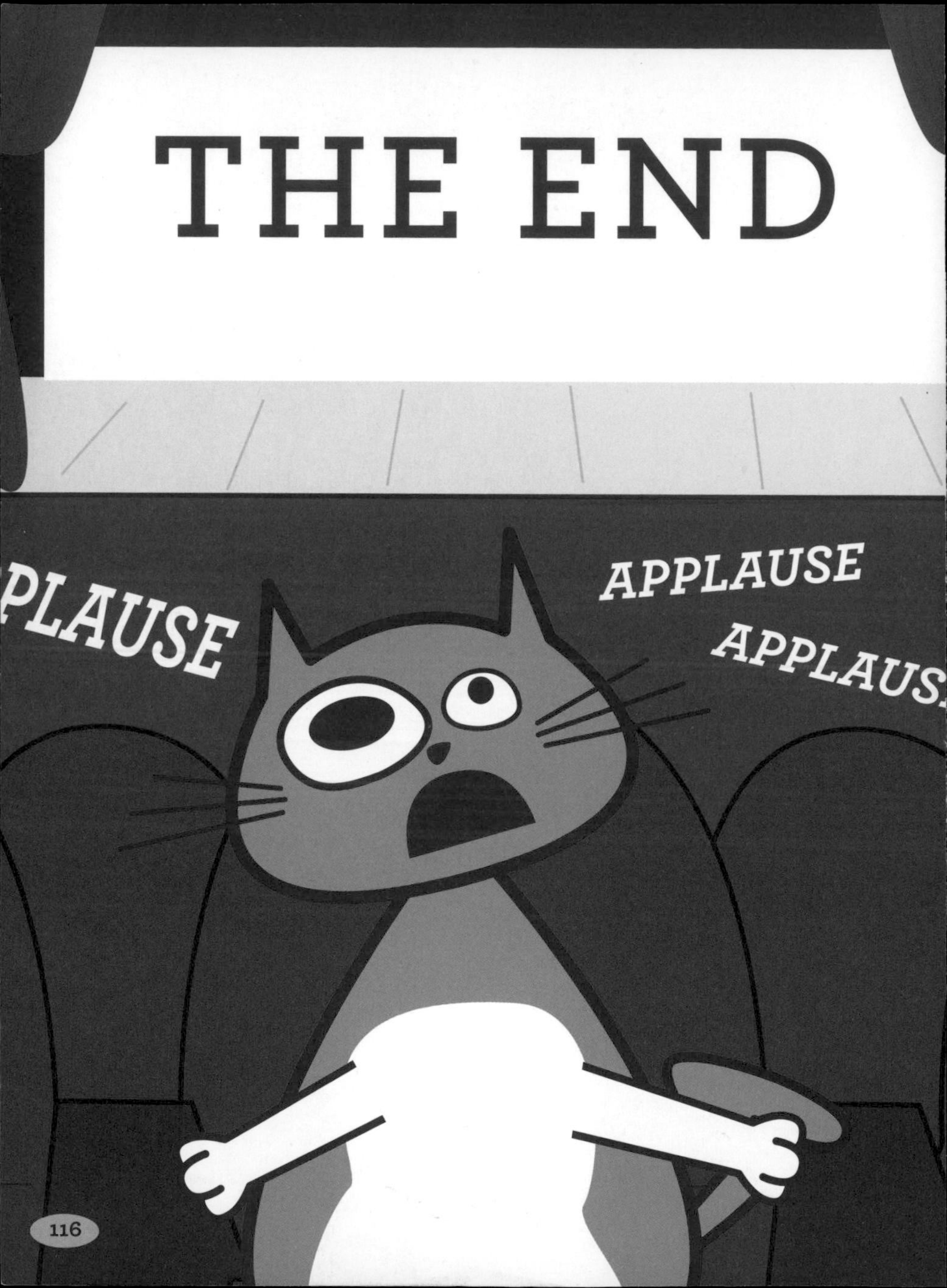
THE END
PLAUSE
APPLAUSE
APPLAUS

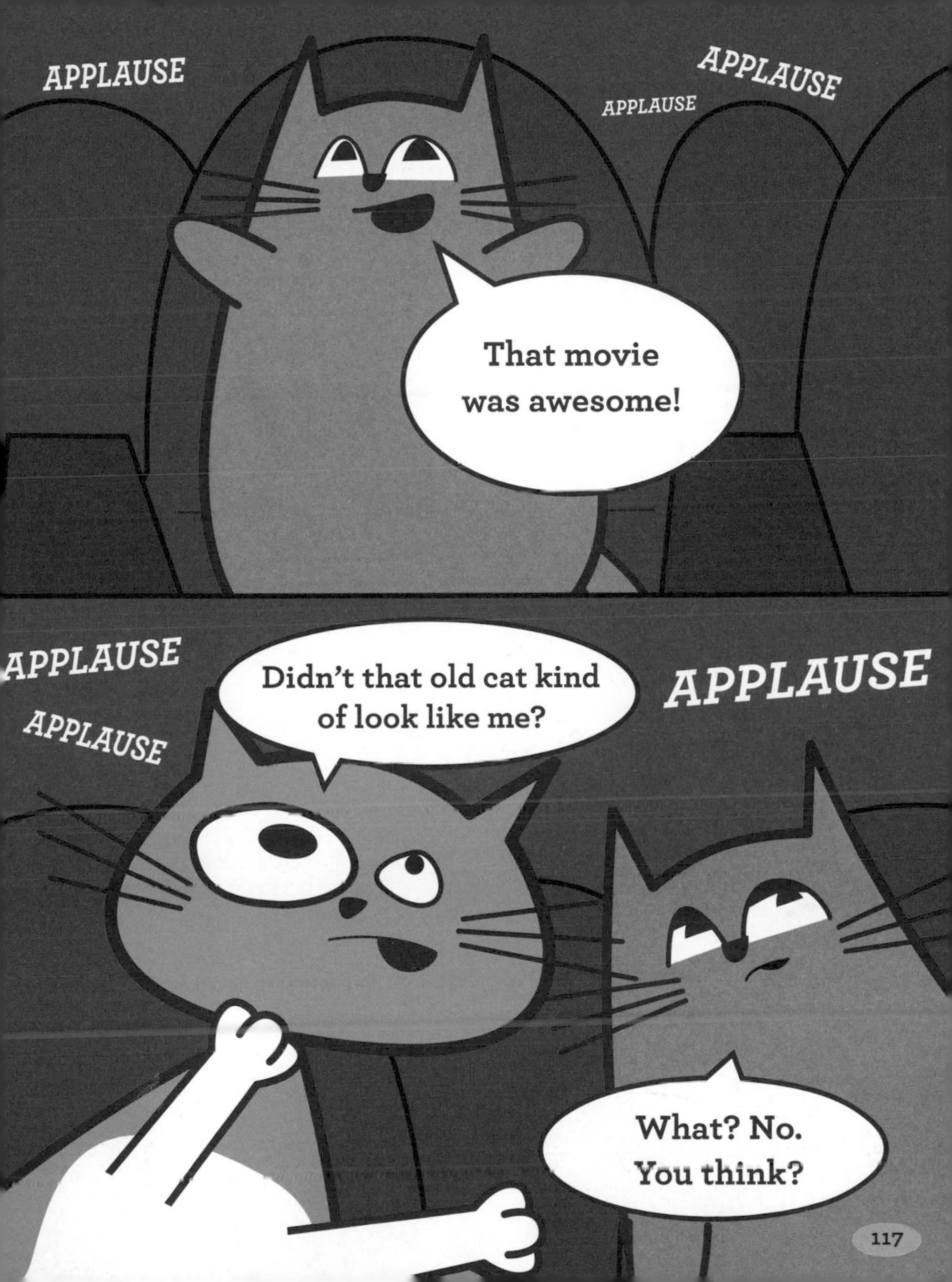
APPLAUSE
APPLAUSE
APPLAUSE
That movie was awesome!
APPLAUSE
APPLAUSE
Didn't that old cat kind of look like me?
APPLAUSE
What? No. You think?

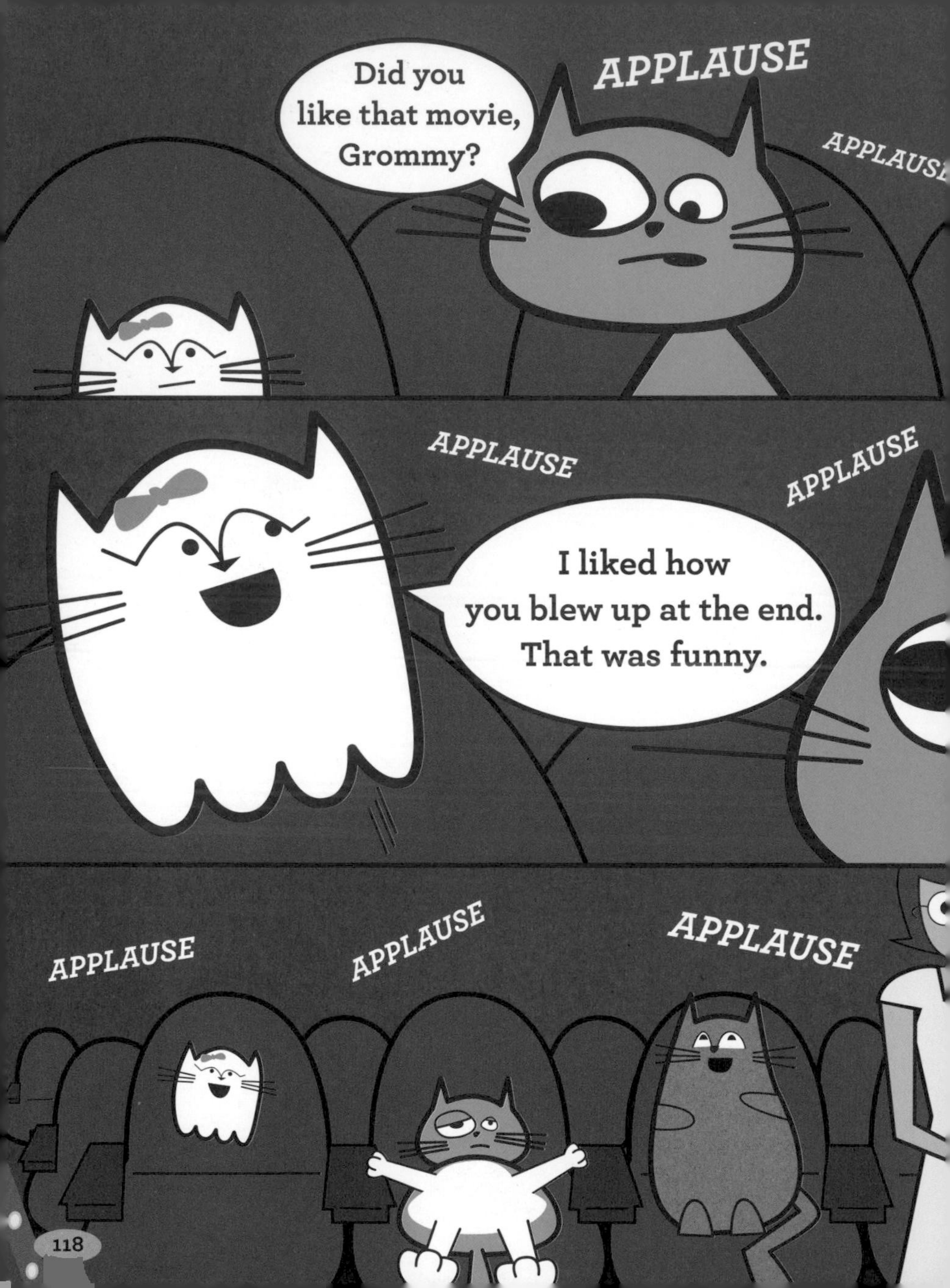
Did you
like that movie,
Grommy?
APPLAUSE
APPLAUSE
APPLAUSE
I liked how
you blew up at the end.
That was funny.
APPLAUSE
APPLAUSE
APPLAUSE

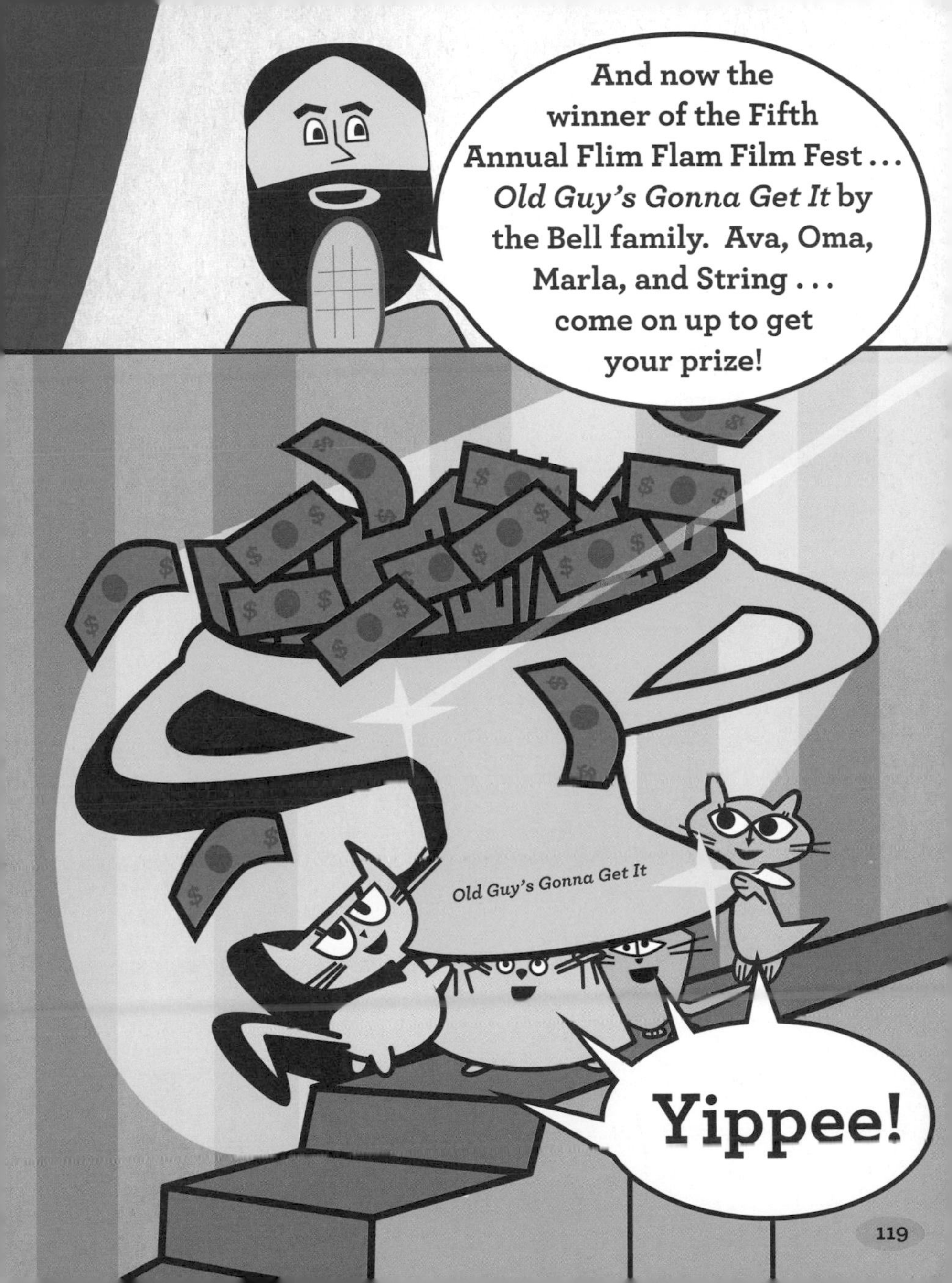
And now the winner of the Fifth Annual Flim Flam Film Fest . . . Old Guy's Gonna Get It by the Bell family. Ava, Oma, Marla, and String . . . come on up to get your prize!
Old Guy's Gonna Get It
Yippee!

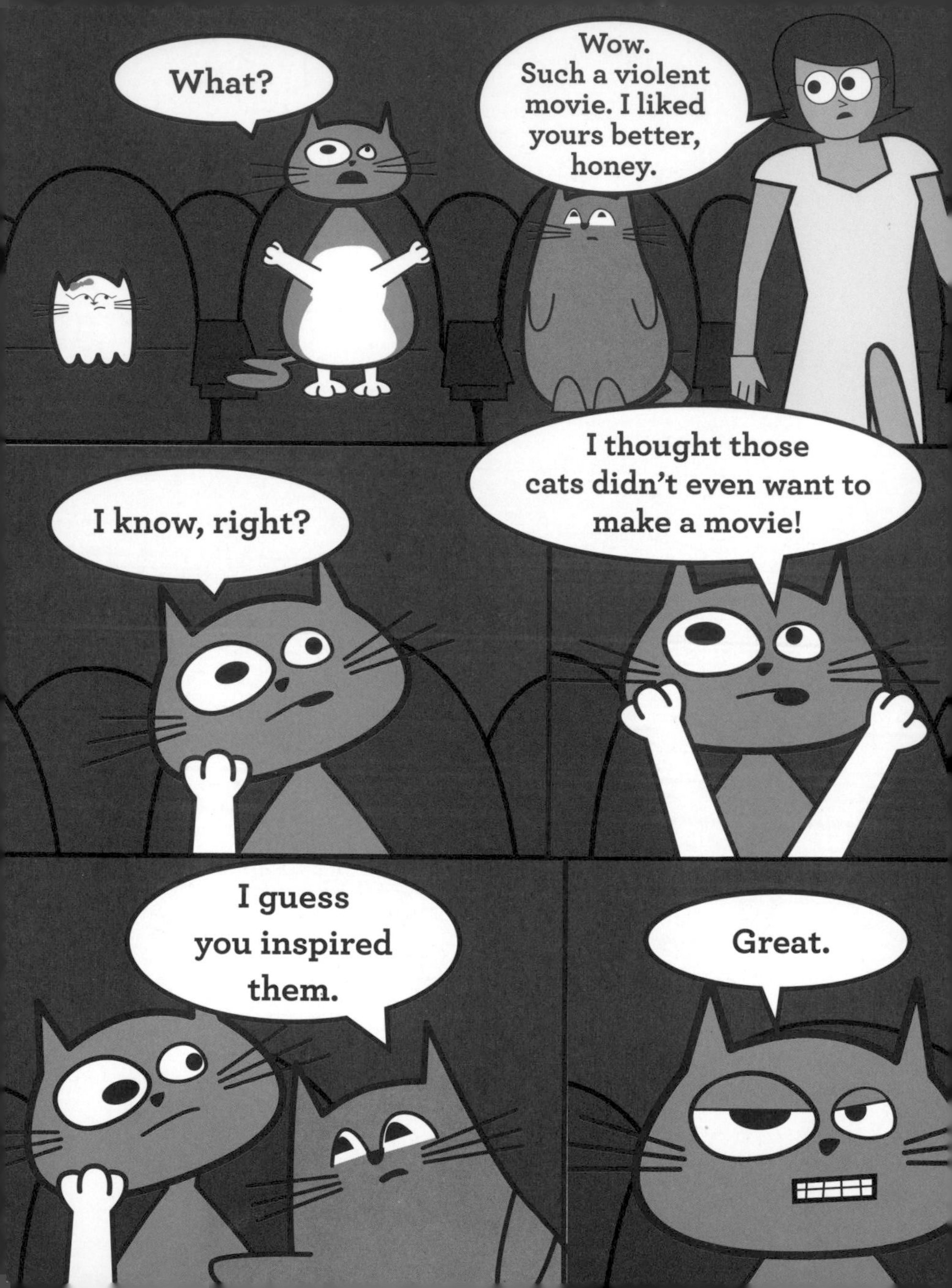
What?
Wow. Such a violent movie. I liked yours better, honey.
I know, right?
I thought those cats didn't even want to make a movie!
I guess you inspired them.
Great.

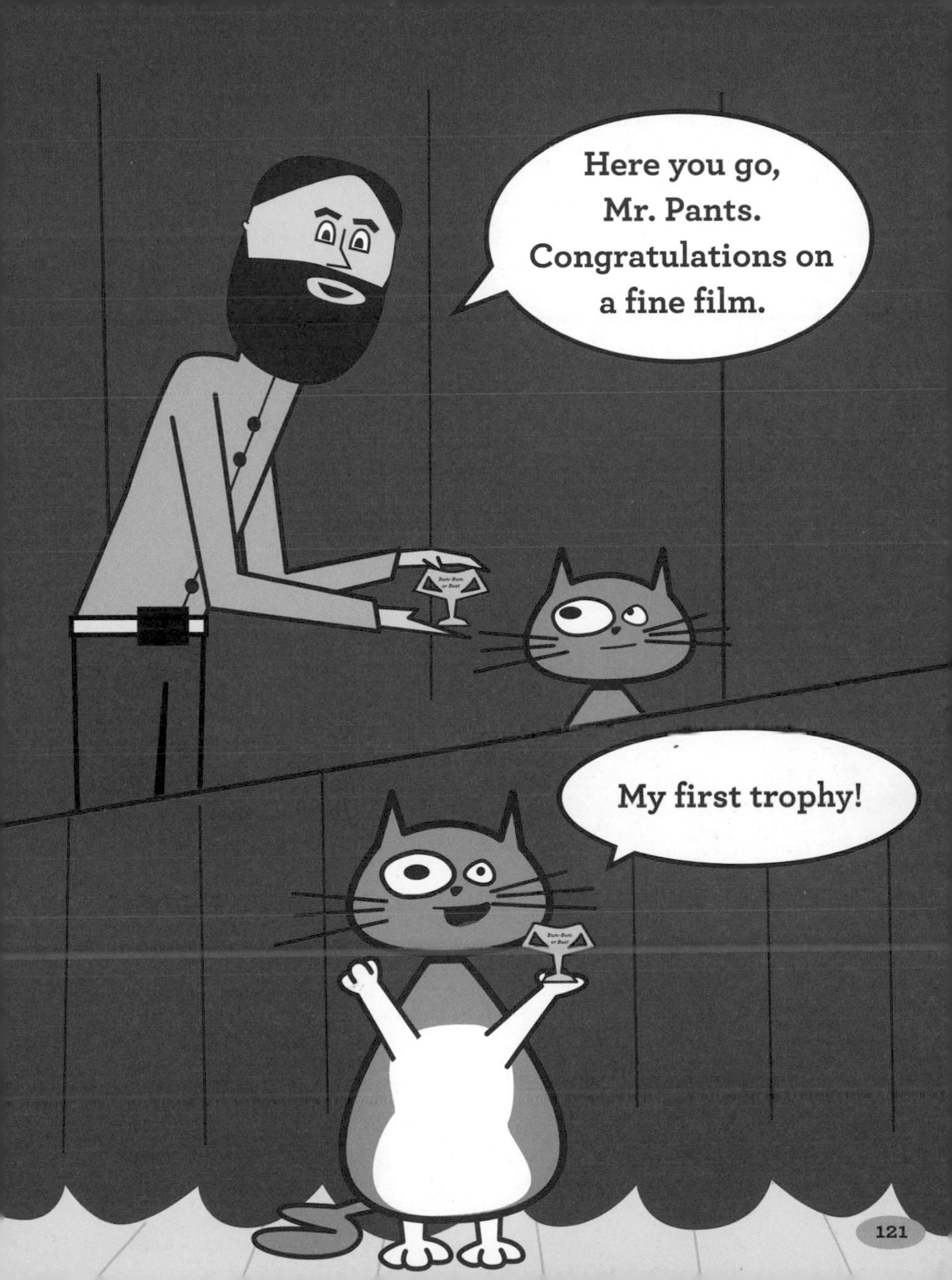
Here you go, Mr. Pants. Congratulations on a fine film.
My first trophy!

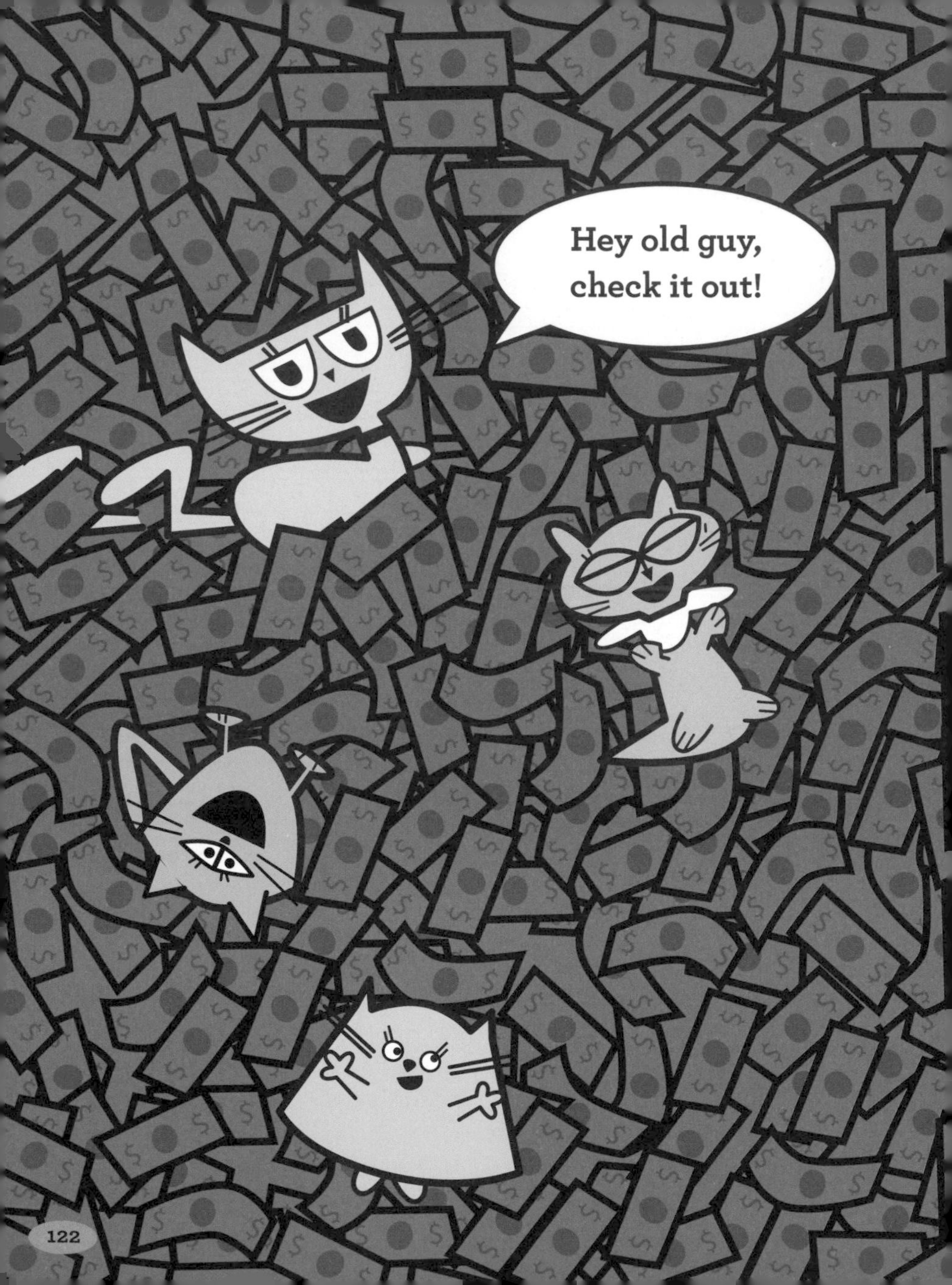
Hey old guy, check it out!

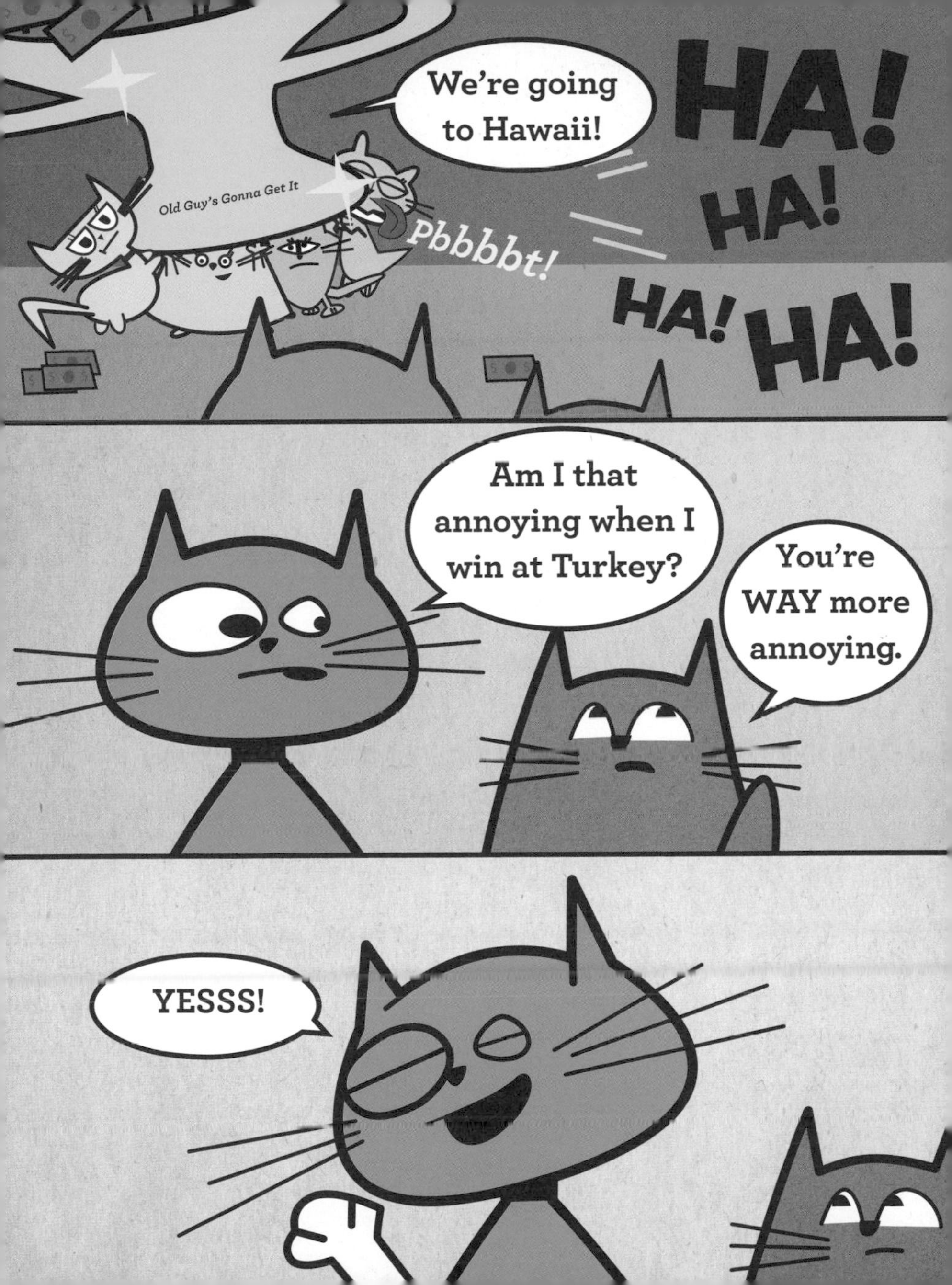
We're going to Hawaii!
HA! HA! HA! HA!
Old Guy's Gonna Get It
Pbbbbt!
Am I that annoying when I win at Turkey?
You're WAY more annoying.
YESSS!

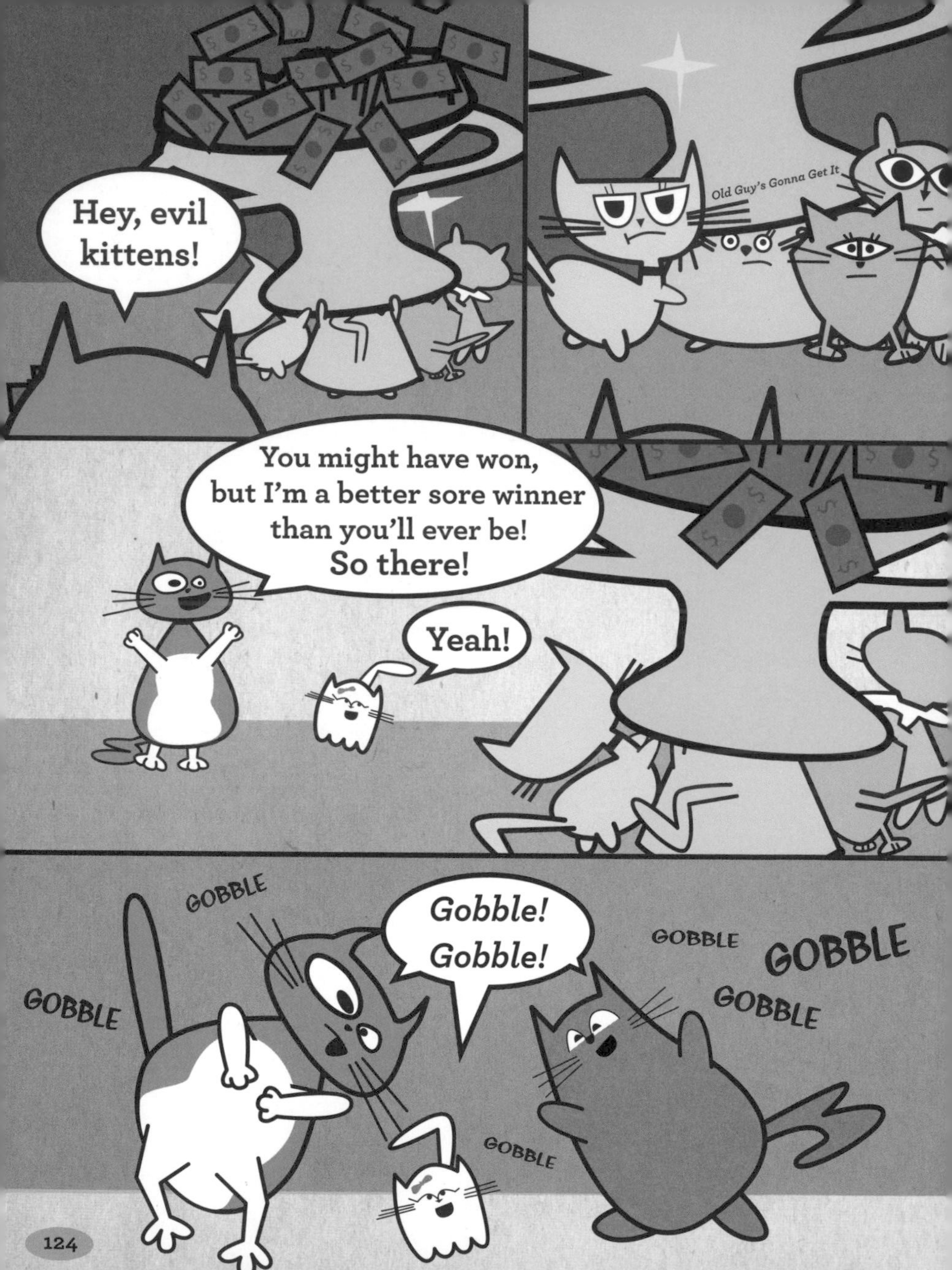

Hey, evil kittens!
Old Guy's Gonna Get It
You might have won, but I'm a better sore winner than you'll ever be! So there!
Yeah!
GOBBLE
Gobble! Gobble!
GOBBLE
GOBBLE
GOBBLE
GOBBLE
GOBBLE

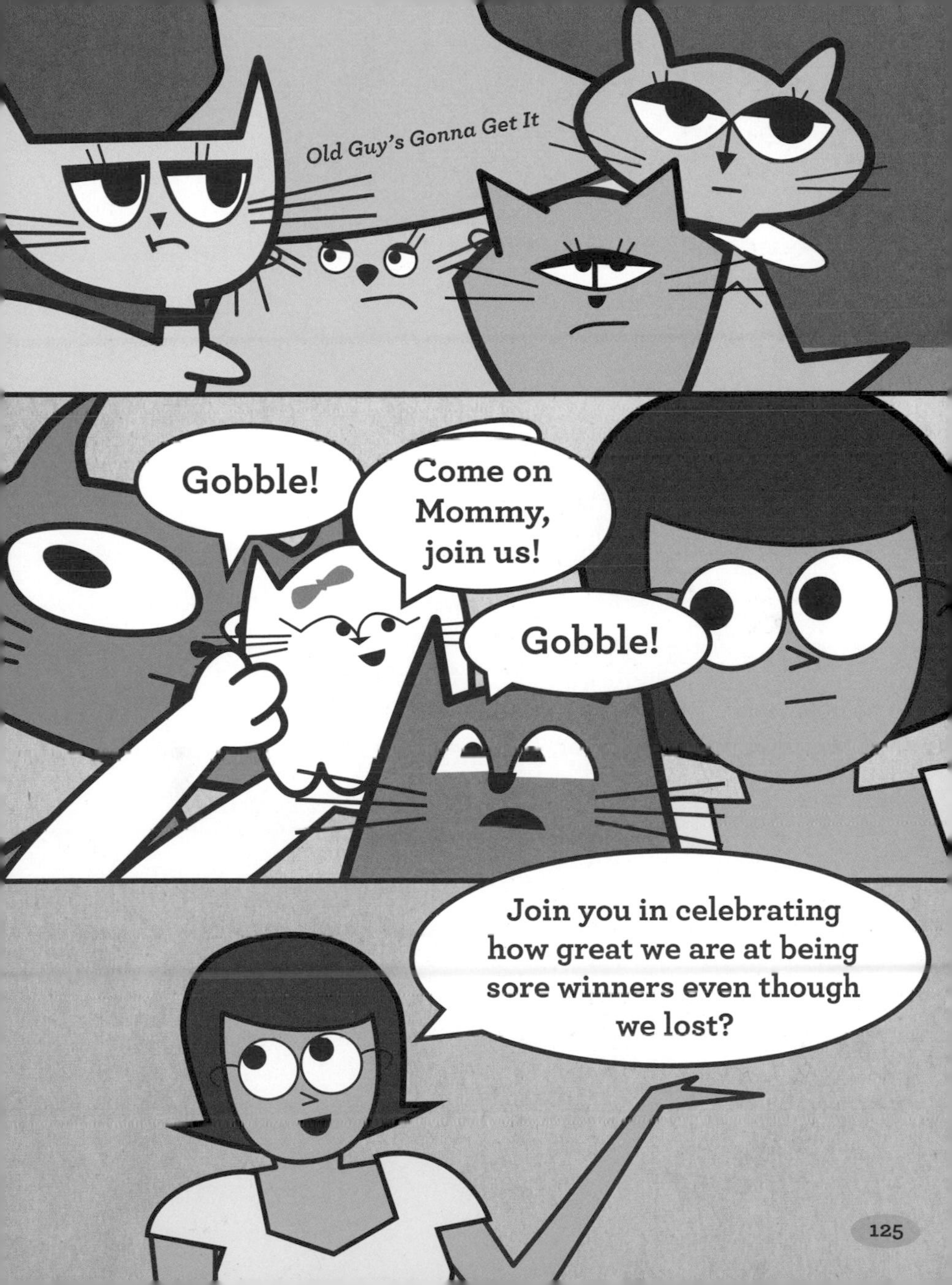
Old Guy's Gonna Get It
Gobble!
Come on Mommy, join us!
Gobble!
Join you in celebrating how great we are at being sore winners even though we lost?

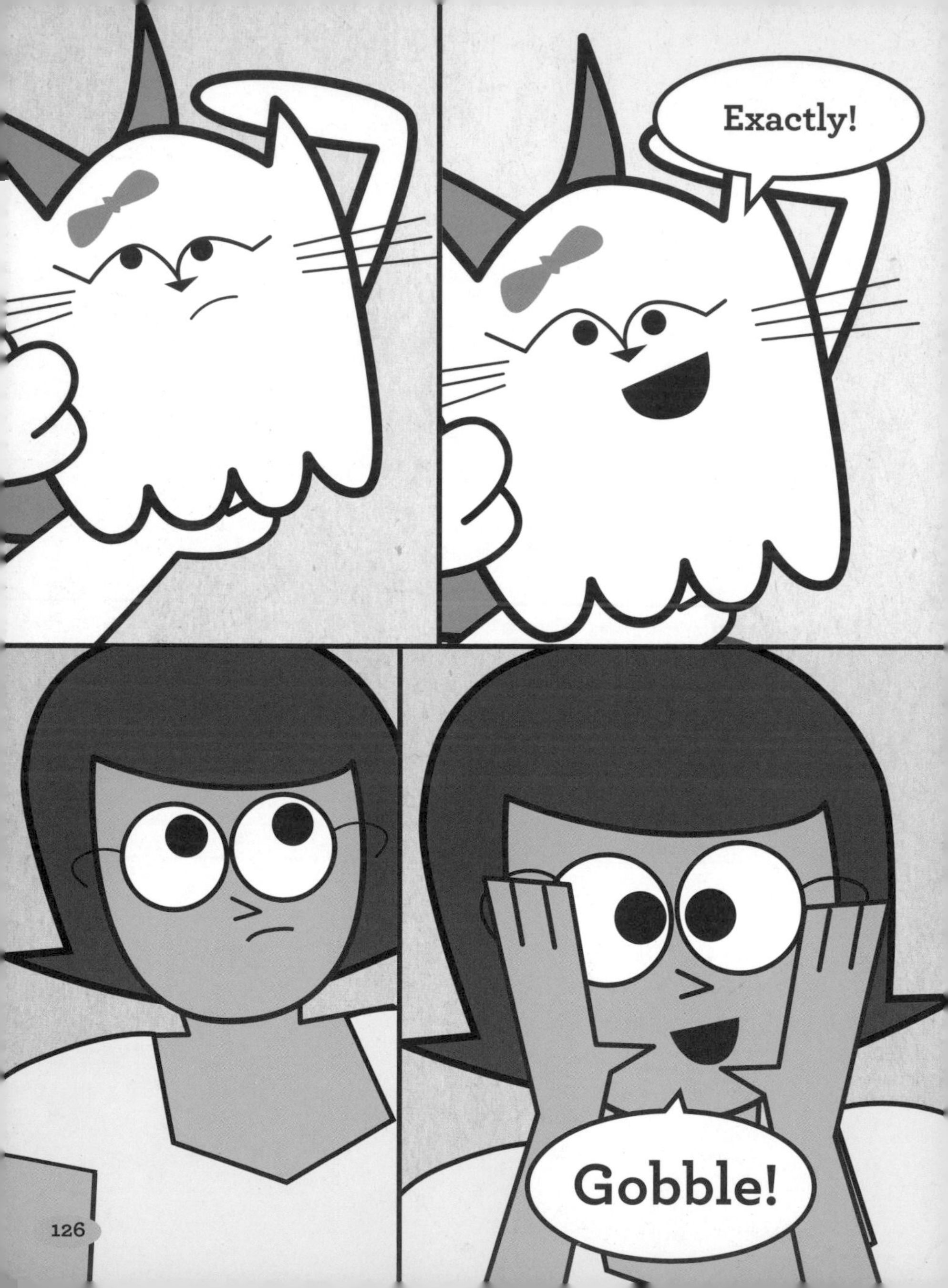
Exactly!
Gobble!

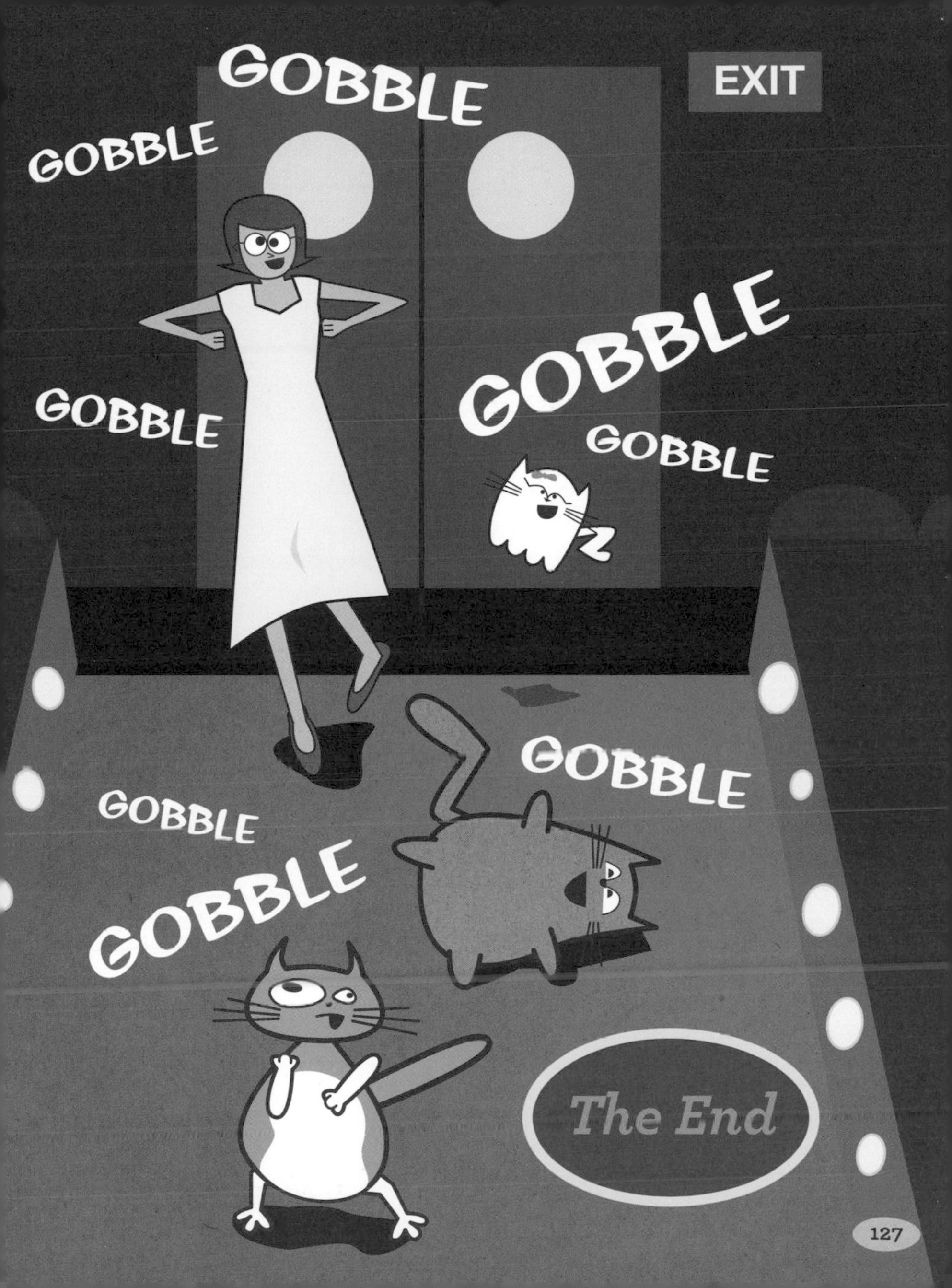
GOBBLE
EXIT
GOBBLE
GOBBLE
GOBBLE
GOBBLE
GOBBLE
GOBBLE
GOBBLE
The End

## *About the Authors:*

**SCOTT MCCORMICK** is the greatest Turkey player in the universe. (Don't tell his kids.) His favorite part of being an adult is that he can have ice cream whenever he wants. He lives in North Carolina with his family and the real Grommy LuluBelle.

**R. H. LAZZELL** is a freelance illustrator who enjoys entering film contests so he can win trips to Hawaii. He lives just outside of Philadelphia, Pennsylvania, and has no cats. (Mr. Pants is enough.)

Visit **PANTSANDFOOTFOOT.COM**
to find out more!

## *And don't miss these cats' first escapade!*

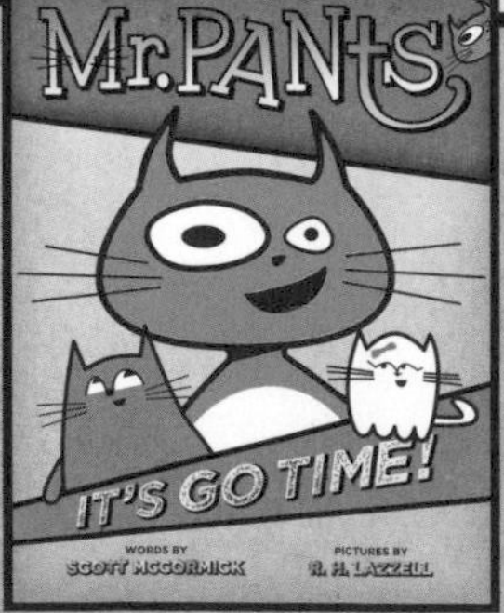
Mr. PANTS
IT'S GO TIME!
WORDS BY
SCOTT MCCORMICK
PICTURES BY
R. H. LAZZELL

"Fans will wait excitedly for the next book in this fun, rollicking series."
—*School Library Journal*

"Readers . . . will find plenty to recognize in this family's harried day of activities and errands, while enjoying Mr. Pants's lighthearted comeuppances."
—*Publishers Weekly*